Former policeman J̶ ̶ ̶ ̶ ̶ ̶ ̶ ̶ ̶ ̶ ̶ ̶ ̶ ̶ ̶ ̶ ̶ ̶ ̶ ̶
investigator for over ̶ ̶ ̶ ̶ ̶ ̶ ̶ ̶ ̶ ̶ ̶ ̶ ̶ ̶ ̶ ̶ ̶ ̶
Bay area. His professional experiences have provided
plenty of material for his novels, which include THE
CONDUCTOR, also published by Headline Feature, and
his highly-acclaimed series of Nick Polo private-eye
mysteries. A native of San Francisco, he lives with his
wife in San Bruno, California.

The Forger

Jerry Kennealy

First published in Great Britain in 1996
by HEADLINE BOOK PUBLISHING

First published in paperback in 1997
by HEADLINE BOOK PUBLISHING

A HEADLINE FEATURE paperback

10 9 8 7 6 5 4 3 2 1

ISBN 0 7472 5090 1

Typeset by
Letterpart Limited, Reigate, Surrey

Printed and bound in Great Britain by
Cox & Wyman Ltd, Reading, Berks

HEADLINE BOOK PUBLISHING
A division of Hodder Headline PLC
338 Euston Road
London NW1 3BH

The Forger

Prologue

Cabris, France

Even at his advanced age, Claude Bresson had not relinquished a bit of his admiration for the female figure. He felt somewhat like a peeping Tom as he watched the young artist go about her work.

But it wasn't Anona Stack, as beautiful as she was, despite being outfitted in paint-smeared khaki shorts and a man's blue button-down-collar shirt, that held Bresson's attention.

The forty by forty-inch canvas, which had been nothing more than a blank white square six hours earlier, was now an intense splash of colors, the artist's impression of the view from the terrace of Château Bresson.

That panoramic view looked out over the rolling carpets of violets, mimosa, lavender, roses, heather and patchouli, all of which were processed, then distilled, the *effleurage* used in making the essences for perfumes, perfumes that since the eighteenth century had made the Bresson family one of the richest in all France. The château, with its multi-turreted roof and coarse-hewn granite walls, had been constructed in the twelfth century and once housed a Benedictine order.

Bresson, short and bulky, with a napkin-length gray beard, had been impressed by all that he had seen and heard of Anona Stack. It was highly unusual for someone who was so young to have the love, the passion, drive and discipline needed to become a great artist, especially someone who had been worth millions of dollars long before having dabbed that first brush on to a canvas. He had often wondered if it would have been different for him, if he had not been born a Bresson.

He had seen her work in the galleries in New York and had been delighted when she accepted his offer of a two-week sojourn at the château. It was considered an honor to be a guest at Château Bresson, joining the illustrious list that in the past had included Cézanne, Renoir, Chagall, Dufy, Matisse and, of course, his mentor and dear friend, Picasso.

Anona Stack was the first American to have the privilege extended. She had arrived with her family, the tall, cruelly handsome husband, Jason Lark, and a beautiful daughter and son. The children had turned out to be charming, the husband not so. A *bon à rien*, good for nothing.

Prior to his marriage, Lark had been an interior decorator, of all things, and had had the nerve to suggest some changes for the château's grand dining room. Luckily, he was seldom seen, having discovered the topless beaches of nearby St Tropez and the casinos at Nice.

Bresson had watched Anona paint, first the flower markets in Cours Saleya, then the wedding-cake Hotel Negresso, then the beaches of the Cote d'Azur. Color. God, she was so good with color! The canvas was ablaze with rich pinks, blues, yellows, greens. The blends, the contrasts. She had the gift, as Monet would say, and, even more importantly, style. Her own, unique style. She copied no one.

Anona reached around with her free hand and massaged her back, then chose a clean brush, dipped it in the small well of black paint and scrawled her signature across the right top portion of the canvas.

Claude Bresson clapped his hands together when she was finished with the ritual and said, simply, '*Magnifique*.'

Anona swiveled around, her golden hair veiling her eyes momentarily.

'Ah, Monsieur Bresson. I didn't know you were there.'

'*Pardon*, Anona. But I could not help myself.' He approached the canvas slowly, as if wading through water. 'I must have this one.' He pulled his eyes from the painting and smiled at her. 'Name your price,' he insisted. 'I must have it.'

Anona's face glowed. 'It is yours, Claude. A thank you for your wonderful hospitality.'

'*C'est impossible*, out of the question. It is a great painting. Your best,' he assured her, then added, 'at least so far. I must pay you.'

Anona wiped her hands on a clean rag, then ran her fingers through her hair. 'No arguments, Claude. The painting is yours.' She leaned against the scrolled iron railing looking out across the valley, then glanced at her watch. 'It's almost five. I didn't realize it was so late. Where are Johnny and Lisa? Pestering your horses again?'

Bresson grinned within the nest of his beard. 'No, today your children are on my boat. Jacques is teaching them the water-skiing.' He could see a look of concern cloud her face. 'They are safe, believe me.'

'And my husband. Have you seen, Jason?'

'No,' Bresson admitted. 'I'm sure he'll be back shortly,' he said with little confidence. He reached out for the canvas. 'You are sure you will not accept payment for this?'

'I'm positive,' Anona said firmly.

Bresson gently plucked the canvas from the easel. 'All right then. Since this is your last night at the château, I shall arrange a little gift.'

Claude Bresson waited until Jason Lark returned to the

château, well after ten o'clock – he had missed many dinners during their stay.

He heard the scream of the Alpha Romeo's engine, the crunch of gravel under the car's tires as Lark skidded the borrowed convertible to a halt in front of the château's massive stone steps.

'Monsieur Lark,' Bresson called out as Lark started up the steps.

Lark stopped in mid-stride. The yellow illumination of the flame-shaped streetlights revealed a tall, thin man, the face narrow, the dark hair thick, parted on one side and falling over his eyebrow. He was wearing a tuxedo, the tie undone, the red carnation in the lapel beginning to wilt.

'Who is it?' Lark asked sharply.

Bresson stepped into a pool of light. 'I am sorry that you missed your family's last dinner at the château.'

Lark feigned a faint smile. 'The roulette tables kept me busy, I'm afraid.' He turned to go up the stairs, stopping when Bresson tapped him on the shoulder.

'Jason, Anona was kind enough to give me her latest painting, *Perfume Fields*. She would not let me pay her for it. I would appreciate it if you would take this.' He pushed out a brick-colored manila packet. 'Give it to her when you are back home in America. It's a small token of my appreciation.'

'What is it?'

'Some sketches. A few of my early efforts . . . and those of a friend.'

Lark undid the packet ribbon and riffled the edges of the linen sketching paper. 'All right,' he said impatiently. 'Where is my wife?'

'In your room, monsieur. *Bon soir.*'

Lark took the steps two at a time, his fingers digging in the packet again. The first two sketches seemed to be of the Château Bresson. Harsh, straight lines. No depth of field. Obviously amateurish. Claude Bresson may have

4

been born to money, but he obviously wasn't born with talent.

Lark shoved the bedroom door open without knocking. Anona was sitting on the bed, dressed in a foam-green nightgown, brushing her hair.

'It's about time you came back,' she said angrily.

Lark responded by waving the packet at her. 'That old fool Bresson tells me you gave him one of your paintings. In return he's giving you some old drawings he made of his precious château.' Lark carelessly tossed the packet into an opened compartment of a Louis Vuitton traveling trunk.

'Where were you?' Anona demanded.

'Out. Having fun. I didn't come over here to be cooped up and watch you paint. Hell, I could do that at home,' he sneered.

Anona pushed herself to her feet. 'It seems your idea of fun includes getting lipstick on your shirt. And that powder under your nose, Jason. I'm sure that it isn't—'

Lark's open palm streaked in a long, curving arc, landing flatly on his wife's cheek, knocking her to the floor.

Anona cried out and the connecting door opened. Five-year-old Lisa, dressed in teddy bear pajamas, came running into the room, dropping to her knees alongside her mother.

'Don't hit Mommy anymore,' she screamed. 'Don't hit, Mommy!'

Lark rocked back on his heels. He looked to the doorway. His son John, just eighteen months older than his sister, was standing there, holding on to the knob with both of his hands, the knuckles white, his eyes wide, his mouth gaping open.

'Get out, Jason,' Anona said, struggling into a sitting position and pulling Lisa to her chest. 'It's over. Get out!'

Chapter 1

Fourteen years later

A sudden gust of warm, sea-scented wind ruffled the palm trees, awakening Robert Duran from a tranquil nap. He yawned lazily and swept a hand out across the towel, reaching for his wife.

He blinked his eyes open and rolled over on to his stomach, the brightness causing him to search the warm white sand for his sunglasses.

Duran put the glasses on and scanned the Jamaican Inn's private beach for Anona. There were several dozen oil-coated bathers, the women young, beautiful, in wispy string bikinis – the men older, thick-bodied, seemingly more interested in the newspapers or books propped on their stomachs than in their companions or the cobalt-blue waters of Sandy Beach Bay.

Duran had never been happier. His business was booming, so much so that it had been hard finding the time to squeeze in this vacation. He and Anona had recently celebrated their wedding anniversary. Six marvelous years.

There were times when Duran would wake up in the morning, stare at his wife's beautiful profile and wonder why Anona had picked him. With all of the rich, talented and famous men chasing her, why had she settled for a widowed insurance investigator whose only claim to fame was locating stolen works of art from time to time.

An enormous, triple-stacked, *Love Boat*-style luxury liner caught his eye. Rainbow-hued, butterfly-winged sailboats rode the wide feather of the liner's wake, bobbing up and down like toys in a bathtub.

Duran got to his feet and stretched his hands over his head. He was of medium height, with a lean, athletic body. His black hair was flecked with gray. His face was angular, well cut, the coppery skin set off by a pair of blue eyes that somehow didn't seem to belong with the rest of the package. A thick scar weaved through his left eyebrow then curled down in a comma to his cheekbone. He was about to run down to the water for a swim when he spotted Anona. She had changed from her swimsuit to a canary yellow basket-weaved dress.

Tall, slender, her hair shades lighter from a week's worth of sun, she had a regal way about her. Although she was in her forties, a good many of the male population on the beach dropped their reading material long enough for an appraising glance as she strolled by.

Duran always marveled at the way she could command attention in a restaurant or at a party.

'Had enough sun for the day?' Duran greeted her cheerfully. Anona's fair skin required massive doses of sun screen, while Duran could lie on the beach for hours and hours and not worry about getting burned.

Anona dropped wearily on to the beach towel. She took off her hubcap-sized dark glasses and stared at her husband. Her azure-tinted eyes were red-rimmed. She'd been crying. He took her hand in his. 'What's happened, Anona?'

'I just spoke to Doctor Feldman, Bob. I didn't want to worry you, but I went in for some lab tests last week.'

Duran brought her hand to his lips and kissed it. 'What is it, darling?'

She dropped her head, causing her hair to screen her eyes. 'I'm afraid it's not good news.'

The Present
Crescent City, California
Pelican Bay State Prison

'Well, well, well. The last night for the artist,' the pot-bellied guard smirked, pronouncing the last word of his sentence as 'arteest'. 'We're going to miss you, Michelangelo.' He slipped the anodized telescoping baton through the cell bars, then flipped his wrist, sending the baton's tip out toward the man on the lower bunk.

'You be a good boy out there, artist, 'cause if we get you back here again, we ain't going to be so nice.'

The man waited until the guard's sharp heel-clicks were a distant echo before jack-knifing into a sitting position.

His cellmate's, Ken Firpo, hairy legs were dangling down from the upper berth.

'He's got a point there. You come back and they'll put you in the SHU again. You couldn't handle that. Are you sure you still want to go through with it and kill them?'

'Definitely,' he promised, pushing Firpo's legs out of his way. 'First her, the same way Arlene died, then Duran. Fourteenth October. Nothing's going to stop me.' He slipped his right hand, his lithe, long-fingered painting hand, under his armpit, then pushed his nose between the cell bars, inhaling deeply, as if the air on the other side of the bars were cleaner, purer. 'Nothing.'

Firpo slithered out of the upper bunk, his feet hitting the cement floor with a thud. He was wearing gray prison-issue boxer shorts – fifty-four years of age, with a power lifter's build, his corded muscles rippling under fish-belly white skin that had been decorated with numerous hot-tipped ballpoint-pen tattoos. His head was shaved, his face that of a heavyweight fighter who had taken too much punishment, his large nose broken and pushed to one side. 'That doesn't give you a hell of a lot of time. Well, I taught you how, and told you where. Now, since this'll be our last night together, get over here and give me a goodbye kiss.'

Paris Tribune

Claude Bresson died last night at the age of 92 at his château in Cabris. Mr Bresson's death was attributed to natural causes. Bresson was a world-famous art collector, as was his father and grandfather before him. His private collection includes works by Angelico, Botticelli, Da Vinci, El Greco, Cézanne, Matisse and Pablo Picasso. The Bresson family owned the building which housed Picasso's studio in Paris. Picasso reportedly took Bresson under his wing and the two men became lifelong friends.

Claude Bresson's passion turned to modern art in his later years. He was recently forced to sell many of his favorite paintings due to the collapse of the family perfume business. Hélène Bresson, his wife, died several years ago. They had no children. Mr Bresson's two brothers are also deceased – although numerous nephews and nieces are expected to challenge for the remains of the estate.

Chapter 2

'You did say cash?' Honest Ed asked, one foot pawing at the gravel alongside the truck.

'Yes.' He took a roll of bills held together by a rubber band. 'All cash.'

Honest Ed's face creased in exaggerated pain. 'Yeah, but at that price, it's almost like you're stealing it from me, son.'

He shrugged his shoulders and started to turn around.

'Now, now,' the used truck dealer cautioned, 'don't get all uppity. All cash. You got a deal. Come on into the office.' Honest Ed paused to take one last look at the vehicle. 'What are you going to use an old bread truck for, son?'

Los Angeles Times

The Santa Barbara mansion of movie producer Alan Fritzheim, whose latest film, Lethal Confession, *has grossed over one hundred and forty million dollars, was burglarized last night.*

Neither Mr Fritzheim, nor his wife, the former actress Danielle Altray, were at home at the time of the robbery.

Mr Fritzheim's attorney stated that the only item taken was a Vincent Van Gogh painting, Sun and Sky, *which was purchased four years ago for twenty-eight million dollars.*

Police say they have no suspects at the present time.

Santa Barbara, California

It was a classic case of the barn door being shut long after the horse had taken off. There were two black and white police cars parked in front of the entrance to Alan Fritzheim's house.

Duran showed his credentials to the uniformed officer guarding the gated entry, then drove into the compound, following an S-shaped cobblestone path that skirted neatly-trimmed topiary hedges.

The largescale two-story structure was an all white, rolling adobe stucco with circular windows. Bright orange bougainvillaea spilled over a low escarpment bordering the front of the house.

He parked alongside yet another black and white, the heavy-jawed officer checking his ID before taking a walkie-talkie from his belt, mumbling an incoherent message and grudgingly allowing him to go up the black tiled steps.

The man waiting for him inside the front door was in his forties, with thinning red hair and wearing a tan poplin suit and rep tie.

He extended a hand. 'Mr Duran? Lieutenant Beeler. Come on in, I'll give you the guided tour.'

Duran shook the policeman's hand, noticing his soft marshmallow grip and the pained expression on the lieutenant's face. It was a look Duran was used to, and he was not unsympathetic to Beeler's frustrations. The police took the heat for the crime taking place in their territory, then were often left out of the picture while the insurance company representatives negotiated with the victims – and the thieves.

Beeler led Duran through the house. The walls were dotted with vintage movie posters: *Casablanca*, *King Kong*, *Bambi*, *The Wizard of Oz*. They passed by the dining room, in which the long table was set between two narrow pools of water. The table top was of granite, matching the floor. An orange and yellow Mark Rothko oil hung on one wall.

Beeler moved into a large room, pointing out the numerous jade statues and figurines encased in a ceiling-high glass case. The adjoining room held a collection of western memorabilia – saddles, hats, rifles, pistols and at least a half-dozen Remington bronzes of cowboys on horseback.

Duran followed Beeler up the stairs to the master bedroom. Here the floors were of gleaming ebony. A round bed dominated the room. Above the terracotta tiled fireplace, in a hollowed-out alcove under a spotlight, sat a gold statue. An Oscar presented to Alan Fritzheim three years ago. Posters from several of Fritzheim's movies hung from the walls. The ceiling-to-floor windows looked out to a quarry-stoned patio. A woman with ash-blonde hair was sitting in a padded loungechair reading a magazine.

'The Van Gogh hung right over there,' Beeler advised, 'over the bed.' He slapped a clipboard against his thigh. 'Do you want to take pictures?'

'No, thanks, Lieutenant. I'm sure you and your crew have taken care of that,' Duran granted. 'What about the alarm system?'

'It was off,' Beeler said, the disgust in his voice obvious. He peeled off a page from the clipboard and handed it to Duran. 'This is a diagram of the system. It cost Fritzheim close to three hundred thousand bucks, but it wasn't on at the time of the burglary.'

'Was anyone at home during the theft?'

'Just the Mexican housekeeper. Eleana Morales. She's in the kitchen now if you want to talk to her.'

'I do, and—'

The sliding doors leading to the patio opened and the blonde came into the room. She looked to be in her late thirties, her hair layered back at the sides, her make-up artfully applied. She was wearing a glimmering red silk dress, carved deeply at both neck and back, and stiletto heels.

'Who are you?' she asked, pointing a red-tipped finger at Duran.

'This is Robert Duran, the man your insurance carrier hired, Mrs Fritzheim,' Beeler informed her. He turned to Duran. 'Do you need anything else?'

'Just to talk to the housekeeper and Mr Fritzheim.'

'I'll take him to my husband,' the woman said dismissively.

Beeler jumped at the opportunity to leave. 'Call me if we can help,' he shouted over his shoulder.

Duran turned to the woman and said, 'Where is your husband?'

She tilted her head to the side and sized up Duran as if he were a side of beef that she was contemplating purchasing for a barbecue. 'You dress too good to be just an insurance investigator. What are you? Someone like Banecek? The guy on the old TV show who solved all those tricky cases?'

'No, Mrs Fritz—'

'Danielle,' she said batting her overly mascaraed eyelashes at him. 'You know they offered me a role in that show, but I never did TV. Just movies.'

'Yes, I've seen your pictures,' Duran lied amiably. 'They were wonderful. It must have been a shock for you, coming home and finding the Van Gogh gone.'

She shook her bare arm, the string of gold bracelets on her wrist making a jangling sound. 'I'm just glad they didn't take my jewels.' She jutted her chin toward a door on the far wall. 'All they had to do was go in there and scoop 'em up.' She tilted her head to the side again and said, 'You want to take a look?'

'No. I'm not interested in what the thieves didn't take.

Maybe I better talk to your husband.'

'Alan's in his library. He stays there all day sometimes. When he's not at the damn studio. The library's downstairs, just across from the kitchen.'

Duran thanked her. 'I think I can find it.'

She headed for the patio, her heels digging into the hardwood floor. 'Yes, but can you find the painting?'

Duran checked the kitchen first. Like the rest of the house, it was all white, with a vaulted ceiling and arched walls. A round-faced girl dressed in a dark skirt and a fluffy off-the-shoulder blouse sat at the butcher's-block table nervously drumming her fingers on her lap.

'*Bueñas dias, Señorita Morales,*' Duran greeted her formally.

'*Habla español?*'

'*Si.*'

Duran conducted the entire interview in Spanish, confident that he had gotten more information from the girl than the police had. He learned that she was nineteen, or at least claimed she was. She had been working at the house for less than three months. The doorbell had rung shortly after noon. She had looked through the peephole and seen two men in coveralls carrying a couch. She had opened the door and let them in. One of the men spoke Spanish and asked her who was home to sign for the delivery. When she told him she was alone the man had pulled a '*grande pistola*' from his pocket. She was tied and gagged, and not set free until Mrs Fritzheim came home later in the afternoon.

Duran went over the incident with her several times, but couldn't get a better description of the two men other than they were tall, possibly in their thirties, looked as if they could be brothers, wore white coveralls and Los Angeles Dodgers baseball hats. She had not seen their vehicle.

The kitchen door swung open and a short, balding man

with a rounded back and caved in stomach, dressed in powder blue shorts, a matching shirt with shoulder tabs and button-down pockets and shower thongs, clomped into the room.

He skidded to a halt when he saw Duran. 'You with the cops?'

'No.' Duran gave him one of his business cards.

Alan Fritzheim glanced at the card then snapped it with a fingernail. 'Lost Art, Inc. You're the guy those morons at my insurance company hired?'

'The manager at Pacific Indemnity hired me,' Duran confirmed.

Eleana Morales tiptoed silently toward the door. Fritzheim gave her a quick look, then shook his head. 'She let them right in the house.' His eyes bounced up to Duran. 'And don't give me a ration of shit because the alarm system wasn't on. And what makes you and those assholes at Pacific Indemnity think you can get the painting back and the cops can't?'

'I don't think the police are going to be of much help. The thieves knew exactly what they wanted. Your wife's jewelry wasn't taken. That Rothko hanging in your dining room is worth over a million dollars. The Remington western bronzes are very valuable, as are the jade items. They left your Oscar behind. They wanted the Van Gogh, period, which means there are two possible scenarios. Either they already have a buyer for the painting, or they'll sell it back to the insurance company.'

'Scenarios,' Fritzheim glowered. 'You sound like a fucking script writer.'

'The Van Gogh's too well-known to peddle on the open market. Either they've got a buyer who'll freeze it, or they'll come to us.'

'What'd you mean, "freeze it"?'

'Put it in storage,' Duran explained. 'For a long time, twenty, thirty, fifty years.'

'You'd have to be nuts to do that,' Fritzheim said angrily.

'No. Just patient. Over time a phony provenance could be carefully detailed – so and so bought it from so and so, who passed it on, and on and on. In the meantime, the buyer has the Van Gogh. He can enjoy it all he wants, as long as he doesn't show it off to the wrong people. Fifty years from now *Sun and Sky* could surface in Europe, South America or Asia. Your heirs would have a tough time getting it back.'

'Heirs! You mean I'm never going to see the fucking thing again?'

'It depends. As I said, if the thieves don't have a buyer, they'll contact us. Do you want your Van Gogh back, Mr Fritzheim?'

Fritzheim squared his shoulders and puffed out his chest. 'What the hell kind of a question is that? Of course I want my painting back. I love that fucking painting! I kept it under plexiglass so it wouldn't get dusty. I even had a little curtain across it. I covered it every goddamn day so the sun wouldn't touch it. I treated that fucking thing like it was my kid, and you want to know if I want it back!' He waved an arm around his head. 'People like you just can't understand what it's like to own a painting like that – a masterpiece. A flat-out goddamn masterpiece.'

'Oh, I understand, Mr Fritzheim,' Duran assured him. 'And I'll do my best to get your Van Gogh back for you.'

It took two hours, but the wait was worth it. He'd found the right van. The couple were young, the man blond, muscular, the girl dark-haired with a heart-shaped face. They were smiling and laughing at each other like honeymooners – like he and Arlene used to.

The courtesy bus pulled up and the young man reached down for a bulging black vinyl suitcase.

'Can I give you a hand with that?' he asked.

17

'Yeah, I'd appreciate it,' the blond man said with a chuckle. 'We're going away for two weeks, but my wife's got enough stuff to last us for months!'

The girl wrinkled her nose and stuck out her tongue at her husband, picked up one of the bags and lugged it on to the bus.

'Where are you two off to?' he asked once all the luggage was stowed away.

'Mexico. Acapulco, Puerto Vallarta, then Baja.'

'Sounds great,' he said enthusiastically. 'Two weeks, huh?'

'Yeah. How about you?'

'Oh nothing quite so exciting. I'm going to New York for a week on business.'

The man nodded, then said, 'You're traveling light. No luggage?'

'I dropped it off at the terminal.' He twisted his neck around and looked back at the long-term parking lot. 'I hope my car will be there when I get back.'

'It'll be there,' the blond man predicted. 'I've used the lot before and never had a problem.'

He nodded and folded his hands in his lap, watching the outline of the San Francisco Airport terminal come into view. Long-term parking lots. A prison lesson. Not from Ken Firpo, but from Darien, a young Aryan skinhead who had murdered two black men who had made the mistake of scratching his car – his own car – in a supermarket parking lot.

Darien's lesson was simple: never steal a car. Stealing a car leads to too many problems. Get stopped for a speeding ticket, the cops had you. If they questioned you and your ID didn't correspond with the vehicle's registration, they had you.

Always take a truck, or a van. A business vehicle. If you get stopped, your story is that you're driving your boss's vehicle.

The second part of the lesson was just as instructive. Spare keys. Darien claimed he could find a spare key hidden somewhere on the chassis of half the vehicles parked on the road. If he couldn't find a key, he'd move on to another vehicle. 'Never break into a car and hotwire it,' Darien had preached.

When he got back to the parking lot, it took him four minutes to find the blond man's spare key – taped behind the rear license plate.

He hummed to himself as he switched on the ignition and familiarized himself with the car's controls – another litany from Darien's gospel of dos and don'ts. 'Know where everything is, the wiper, the lights, the radio. Cops see you fumbling around like you don't know what you're doing, they'll jump on you.'

The registration papers were conveniently located in the glove compartment. He switched on the ignition, his thin lips pinching in a smile when he noticed the gas gauge. Full.

The young lovers would be in Mexico for two weeks. That would give him enough time. Just enough time.

Danielle Fritzheim slowly ran her fingers over Jason Lark's face, tracing his features.

'You're so damn good-looking, you should have been an actor, Jason.' Her thumb and forefinger traced the outline of his nose. 'Who did this? Hassend? Do you know he's married to that stupid bimbo who does that spy show on NBC? Forty-two years old and she claims she's never had anything done to her. She's married to the best plastic surgeon in Hollywood and she acts like a virgin.'

Lark pushed her hand away. 'Tell me about Alan. Is he still upset about the stolen Van Gogh?'

'Upset?' she laughed. 'He's furious. The insurance company is stalling, so he's hired an attorney to sue the bastards.'

'What's the insurance company's position?'

She got to her knees and leaned over Lark, her hard-ened nipples brushing across his lips. She dragged her Gucci purse from the nightstand, her fingers digging inside until she found the circular gold compact. 'They say it was our fault. That the security system should have been operating. As if we have to live like we're in a Third World country or something.'

Her fingers went back into the purse, this time coming out with a tiny silver spoon. 'It's that little bitch Eleana's fault for letting them in the house.' She dipped the spoon in the compact, then shook a line of the powder from the middle of Lark's stomach down to his belly button.

'What do you think of her?'

'Who?' Lark asked, pressing the back of his head into the bed pillows.

'Eleana. Did she ever make a move on you while you were decorating the house?'

'Hell, no.'

Danielle bent over and vacuumed up the cocaine with her nose, her tongue licking up the remaining granules. 'I think Alan may be fucking her. I can't think of any other reason to keep her around.'

Lark reached down and grabbed Danielle's mane of ash-blonde hair. 'So is the insurance company going to pay or not?'

'Oh, they think they'll get the painting back. An inves-tigator was at the house yesterday.' Her fingers reached out to his penis, slowly stroking it. 'He was from San Francisco. A hunk. He said it was obvious the thieves were interested in the painting and nothing else. In cases like this they usually always sell the stolen item back to the insurance company.'

'What do you mean "cases like this," Danielle?'

She jiggled her wrist. 'My jewellery. They left it all behind. The jade collection. Even Alan's Oscar. They could have taken everything, but they didn't.'

Lark pushed the extra pillow under his head so he could watch Danielle's hand. 'The San Francisco investigator. What did he look like?'

She dropped her head to his stomach, her tongue exploring his belly button. When she came up for air, she said, 'He was cute. Dark, but with blue eyes. Paul Newman eyes.'

'Did he have a scar over one eye?'

Danielle pulled her hand away, satisfied that Lark's manhood stood at attention on its own. 'Yes.' She squinted up at Lark. Without her contact lenses his face was a hazy blur. 'Do you know him?'

'Perhaps. Robert Duran, right?'

'Right. Like the fighter. The one that quit in the ring.' She picked up the compact again. 'This one doesn't look like a quitter. I hope he gets Alan's painting back. He's been a fucking bear.' She swirled her finger in the cache of cocaine, coated her lips with the powder, then leaned down and engulfed Lark's penis with her mouth.

Lark lay back and stared at the ceiling. Robert Duran. Of all the luck. Of all the rotten fucking luck.

Danielle Fritzheim dressed hurriedly after showering.

'I've got to get home. Alan's bringing some people over to the house. He's thinking of making a costume flick. One of those Three Musketeer type things.' She looked around for her shoes.

'Put your glasses on,' Lark suggested, already dressed and waiting impatiently at the door.

She gave him a nasty look, found her shoes, then patted Lark gently on the cheek. 'Give me a five-minute head start, Jason. It was nice seeing you again. It's been too long. Over six months. Get some rest. You tired out awfully fast today.'

Lark watched as her lipo-suctioned fanny sashayed

toward the elevators. Once she was out of sight he closed the hotel room door and took the stairs to the back exit.

No one was taking advantage of the inviting sky-hued swimming pool, but the surrounding beach chairs were packed with vacationers and the flight attendants who used the hotel on a regular basis.

It was there at the pool that he'd met his last wife, Ilsa. His fourth and, he swore to himself, positively last wife. He crossed through the lobby and out on to the street. The hotel was over-priced and beginning to look a little seedy. Its appeal was its location, less than two blocks from his office.

Adam Sheehan, his assistant, a terrier-like man of fifty who wore tweeds no matter what the weather, was showing a customer swatches of paint.

'Ah, here's Mr Lark now.' Adam approached Lark cautiously, his voice in a whisper. 'Mrs Quiller. She's driving me crazy.'

Mrs Quiller was a tall, red-headed woman with a diet-hard body and a house overflowing with valuable antiques. Lark gave her a friendly wave, then told Adam 'You'll have to handle her. I've got an important call to make.'

Lark weaved his way through tables covered with upholstery and drapery fabrics. The showroom walls were festooned with oil paintings and ornately-framed mirrors. He heard Mrs Quiller call out something to him, but he ignored her. He reached his office, entering quickly, slamming the door behind him.

He flopped into the Eames leather deskchair, slipped a black-lacquered cigarette case from his jacket pocket, extracted a ready-rolled joint and lit up.

He held the smoke in as long as he could, then let it stream out of his nose – the nose that Danielle Fritzheim had rightly diagnosed as having had reconstructive surgery, the cartilage having been chewed up by cocaine.

He flipped the Rolodex to the letter M. There was just the name: Mario – and a Las Vegas telephone number. He often wondered just where the telephone that Mario always answered so abruptly was located. His home? Office? Do men like Mario Drago have offices? Lark's only personal meeting with Drago had taken place in an empty room in the basement of the Sandbar Casino. He took another hit of the marijuana then dialed the number.

'Yes?'

Mario. As abrupt as ever.

'It's me, Jason.'

'What did you learn about the Fritzheim robbery?'

'Fritzheim has hired an attorney. He's threatening to sue the insurance company.'

'Yes, we know about that. Have the thieves contacted Fritzheim?'

'No, and apparently the cops don't have a clue.'

'The police are useless in cases like this,' Mario imparted.

'The insurance company has hired someone who has a good track record in recovering these types of things.'

'Yes. We know that too, Jason. Robert Duran. And that's bad news for you, isn't it? He's married to one of your ex-wives, isn't he?'

'Yes, Anona Stack,' Lark confirmed.

'Duran lives with her, and your two children, John and Lisa, in San Francisco, doesn't he?'

Lark felt his throat muscles tighten. He had been debating about whether or not to even bring Duran's name up.

'You seem to know all about it, Mario.'

'I do. I do indeed. What kind of a relationship do you have with your ex-wife?'

'We're on speaking terms.'

'And the children?'

'We get along fine. Why?'

23

'I want you to go to San Francisco. Find out what Duran's up to. Check on his investigation. If he negotiates with the thieves and finds out the Van Gogh is a fake, he'll start looking into the Fritzheims, Jason. And he'll find you there. It won't take him long to put it all together. And once he targets you, he might get to me.'

'Can't you find out who the thieves are?' Lark asked.

'I'm working on it. But if Duran gets to them first, *someone* will have to be eliminated.'

Lark didn't like the way Drago emphasized 'someone.' He knew the bastard wouldn't think twice about killing him if he thought it would blunt his connection to the Van Gogh. 'I've got something that looks good,' he said hurriedly. 'A woman in Beverly Hills. She's in her eighties, with no close relatives living close by, and doesn't remember her name half the time. There are some real treasures in the house. A Renoir that I'm sure you'd like.'

'Solve the Van Gogh problem first. Take care of Duran. Then we'll talk.'

The phone line crackled a moment, then purred. Lark crashed the receiver on its rest.

'Shit,' he said aloud, then flopped back into his chair. He had done four jobs for Mario – each time switching a forgery for a valuable painting: a Paul Gauguin, a Botticelli, a Matisse, the Fritzheim Van Gogh. Alan Fritzheim. It had seemed so easy – almost too easy. He was at the studio all day, every day, and Danielle went shopping every afternoon. All afternoon. That gave Lark all the time he needed to allow Drago's man to photograph and laser-scan the Van Gogh. The forgeries were always perfect. There had never been a problem. Until now. The damn thieves taking the forged Van Gogh.

'Take care of Duran.' Meaning that Mario wasn't going to be much help. If Duran did somehow tie the Van Gogh to him, he'd check his other clients, find the other switches. 'Take care of Duran.' Why the hell didn't Drago take care of Duran himself? It was his kind of business.

Lark moaned inwardly. Mario Drago. He would never forget meeting Drago. He had been at the roulette wheel when a man with a beach-ball face and chunky body tugged at his sleeve and told him that the casino manager wanted to talk to him.

Lark had expected to be escorted into a plush office, but the goon had taken him to the elevator and pushed the button for the basement, then shoved him down a narrow corridor to a cold room, its ceiling criss-crossed with air ducts.

Drago had been waiting behind a small wooden desk. He got to his feet slowly, a short, pudgy man with thinning gray hair, carefully combed across his scalp. *Unimpressive* was Lark's first impression, but that impression didn't last long.

Drago waved Lark's gambling debts under his nose, then began telling him what he was going to do to Lark, pulling a pen from his tuxedo pocket and placing it on the areas of Lark's body that would be fractured first.

When Lark was sweating sufficiently, Drago widened his hooded eyes and explained how 'things could be straightened out. To the advantage of both of us.'

Lark didn't need much convincing. The work was easy. He'd get a redecorating job and tell Drago of the treasures available. The gambling debts were canceled after the first job, then he got paid for his efforts. And the money was good. And was always paid in cash. Cash that somehow didn't last long. His last divorce had cost him a bundle. All of his marriages had cost him a bundle, he reluctantly admitted. He should have stuck it out with Anona.

Robert Duran. Lark was sure he could have gotten Anona back if it hadn't been for Duran. He had started visiting the kids in San Francisco. Seeing Anona. Taking her out to dinner. She was coming around, her attitude toward him softening. That was what? Seven years ago? Then she came to Los Angeles to testify against some bungling forger. Some bungling forger that Duran had caught. Anona was infatuated with this rugged "art cop." Infatuated enough to marry the bastard. Now Duran was sleeping in Stack House. With Anona.

Duran had made it clear that he didn't want Lark around. Didn't want him near Anona, and that he was more than willing to make life physically unpleasant for Lark if he 'ever touched Anona or the kids again.'

He flipped through the Rolodex again then dialed San Francisco.

The all too familiar voice of George, the pompous butler, greeted him formally: 'Stack House. Whom do you wish to speak to?'

'George, this is Jason Lark. Is Johnny there?'

'No, sir. He is not.'

'What about Lisa?'

'No, sir. She is not.'

'Well, then let me speak to Anona.'

'I'm sorry. She is indisposed. She is not feeling well, sir.'

Lark remembered Johnny writing to him some months ago, saying something about Anona being sick, but he hadn't paid much attention at the time.

'What's wrong with Anona?'

'I'm not at liberty to say, sir.'

'I'm coming up, George. Prepare a room for me. And let my son and daughter know I've called.'

'Yes, sir.'

Lark broke the connection. 'Indisposed.' How sick was she? Sick enough to keep Duran from his work?

A knock at the door interrupted Lark's thoughts.

It was his assistant, Adam.

'Mrs Quiller is becoming impatient, Jason. What shall I do with her?'

Lark was about to suggest in a most vulgar way that Adam do to Quiller what he had done so often to Danielle Fritzheim, but then he realized that, given Adam's sexual preferences, it wasn't possible.

Chapter 3

He was getting nervous. Four days spent watching the house and there was no sign of Anona Stack. Her husband, Duran, jogged regularly in the morning, right by the spot he had picked out as his surveillance post – just inside the Broadway Street pedestrian gate to the Presidio.

It had been a break, Stack House being located so close to the heavily wooded Presidio, the sixteen hundred acre former army post that was now a National Park.

He found it easy to hide amongst the pines and eucalyptus trees. The stolen van was parked a block away. As long as he moved it every few hours, the police wouldn't bother with it – and he certainly didn't have to worry about paying parking tags.

He kept a sketch-pad with him, so if anyone spotted him he could start drawing. Have a prop, Firpo, his cellmate had preached to him. A prop of some kind to validate your reason for being where you are. The sketch-pad was perfect, and it gave him something to do while waiting for his quarry. Where was she? He wanted her. Wanted her more than he wanted Duran. He had telephoned the house, asking for Anona. The response had always been the same: 'Madam is indisposed.'

He hadn't seen Anona, but he had seen Duran. He remembered Robert Duran from Duran's visit to the gallery seven years ago. He had barged in with the police – the day of the arrests.

Marrying the rich and famous Anona Stack and having access to all her money didn't seem to have changed Duran. He looked what? Tough? Competent, he decided. A 'stone' was what he'd be called in prison. Someone not to fool with – until the time was right.

He smiled, his upper lip riding over his teeth. The time was coming. Soon, very soon.

Duran had not testified or made an appearance at the trial, but the prosecutor had mentioned his name, mentioned how Duran had been responsible for identifying the gallery and the forged Anona Stack painting, responsible for sending Arlene and him to prison. Seven years ago. A lifetime ago. An eternity ago for Arlene.

Each morning, an hour or so after Duran returned from his morning run, he would take off in his fancy green Jaguar sedan. He had followed Duran on two occasions – both times the Jag had ended up in a parking lot alongside Duran's office on Taylor Street, by Fisherman's Wharf.

A cab pulled to the curb in front of Stack House. He lowered his sketch-pad and picked up the binoculars that dangled from a cord around his neck. A tall man with silvery hair exited the taxi, a raincoat draped around his shoulders like a cape.

He zoomed in on the man's face. Handsome, arrogant. He'd seen that face at the trial. Who was he? Someone who had been with Anona Stack, sat with her in the court room.

He lowered the binoculars and grabbed the sketch-pad.

'You look exhausted,' Peggy Jacquard advised Bob Duran when he came into the offices of Lost Art, Inc. 'How's Anona?'

'She had a tough night, Peg. A real tough one.' He walked to the fax machine. 'Anything new on the Fritzheim heist?'

'No. Nothing. Are you expecting the bad guys to give us a call?'

'It's a strong possibility.' Duran took off his sports coat and hung it on a rack near his desk.

He poured two cups of coffee and handed one to Peggy. Peggy Jacquard was a sleek-figured Jamaican, with jet-black, close-cropped hair. Mocha-colored skin and coffee-brown eyes, was the way one hopeful office Romeo had described her. She was graceful in her movements and had a delightful sing-song accent. She favored brightly-colored blouses and black tailored business outfits. Today's blouse was a solid cyan blue. She had worked with Duran at the Centennial Insurance Agency and had left to join Duran when he opened his own office.

'Tell me about Alan Fritzheim,' she urged, settling into her chair.

'He's short, bald and pissed off,' Duran said. 'He was ranting and raving the whole time.'

'What about his wife? Danielle. How does she look now? Tell me the juicy details.'

Duran grinned. Peggy was a devotee of *People Magazine* and supermarket tabloids. 'She's blonde, flashy, and likes to flirt.'

'Hmmm. What's the house like?'

'Unbelievable. It looks like a beached ocean liner. All white, half of it hanging over a cliff.'

'I read it cost over thirty million dollars,' Peggy disclosed.

'I wouldn't argue with the estimate. Everything was state of the art – including the security system.'

'So how did the burglars get away with it?'

Duran sipped his coffee, then smacked his lips in appreciation. It was a strong French roast. And he needed a jolt of caffeine badly. 'They showed up in the afternoon in a van posing as delivery boys with a sofa. Fritzheim was at his studio, his wife was out shopping. A young Mexican housekeeper was the only one there. Eleana Morales. Poor kid was scared to death when I talked to her. She doesn't speak much English.'

Duran settled behind his desk and absent-mindedly flicked on the computer. 'Fritzheim's got this super hi-tech security system, but it wasn't activated.'

'Do you think Morales could be in on it, Bob?'

'No. I talked to her for half an hour. I'm sure she's not involved,' Duran covered his mouth to stifle a yawn. 'The local cops showed me the blueprints for his security system. And the price-tag. Two hundred and eighty-nine thousand dollars. He's paying Eleana, the kid house-keeper, seven bucks an hour.'

Peggy made a clucking sound with her tongue. 'Was anything else taken?'

'Nope. Just the Van Gogh, and there are plenty of valuables throughout the house, that's why I think they'll contact either the Fritzheims or the carrier, Pacific Indemnity, who will pass them on to us.'

'How did they know about the painting?'

'Fritzheim must have bragged about it to the press more than once. Run a Nexis search on him, see if there are any articles in any newspapers or magazines about the house and the painting.'

He watched Peggy saunter back to her desk, the liquid movement of her hips made it look as if there was a samba playing in her mind. Maybe there was, he thought. She was currently dating a halfback who played for the Oakland Raiders.

He logged the computer on to the Art Index, a database set up by the museums, auction houses and galleries in the United States. When a major work was stolen, it was reported to AI, which then listed it on their 'missing' bulletin board, along with a description of the work, a color photograph when available, and the name of the last registered owner.

Over nine thousand works of art had been listed as stolen in the last twelve months. About seven per cent were recovered. The going fee for recovery was ten per cent of the insured value, so it certainly gave investigators like Duran a good reason to go looking for them.

The problem was that there was nothing close to the Art Index for Europe, Asia or South America, where most of the stolen items eventually ended up.

From the beginning of his career as an insurance investigator the art world had fascinated Duran. The staggering amounts of money involved and the secrecy in which transactions were conducted made art an especially inviting target for a thief.

Billions of dollars changed hands every year, but there was no watchdog agency, such as the Security Exchange Commission which monitored the stock market. Deals were often made in cash, the money spirited away to a numbered Swiss or Bahaman bank account.

The Internal Revenue Service had an Art Advisory Panel, which consisted of dealers, museum directors and collectors – an incestuous group if there ever was one, in Duran's view. The auction houses weren't much better. The inflated sales that made headlines were often rigged. The price of one wildly overpriced painting would then elevate the rest of the offered items. Quite often the buyer would donate that multimillion dollar painting to a museum, thus getting him or her an enormous tax write-off, so the tax payers were ripped off as well.

The artists themselves were part of the shady mix – selling their work directly to a client at a drastic discount, taking a small chunk of cash rather than paying the dealer a third, Uncle Sam a third and their agent his slice of the dwindling pie.

Duran scanned the latest items listed on the bulletin board. At least a dozen since yesterday, but there was no mention of the painting stolen from Alan Fritzheim. The insurance company was holding off for ten days. If the thieves didn't contact them, or Duran, by that time, the information would go on-line.

'Help the driver with my bags, George,' Jason Lark ordered when the butler greeted him at the door of Stack House.

Lark stood with his hands on his hips, surveying the entry hall while he waited for his luggage. He shook his head sadly. Stack House, a massive, half-timbered, English Mock-Tudor designed by Bernard Maybeck in 1911 for Anona's grandfather, Sean Stack. It stretched out some 19,088 square feet, with twenty-two rooms, twelve bathrooms, an indoor swimming pool, a game room, and a media room in the basement.

Old Sean had arrived in America from Ireland with little more than his confirmation suit. He'd started his life in the New World as a blacksmith, worked his way into the steel business, eventually building ships and bridges. Very large ships and very large bridges.

His son, Conrad Stack, wasn't quite the businessman his father had been, but he carried on the family enterprise, marrying a young secretary, Grace Hanlon, who died just two days after their only child, Anona, was born.

While Bernard Maybeck may have been a genius in his time, back in 1911 he hadn't had to worry much about garage space. Later on, it just wasn't fashionable to leave those Dusenbergs and Rolls Royces lined up along the sidewalk, so in the sixties Anona's father did what he thought was the sensible thing. He bought the property alongside, tore down the house, and built a garage.

The garage was hidden from the street by a fifteen-foot privet hedge and was designed to resemble an English countryside stable, but instead of gravel, mud and straw, the flooring was of herringbone-patterned brick.

'Early twentieth-century', Lark had dubbed the interior

of Stack House when he first saw it: 20th Century Fox. It looked as if old man Stack had brought in Cecil B. DeMille or some other Hollywood dinosaur to furnish the place. Jason had tried to lighten it up, bring in some color, some life, but Conrad Stack would have none of it.

The mail was bundled neatly on a Regency period mahogany table. Lark glanced over his shoulder to make sure the butler was out of sight, then quickly thumbed through the mail, hoping to find something addressed to Duran. He was disappointed. It was all for Anona. One envelope caught his interest. The return address was for the Gerhow Gallery in Zurich, Switzerland. Perhaps the most famous and influential gallery in the world. He slipped the envelope into his coat pocket, then strolled into the living room and was pleasantly surprised at the changes. The dark coffered ceiling was now pale yellow, and backlit under frosted glass. The walnut paneling was painted a light beige. The massive carved oak furniture was gone, supplanted by a hotchpotch of brightly upholstered chairs and couches.

The fifteenth-century tapestries were gone too, replaced by one of Anona's paintings.

'I'll take your bags to your room, sir,' George said, in his clipped baritone. 'You're on the third floor. You may remember the guest room.'

Lark's jaw flexed. Old George reminding him of the times he'd spent in the guest room during his marriage to Anona. Impertinent old prick!

'Is John home?'

'No, sir. Master John has purchased a houseboat in Sausalito. He spends much of his time there.'

'What about Lisa?'

'Not in at the moment, sir.'

'You told them I was coming?'

'I did indeed, sir.'

Lark slid the coat from his shoulders and tossed it over

the luggage at the butler's feet. 'What about Bob Duran?'

'I believe he's at his office, sir.'

'Well, I'll go and see Anona.' He edged up close to the butler. George had to be in his seventies now – tall, gaunt, a seemingly emotionless man with thick, billowy white hair. He had been in the Stack family employ since before Anona had been born. Lark and George had taken an immediate dislike to one another. Lark had tried to persuade Anona to fire George several times, but she wouldn't hear of it.

'You don't mind if I visit with Anona, do you, George? I still remember the way to her room.'

'I'm afraid she's not receiving anyone at the moment, sir. The doctor left less than an hour ago. He gave her something to help her sleep.'

'Just how sick is she?' Lark asked.

The stern face folded in a rueful smile. 'Very, sir. Very, very, sick.'

Chapter 4

The area was just as Ken Firpo had described it: thickets of pine, oak and redwood trees, and head-high scrub bushes soaked up every sound of movement.

There were numerous possibilities – he'd chosen a road that was totally grown over by low-lying vegetation. A rusty iron gate held together by an equally rusty lock had been the only barrier.

He had sawn off the lock, replacing it with a new one that quickly achieved a patina of rust from the thick, ocean-drenched fog that coiled in through the woods.

A warren of trails used by small animals led him to the caves. There were at least a dozen, and the one he had chosen was perfect.

He had considered several vehicles: trucks, moving vans, campers, but had settled on the bread truck after his cellmate Ken Firpo convinced him it would be the easiest to convert into a likeness of the SHU at Pelican Bay.

The truck's checkerboard blue and white coloring was faded. The Kilpatrick's Bread lettering was chipped and oxidized. The engine's front cowling was missing and it tilted to the right, the result of two tires being almost flat. But that didn't matter. It had just a short trip left.

The cave was hollowed out deep enough to engulf the entire truck. He turned the ignition and eased the clutch in, inching the vehicle over the plywood boards leading into the opening. He butted the bumper against the dirt wall, then edged himself out of the driver's seat and observed the results. Not bad, not bad at all, he surmised. Nothing like the real thing of course. His cell, called the SHU, for solitary housing unit, was six feet by ten feet – no windows, just raw concrete walls and floor, the door of perforated steel sheets, with a small slot for the passing of food, fresh linen and blankets. He had counted the bullet-sized holes in his cell door – a total of 3,864. He had counted them over and over, outraged when he was off by a number or two, determined to pinpoint just which holes he had missed. There had been no television, and books or magazines weren't allowed. No one to talk to, to touch. No view of neighbouring prisoners. Dark, cold, desolate. Not a ray of sunlight ever reached his SHU. The three daily meals were delivered by a close-mouthed guard – starchy prison food: potatoes, rice, beans, overcooked meats, white bread sandwiches, fruit, potato chips, stale pieces of cake or pie. A hard plastic cup and an unbreakable spoon were provided. If the spoon was not returned with the cup and tray, four of the guards would enter the cell, batons and stun guns flying.

He had saved pieces of dessert – crumbs of cookies, cake or pie – and sprinkled them around the floor, hoping that something, anything: an ant, a spider, a fly, something alive would visit, if only for a short time. But nothing ever came.

His options were limited to praying, masturbating or exercising. He had long ago given up his belief in a god. He opted for masturbation and the exercises, and since he was not allowed access to weights or machines, he built up a regimen of running in place, sit-ups and isometrics, contracting one set of muscles against another.

His hand massaged the back of his head, behind his right ear. That was where the migraines usually started. First the dazzling light, then the blurred, double images, followed by the pain that echoed throughout his head.

Pain that the prison doctor claimed was nothing more serious than headaches brought on by anxiety. Not the batons, or the guard's steel-capped shoes, but anxiety.

He selected a pick from the tools littering the area and eased his way back into the cave, sweating with the effort it took to swing the pick in the narrow quarters, aiming at the tires, listening to the air hiss out as the truck's rims settled ever so slowly down into the mud.

There was a three-foot clearance above the truck's roof, more than enough room to run the electrical wiring.

The truck's original rear doors had been discarded. He examined the interior. The half-inch steel plates bolted to the walls had a wet, silvery look. The makeshift toilet was just a hole in the floor. Anona Stack would have to put up with it. No shower. They had always watched him when he showered, as if they were afraid he would somehow try and escape through the drain. They'd watch, laugh, and make crude jokes. The single bunk was nothing more than angle iron, welded together and bolted to the wall.

A donut-sized eye-bolt had been welded and bolted to the ceiling. He slipped a finger through the bolt and tugged, then removed the garment from his back pocket and carefully threaded it through the bolt, fastening the back straps of the bra in a solid square knot. He grasped the bra with both hands and pulled himself upwards, his feet dangling free for several seconds. The nylon stretched under the strain, but he outweighed Anona Stack by at least seventy pounds. It would hold her.

A light in the ceiling, a mattress, that was all that was missing. Except for the new door, of course. He still had to work on the door.

He strolled over to the saw horses holding the heavy steel sheeting. It would be too much work to drill 3,864 holes in that thick metal. He decided to compromise: four rows of holes, three in the first row, then eight, then six and finally four.

★ ★ ★

Jason Lark showered and changed his clothes. George had left the luggage on the bed. Lark remembered the bed, and the room with its pot-bellied, bow-legged French Provincial pieces. The print on the wall was of Van Gogh's *The Night Café*. It made him think of the original Van Gogh from Alan Fritzheim's collection, *Sun and Sky*, the one he had helped to scan, photograph and then switch. The one that was causing him so much trouble.

It had seemed such an amazingly safe scheme. Foolproof. The replaced paintings didn't change hands often. Most people held on to works of art like the Van Gogh for years. For lifetimes. When, and if, a sale was made, who was to say just when the forgery had been switched?

'Goddamn thieves,' he murmured under his breath. He unsnapped his suitcase and began hanging up his garments. He remembered the letter to Anona he'd pilfered from the morning mail. He slipped it out of the raincoat pocket. The Gerhow Gallery. The envelope was creamy-white, heavy cotton. He slit it open with his fingernail. He scanned the first paragraph, then began reading carefully.

Dear Madame Stack
We have been hired by the Bank of Zurich to catalog and evaluate the paintings and sculptures of the estate of Claude Bresson.

One of your paintings, Perfume Fields, *is among the items in question. There seems to be no bill of sale, or mention of payment in the personal records of Mr Bresson, other than a hand-written diary notation – showing the date and the words – 'A gift.'*

There is a further notation in Mr Bresson's diary – the same date – 'Cinq Putaims and my sketches of Château Bresson to Anona.'

We would appreciate it if you could enlighten us as to whether or not Perfume Fields *was given by you to Mr*

Bresson, and your estimate of its approximate value at that time.

In addition, would you please clarify whether or not Mr Bresson presented Cinq Putaims *to you.*

Our research shows that Mr Bresson obtained these sketches from the artist, Pablo Picasso, in approximately 1925.

Your earliest attention to these requests would be appreciated.

Very truly yours,
R. G. Gerhow III

Lark groaned and flopped down on the bed. Bresson! He vaguely recalled Bresson having given him a packet of sketches for Anona. He remembered the ones he saw were amateur drawings of the château. There had been others, but he hadn't bothered to look at the damn things. What was it that Bresson said to him? Something about the sketches being some of his early works and those of a friend. Friend! Pablo Picasso! *Cinq Putaims*.

Lark's knowledge of French wasn't extensive, but he knew the *cinq* was five and *putaims* was slang for whores. Five whores. Picasso was a known whoremonger in his youth. He pounded his bunched fists into the mattress in frustration. Why hadn't he looked at all the drawings? He could have easily kept them. What the hell became of them? What would five Picassos, Picassos that had never been on the market, be worth now?

He went to the bathroom, ran a comb through his hair, sprinkled on some aftershave, then took the stairs to the second floor. To Anona's room. The hell with asking George's permission to see his ex-wife. He eased the door open a crack. He could see her silhouette under the bedspread.

'Anona,' he whispered, then entered the room and silently closed the door behind him.

A large-screen TV was situated in front of her bed. The sound was off, the screen showing an old movie. Lark recognized the figure of a young John Wayne on horseback.

He crept around to the side of the bed, his slow breathing becoming a gasp when he saw Anona's face. God, she looked like hell! It had been several years since he'd last seen her. She'd aged considerably in that time. Her thin hair had patches of scalp showing through the brittle-looking grey-red strands.

Lark took a step back, his eyes skimming the walls. One of Anona's paintings hung over the bed. The rest of the walls were bare, except for several mirrors.

The figure beneath the covers stirred. Anona fluttered her eyes open. When she saw Lark she squeezed them shut for several seconds. When they popped open she said, 'Good Lord, have I died and gone to hell? Is that you, Jason?'

'Yes,' Lark said, nervously flashing his perfectly capped teeth. 'It's me, Anona. I hope I didn't wake you.'

Anona dug her elbows into the pillows and slowly levered herself up into a sitting position. 'What are you doing here? I suppose Johnny or Lisa told you.'

'Told me what, Anona?'

'That I'm dying, obviously.' Her eyes narrowed to slits. 'You look as handsome as ever, and disgustingly healthy. I've lost track of you. Are you still married?'

'No. I'm single again. Ilsa left me months ago.'

'Ilsa? Was she the blonde or the brunette?'

'It depends on your vantage point,' Lark disclosed.

Anona started to cough. A deep, hacking cough. She pointed a finger to the nightstand. 'Water, please.'

Lark quickly poured a glass from a swan-shaped decanter and handed it to her.

Anona took small, bird-like sips until the glass was empty.

'Is there anything else I can get you? Some pills, a brandy or something?'

'A syringe full of morphine seems to be the only thing that helps me. I have a glass of wine with Bob every night, although I can seldom keep it down.' She patted the bed. 'Sit down. Don't worry, it's not catching.' She coughed lightly into her hand. 'Have you seen the children?'

'No. I just got here. Are you sure there's nothing—'

'There's nothing anyone can do,' Anona revealed. 'I'm dying. I just pray it comes quickly.'

Lark was startled by her matter-of-fact response.

Anona's face clouded in pain. She gestured with her hand. 'The drawer. A smoke, please.'

Lark opened the nightstand drawer, his nostrils twitching like a rabbit's in a carrot field. 'Marijuana? You wouldn't even try it when we were married.'

'I wasn't dying then. It helps.'

Lark held one of the cigarettes and ran it under his nose. 'Ummm. Good stuff.'

'Bob gets it for me. I don't know who from. Help yourself, Jason.'

Lark used his lighter to get two of the cigarettes going, handing one to Anona. They blew smoke at each other.

Lark looked up at the painting over the bed. 'I've been thinking of you a lot, lately. Remember when we were in France? The Riviera? Claude Bresson's magnificent château?'

'What I remember is you casino crawling and chasing all those naked girls on the beach.'

'I acted stupidly, I know. I never really thanked Bresson. He died recently, didn't he?'

Anona took another hit on the cigarette. 'Yes. In his sleep. Lucky man.'

'I remember you giving Bresson a painting. What was it called? *Perfume Fields*? Something like that. And he gave me some sketches for you. Remember?'

Anona shook her head slowly from side to side. 'I remember the painting – those beautiful fields of flowers. But sketches? No. What were they like?'

'They were of the château and some young women. Bresson did them himself. Don't you remember seeing them? I gave them to you, or I put them in our luggage.'

Anona sank back into the pillows. 'No, I don't remember, Jason. But if Claude gave them to me, they must be around somewhere. I wouldn't have gotten rid of them. He was such a wonderful man, he—' She bit down on her lip, her face a fan of wrinkles. 'Damn it. Get George for me. Jason. Tell him to get ahold of Dr Feldman.'

Lark got to his feet. 'Right away, darling.' He stared down at Anona. 'I hate to see you like this.'

'I hate to be like this,' she confessed. 'I want this to end. And the sooner the better.'

Peggy stuck her head into Duran's office. 'Telephone. It's Harry Lawson.'

'Lawson,' Duran gave a curt laugh. 'It looks like we're in business.' He picked up the phone. 'Good afternoon, counselor.'

'Robert. Good to talk to you again.' The attorney's voice was smooth and oily. 'I had a call this morning. The caller was quite cryptic. He mentioned that he had come into possession of a painting. A rather valuable painting, he thought.'

Duran reached out gratefully for the cup of coffee in Peggy's hand. 'Let me take a wild guess. A Vincent Van Gogh. *Sun and Sky*.'

'That's an excellent guess,' Lawson admitted. 'My impression was that the gentleman was thinking of shopping the item around.'

'And what did you advise him to do, counselor?'

'My advice was that if the item was obtained illegally, it

should be returned to its proper owner or turned over to the police.'

'I bet that went over real big with your client, Harry.'

'The gentleman is not my client. Yet. However, if in fact he does contact me again, what do you suggest I should do, Robert? I'm told that you are handling the Fritzheim incident.'

'Who told you that?'

'The newspapers reported that Pacific Indemnity is the carrier. They told me you've been hired to get the painting back. And I think it was a very wise choice on their part. We've been able to solve these problems together in the past.'

Duran was tiring of the verbal sparring. Harry Lawson was a criminal attorney who was known in the trade as the 'Holy Redeemer.' He was the connection between the thieves and the insurance companies. Neither Duran nor anyone else could ever prove that Lawson was directly involved in any of the thefts.

'I think you should do what you usually do, Harry. Tell the crooked bastards that we're ready to deal and take your cut.'

'My, my. A little testy today, Robert. Wrong side of the bed?'

Duran took a deep breath and sighed. He wasn't in much of a position to give Harry Lawson a 'holier than thou' speech. They both dealt with the same clientele. 'Sorry Harry. If the gentleman calls again, tell him I am interested.'

'Yes, I'll do exactly that, Robert. The usual conditions?'

'Yes, I think that can be arranged.' The usual conditions were that the payment would be in cash and once the painting was returned, the owner would advise the police that he would not press charges.

'Give my love to Peggy and your wife,' Lawson urged before hanging up.

Duran dropped the phone on its cradle and turned to see Peggy's smiling eyes. 'Lawson says to give you his love.'

'I know what his idea of love is. A room-service dinner in his hotel suite. I'd rather he tempted me with a percentage of his profits. What do you think he makes on these deals?'

'More than we do, Peg. That's for sure. I better call the insurance carrier and tell them that it looks like a go.'

Chapter 5

It had become an evening ritual. Duran carried the tray with the wine bottle and the crystal glasses into Anona's bedroom. He was encouraged to see she was sitting up in bed. Her hair was covered with a gold-colored turban and she had lipstick on.

'Hi,' he said, setting the tray down on the nightstand. He bent over and kissed her lightly on the lips. 'You look great.'

Anona gave him a sour look. 'Liar. How was your day?'

Duran poured the wine and Anona used both hands to hold on to the glass. She ran her nose over the rim and inhaled.

'A 1983 Musigny,' Duran whispered.

'There was a time when I would have known.'

'*Siempre,*' they said in unison, then Anona took a small sip and handed the glass back to Duran.

'My day wasn't very exciting, though it looks like I am to be involved in the Fritzheim theft. Harry Lawson is representing the crooks.'

'Bastards,' Anona hissed.

'George tells me we have a house guest.'

'Yes. Jason. The devil himself. Unfortunately we can't very well kick him out, Love. He is their father.'

'Have you talked to him?'

'Yes. He looks disgustingly well. I'd bet he's had his face tightened with a little surgery.' She reached out for

47

Duran's arm. 'I'm sorry he showed up. I was hoping he wouldn't find out about me until after I was gone. He'll be after the children, Bob. And all their money. Jason will try to get back in their good graces, somehow.' She dropped her arm to the bed. 'The money can be a curse. I'm worried about them. Especially Johnny.'

'Have you talked to John or Lisa about Jason?'

'No. Not lately. I know Lisa's never forgiven him for the way he treated us and the way he's neglected her all these years. But he's evil, Bob. And Johnny's vulnerable. So vulnerable.' Her hands grabbed Duran's arm again. 'You will look out for them, won't you? Protect them from Jason. I know it won't be easy, but you'll do it, won't you?'

'I will,' Duran promised. 'Now tell me about your day. What did Dr Feldman say?'

Duran stayed until he saw Anona's eyes starting to droop. He made sure she was covered by the bedspread and that the TV remote control was within reach. She was sound asleep by the time he closed the door behind him.

George informed Duran that 'Mr Lark is in the game room.'

The game room had both a regulation-sized billiard table and a pool table. A rectangular-shaped Tiffany lamp hung over each table, and above the circular oak one where Conrad Stack and his cronies reportedly indulged in very high-stakes poker marathons. The walls were paneled with thick French walnut, the floor covered by overlapping three-hundred-year-old Bahkshayesh oriental rugs.

Lark was leaning over the pool table, lining up the cue ball on the three-ball when he heard Duran's footsteps.

He waved the cue in Duran's direction. 'Hello, Bob. Long time no see.'

Duran nodded, making an effort to disguise his feelings toward Lark. He was an imposingly handsome man, with a narrow-shouldered body, a movie-star face and silver hair worn long and winged at the side. He was wearing a brass-buttoned blue blazer and gray cashmere turtleneck sweater. His twill slacks were creased saber-sharp.

Lark extended a hand and Duran grasped it by the fingers and gave an extra-hard squeeze, taking satisfaction in knowing it was the same hand that Lark had struck Anona and the children with.

'What are you doing here, Jason?'

'I had some business in town. I thought I'd stop by and see the kids. I . . . I didn't know about Anona. I saw her this afternoon, she . . . doesn't look good. What does the doctor say?'

'He's optimistic that she will go into a remission period again. How long is your business going to take?'

'Oh, just a few days. Johnny's coming over and we're going out to dinner,' Lark said, turning back to his shot. The cue ball hit the red ball, then banked off the cushion and rolled into the corner pocket. 'I never was any good at this,' Lark confessed with a smile. 'Johnny tells me he's opened a nightclub. Have you seen the place?'

'No. Not yet.' Duran knew Anona was the prime backer of the project, but she was in no condition now to visit the club and John had made it clear that Duran would not be welcomed.

Lark racked his cue stick, picked up the eight-ball and rolled it slowly down the green felt. 'Look, I know you don't think much of me, and . . . well, there were times when I didn't think much of myself,' he admitted genially. 'But, I'm still fond of Anona and, though I know I've had a funny way of showing it, I love my kids. But, if you want me out of here, I can understand that. I—'

'You can stay for a couple of days,' Duran proposed, knowing that Lark would put on a martyr scene if he was asked to leave. 'Have you seen Lisa?'

'No. She hasn't been home since I got here.' Lark

pointed to the fully stocked bar on the far side of the room. 'Have a drink with me?'

'No thanks.'

Lark selected a bottle of Scotch malt whisky and dribbled a measure or two into a cut-crystal goblet. His eyes circled the room. 'Did Old Man Stack ever get you in here and give you the third degree?'

'No, he chose the wine cellar for that session.'

Lark laughed loudly. He pointed to the poker table. 'He sat me down right there and put me through the wringer. He was a tough old bastard. But he was right. That time. How's business, Bob? Still an art gumshoe?'

'Still working at it,' Duran confirmed. 'How about you? How are things in the interior decorating world?'

'It's a living. Nothing exciting, like what you're doing. I was wondering if—'

'Hey, Jason.' Johnny Stack entered the room with a swagger. Twenty-three now, with reddish-brown hair worn ear-lobe length. His mustache, all of six months' old, was slightly darker than his hair.

He slapped his father on the shoulder. John was wearing blue jeans and a black shirt with a silk-screened Grateful Dead caricature across the chest. 'Good to see you. Come on, let's get out of here. I want to show you my club.'

'Sure, son. I was just having a drink. Join me.'

Johnny gave Duran a strained look. 'No. Let's go.'

'Your mother just nodded off to sleep,' Duran advised.

'Yeah, well I'll look in on her later. Come on, Jason. Let's go.'

Lark gave Duran an exaggerated shrug, took a long sip of the whisky, then slipped his arm around his son's shoulders.

Duran watched and wondered what that little scene was all about. Jason Lark was acting like a long lost sheep ready to come back to the fold. The rich fold of Stack

House. Once you saw Anona, you didn't need a medical degree to know that she was dying. Dying and leaving her estate to her children. Lark's children. How the hell was he going to keep his promise to Anona to protect them from their father?

The nausea was back. Anona's stomach was churning and when she opened her eyes the room was spinning. Pain and nausea. God, she was tired of it. *God. Do you hear me? I'm sick and tired of it! Take me out of here, take me, damn it!*

There had been several periods of remission over the last eighteen months, but somehow she knew there wouldn't be another one. She couldn't take another one, knowing that she'd drop back, back into this hopeless, miserable state.

She'd actually tried taking an overdose once. It had turned out disastrously. All it had accomplished was to make her sicker than she'd ever been, but not as sick as she was feeling now.

She'd chided herself endlessly for not having been successful. She'd thought about the different methods available. Use a gun – there were several of her father's shotguns and rifles in the house? Or do it the old-fashioned San Francisco way, by jumping off the Golden Gate Bridge? One last look at the city's beautiful skyline, then over the rail. She should have done it a year ago, while she was still able to function.

She sensed the presence of a person in the room. She opened her eyes and saw someone with what appeared to be a halo around their head hovering over her. For a brief moment she thought she had died and gone to Heaven.

She could make out a pair of hands opening a medicine bottle, breaking open the capsules, sprinkling the powder into a glass of wine.

I hope you know what you're doing, she prayed. She used all her remaining strength to focus her eyes, to stop the room from spinning. She could see the medicine bottle. 'Improvane,' she said in a groaning whisper, then another thought came to her mind. *I hope you don't get into any trouble. Don't get in any trouble. It's what I want, what I . . .*

She was helped into a sitting position, her head gently tilted back and, as her cracked lips parted, the liquid slowly flowed into her mouth a sip at a time.

It tasted bitter and she pulled her head away for a moment and managed a weak smile. It was the first time that she had really smiled in weeks. The damn wine probably cost a couple of hundred dollars a bottle and it was bitter now. But she wanted more. More.

She sipped at the wine steadily, swallowing teaspoons at a time, and finally it was done. The glass was empty. She slid back down into the sheets, curling her legs up toward her chest. It was working. She was getting sleepy. A soft, sweet, painless sleepiness. Then the nausea came back, along with a jolting pain in her stomach.

'Don't let me throw it up, don't let me throw up the wine, please don't . . .'

She opened her eyes. 'Where are you? Help, please.'

She saw something coming at her, floating over her head. White. A pillow. 'I love you,' were her final words as she opened her mouth wide, welcoming the pillow like a lover's kiss.

Jason Lark had waited until Bob Duran left for work the following morning, then used the phone in the library to call the Gerhow Gallery in Switzerland. Johnny had told him that Hugh Stringer was still Anona's attorney, so he decided to use Stringer's name.

He was put through to R. G. Gerhow III almost immediately when he identified himself as Anona Stack's attorney.

'We received your letter yesterday, Mr Gerhow. I'm

sorry to inform you that my client is quite ill. She does recall giving her *Perfume Fields* painting to Mr Bresson. It was purely a gift.'

'I understand, monsieur. It was very generous of her.'

'Quite,' Lark concurred. 'I am afraid there is some confusion regarding the Picasso sketches. Anona remembers Claude Bresson giving her some sketches – but they were ones he himself had done. Of the château.'

Lark could hear the shuffling of papers over the long-distance line.

'Claude's records show that, in addition to his drawings, there were the Picasso sketches, six of them, one of his old flat in Paris, the other of five women: *putaims,*' Gerhow said with a polite chuckle.

'I assume these would be quite valuable.'

'Monsieur, I know that Mrs Stack's canvas is worth a great deal now, but the Picassos, ah, these could be special. Very special.'

'How so?' queried Lark.

'Two of Monsieur Bresson's nephews, as well as several friends, had seen the Picassos. They are unique in that they are signed *in verto*, on the back – just the initials – P.R.P. for Pablo Ruiz y Picasso, but there is the name of each of the young ladies there also and, according to those who have seen them . . . a toast to the earnestness in which they performed their duties.'

Lark involuntarily sat up straight and squared his shoulders. Five unknown Picassos with a ribald history!

Gerhow seemed to be reading Lark's mind from a distance of over six thousand miles. 'It is almost impossible to estimate the value of these sketches, Monsieur Stringer. The originals, then the value of the reproductions.'

'I'm an attorney, not an art dealer, Mr Gerhow. If I suddenly walked into your gallery now with the Picassos, what would you give me?'

'First, a heartfelt thanks, then, oh, something like

53

twenty million dollars, Monsieur Stringer.' Gerhow paused. 'Do you think that such an event is possible?'

'I wish it were but, as I say, Mrs Stack has no recollection of the sketches.'

'Perhaps if I spoke to her?'

'I couldn't allow that,' warned Lark. 'She is seriously ill. There . . . there is a strong possibility that she will not recover.'

'Then my condolences, monsieur. But do everything you can to find those sketches. Your cooperation will be greatly rewarded, I am sure.'

Lark bid Gerhow goodbye, then leaned back in the chair. The Picassos. He jumped to his feet and started his search. He definitely remembered throwing the packet that Claude Bresson had given him into Anona's huge Vuitton traveling trunk. He decided on the basement first – the storage area, adjacent to the wine cellar.

There he found a jumble of lawn furniture, old toys he remembered belonging to Johnny and Lisa: a wooden rocking-horse, a white doll's house that Lisa had played with hour after hour. Golf clubs, tennis rackets, fishing equipment, all neatly lined up against the brick walls. Sealed cardboard boxes reaching to the ceiling, and luggage. Mounds of luggage. Lark dug his way through the pile until he found the trunk. He ran his hand across the distinctive patterned fabric and the brass hardware, then unsnapped the locks and began digging through the drawers. Empty. All of them empty.

He stood back and dusted his hands together. He hadn't expected the Picasso sketches to still be there, but it was an obvious starting place.

Anona certainly would have recognized anything by Picasso – maybe not immediately – but she would have known that the sketches were quality work, yet she claimed no knowledge of them. He had questioned her again last night. Thoroughly. He was sure that she'd never seen them. Could they have been discarded? Thrown out? No. Anona was just as certain that she would have never gotten rid of a gift from 'wonderful old Claude.' But she had to know. Had to! Somewhere in her confused, sick, pain-filled mind she knew. He had patiently probed at her for an hour, while Duran was out at some business meeting, spiking her marijuana cigarette with a little cocaine base, when she started to dose off, coaxing her to drink a little of the fine Burgundy on the nightstand, but it hadn't helped. Would she wonder about his interest? Discuss their conversation with Duran? Did he have the Picassos? Lark doubted it. If Duran knew of them, then so would Anona. He'd have to find them. Find them fast.

So where were they? Stuck in some bureau drawer in the house? At the bottom of a pile of magazines in some cupboard? They had to be here somewhere.

'Is there something I can help you with, sir?'

Lark whirled around, almost losing his balance. 'Oh, George. It's you. No, I'm just . . . chasing memories.'

The butler nodded solemnly and did an abrupt about-face.

Lark waited until George was gone before surveying the storage area, his eyes falling on the cardboard boxes. Most were neatly labeled: Christmas lights. Christmas ornaments. Tax records. Silverware. China settings. There were at least a dozen with no labels at all. It would take time to go through them. Time when George wasn't around peeking over his shoulder.

The Picassos. They could be his salvation. Get him out from under. Get him out of California, away from Mario Drago. But there was still Duran. Drago was right about the miserable bastard. He'd start digging into the Fritzheim job. The Picassos wouldn't do him any good in jail. He'd have to take care of Duran, get rid of him, then find the Picassos.

He took the elevator to the third floor, then walked

down a flight of stairs to Duran's room. Anona had told him that Duran had taken the room adjacent to hers. The door was unlocked. The bedroom was large, but sparsely furnished, as if the tenant spent little time there. A bed. Two dressers. A closet. A few paintings on the walls. None of Anona's. None of anyone who Lark recognized. Certainly no Picasso sketches.

He checked the dresser first, then the closet. He found nothing. A ceiling-high armoire held sweaters and underwear. A middle drawer revealed Duran's jewelry: watches, cuff-links and a zip-lock plastic bag filled with keys. Spare keys! He slipped them into his coat pocket and was about to leave, when he decided to look under the bed. He was on his knees when he heard someone enter Anona's room next door. He got to his feet and gently eased the connecting door open an inch.

Old Dr Feldman on his morning rounds. Lark watched through the crack as Feldman leaned over to talk to Anona. He was about to close the door when he saw the expression on Feldman's face.

The neatly dressed little man who drove the tan Lincoln Continental was right on time. He'd had no doubt from the beginning of his surveillance that the man was a doctor – he carried a black leather bag, and his visits were regimented. Nine thirty in the morning, and four in the afternoon.

To confirm this, he had checked the Lincoln's license plate number. He simply looked in the Yellow Pages under Information Services, picking a firm with an 800 number. For a fee of thirty-five dollars, they were happy to supply the registered owner of the vehicle. The clerk barely listened to his explanation of having accidentally bumped into the car, and wanting to contact the owner to pay for the damages.

'We can give you the name, sir. But not the address.'

He wasn't worried about the inquiry being tracked back

to him. He'd used one of a half-dozen credit card slips picked up from the waste can at a gas station. It was one of the first lessons he learned in jail, after getting out of the SHU. Self-service gas stations. Customers pump their gas, pay with a credit card and dump the smelly receipt in the nearest receptacle, where it just sits and waits for someone to pluck it out and use the card number for whatever he wished.

Dr Paul Feldman was the owner of the Lincoln. The phone book listed his office at 450 Sutter Street, San Francisco.

A doctor who made house calls. To Anona Stack's house. He worried about that. About her health. It wouldn't do to have her sick. He had the bread truck just about finished, just about perfect. It was waiting for her.

He checked his watch. Robert Duran had gone to work, and there was no sign of the tall stranger this morning. He paged through his sketch-pad, studying the man's face. Who was he? Why had he been at the trial in Los Angeles?

He took a sandwich and a thermos from his tote bag and unscrewed the top. He was thinking about the stranger when Duran's Jaguar showed up, skidding to a stop behind the doctor's Lincoln.

Bob Duran leapt from the car and ran to the front door. It was almost an hour later when the white van arrived. He read the lettering on the side of the van through the binocular lenses: San Francisco Medical Examiner. He pulled the binoculars from his eyes and looked at his hands. Suddenly it was there – the dazzling, radiant aura, giving his fingers a faded, twinkling glow. He knew it would be only a matter of minutes before the blinding pain of the migraine would jolt his brain, drain the strength from his limbs, and the excruciating sensitivity to sound and light would drive him to darkness. Darkness and pain. 'The bitch is dead,' he moaned in anguish. 'The bitch is dead.'

Chapter 6

The crowd moved at a leaden pace as Anona Stack's friends, fans and the just plain curious came to pay their respects and take a last look at the famous artist. He shuffled along the marble path dividing the funeral chapel rows of pews, his head pulled down to nullify his height. The column of mourners was two and three abreast and every minute or so would come to a complete stop as someone paused to pray at the coffin.

The walls of the chapel were lined with rainbow-like wreaths and garlands sculpted in the shapes of hearts, crosses and prayer books. The overpowering fragrance of the flowers assaulted his nose. The two women in front of him, both middle-aged, over-weight and over-dressed, were complaining of the heat.

His eyes drifted over to the alcove where the bereaved family was gathered. He tucked his right hand under his armpit, took a deep breath and contracted his stomach muscles. He didn't need to count the seconds. The exercises were an unconscious habit now.

He peered over the shoulders of the two women in front of him as they knelt down on the cushioned bench in front of the coffin to silently recite a prayer.

Anona Stack was obviously wearing a wig. The thick, bronze-tinted make-up could not veil the deep, pain-etched wrinkles chiseled into her face by her illness. He remembered her beautiful, taunting face as it was when she testified against him and his wife at their trial.

He had fantasized about Anona Stack often in his prison cell – detailed, bizarre fantasies on just what he would do to her face, and her body. She would find out what it was like to have her own little SHU. He would be the guard with the club and the stun gun – she'd be the one with her hands cuffed behind her back, her legs spread apart, shackled. He had taken it for eighteen months. Five hundred and forty-seven days. And nights. He wanted her to have a taste of it. A week, a few days, but her death had cheated him out of the realization of his fantasy. He felt some satisfaction in that her last year on earth must have been a painful one. Robbed of her health, her beauty, her talent. Maybe there was a god after all. A cruel, punishing, vengeful god.

Anona Stack lay there, dressed in a silk cream-colored dress. Her slack hands rested across her chest, clasping a string of black rosary beads. There was a plain gold wedding band on the proper finger of her left hand. His face tightened sharply. Yes, he would make good use of the dress, use the beads. Perhaps the ring, too.

He felt a bump from behind and shifted around to see an elderly white-haired woman smiling up at him.

'Can I kneel down?' she asked in a faint, shy voice.

He nodded, took her by the elbow and led her to the prayer dieu. 'By all means. Say some prayers for her. She'll need them.'

He slipped his hand under her arm, then glanced back toward the family and friends gathered in the alcove. They were all absorbed in conversations with the visiting mourners. Anona Stack's daughter, Lisa. Young, beautiful, but nothing like Anona. Lisa's hair was long and dark, like Arlene's had been. Her face bore a distinct resemblance to her father's. The photos in the newspapers had identified the tall silver-haired man as Jason Lark, Anona's first husband, and the father of her only two children.

He discounted the possibility of Lark or Duran recognizing him. His hair had been shoulder-length then. It was short now, slowly growing out from the prison buzz-cut. Lark was standing between his daughter and his son, John. John resembled his mother, reddish hair, fair skin.

He focused on Robert Duran, his eyes documenting every feature. He had glared at a guard like that once, the hate in his eyes so obvious that the guard had reacted by shooting him with his stun gun, then clubbing his ankles and knees so hard that he couldn't walk for three days.

Duran's head snapped around toward the coffin. Could Duran feel his eyes? Feel his hate? He wondered as he turned away quickly and made his way through the mourners, exiting the funeral home by a side door. The stolen van was parked three blocks away. He looked up at the gloomy, battleship-gray sky and decided to skip the church service and drive directly to the cemetery.

Robert Duran was a bit dizzy. He wasn't sure if it was from lack of sleep, or because he hadn't been eating much since Anona died. He squeezed the bridge of his nose between thumb and forefinger, then shook his head.

'My sympathies. It's such a beautiful casket,' a soulful mourner with pencil-line eyebrows and protruding eyes assured Duran.

'Yes, it is,' Duran granted, suddenly feeling a chill. He looked toward the front of the chapel where Anona's shrunken body was enveloped in the white silken shrouds of the imposing brass and bronze casket.

Anona had designed the casket herself, while lying in her sickbed, sketching it out on thick watercolor paper as the funeral director watched in amazement.

He'd brought along dozens of brochures, but none of the designs had satisfied Anona. The finished product was a bit avant-garde – tapered, with rounded corners, giving it the look of a vintage, expensive roadster, minus the wheels and fenders.

Duran wondered what the funeral director had done with the sketch, if he had framed it or put it away for another day, when he could make a nice profit. After all, it was an original Anona Stack. Duran's mind flickered back to a luncheon at a three star bistro just outside of Paris. They'd sat on a balcony with a view out to the Monet-inspired garden. Anona introducing him to some of her friends, using a ballpoint pen, a lipstick and an eyebrow pencil, dipped into her wine glass to make a rough outline of her latest painting on the white linen tablecloth. The meal, which included several bottles of wine and after-lunch cognacs, must have been quite expensive, but the proprietor wisely told Anona the lunch was on him, if only she would sign her name alongside the drawing.

Monsignor Wagner touched Duran lightly on the shoulder, causing his body to twitch as if he'd received an electric shock.

'Are you all right, Bob?'

Wagner was a big, rugged man who looked as if he'd be more at home coaching a high school football team than saving lost souls.

'I'm fine, Monsignor,' Duran responded, his voice almost a croak.

Wagner glanced at his watch. 'You'll have to shut this down pretty soon. I'm leaving now. See you at the church. We don't want to keep the bishop waiting,' he cautioned, giving Duran's shoulder a final pat, then edging over to the alcove to say a few comforting words to the rest of the family.

Duran watched as the priest spoke first to Johnny.

Alongside Johnny, teetering on high heels, was his sister Lisa. Her chestnut-brown hair fell around her face and every so often she hurled it back with a brief shake of her head. She nodded her head in unison with her brother as they listened to Monsignor Wagner.

Jason Lark was standing directly alongside Johnny, straight-shouldered, erect, a mournful frown stitched across his elegant face.

Another mourner grabbed Duran's hand, shook it lightly, and whispered condolences. 'So sorry about your wife, Mr Stack.'

Duran nodded his thanks. He'd long ago given up telling people his name was Duran and that, since their marriage, so was Anona's. It never stuck. She was Anona Stack throughout her life, and that's how she'd be remembered. Even her marriage to Jason Lark hadn't changed that. Anona's father had used his powerful connections with the church to have the marriage annulled, rather than end in a divorce. He'd had no difficulty at all in having the two children's names legally changed to Stack.

From what Anona had told Duran, Lark was less than happy with the separation or the settlement her father had reluctantly bestowed upon him. Lark thought that he was worth more than what Conrad Stack was offering, but Stack was a persuasive man.

Conrad Stack had offered Duran a settlement, too. Before their wedding.

Every detail of that meeting was still vivid in Duran's mind – the taste of the food and fine wines, the smell of Stack's cigar, their verbal sparring. Conrad Stack had invited Duran for a 'man to man' dinner, at Stack House, in Conrad's favorite room, the wine cellar, a vast, brick-floored vault catacombed with long racks of expensive dust-coated wine bottles. Conrad Stack was a tall, heavy-shouldered man, with shovel-like hands. He had worn a formal business suit and somber tie in contrast to Duran's casual slacks and sports coat.

Stack was a meat and potatoes man with a complexion that rivaled the prime rib they dined on. It had been an elaborate, but tension-filled meal, Stack snobbishly explaining the vintages of the wines that accompanied each course of their meal.

When they'd finished dinner, Stack lit up a long Cuban cigar, smiled at Duran through the smoke then pulled an envelope-sized leather notepad from his well-tailored suit coat. 'I made a terrible mistake by not doing a better job of checking out that bastard Jason Lark. I'm not going to make the same mistake with you.' He locked his eyes on to Duran's. 'Do you object?'

'Damn right, I do. But I don't suppose that makes much difference to you.'

Stack snapped open the notebook. 'Robert Duran. Born in Otay, just south of San Diego. Father, Mexican, born in Tijuana. Mother, Danish, born in Copenhagen. Father a salesman for a paper goods company. Mother worked in a . . . a bakery. Mother deceased. Father? Unknown. Just sort of disappeared, did he?'

'Yes. He had a habit of doing that. One day he took off on a business trip and never came back.'

'You did make it to college, for a short time. A city college down there, wasn't it?'

Stack pronounced 'down there' as if it were some terrible disease. 'Yes.'

'But you didn't graduate, did you?'

'No.'

'Why not? Your grades weren't all that bad,' Stack conceded.

'I was restless. Uncle Sam called. I listened.'

Stack drew deeply on his cigar, fanning the smoke away with the back of his hand. 'Restless. Did it have anything to do with your being arrested?'

'Yes. It did. I got into a fight with a man. I hit him a little too hard and ended up in jail for a few months. When I got out, I joined the army.'

Stack smiled knowingly. 'You seem to have been quite restless, Robert. There was more than just the one fight.

Is that how you acquired that scar?'

'I grew up in a *barrio*, Mr Stack. Near the border. I was a half-breed to most of the kids. The Mexicans didn't like the blue eyes, the whites thought I was an uppity Latino. If you didn't fight, you didn't survive. If your investigator did his job thoroughly, then you would know that my mother committed suicide. She was very beautiful, and didn't speak either English or Spanish very well. Most of her time was spent waiting for my father to come home from his sales trips. He'd be gone for weeks at a time, then finally he just never came back. I suppose that's when she decided to kill herself. With his shotgun. I was seventeen years old. I found her in the bathtub, a plastic laundry bag around her head, and the shotgun.' He paused a long moment. 'My mother was always very neat. Even in death.'

Conrad Stack flicked the pages of his notepad. 'United States Army. Fairly distinguished record. You were in for six years. Then you went to work as an insurance investigator. What pointed you in that direction?'

'The army. I spent some time in the Intelligence Division. I liked the work, so when I was discharged it seemed a natural choice.'

Stack made a non-committal humming noise. 'Then you were married in New York. Your wife's name was Teresa, wasn't it?'

'Yes.'

'And she died quite unexpectedly.'

'An aneurism. There was no warning. She just felt ill one day, complained of a terrible headache. I took her to the hospital and she died shortly after we got there.'

Conrad Stack slid the notepad back into his suit pocket. 'I'm not saying that you aren't an honest man, Robert, and in many ways I admire your grit. Your work record at the insurance company is quite good. However, I don't think that you are the right person for Anona.'

'You're wrong,' Duran replied bluntly.

Stack worked the cigar thoughtfully from one side of his mouth to the other. 'Let's get down to business. How much?'

'I'm not marrying Anona for her money, or your money,' Duran declared, knowing that the statement, true as it was, sounded trite.

'Then you won't mind if there's a pre-nuptial agreement?'

'Not at all. You have the document drawn up, and I'll sign it.'

Stack dug out his notepad once again. He thumbed through the pages. 'You have a few dollars put away. Close to sixty thousand dollars, most of it invested in mutual funds. I'll double that amount. In cash. It's my one and only offer.'

'Keep your money,' Duran advised him, annoyed that Stack knew his financial holdings. He leaned forward. 'Anona was a very young girl when she married Jason Lark. But she's a woman now. A strong woman, with money of her own. Don't try to make me into something I'm not. I'm thinking of leaving the Centennial Insurance Company and starting my own business.'

'Are you really?' Conrad Stack scoffed. 'Starting your own business. Your business will be squandering my daughter's money.'

Duran stood up, the legs of his chair making a screeching noise on the brick floor. 'I love Anona, and I'm going to marry her. Get used to it, Mr Stack. It's as simple as that.'

Conrad Stack stared at Duran a long time, then pushed his chair away from the table and stalked out of the room without saying a word. Duran had made his way out of the mansion on his own, deciding not to mention her father's offer to Anona. Two months later Duran and Anona flew to Mexico and were married. Three months after that, Conrad Stack died of a stroke.

Chapter 7

Cars were double- and triple-parked along Geary Boulevard, outside the mortuary. He swung to his left to avoid a dark sedan that had darted out from a line of parked cars, momentarily crossing the double yellow line separating the flow of traffic.

A motorcycle officer pulled alongside the van signaling for him to stop. He felt the sweat break out on his forehead as he eased his right hand down to his boot top, fingering the small pearl-handled Derringer. The gun was the first thing he'd purchased after his release from Pelican Bay. There was a risk in carrying the weapon. A mere possession charge would send him back to prison, but there was no way he would ever again let them send him back there.

The officer pushed up his helmet visor with a leather-gloved hand. 'Are you planning to join the funeral procession, sir?'

Sir. When was the last time a policeman had called him sir? He released his grip on the Derringer, his hand moving up and settling under his armpit. 'No, officer, I'm not,' he responded in what he hoped was a calm voice.

'Well then, I'd appreciate it if you'd move out of this area.' The cop pulled his visor down and revved the bike's motor. 'Thanks for your cooperation.'

A polite policeman. It was a new experience for him.

'Want some?' asked Lisa Stack, holding out a plastic bottle of Evian water to Robert Duran.

Evian water. Plain out-of-the-tap water wouldn't do for Lisa.

Duran declined the offer. 'No thanks. How are you doing?'

Lisa took a sip from the bottle, then did her little tossing of the head gesture. She was wearing a black hourglass knitted dress that came to an abrupt halt half-way between her knees and thighs. 'God, I can't wait to get out of here. Will the mass be long?'

'I would imagine so.'

'Shit,' she said peevishly, then slowly sauntered back toward her brother, whose head was bowed down, speaking to an elderly woman dressed in black from veil to shoes.

Hugh Stringer, Anona's attorney, his attorney now, recognized Duran, walked over, tugging a pair of white gloves on to his hands.

Stringer was in his early sixties, a burly man with a fleshy face and meaty chin. His pale gray eyes were buried deep under bristly eyebrows. His shoe-polish-brown hair was combed straight back from a widow's peak. He was wearing a perfectly tailored pin-stripe, double-breasted suit and solid black silk tie.

'Time to get things moving,' Stringer announced in a professional tone. Then his voice lowered. 'Beware of the wolves. And the lambs, Robert.'

Duran was well aware of the wolves. In fact he considered Stringer one of the hungrier ones.

'Lambs?' he inquired, his forehead crinkling in confusion.

'You're rich, Robert. You're a catch. They all will be after you now.' His voice rose a few discreet decibels. 'We'll have to get together. The sooner the better. Let me know when.'

'As you say, Hugh. The sooner the better.'

68

Stringer was right about the lambs. Some of Anona's friends, women who in the past had barely acknowledged him at dinner parties or social functions, had lately taken to batting their eyes and trailing their fingernails across his palm.

Stringer sidled over to Lisa and Johnny Stack, giving them their marching orders. Duran was relieved that Stringer was taking charge. He wasn't sure just how Johnny and Lisa would react to directions from him.

It took another forty-five minutes to clear the room and have Anona's casket closed for the final time, then taken to the waiting hearse.

There was a flood of people waiting on the steps of St Mary's Cathedral. St Mary's, with its signature roof of four 190-foot hyperbolic paraboloids, which had defied description until a local wag likened it to the insides of a washing machine. Duran thought the description was dead on. Under that massive roof was seating for twenty-five hundred worshipers. It was filled to capacity for Anona's funeral. The ceiling-high Wizard of Oz organ operated at full volume during the service.

When the mass was over, Duran, Johnny, Lisa and Jason Lark piled into a limousine and led a snake-like body of cars, ten blocks long, flanked by San Francisco Police Department motorcycle officers, down to Colma, the small town on San Francisco's southern border.

Colma had been selected as cemetery ground around the turn of the century, when land in San Francisco became too valuable to house the dead.

The stretch-limo was a black Mercedes with darkened windows so no one could see inside. Which was just as well, in Duran's opinion.

Lisa and her father were sprawled out on the back seat while Duran and Johnny sat in the jump seat, Johnny hugging the window, seemingly to get as far away from Duran as possible. Or was it to keep a distance between him and his sister? Duran had noticed that a tension had developed between the two of them. They had always had their fair share of fights and disagreements, but lately they seemed to jump at one another at the slightest provocation.

'This is really stupid,' Johnny said angrily. 'Mom never gave a damn for the Church until she got sick.' He ran a finger around his shirt collar. He wasn't accustomed to wearing a closed collar and tie.

Duran surveyed his fingertips. He had never gotten as close to Johnny as he would have liked. The boy was already spoiled rotten when Duran married Anona. Bright, good-looking and headstrong. There was no way that Duran could have disciplined a sixteen-year-old who had his own Harley-Davidson motorcycle and an allowance of several hundred dollars a month. Duran had tried to form a bond – fishing trips, golf lessons, 49er football and Giants baseball games. But John wasn't that interested, especially by the time he graduated from high school. When he got kicked out of Stanford, Anona had come down hard on him, cutting back on his allowance, taking away his car for a time. John had blamed Duran for those decisions.

Somewhere under that whining, cocky attitude was a good kid, he hoped, though lately he'd been disappointed in both Johnny and Lisa. He knew they loved their mother, but toward the end they had treated her somewhat like a leper. They'd visit her room, talk to her, sometimes cajoling Anona for more money, but they were reluctant to touch her, hold her, kiss her, as if they were afraid her cancer was contagious. 'This is what your mother wanted, Johnny. We should grant her her last wish.'

Jason Lark took a pewter-colored flask from his coat pocket, took a sip, then pushed the flask toward his son. Johnny accepted it gratefully and held the flask to his lips, his Adam's apple bobbing twice before he handed it back to Lark.

Lisa took a swig from her Evian bottle. Her face was flushed and Duran wondered if she'd spiked the mineral water.

'Can't we get some music in this damn thing?' she spouted angrily.

Her short dress had ridden up to her thighs. Lark patted his daughter's knee, said, 'Good idea,' then began fiddling with the limo's stereo console.

Johnny unbuttoned his shirt and pulled his tie down to half-mast. 'And what about the wake? How long is that damn thing going to last? How long are we going to have to stick around?'

'A lot of your mother's friends will be there,' Duran predicted, trying to keep the anger out of his voice.

'Friends,' Johnny snorted. 'Deadbeats.' He ran the back of his hand viciously across his mouth, as if he wanted to hurt himself. 'Creeps. All they're interested in is Mom's money.' He glanced at Duran – the message clear: you're one of the creeps.

Lark's fiddling with the stereo controls stopped and the screeching of an electric guitar poured out of the speakers.

He patted Lisa's knee again. 'Is that better?'

Lisa didn't bother to answer. Instead she had a question. 'What about Mommy's will? When are we going to hear about the will?'

Duran reached over and adjusted the volume. 'I'll meet with Hugh Stringer in the next couple of days.'

'I hear you're the executor, Robert,' Lark prompted.

'You heard right.'

Johnny Stack mumbled something under his breath, then asked his father for the flask.

Chapter 8

The late afternoon sun cast long shadows on the sidewalk as he joined the queue in front of the San Francisco Museum of Art. He was slightly amused. The gall of the woman. Charging fifty dollars for admittance to her own wake.

The ceremony at the cemetery had been tedious. He'd learned nothing of interest. He already knew where Anona Stack was to be entombed. The tears streaming down Robert Duran's face as his wife's casket was wheeled into the cemetery's receiving chapel had proved to be the only worthwhile event.

He had two twenty-dollar bills and a ten in his right hand ready for the oval-faced attendant dispensing tickets. The ticket popped up from the machine like a piece of toast. He grabbed it, then joined another queue, waiting to gain entrance to the museum. The people in front and back of him were all cheerfully jabbering away, as if they were attending a Streisand concert or an opera, rather than paying their last respects to a famous artist.

He never could quite figure out just what it was about Anona Stack's style that had caught on with the public. He found her to be too organic – a raw blend of Abstract Expressionism with amorphous shaping of nature: trees, flowers, skies. She was wonderful with colors though. And, best of all, he and Arlene had found her work easy to duplicate. The guard accepted his ticket without as much as a glance and said a non-enthusiastic 'Thank you.' Even if the guard had done more than just glance, there was no way he could have detected the weapon holstered under his left arm.

'You're welcome,' he responded solemnly, as he entered the museum searching for his target.

Johnny and Jason Lark headed straight for the bar.

Robert Duran stayed back, walking slowly around the indoor piazza, the flooring of zebra-like, alternating bands of black and gray granite. Natural light flooded through the 140 foot-high skylight. The Italian architect Mario Botta's contemporary designed museum had stirred quite a bit of controversy when it was first presented. A massive three-tiered building of textured red brick, the forty-five degree upslanting skylight was its most controversial feature. The architect intended the skylight to 'look out at the city like a big eye, like a cyclops.'

Anona Stack had been one of Botta's most ardent supporters. Both verbally and financially. Duran studied the crowd, remembering his wife's rather unusual wish list. 'A wake. A knock-down-drag-'em-out Irish wake. Lots of music, food and booze. The works.'

That was what Anona Stack wanted, and what she wanted, she usually got. Alive or dead. Plans for her wake had consumed her toward the end. She considered various locations. Stack House was certainly big enough to hold her close friends and admirers. 'But there'd be no way to keep out the rest of them. And the press. George would have a fit.'

George had fits a little too often for Duran's taste, but he'd been working for the family since before Anona was born, and his say over the household carried a lot of weight.

So Anona decided to hold the wake at the recently opened Museum of Modern Art on 3rd Street.

The powers at City Hall wanted no part of the deal, until Anona pledged to donate one of her last paintings, *Rondeau #8*, a pastel abstract. She fully acknowledged it was not one of her best. Duran remembered how difficult it had been for her to finish the canvas. The trips to her studio on the waterfront tired her out so much that when she got there, she had to sit and rest before starting to work. Still, it was an original Anona Stack and the Art Commission decided they'd grant her wish and open the museum doors for her. However, there would be an additional cost. Each mourner would have to pay fifty dollars as a donation to the museum to gain entrance.

Anona loved the idea, only sorry she hadn't thought of it first. 'They say you can't take it with you, but damn it, I'm going to make them pay to see me go.'

And pay they did. Duran estimated the crowd at five hundred plus. All sipping cocktails or Napa County champagne and nibbling on upscale *hors d'oeuvres*, while listening to a six-piece band play soft jazz.

The music floated through the piazza. The conversations were hushed and quiet for the first hour or so, then the liquor began loosening tongues, and feet.

'Bob. I've been trying to talk to you all day.'

Duran shrugged his shoulders and smiled at Laura Ralston. 'It's been hectic, Laura.'

Laura Ralston was wearing a gracefully tailored gray crêpe dress, one button fastening it at the side. The ruffle collar scooped just low enough to allow a glimpse of the swelling of her breasts. Her skin was lightly tanned, her highlighted-brown hair stylishly feathered.

'You look wonderful,' he told her sincerely.

Laura had two glasses of champagne in her hands. She held one out to Duran. 'You haven't returned my calls.'

Duran accepted the glass, looked around, saw no one was within earshot and said, 'I'm sorry, it's just that I haven't been up to calling anyone.'

'Yes,' Laura agreed readily. 'I know how rough it's been for you. I do. Really. Anona was my friend, too, Bob. A good friend. I know how sick she was, and how lonely you must have felt at times.'

Duran took a shallow draft of the champagne.

'Am I going to see you?' Laura Ralston asked plaintively.

'I've had so many things to deal with. I think—'

'You do want to see me, don't you?' she insisted. 'We have a lot to talk about.'

Laura was a real estate broker. She was no doubt interested in handling the sale of Stack House and the cottage in Carmel. 'I'm sure we do, Laura.'

Laura touched her fingertips to Duran's arm, then retracted them quickly. 'Is there any truth to the rumor I've heard that Johnny and Lisa are upset about you being named the executor?'

'Who told you that?' Duran asked sharply.

She motioned her head toward the dance floor. 'Jason. I suppose he's still staying at Stack House.'

Duran was surprised to see Lark dancing with his secretary, Peggy Jacquard. 'Yes, but I hope not for much longer,' Duran said glumly. 'I don't know how much longer any of us will be living at Stack House. It's certainly too big just for Lisa, and I don't think Johnny wants anything to do with it, except for the money it will bring in, and there are too many memories there for me.'

Laura reached out, her hand encircling his wrist. 'You're going to need a friend, Bob. Call me. Soon.' She leaned forward and kissed him lightly on the ear, her tongue taking a quick cat-like lick before retreating.

Duran watched Laura work her way into the crowd, grab Hugh Stringer by the elbow and coax him out on to the dance floor.

Peggy Jacquard came over and snatched the silk handkerchief from Duran's breast pocket. She blotted her sweating face and blew air through her lips. 'Bob, you didn't tell me that Anona's first husband was absolutely gorgeous.'

'There's a lot I haven't told you about Jason Lark. None of it is good, believe me.'

Peggy expertly refolded the silk and tucked it back in Duran's suit. 'He's got his charm button on full throttle at the moment. He wants to take me out to lunch.'

'Make sure he pays and don't let your purse out of your sight,' Duran suggested.

Peggy rolled her eyes at him questioningly. 'Is he really that bad?'

'He makes Harry Lawson look like a choirboy, Peg.'

'Why's he being so nice to me?'

'Because you're beautiful, kid.'

Peggy smiled and gave him a full-armed hug. 'You're doing good, Bob. Anona would be proud of you.'

Duran headed for the bar, exchanging his champagne glass for a Scotch and water, his thoughts once again on Anona. Another museum. The Guggenheim in New York. Four of her canvases had been on display and the reviews were wonderful. She'd been surrounded by influential admirers who'd fawned all over her with invitations to parties, dinners, shows. But Anona had refused them all and they'd spent the entire weekend together, almost never leaving their room at the Algonquin Hotel.

'A penny for your thoughts?' Lisa Stack asked, dragging Duran back to the present.

'I was just thinking about your mother.' Duran smiled down at his beautiful stepdaughter, with her high, pronounced cheekbones, the well-cut nose and light, full lips. The champagne glass in her hand was tilted at an angle, the wine ready to cascade on to the floor. It appeared to Duran that she had a pretty good buzz on. 'How are you feeling?'

Lisa Stack made an exaggerated pout, then sucked her

lips back, and ran her tongue along her lower lip.

Lisa had been in her early teens when Duran first met her, shortly before Anona and he were married. Even then Lisa was a first-class prick-teaser. And one prick she particularly delighted in teasing was Robert Duran's.

She draped an arm around Duran's waist, hugged him to her, pushing her breasts into his side.

'I'm fine, Bob. Got any humbie on you?'

'Humbie? What—'

'You know, bo, grass.' She grinned and hugged him harder. 'I think they called it reefers when you were a boy.'

'Lisa, I don't—'

She augured a long-tipped fingernail into his side. 'I know about you supplying Mommy with grass. Why not share a little with me?'

Duran wasn't surprised that Lisa knew about the high-grade Humboldt County marijuana that Anona had been using – some nights the sweet smell of the smoke hung over her bed like a curtain.

'I got that for your mother because it helped her with her pain and nausea.'

'But it's against the law.' She dipped a finger into the champagne, pulled it out and licked it. 'Are you fucking Laura Ralston?'

'Don't be stupid. Whatever gave you that idea?'

Lisa ignored the question, her eyes mocking Duran. 'What about Peggy?'

'Lisa, you've had too much to drink.'

'Mommy's jewelry. The emerald necklace in particular. I'd like that. Right away. There's no problem with that, is there? Mommy would want me to have it.'

'I know she would,' Duran agreed. 'There are procedures that need to be followed. Everything in the estate has to be evaluated. But I don't see any problem if you want to wear the necklace. Or anything else.'

Lisa's pink, snake-like tongue pushed out from between

her lips, swirled around, then retreated. 'Jason says you're the executor and that everything has to go through you.'

'It's just a legal formality,' Duran clarified, the annoyance clear in his voice.

'Johnny's upset. He thinks there should have been an autopsy.'

'When did he tell you this?' Duran demanded.

A man in his late twenties with a long, bony face moved in and draped an arm around Lisa's shoulders. He wore his hair in a lion's-mane style. He gave Duran a vulture-like smile.

Lisa cleared her throat, like someone with a cold coming on. 'Last night at dinner. Johnny says someone called him and told him that Mommy was murdered.'

'That's ridiculous,' Duran responded hotly, his voice drowned out by a loud scream.

There was a chilling silence, then another scream and the nervous static of a crowd at a disaster site rumbled through the museum's lobby. Everyone seemed to stand in freeze-frame for a moment, then the rumbling intensified.

He was getting anxious. He never did have much of a taste for alcohol, and the one glass of champagne that he'd consumed had done nothing but trigger another headache. He kept an eye on Robert Duran, watching him talking to the woman in the gray dress, then the black woman, his secretary, then his stepdaughter, Lisa. All of them looked attracted to Duran. Even his stepdaughter.

He checked his watch and decided it was time. He got himself into position and waited, finding an opportunity when the band played a swing number and the audience's attention was drawn to the dance floor. He quickly unholstered the fiberglass pistol, placed the barrel under his armpit, turned sideways and pulled the trigger. Powered by a CO_2 cylinder, the .68 caliber cartridge traveled the fifteen foot distance, striking its target with a soft, splatting sound.

The woman standing next to him had her attention focused on the dancers. He shoved the pistol in his waistband, tapped her on the shoulder and said, 'Look at that.'

The woman turned, saw *Rondeau #8* and let out a high-pitched scream.

Robert Duran elbowed his way through the crowd that had gathered around the area where Anona's painting was on display. He could see Hugh Stringer's large sweating face contorted into a mask of rage as he questioned a security guard.

Stringer spotted Duran and waved him over.

'Bastard,' Stringer sputtered as the guard began herding the crowd backwards.

'What happened, Hugh?'

Stringer didn't seem to know what to do with his hands, holding them before him first, then clasping them behind his back. 'It's Anona's painting. Some bastard has ruined it!'

Rondeau #8 was displayed on a simple easel, a series of ceiling track-lights focused on it. A wrist-thick purple-colored rope, threaded through brass posts, encircled the painting.

A dripping ketchup-red blob the size of a fifty cent piece was splashed across the canvas.

'What is it?' Duran asked in a back-of-the-throat rage as he slipped under the roping. He approached the painting cautiously, a finger tentatively reaching out, dabbing at the obscene red markings. He sniffed his finger. 'It's some kind of paint.'

Stringer stood beside him, his heavy jowls shaking as he put his nose just inches from the painting. 'Who the hell would want to do something like this? It's crazy!'

Duran turned, his eyes patrolling the crowd. A maze of open-mouthed faces stared back at him. He looked back at the painting and groaned, repeating Stringer's question to himself. Who the hell would want to do something like this? At Anona's wake?

Chapter 9

Seven quarters, fourteen dimes and more nickels and pennies than he bothered to count. All scattered across the base of the modest old tombstone, as if it were some kind of wishing-well. The worn inscription read: WYATT EARP 1848–1929.

He wondered how the notorious lawman had ended up with his bones interred in a graveyard in Colma, California. A famous man like Earp, with nothing more to show for his life than a cheap cement slab, while Anona Stack was entombed like an Egyptian princess.

He knelt down and picked up one of the quarters. 'For luck, Wyatt. Just for luck.'

He stood, pocketing the quarter, and hitched the nylon tote bag over his shoulder. A low-lying fog was spreading like mercury across the cemetery. He tilted his hat and hummed a tuneless song as he strolled back toward the Stack family mausoleum.

The Colma Police Department squad car cruised around the serpentine cemetery road, its headlights barely penetrating the fog, sliding past the tombstones. He checked his watch. Fourteen minutes after midnight. The previous patrol car had made its rounds shortly after eight o'clock. Four hours. If they kept to their scheduled patrols, he'd have more than enough time.

He rested the bloated end of the war surplus Russian-made night-vision scope on his forearm and took a slow infra-red tour of the area. He was certain there was no caretaker. His main concern was that some kids would show up to play pranks or to party in the graveyard. There was nothing in the viewfinder now, nothing but the orderly rows of graves, the wind-sculpted trees and shrubs and the outlines of the pretentious private mausoleums. The fact that Anona Stack was entombed in a mausoleum was actually a bonus for him. It would make everything much easier.

He slipped his right hand under his armpit. Another ten minutes. One of the things he'd learned in prison was patience. He still woke up in a sweat dreaming he was still in prison. The first eight months hadn't been bad. It was almost a country club atmosphere. Dormitories instead of cells. Tennis courts, a fully stocked library, unlimited access to art supplies. There was a fear at first, the fear of sexual attack, expecting to be gang-raped at any moment. He soon learnt that it was the young ones, the pretty ones, they were after. If a man minded his own business, made his intentions known, and kept some kind of weapon with him at all times, he had little to worry about, unless the loneliness became too much and he went looking for sex, became one of the predators, and one day woke up and decided there was no sense waiting any longer and willingly joined the scene. He'd seen men who had succumbed to the pressure, the temptations, and late at night pulled lipstick and mascara from beneath their pillows and went 'cruising for a train.'

That all changed after Arlene's death, after the transfer. The transfer to hell – the Pelican Bay State Prison. A cold, clammy hell. Just fifteen miles from the Oregon border. His first eighteen months there had been an eternity. Twenty-three hours alone in the SHU – then every afternoon the guards would come. Three of them. Then the handcuffs, a humiliating strip search, a short march to the cramped confines of the exercise yard and an hour alone in the fresh air, surrounded by a twenty-foot-high concrete wall. The yard floor was cement, too. There were no trees or shrubs. The few weeds that dared show through the cracks were quickly uprooted. Nothing to see but the sky, and that was all too often gray, threatening, bursting with rain clouds. He remembered a movie he'd seen as a child: *The Bird Man of Alcatraz*. Burt Lancaster. At least Lancaster had birds to talk to. To hold, to fondle. The few birds he'd seen had been high up in the sky. Free-wheeling, soaring. Once in a while a flock of ducks came by. They never got close. Even the birds were wary of Pelican Bay Prison.

It was different once he was released from the SHU and placed in the main yard and was able to mix with the other prisoners. Many of them were lifers: murderers, rapists, career criminals with sentences stretching out far past their life expectancies. But he could talk, communicate, touch.

The main yard had two-man cells. His cellmate, Ken Firpo, was a professional criminal, a man who had followed his grandfather and father into a life of crime and who had taught him how to 'beat the clock.' Don't count the minutes, the hours, the weeks or the months.

The guards utilized his painting skills, first elementary chores like painting bathrooms, the galley, then more personal jobs for their offices, canvases for their homes.

Once his forgery talents had become known to the other inmates, he'd found himself in demand. He joined the 'staff', passing on his skills in return for learning new ones: lock picking, breaking and entering, survival techniques. It was a long, grueling education, and now it was payback time.

The headache was starting again. He reached into his jacket pocket, his fingers rooting around for the capsules.

He swallowed three of the pain killers, took one final sweep with the night-vision scope, then got to his feet, stretching, loosening his muscles. He slipped the scope into his backpack and headed toward the gardener's tool shack.

He selected a wheelbarrow and cautiously made his way to the mausoleum. He used a chisel on the metal door. It opened with a sharp, cracking noise. He stood rock-still for a minute before proceeding inside. He groped in the sack for a flashlight, snapped it on, the beam licking over the walls, settling on the crypt. His gloved hands touched the cement. It still had a damp feel about it.

He dug a small battery-operated camp lantern from the sack. It provided all the illumination he needed. He started to work with the chisel, pounding at it with a rubber-tipped hammer. After no more than a dozen blows he was through the concrete. He widened the hole with the chisel until he could get a hand inside. Sweat was running down his forehead into his eyes, his gloved hand clawing, coming away with hunks of the still damp cement. Finally he had the section cleared and he could touch the coffin. It felt icy cold even through his gloves. He pulled at the brass handles, placing his right foot against the lower portion of the wall for leverage. His grunts and groans sounded like those of an animal, but gradually the coffin moved, making raw, scraping sounds as it ground against the cement, sounds of protest much like a wild creature being forced from its cage.

He finally pried one end of the coffin free, then, when it reached the balancing point, it tilted and teetered briefly before crashing to the ground.

He ran to the door and used the night glasses to check the cemetery perimeter before returning to the coffin. He unsnapped the locks, took a deep breath, pinched his nostrils shut, then pried the lid open.

There she was, her head tilted at an angle, her wig askew, like a rag doll that had been thrown against a wall. He knelt down, reaching for her hand, fingering the gold wedding band. 'You're going on a journey, Anona. And Robert will be joining you soon. I'm sure you'll like that.' He tugged at her wedding ring, but it was stuck to her spongy flesh. He kept twisting on the ring, but couldn't get it past her knuckle. He decided to leave it for now, he would get it later. He pocketed the rosary beads, then slid the hunting knife from its sheath and began cutting the dress away from her body.

Robert Duran woke early. He slipped out of bed and by force of habit began tiptoeing to the adjoining bedroom, to check on Anona – stopping half-way from the open door that separated their bedrooms, the reality of her being gone sweeping the last of the cobwebs from his alcohol-clouded brain. They had shared a room and a bed during their marriage, up until Anona began feeling uncomfortable during those last months. Her radiation-crisped scalp covered by a wig, rather than her luxurious golden hair. Her once voluptuous figure withering away to where she was only an emaciated shell. Duran had fought the move at first, but agreed to the adjoining room when he realized how much Anona needed her privacy. Her schedule was never the same. Sometimes she'd sleep most of the day away, then lie in bed, watching the large-screen TV all night, surfing the channels, or re-watching favorite movies on the VCR. Duran recalled one of their last conversations, asking her if there was anything he could do for her before he retired to his room. 'No, Love, just leave me alone. I don't want to see anyone. And I don't want anyone to see me. I just want to die.'

Duran ground the heels of his hands into his eyes,

trying to ease the pain, wondering if the women in his life were all cursed: his mother's suicide, his first wife's sudden death, and now Anona. He, Johnny and Lisa had a ten-thirty meeting scheduled with Hugh Stringer. A formal reading of the will, then lunch at Stringer's club. He donned a sweat suit and running shoes and moved silently through the sleeping house, out on to the street. A low-lying, wall-like fog obscured the Broadway Street pedestrian-only entrance to the Presidio.

As was his practice, Duran kept to a little-used path bordered by towering groves of pine, cypress and eucalyptus trees.

He slowed his pace as the path skirted the golf course, then picked it up again as he found himself alone on a narrow dirt trail. The air was cool and so thick with the overpowering scent of eucalyptus that it felt as if he had a cough drop in his mouth.

He rounded a turn and came to a skidding halt, holding up his hands in front of his face to protect himself. His first thought was that he'd run into someone coming from the opposite direction. But no, it was a cream-colored dress, flapping back and forth as it hung from a tree branch. He pushed it away, took a step backward then froze. It looked like Anona's dress, the one she was buried in. He reached out to touch it, fingering the silk, feeling the ragged rips in the material.

He didn't hear the footsteps until they were almost alongside him. Something hit him hard on the left shoulder, knocking him off-balance. He swayed for a moment, then there was another blow, harder this time, and suddenly he was falling over a cliff, his head twisting as he tumbled downward, trying to see who had struck him, his hands grasping at shrubs and tree branches. He came to a jarring halt in a thick patch of ferns. He slowly got to his feet. His shoulder, back and knee were sore and the skin of his right wrist was cut and bleeding, his hands were covered with nicks and scratches.

He cursed, then began climbing, flopping down to his knees once he reached the trail. The dress was gone. He heard something in the distance. It sounded like someone laughing.

Chapter 10

Hugh Stringer's office was located on the thirty-fifth floor of the 101 California Street Building, a sleek, graceful, forty-eight-story glass silo that would for ever be remembered as the site where a crazed gunman wandered through the floors, armed with several semi-automatic weapons with extended clips, killing eight people and wounding six more hapless victims. The killer was upset at an attorney for allegedly cheating him out of a great deal of money in a real estate transaction some years earlier.

Security at the building had been upgraded after the tragedy: armed guards, metal detectors, and patrol dogs. But time had eroded the memory, and the fears, and there wasn't a guard or dog in sight when Duran passed through the glazed street-level atrium and boarded an elevator.

Hugh Stringer squinted at the wall clock as he waited impatiently for Robert Duran in the office conference room, a long, narrow affair, expansively windowed with oak wainscoting and matching molding rimming the coffered ceiling.

'Ah, here's Robert now,' Stringer announced nervously. 'I think you know everyone here, except Mr Abbott.'

A gray-haired, gray-suited man in his fifties with a full-jawed face and whisky-brown eyes rose from his chair, said, 'How do you do,' then handed Duran a business card.

Duran glanced at the card. Victor Abbott, Attorney at Law, an address on Sansome Street. 'And why are you here?' Duran asked, his eyes wandering over to Johnny and Lisa Stack, who were seated next to each other at a long, polished mahogany table. Duran had tried to talk to Johnny about the allegations that someone had called him, and told him Anona had been murdered, but Johnny had been avoiding him.

Abbott noticed the bandage on Duran's wrist. 'What happened, Mr Duran?'

Before Duran could respond, Hugh Stringer said, 'Why don't we all sit down and get started?'

Stringer plopped a royal blue leather-bound three-ring binder in front of John and Lisa Stack. He handed another one to Abbott, the last to Duran.

Johnny Stack kept his eyes focused on the binder, flipping the pages. He was dressed all in black, not in mourning for his mother, but as homage to his idea of fashion: leather pants, cotton T-shirt and a leather motorcycle-style jacket with zippered pockets and cuffs.

Hugh Stringer coughed into his fist, then offered, 'Now then, shall we get started?'

'Not yet,' Duran insisted. 'I still don't know why Mr Abbott is here.'

'To represent my client, John Stack,' Abbott disclosed with the calm of a man holding four aces.

Stringer slapped open his binder and began reading from his copy of Anona Stack's will. 'I, Anona Stack Duran, being of sound mind . . .'

While Stringer's voice droned on, Duran glanced across at Johnny and Lisa. They were reading along with Stringer.

Victor Abbott looked directly at Duran, as if he had no need to see the legal document. Duran wondered if he already knew its contents.

Hugh Stringer finished his oratory and closed his

binder with a snap. 'There. Now. Any questions?'

'Several,' Abbott announced loudly. 'Have you come up with an approximation of the estate's value?'

Stringer bulged his lower lip with his tongue. 'That's rather difficult, as you can imagine, Mr Abbott.' He tapped the blue binder with his index finger. 'All of the assets and properties are listed. However, until we get a full accounting of their current market value, it's almost impossible to say. There's the house here in San Francisco. Have the three of you come to a decision as to whether or not it will be sold?'

'We're going to sell,' Johnny said adamantly. 'There's no reason to keep the place.'

Stringer looked at Lisa, who pouted, then said, 'I guess we should sell.'

Duran nodded his head in agreement. 'I think that's the wise thing to do.'

'It will not be an easy property to liquidate,' Stringer advised. 'We are waiting for estimates from the real estate people. Then there's the Carmel cottage, the stocks, bonds, jewelry, personal property. They're all itemized, but coming up with an accurate figure isn't really possible at the moment. And finally, there are the paintings.' He moved his eyes in Duran's direction. 'There are only two of Anona's paintings in the house. However, as you know, Anona left *Evening Field* to George Montroy, the butler. Robert says that Anona had a work in progress and a number of sketches in her studio. We'll have to have them all appraised.'

'I can't believe Mom left the painting in her bedroom to George,' Johnny said disgustedly.

Stringer didn't bother to respond to the statement.

'What do you think? Give us a guess,' Johnny insisted. 'How much are we talking about?'

'John, it's not that easy,' Stringer explained patiently. 'I can't just pick a figure out of the air.'

'But if you had to make a guess,' Johnny pressed. 'How much? Come on, I'm not going to hold you to it, but give me an idea.'

Stringer squirmed in his chair and fluttered his lips. 'You must realize, John, that when your grandfather died, tax liabilities were a major expense. What income has been generated since that time has come from your mother's paintings and her investments.' His eyes drifted to John and Lisa. 'More importantly, a great deal of money has been going out.'

Duran had purposely avoided any involvement with Anona's financial assets, so he was as much in the dark about the estate's worth as his stepson.

'You must have an idea of how much money we're talking about, damn it,' Johnny argued. 'I want to know how much.'

Stringer continued on in a voice heavy with regret. 'There is no way to avoid another heavy tax bill, though I'm doing the best I can.' He looked across at Abbott for support, but found none. 'After the charities, the bequest to George and the household staff your mother mentioned in her will, I would estimate that the estate would be somewhere around ten million dollars.'

'That's all?' Johnny Stack protested irritably. 'One of Mom's paintings sold for well over a million dollars at Christie's last year.'

'Yes, that's true,' Stringer explained patiently. 'But Anona painted that particular canvas fifteen years ago. It originally sold for less than eighty thousand dollars. Unfortunately, there are no royalties on paintings, John.'

There was a silence that lasted several moments, then Victor Abbott spoke. 'We are going to protest the will and we expect Mr Duran to be relieved of his duties as executor.'

'I don't understand the problem,' Duran challenged, trying to keep the heat out of his voice. 'It's a simple will.

The entire estate is split three ways, minus the charitable contributions and the gifts to friends and household staff. Mr Stringer formulated the will for Anona just two months ago.'

'Two months ago,' Abbott agreed with a nod of his head. 'We don't contest that, Mr Duran. What we do contest is your undue influence over your wife.'

Duran started to rise from his seat. Stringer waved him down, then said, 'This is outrageous, Mr Abbott. The will was drawn exactly as Anona dictated it. As you see, my secretary was one of the witnesses to Anona's signature.' He waggled a finger at Johnny Stack. 'I don't know what you expect to gain from this, John.'

Johnny Stack kept his eyes centered on the blue binder. Lisa gave Stringer a blank look then drifted her eyes in Duran's direction. She was wearing a butter-yellow V-necked sweater and skirt. Her hair was tied back with a matching ribbon. She looked impossibly young and beautiful.

Victor Abbott smoothed his tie and examined both of its ends to see if they matched in length. 'We can prove, if necessary, that Mr Duran was indeed executing undue influence upon my client's mother.'

Duran's voice turned frosty. 'That's just plain ridiculous.'

Abbott pressed his lips into a kiss of disapproval, then, seemingly reluctantly, he reached down and picked up a scuffed leather briefcase. He unsnapped the case and selected a thin folder. 'I am not going to reveal the entire contents of our investigation at this point, however,—'

'Investigation?' Duran responded hotly. 'What the hell are you talking about?' He looked at Stringer who shrugged his shoulders and upturned his palms.

'Gentlemen, may I continue?' Abbott asked, then went on without waiting for an answer. 'Our investigation indicates that Mr Duran has been supplying his wife with narcotics for several months, that he encouraged her to use the said narcotics. There is also evidence indicating that Mr Duran supplied Anona Stack with a lethal drug overdose.' He pulled a single page from the folder. 'Marijuana and cocaine combined with alcohol.'

Duran leaned forward, his hands knuckled down on the desk, the heavy blue veins standing out like ropes. 'Are you accusing me of murdering my wife?'

Victor Abbott folded his arms across his chest and gave Duran a patronizing smile. Johnny was staring at Duran, a look of loathing on his face. Lisa's head was tilted upward toward the ceiling, like royalty ignoring the crowd.

Victor Abbott broke the strained silence. 'If Mr Duran has nothing to hide, then I assume he will have no objection to our plea for an autopsy. That way we can determine once and for all just how Anona Stack died.'

'Of course I object. Damn it, John. Lisa. Your mother went through hell the last months of her life. The very least you can do is let her rest in peace!'

Abbott's mouth pursed for a moment, as though he was considering or rejecting a thought. 'My client received a phone call from a man saying that Robert Duran had indeed killed Anona Stack.'

'What man?' Duran demanded. 'Some crazy bastard makes a phone call and on that basis you accuse me of killing my wife?'

Abbott slipped another document from his case. 'I received a fax making the same claim.'

'This is ridiculous,' Duran said between clenched teeth.

'You can clear it up easily enough,' Abbott retorted. 'As next of kin, you can request an autopsy.'

'I won't do that.'

Johnny Stack leaned across the table and shook a fist at Duran. 'Why not? What are you afraid of?'

Abbott jumped back into the skirmish. 'If you do not request the autopsy, I will obtain a court order on my client's behalf. I know I can get a judge to sign one this afternoon.'

Duran looked at Johnny, seeing the hatred in his eyes. *He believes it, damn it. He actually thinks I killed his mother.*

'In addition, if Mr Duran rejects our request for an autopsy,' Abbott continued in a bland, impersonal tone, 'we shall have to bring to light other facts.' He paused for dramatic effect. 'Those facts being that Mr Duran committed adultery several times prior to his wife's death. And that he is responsible for the mismanagement of the estate.'

The room turned deathly silent. Hugh Stringer placed both palms on the table and slowly heaved himself to his feet. He was about to say something when the telephone rang. He picked up the receiver. 'No calls,' he growled, then broke the connection.

The phone immediately rang again. Stringer's normally red face deepened in color. 'I said no calls!' he repeated, this time slamming the phone into its cradle.

Victor Abbott went back on the attack. 'What about it, Mr Duran? Mr Stringer? I already have a declaration signed by Dr Feldman. He has no objections to an autopsy.'

Stringer finally entered the fight. 'Then why the devil didn't the man request one at the time of Anona's death? Good God, he arrived at the house that morning. He found her dead in her bed. There's no question that—'

The conference room door opened and a nervous-looking woman in an equestrian-style red blazer cautiously entered the room.

'I'm sorry, Mr Stringer. But there's a call for Mr Duran. It's the police. They say it's urgent.'

Stringer shooed her away with a hand. 'All right, all right. You better take it, Robert.'

Duran picked up the phone. The man on the line identified himself as Chief Saylor of the Colma Police

Department. Duran's face paled and his legs turned rubbery. He dropped into his chair with a thud, mumbling, 'Yes,' several times, then 'No,' finishing with, 'Right away.'

'What is it?' Hugh Stringer bellowed, prying the phone from Duran's hand. 'What's the matter, Robert? You look ill.'

'That was the Colma Police Department. Anona's body. It's been stolen.'

Victor Abbott was the first to respond. 'How convenient.'

Chapter 11

The Stack family mausoleum was the size of a small house, constructed of quarried stone in a Greek Revival style complete with Corinthian columns and grotesque demon-headed gargoyle water spouts. It sat on a small knoll overlooking a few similar but less grand structures and serried rows of tombstones.

A time-stained brass door afforded the only entry. There were fresh, bright, gold-colored scars around the lock and the greenish metal at the edge of the door.

The interior floors were of variegated marble, laid out in a geometric pattern with scrolled inserts indicating the points of the compass. Benches of red-veined marble were built into the walls. The crypts holding Anona Stack's parents and grandparents were set in the east wall, their coffins entombed behind six inches of concrete.

Anona Stack's coffin had been placed in a crypt in the west wall. Jagged chunks of broken concrete, ranging in size from that of a football helmet to a fingernail, littered the floor. The coffin had been pulled free of its niche and lay on its side, empty, except for the white silk pillowing.

'Are you the husband?' asked a tall, restless-looking man with dark hair and tightly-drawn features. He wore a policeman's beige uniform.

'Yes. I'm Bob Duran. This is Hugh Stringer. My attorney.'

'I'm Chief Bill Saylor.' He strolled over to the brass

door. 'Whoever did this had no problem breaking into the place. That lock had to be fifty years old. A simple warded lock. Oldest and least secure lock there is.'

'But Christ man,' Stringer growled menacingly. 'How could anyone get away with something like this?'

Saylor pushed a pair of tinted, aviator-style, gold-rimmed glasses up on top of his head. 'We've got fourteen cemeteries under our jurisdiction: Catholic, Protestant, Greek, Italian, Serbian, Jewish, Chinese, Japanese, you name it, we've got it. There's even a pet cemetery. I haven't got enough men to make passes at all of them.'

Stringer wasn't satisfied. 'Maybe, but there had to be a hell of a racket. Whoever did this had to make—'

'Enough noise to wake up the dead,' Saylor interjected smoothly. 'These stone walls are over two-feet thick. They absorb a lot of sound.' He propped his glasses back on his nose and stirred some of the cement fragments with the tip of his shoe. He looked directly at Duran, like a prize fighter surveying his opponent before a fight. 'Whoever did it was strong. Damn strong.'

'You think one man could have done it?' Duran queried.

Saylor surveyed the rubble-strewn floor. 'Like I said, he'd have to be real strong. It'd be a lot easier for two people. Once they broke through the cement, they had to dislodge the coffin. Then there's the body. Lugging the body out of here wouldn't be an easy matter, either.'

Duran walked to the coffin, reaching out to touch it, then pulling his hand back abruptly.

Chief Saylor's eyes strayed to Duran's bandaged wrist.

'When . . . when did this happen?' Duran asked.

'We're not sure,' Saylor said, hooking his thumbs into the belt holding his holstered revolver. 'One of the maintenance men noticed the scratches on the door. He looked inside and saw all this mess.'

'You mean you don't even know when this maniac broke in here?' Hugh Stringer protested contemptuously.

100

Saylor gave Stringer an icy look, then turned his attention to Duran. 'Your wife was buried two days ago. From what the lab has told me so far, from the condition of the cement, the crypt was most likely broken into that night, or early the next day.' His hands moved as if to explain, then dropped to his side. 'But, it could have happened last night, or possibly early this morning. Why don't we go to my office and talk about it?' Saylor suggested.

Stringer wasn't pleased with the idea. 'Robert, before you start giving statements, perhaps I should call someone with more experience in these type of matters than I have. I can get a—'

'It's not necessary, Hugh.'

Stringer put his arm around Duran's shoulder and steered him out of the mausoleum. 'Robert, you shouldn't be talking to the police. Not alone. Not now. Especially after those charges that Victor Abbott made.' He gave Duran a quick, probing look. 'The drugs. The overdose. What the devil is Abbott talking about?'

Duran took a deep breath. The air smelled of freshly cut grass. A soot-colored sky blanketed the horizon. He walked across a gravel road to a row of knee-high tombstones.

'I don't know, Hugh. Anona smoked marijuana, you knew that.'

'I did not,' Stringer protested.

'It was medicine, Hugh. Nothing more. The cocaine charge, that's out of left field. Anona never used cocaine, and there was no reason for Dr Feldman to prescribe it. It's ridiculous, just some nut making phone calls and sending faxes. See if you can get a hold of a copy of the fax that Abbott waved at us during the meeting.'

'I don't think that will be necessary.' Stringer took a paper from his suit coat and handed it to Duran. 'This was faxed to my office this morning. Some fifteen minutes prior to the meeting. I tried calling you.'

Duran examined the fax. The wording was just as Victor Abbott had announced: Anona Stack was murdered! Her husband killed her with an overdose of marijuana, cocaine and alcohol. Don't let him get away with it!!

The letter was typed in capital letters and double-spaced. No signature.

Duran's fingers clenched as if he was going to crumple the paper up, then stopped. He looked at the top portion of the document. The date and time of transmission were neatly typed in: today's date, the time ten-fifteen. Had the sender known of the meeting? When had Victor Abbott received his fax? Much earlier, obviously. He had brought the damn thing to the meeting. Alongside the date was the telephone number of the sender: 415-555-2828.

'See if you can get a copy of Abbott's fax,' Duran said, slipping the fax into his pocket.

Stringer gnawed at his lower lip. 'Abbott all but accused you of murdering Anona. And the adultery charge. These are very serious accusations. He must have had someone following you.' He paused, pulled at his chin, then said, 'If there's something there, we have to talk. Right away.'

A primer-spotted pickup truck rumbled by. The back of the truck was loaded with power-mowers, shovels and hoes. The driver, a solemn-faced Latin wearing a straw cowboy-style hat, pulled the truck to a halt.

Duran turned back to the mausoleum. Chief Saylor was waiting, arms folded across his chest. The sunlight reflected off his glasses, making him appear sightless.

'Hugh, there is nothing to any of the charges. But, I think you should know the reason I was late for the meeting this morning is that while I was out jogging, someone set a trap for me.'

'Trap? What are you talking about?'

'I jog in the Presidio just about every day. I always take the same route. This morning I ran into a dress hanging

from a tree. A dress that looked like the one that Anona
had on when she was buried. While I was looking at the
dress, someone came up behind me and knocked me off
the trail, and over a cliff.'

'Someone? Who? Did you get a look at him?'

'No. I didn't.'

'What time was this?' asked the lawyer.

'Oh, a little after eight o'clock.'

Stringer stared at the ground at his feet. 'Are you sure it
was Anona's dress?'

'I am now. It was the same style, the same color, and it
was ripped to shreds. Tell me, what kind of a reputation
does Victor Abbott have?'

'I don't know much about him. He moves in slightly
different circles than I do. Lots of rough civil stuff and
some criminal work, I believe. I can check him out.'

'I wish you had checked him out before today's meeting.'

Stringer's heavy face crimsoned. 'I didn't know he was
involved until today,' he pointed out. 'Neither Johnny nor
Lisa mentioned anything about this to me.' He sounded
hurt, as if Anona's children had betrayed his trust. 'I've
been the Stack family attorney for over thirty years. I can't
believe that Johnny wouldn't come to me and let me
handle everything.' He lowered his voice to a whisper.
'Here comes that policeman. I don't think you should be
talking to him, Robert. I strongly advise you not to.'

'I have to, Hugh. Sooner or later, so it might as well be
now. He looks like a capable guy, and the important thing
is to help him find Anona. I'm sure I'll get along just fine
with Chief Saylor. I'll call you later.'

Robert Duran really wasn't sure just how well he'd get
along with the policeman. He did know that in cases of
homicide, when the victim is a married woman, statistics
showed in overwhelming numbers that the husband was

the culprit. This wasn't a homicide, but from Saylor's demeanor, and the way that he looked at him at the mausoleum, Duran felt that he was right at the top of the Chief's suspect list. He wanted to talk to him before Johnny Stack or his attorney did.

Saylor's office was located in a small two-story Spanish-style building less than a half mile from the cemetery.

A cameo-faced woman working behind a bullet-proof, glass-enclosed, front desk buzzed them into the restricted area. Duran followed Saylor past a small kitchen area, then up a cramped stairway to the second floor and into a medium-sized room. Two desks butted against each other. Each desk was littered with file holders, pencil caddies, telephones, and Rolodexes.

A coffee machine sat in one corner, perfuming the air.

'Coffee?' Saylor asked, unhooking his belt and laying his revolver on the desktop.

'Thanks.'

'I hope you like it black. It's all we've got.'

'Black's fine.'

Saylor handed Duran a chipped white mug with a Highway Patrol emblem on the side, then flopped down in his chair like a man who'd put in a hard day's work. 'That's Sergeant Miller's chair,' he said, waving a beefy hand. 'He's off today. Make yourself at home.'

Saylor studied Duran over the rim of his coffee cup for a moment, then wheeled his chair around so he was no more than four feet from him. He picked up a pen and pad of foolscap paper and started asking questions, banal questions at first: current address, previous addresses, telephone numbers. Going by the rules.

Duran knew the rules. Over the years his former employer, the Centennial Insurance Agency, had sent him to a half-dozen workshops dealing with the black art of suspect interrogation.

Develop a comfortable feeling between you and the

suspect. Sit directly across from him/her. Establish eye contact.

According to experts in the field, in a normal conversation eye contact between two individuals should range between forty percent and sixty percent.

There had been special classes on body movement and facial expressions: shaking of the head, frowning, raising eyebrows, taking deep breaths, tightening of the mouth, all little tips that were supposed to give the interrogator clues as to the suspect's truthfulness.

The crossing of arms or feet is considered a defensive posture and indicates an untruthful person, so Duran sat up straight, hands folded in his lap, answering each question calmly, making sure he didn't overdo the eye contact.

Saylor must have gone to some of the same workshops, Duran thought. His questions had a nice rhythm, zigzagging from Anona's wake, the funeral, then into Duran's background.

'An insurance investigator, huh? That must be interesting.'

'Just a way to make a living, Chief.'

Saylor drummed his pen against the legal pad. 'Still, you must have learned some things about the criminal justice system.'

'I worked for the Centennial Insurance Agency, or the CIA as they liked to joke. I was with them fifteen years, first in New York, then Dallas, then Los Angeles, finally in San Francisco. Thefts from museums, private galleries, and forgeries. After I was married I started my own business, Lost Art, Inc. I handle art thefts and recoveries exclusively.'

'Keeps you busy, does it?'

'You'd be amazed at the amount of forgery going on in the art world. It's so damn easy to do now, with computers and scanners.'

'They use computers to forge paintings?' Saylor asked skeptically.

'Sure. Someone brings in an original, say for a cleaning, or a new frame. The forger runs it through a scanner. There's software now that will give you the exact measurements and, more importantly, the depth, thickness, the viscosity of the paint. You can—'

Saylor held up a hand. 'I get the picture.' He chuckled at his own joke, then said, 'You must have put some people in jail. Or at least made them surrender whatever it was they stole.'

'Yes,' Duran acknowledged. He had helped to recover millions of dollars of stolen art, and in doing so had angered a lot of people, rich and poor. Professional criminals as well as not very clever amateurs. The Mafia in New York had been involved in a couple of his investigations. 'But I don't think that any of my cases would have anything to do with . . . with this . . .' He tried to think of a description for what had happened to Anona – grave robbery, it sounded so grotesque, like something out of an old horror movie.

'You never know, Mr Duran. People harbor grudges for years and wait until their victim has forgotten about them, then they strike. Are you working on anything in particular at the moment?'

'Yes. Alan Fritzheim, the movie producer. His house was robbed of a very valuable painting. A Vincent Van Gogh, *Sun and Sky*.'

'Yeah. I read about that. Millions of dollars involved, right?'

'Right.'

'Have you any idea who pulled off the heist?'

'Not yet,' Duran answered truthfully. He saw no reason to inform Saylor that there was a good chance he'd be negotiating with the thieves shortly. The police hated it when they weren't involved in the transactions. Hated it even more when the thieves walked off scot-free with a bundle of cash.

Saylor said, 'Well, it's an angle worth thinking about. What caused your wife's death, Mr Duran?'

'Cancer. How did you know I'd be at Hugh Stringer's office today?'

'I contacted your house. The man who answered the phone, the butler, I guess. He gave me Stringer's number.'

'Well, the reason I was there is that we, we being myself, my wife's son John and her daughter Lisa, and John's attorney, were there for the reading of my wife's will.'

Saylor scribbled something on his pad, then said, 'You and your wife didn't have any children together?'

'No.'

'What was the gist of the meeting?'

Duran steepled his hands together, a gesture that indicates a confident, truthful attitude. 'John's attorney said they want to have an autopsy performed.'

Saylor inched forward on his chair. 'Why wasn't an autopsy performed in the first place?'

'My wife's doctor, Paul Feldman, visited the house regularly. He found my wife dead in her bed on Wednesday morning about nine-thirty. He examined her, and signed the death certificate then and there. His opinion was that she had died no more than a few hours before he found her. There was never any doubt that Anona was terminally ill, Chief. It was just a matter of time.'

'That's true for all of us,' Saylor said.

'I'm talking about days, weeks, perhaps a few months at the most.'

Saylor nodded and slid forward on his chair. Weeks. Months. A lot could happen over a period of months. 'What's the name of this attorney who wants the autopsy now?'

'Victor Abbott.'

Saylor's eyes widened sharply. 'Abbott. I've heard of him. What reason did he give for the need of an autopsy?'

'He suggested that my wife died from an overdose of drugs and alcohol, and that I was responsible.'

Saylor leaned back in his chair until it creaked. 'And what was your response to the accusation, Mr Duran?'

'I said it was ridiculous. Someone has been making phone calls and sending faxes saying I killed Anona.'

'Calling who? Faxing who?'

'My stepson, his lawyer, and my lawyer, Hugh Stringer.'

'Why do you think someone is doing this?'

'I wish I knew, Chief.'

'Did your wife have any enemies?'

'No. She was a much loved woman.'

'How big a person was she?'

'Anona was about five feet five inches. She weighed, oh, a hundred twenty-five pounds before she became ill.'

'At the time of her death, what do you reckon she weighed?'

Duran closed his eyes momentarily, picturing Anona. 'A hundred pounds. Probably closer to ninety.'

'Doctor Feldman. You have his address?'

'Yes. 450 Sutter Street, in San Francisco.'

Saylor wrote the information down on his pad, then said, 'Doctor Feldman signs the certificate, so no autopsy. How about the funeral arrangements? Was her body embalmed?'

The question startled Duran. 'Embalmed? I guess so. It's the law, isn't it?'

'No. People think it is, but it's not. It wouldn't make much difference regarding an autopsy, as long as the examination is performed in a reasonable time, they'd still be able to determine drugs, alcohol, toxins.' Saylor looked down to his polished cowboy boots, then brought his eyes up to interrogation level. 'If your wife weighed ninety to a hundred pounds at the time of death, she'd weigh just about the same at the time of burial. You hear a lot about "dead weight", but a hundred-pound corpse wouldn't really be that hard to maneuver.'

He removed his glasses and polished them with a handkerchief, polishing them longer than was necessary, waiting to see if Duran would say something.

'I hate to be blunt, Mr Duran, but whoever took your wife's body had to either hide it somewhere or dispose of it. Was your wife wearing any valuable articles when she was buried?'

'Just her wedding ring. A plain gold band. Worth no more than a few hundred dollars. And rosary beads. Certainly nothing worth breaking into a coffin for, Chief.'

'You'd be surprised. Nowadays some of the characters on the street will chop off an arm, just to get a ring. Was there an inscription of any kind on the ring?'

'Yes. One word. *Siempre.*'

'*Siempre.* Spanish for always, right?'

Duran nodded his head in agreement.

Saylor tugged at an earlobe. 'Mrs Stack. She was Irish, right?'

'Yes. I'm half Mexican, Chief.'

'The blue eyes fooled me. I've seen a lot of blue-eyed Italians. My wife is one of them. But never a blue-eyed Mexican.'

'My mother was Danish. That's where the eyes come from.'

'Was this your first marriage, Mr Duran?'

'No. I was married before. My first wife, Teresa, died years ago. In New York City. An aneurism.'

'Can you think of any reason why anyone would want to steal your wife's body?'

'No. Not one.'

'And there obviously haven't been any ransom calls.'

Duran was caught off guard by the statement. 'Ransom?'

'It's a possibility. The same type of thing happened in Seattle a couple of years back. Some nut would steal a body, some rich person that had died recently, then call the family and demand money.'

Duran grimaced. 'Did they catch whoever was doing it?'

'Yes. Some punk kid, just twenty-one.'

'Is he still in jail?'

'Yep. That was the first thing I checked on. About your wife's will. Who are the benefactors?'

'My wife's son John, her daughter Lisa, and me divide the bulk of the estate equally.'

'I . . . I would imagine it's a pretty substantial estate, Mr Duran.'

'Yes.'

'Are you planning to keep your business?'

'I tried retirement for a few months after Anona and I were first married. I didn't like it much.'

Saylor's gaze settled on Duran's hands. 'How did you hurt yourself?'

Duran held up his hands, like a surgeon waiting to have a nurse slip on gloves. 'I was jogging this morning. I ran into something. It was hanging from a tree. A cream-colored dress, very much like the one my wife was buried in. Then someone bumped into me, knocked me over a cliff and I took a fall.'

'Where was this?'

'In the Presidio. It's not far from Stack House.'

'Are you sure the dress was your wife's?'

'I wasn't sure at the time. It was pretty much in shreds, but it was silk, and the same color.'

'Where's the dress now?'

'It was gone by the time I got back up to the trail.'

'Did you see who knocked you over the cliff?'

'No.'

'The Presidio. That's the jurisdiction of the United

110

States Park Police. Did you notify them?'

'No. I thought it was some kind of sick joke. I didn't know Anona's body had been stolen at the time.'

'I read where someone damaged one of your wife's paintings at her wake. Do you think it's the same person?'

'I'd hate to think there are two bastards like that running around.'

'This autopsy. When we find the body, what do you think it will show?'

'Nothing. Anona died of natural causes. I'm against having an autopsy. She's been through enough. I just want her found, Chief. Found and laid to rest.'

Chief Saylor opened his mouth as if to say something, changed his mind, stood up, dropped the notepad on his desk and held out a hand. 'Well, I'll do my best, Mr Duran. You can count on that. I'll be in touch. Come on. I'll show you out.'

Duran's car was sandwiched in between two black and white patrol cars. Saylor gave the Jaguar an admiring look.

'Nice wheels. What year is it?'

'1975.'

'I like the color. British racing green.'

Saylor ran the back of his hand lightly across the trunk. 'Looks like new.' He peered into the window. 'They knew how to make them then. Leather looks like real leather. And wood trim, not that plastic stuff they put out today. I've got a classic 1958 MG convertible, but I'm getting tired of it. This is just what I'd like to move up to.' He pointed to the rear of the car. 'How about the trunk? Much space?'

Duran unlocked the trunk lid. 'Enough,' he said. Enough for a reasonable amount of luggage, golf clubs, or for the Chief's unspoken question. A body.

Saylor bent down and stuck his head inside the trunk. 'You sure keep it clean, Mr Duran.' He swept his hand across the car's carpeting, his fingers coming in contact with what appeared to be a small pebble. 'Beautiful piece of machinery,' he said, scooping the pebble up. 'Just beautiful.' He held the pebble between his thumb and forefinger, squeezing one eye shut like a jeweler examining a rare stone. 'There's a little hole in this thing.' He handed it to Duran. 'You said your wife was buried with her rosary beads, didn't you?'

Duran nodded, rolling the bead around in his palm. 'Yes, yes she was.'

Saylor plucked the bead from Duran's palm. 'How do you suppose this got into your trunk?'

'I . . . I don't know, it could have been there for some time, perhaps it was a—'

'You mind if I look a little closer?' Saylor asked, not waiting for an answer as his hands explored the trunk carpeting, rolling it back, exposing the plywood board covering the spare tire. He slid the board loose, and when he lifted the tire free, there was a clattering sound. He lay the tire against the bumper then reached down into the circular, hollowed out compartment, his hand coming out with a cluster of rosary beads. 'Are you a religious man, Mr Duran?'

Duran stared at the chief's hand in wonderment. 'I don't know how those got there.'

Chapter 12

He tore the binoculars from his eyes in disgust. What the hell was Duran doing? Opening his trunk up to the police! What had prompted the policeman to look in the trunk? Duran would be the logical suspect, and that wasn't all bad. But he didn't want Duran arrested. Not now, and he didn't want him followed by the police. He wanted Duran for himself. At the right time. There were just a few days to go. A day or two in the SHU, then Duran would go in the ground with his wife. It wasn't perfect justice but, as he knew all too well from Pelican Bay Prison, there was no such thing as perfect justice.

He focused the binoculars again. Duran was gesturing with his hands, the policeman was gesturing back, holding out a palm full of rosary beads. Duran was supposed to find the rosary beads – not the cops! Not now! He had planned to puncture one of the Jaguar's tires while it was parked on the street. He wanted to see Duran's expression when he found the rosary beads. He slipped his right hand under his armpit, then withdrew it and reached for the sketch-pad. The policeman. Another face he'd have to be wary of.

The afternoon fog had penetrated the coastside trees and worked its way inland, causing traffic on the freeway to throttle down to near loitering speed.

Duran exited the Junipero Serra Freeway at Brotherhood

Drive. There was a break in the fog as he skirted Lake Merced, which was encircled by a determined crowd of walkers, joggers, runners, young women pushing strollers, Spandex-encased cyclists, their heads topped by salad-bowl-style helmets, weaving their way around the pedestrians as if they were nothing more than barriers put there to make the biker's ride more interesting.

Robert Duran saw none of the scenery. His eyes kept bouncing to the rearview mirror, looking for a police car, thinking about the interrogation by Chief Saylor. The rosary beads. Who planted them? Had Saylor known they were in the trunk? And set him up with that story of being interested in an old Jaguar? Had someone called him, or faxed him a message telling him the beads were there?

Who had access to his car? The Jag was left unattended in the garage area at Stack House. Anyone in the house could get to it. And what about the parking lot at work? He was in and out all the time, so the car sat in the back of the lot, the keys in the ignition. It wouldn't have been difficult for someone to get the keys.

He took a deep breath, trying to reason it out. Someone wants me to look guilty of killing Anona, and taking her body from the mausoleum. The dress, the beads. That left her wedding ring. Where was it and when was it going to turn up?

Duran wrenched the wheel to his right, pulling into a parking lot near Lowell High School. Could it be as Chief Saylor suggested? Someone who he'd come into contact with during an investigation? Someone with a grudge. The chirping of the carphone startled him.

'Bob, it's Peggy. I heard about Anona. Are you all right?'

'I'm not sure,' Duran conceded.

'Have there been any arrests?'

'No. But the cops have got me in their cross hairs.' He told Peggy what happened on the jogging trail, of the accusations made at the meeting at Hugh Stringer's office and Chief Saylor finding the rosary beads.

'Jesus,' Peggy said, 'that explains the call.'

'What call?'

'I went out for a while, this was on the answering machine when I got back. Listen.'

Duran didn't recognise the tune or the singer at first, then it came to him. Louis Prima, a long dead trumpet player and vocalist who somehow, even in death, had caught on with the so-called X generation.

'I-I-I-I ain't got no boooody, and no body cares for me. I-I-I-I'm so sad and lonely, won't some body care for meeeee.'

The music stopped abruptly. Then there was laughter. Scornful, evil laughter. Then silence.

Peggy came back on the line. 'What's going on, Bob?'

'I wish I knew,' Duran confessed. 'Save that tape. And Peg, lock the office door. I don't want anyone coming in there when you're alone. And check this phone number for me right away.' He took out the fax sheet and read off the number. 'I'm on my way home. Call me as soon as you get the information.'

He watched the traffic zoom for several minutes, then began digging through the car – the glove compartment, under the seats, alongside the narrow spaces between the seats. Chief Saylor had wanted to search the entire vehicle, but Duran had put him off. Anona's wedding band. If Saylor had found Anona's ring, he probably would have thrown Duran in a cell right then and there.

No ring. Not in the car, but it was out there somewhere. He pounded the steering wheel in frustration.

Someone was trying to rattle him, shake him up. Why? On the jogging trail this morning. The ripped dress. The shove over the cliff. Was it meant to kill him? No, the cliff wasn't steep enough to cause a fatal injury. A broken bone or two, maybe, but not death. The laughter he heard on the trail. Was it the same person who had phoned his office? He looked at his bandaged wrist and sighed. Saylor had taken notice of the bandage and the cuts and scratches on his hands at the cemetery, then again at his office before inquiring about them. If someone breaks into a mausoleum, then into a crypt, rips out chunks of concrete, that someone gets scratches and cuts on his hands.

Who would do such a thing? Jason Lark? Everything seemed to happen after Lark turned up. Was Lark the one feeding Victor Abbott those telephone calls and faxes? But what motive could Lark have? Revenge? No. Lark wasn't the type to seek revenge. He'd go after money, but there was no money in taking Anona's body, or in framing Duran. Unless – unless the plan was to get him knocked out of the will. Then there'd be a two-way split between Johnny and Lisa. He shook his head in disgust. Anona's body. Lark was a bastard, all right. But even he wouldn't stoop to that. Or would he? With Duran gone, Lark would be free to deal with his children.

He edged back into traffic and headed home.

Duran parked the Jag in its slot alongside a silver Bentley that had seen little of the road since Anona's illness. Beside the Bentley was a maroon Jeep 4x4; next in line a gun-metal gray Lincoln Mark VI, and finally Lisa's red Mercedes convertible.

All the cars were showroom polished except for Lisa's. White walls blackened, a fresh dent in the grill, half-moon marks from the wiper blades visible on the gritty windshield.

Duran sighed. Lisa Stack was hard on cars. Lisa was hard on everything.

There was no sign of Johnny Stack's inky-black shark-jawed Porsche. Johnny had moved six months ago, to a houseboat in Sausalito, and had been an intermittent visitor during Anona's illness.

George Montroy, the butler, was waiting for Duran at

the front door, his face set, as if fighting to remain silent.

George had always been very protective of Anona. At first he had thought that Duran was nothing more than another fortune hunter. A mistake commonly made by women in their middle years. Someone who would be gone after a year or two. But after a while, George seemed to grudgingly accept Duran.

'Good evening, sir,' George said in his clipped baritone. 'You have a visitor.'

'Friend or foe?'

'A foe would be my estimate. A young man. None too tidy. He's waiting in the parlor.'

Duran raised his eyebrows in a question. George didn't let just anyone into the house. Especially an unknown who was 'none too tidy.'

'Miss Lisa arrived while he was at the door,' the butler explained. 'She suggested that he be allowed in.'

'Is Lisa still here?'

'Come and gone, sir.'

'What about Jason Lark?'

'No, sir. The policeman who called told me about Mrs Anona,' George said in a pained voice. 'I'm terribly sorry. I just can't believe it. Have there been any developments?'

'No. I spoke to the police, but as of now they don't have a clue as to who broke into the mausoleum or what's become of Anona's body. Let me know right away if Mr Lark returns.'

'Yes, sir, and let me know if there's anything I can do, sir. Anything at all.'

Duran nodded his thanks and headed for the parlor.

The man sitting in one of the club chairs was staring quizzically at Anona Stack's *Leaf in Transit*. He appeared to be in his early twenties, with disheveled mud-colored hair and scaly sunburned skin.

'You wanted to see me?' Duran asked.

He got to his feet quickly and looked at Duran with an

almost apologetic look on his face. 'Are you Robert Duran?'

'Yes.'

The young man pulled an envelope from his faded blue parka and touched it to Duran's shoulder. 'You're served,' he said quickly, letting the envelope flutter to the floor as he hurried to the door.

George was there to open it for him and close it after he was gone.

Duran bent down for the envelope. The lettering in the left-hand corner read Ace Attorney Services. Inside were several legal documents. A probate citation and petition for suspension of powers and removal of Robert Duran as the estate representative. Victor Abbott, attorney for Petitioner John Stack, vs Robert Duran, Executor of the estate of Anona Stack Duran.

He didn't bother with the fine print. At least he had seen his wife's last name listed as Duran. He headed for the nearest phone and dialed Hugh Stringer's number. He was put on hold for a couple of minutes, his string of silent curses broken only when George presented him with a Martini in a frosty glass.

'Bless you,' Duran said, gratefully accepting the drink and passing the legal documents to the butler.

'I was afraid of that, Mr Duran. I shouldn't have let him in.'

'You did the right thing. I want to tell you—'

Hugh Stringer came on the line. 'I know what you're calling about, Robert. A messenger dropped off copies to me an hour ago. You were served by Abbott's office, right?'

'Yes. Just a few minutes ago. What are you going to do about it?'

'Well, I've got to get ready for the hearing, which won't be for at least two weeks. Under the circumstance, I'm sure I can get a postponement. I think it would be wise for you not to write any checks on the estate account until we get this straightened out.'

Duran took a long sip of the Martini then settled into one of the stuffed chairs. 'Do you want to represent me in this Hugh, or should I look for another lawyer?'

'I'm your attorney of record,' Stringer insisted. 'Don't get excited. I am representing you, and I'll do my best for you, just as I did for Anona, and her father. But there's nothing we can do now except prepare for the petition in court.

'Victor Abbott has made some serious charges. We have to be ready to refute them. That means we have to work together.' He paused, and when he spoke again there was a hard edge to his voice.

'I know how badly Anona was feeling. Did she . . . take something?'

'Anona was very sick, and she died, Hugh. Nothing could have prevented it.'

'What happened during your meeting with the policeman?'

'He's a pro. The questioning went fine. Then he conned me into opening the trunk of my car.'

'What the devil for?' Stringer asked in a confused voice.

'He was fishing. And he found something. Rosary beads, the same type Anona was buried with.'

Duran could hear the sharp intake of Stringer's breath. 'Anona's beads?'

'I don't know who else's they could be, Hugh. And I have no idea how they got there.'

'I wonder if Victor Abbott knows of this?'

'I wonder if he had something to do with planting them,' Duran countered. 'If he doesn't know now, he'll find out soon. I don't think Chief Saylor will wait very long before calling him.'

'Poor Anona. It's ghastly.'

'Yes,' Duran agreed readily. 'And this subpoena. The

charges are outrageous and you know it.'

'I do, Robert, but obviously John does not. He wants you removed. Let's get together, uh, how about Wednesday morning? Ten o'clock.'

'That's three days from now,' Duran protested.

'Yes. Well, I need that much time to have my staff research the documents Victor Abbott served on you. I won't have the results until then. Use your time wisely, Robert. Think about the charges. Write down your responses. List any witnesses you can think of to refute them. I'll talk to Dr Feldman. We have to be well prepared. I've made some calls regarding Victor Abbott. He's tough. Very tough.'

'When I mentioned his name to Saylor, I got the impression he knew who Abbott was.'

Stringer's voice became official-sounding. 'When Anona is found, I don't know if I will be able to prevent an autopsy.'

Duran drained the remains of the Martini in a gulp. 'Find a way, Hugh. Under no circumstances will there be an autopsy.'

Stringer started to ask why, then stopped, not sure he was prepared for the answer. 'All right, I'll see you Wednesday morning here at the office. Or perhaps before that. I want to speak to Lisa.'

They said their goodbyes, then Duran rolled the empty glass across his forehead, the reality of Anona's body being stolen hitting him again. He shuddered, like a dog shaking off water. The phone call. Would the man call again? And Victor Abbott. What did Abbott have on him? The overdose charge. Drugs: cocaine, marijuana and alcohol. Where the hell was Abbott getting information like that? Anona had a nightly glass of wine. The marijuana had been a blessing. But cocaine? No. Not Anona. Johnny had been caught with some coke on him a year or so ago. Hugh Stringer had gotten him off with a warning.

Would John have given his mother cocaine? Why? It was a stimulant, certainly not what Anona needed. He remembered reading something years ago about the drug having been pushed by Sigmund Freud as a magic elixir, but that had been debunked. It was a drug, a highly addictive drug. Anona would never touch it.

The adultery claim. There was nothing there. He and Anona hadn't made love in months. There had been times when Duran was sorely tempted to have an affair, but he hadn't. So what was Abbott talking about?

'A refill, sir?'

Duran's head snapped up. George was stooped over, a sweating silver cocktail mixer in hand. 'Is there enough in there for two?'

George bobbed his head as he poured.

'Pour yourself one, Mr Montroy, and I'll tell you about the will.'

A quizzical expression settled on the butler's features. He could never remember Duran, or anyone else in the household calling him by his last name. 'If you wish, sir,' he said, 'I'll be right back.'

Duran sipped at the Martini. Anona's recipe. Kettle One vodka straight from the freezer, a drop or two of vermouth to make it legitimate, and a twist of lemon.

George returned with glass in hand. 'I must admit, I am curious about the will, sir.'

Duran satisfied his curiosity. 'There's a lump sum bequest for you of a hundred thousand dollars.' Not as much as expected, Duran could tell from the way George's eyes narrowed. 'And the Bentley, and the contents of the wine cellar, plus a pension, George. Anona made sure that the pension was fully funded. And last, but not least, *Evening Field*.'

George's eyes blinked rapidly. *Evening Field* was one of Anona's first paintings, and hung in her bedroom. It had never been offered for sale.

'The estate is split equally three ways,' Duran reported. 'Johnny, Lisa and myself. There are special bequests: yours, to friends and various charities.'

'It's more than I expected, sir. And much more than I deserve.'

'Anona didn't think so, and neither do I.' Duran held his glass up in a toasting gesture. 'I'm afraid that not all the other beneficiaries agree.'

George nodded knowingly. 'I understand, sir.'

I hope so, Duran thought. He needed an ally.

The phone rang. It was Peggy Jacquard.

'That telephone number was unlisted, Bob, that's why it took me a while to get it. It's a fax machine in the lobby of the Hyatt Regency Hotel. You know the kind. Anyone can use them. They're coin-operated, like a telephone. Has this something to do with Anona?'

'Yes.'

'Does it help in any way?'

'No,' Duran said between tight-together lips. 'Not a damn bit.'

Chapter 13

A rigging of yellow crime-scene tape sealed off the area in a fifty-yard circumference around the mausoleum.

Chief Bill Saylor ducked under the tape, feeling the TV camera lens zoom in on his back as if there was a bull's-eye painted in the middle of his jacket. His shoes made crunching sounds on the gravel. He turned to face the camera. 'Sorry, fellas. There's nothing doing now. I'll be holding a press conference in my office at ten o'clock. I'm going to ask that you move on now. I'll give you everything I've got at the conference. Later today you'll be allowed in here, at which time you may take all the pictures you want.'

There was some grumbling as the reporters picked up their equipment, tucked it into a van and drove off.

'All finished, Chief,' said the lead crime-lab technician, a bearish looking man with a full beard. He stripped off his rubber gloves as Saylor approached the crypt.

'Find anything, Tony?'

'Not much. Nothing in there except all that debris. The concrete hadn't really set yet, but it still required a hell of a lot of work to dislodge the coffin.'

'Did you look for the rosary beads, like I asked you?'

'Yes. Didn't find one.'

Saylor ran a hand down the edge of the mausoleum door. 'Nothing fancy here, huh?'

'No. It was simply pried open with a screwdriver or

chisel. It didn't take much to break the lock.'

'Were there any trace samples of blood?'

'We didn't find a drop, Chief.'

The smell of concrete dust hung in the air. The gaping hole in the wall where Anona Stack's coffin had lain had been swept clean.

'We picked up a lot of prints from the coffin, Chief. It'll take a while to identify them all.'

Saylor nodded his head and studied the coffin, now positioned directly in the middle of the marble floor. He had already taken statements from the members of the cemetery crew who originally sealed the crypt. He'd also taken their fingerprints, which were probably the ones Tony had pulled from the coffin.

Tony was right. It had taken a hell of a lot of work. How had he done it? A pick? Or did he just bust it open with a sledge-hammer? No, the noise. No matter how thick the walls were, he'd have to consider the noise. But, if he started with a small hole, maybe a drill, then a bigger drill bit, until he could get a chisel in there and then just start pulling out chunks of the concrete, it wouldn't be too difficult. Then there was the coffin itself. The crypt was set some four feet above the floor. He'd have to edge it out, slide it down. Then open it. Saylor cringed at the thought of opening a coffin in a mausoleum. At night. In the middle of the night, probably.

Then the body. Picking it up, carrying it away. Where would he take it? The young grave robber in the Seattle cases had buried the bodies in makeshift graves in the woods.

While it was no problem to walk into the cemetery grounds at night, driving in was another matter. A chained gate was in place at all entrances and exits after six in the evening. His officers had to unlock the chains to make their rounds.

And even if he had been able to get a vehicle by the

chained gates, would he chance it? A car or truck would stick out like the proverbial sore thumb. His patrolling officers would notice a vehicle. Headlights in a cemetery. Saylor smiled thinly. Or at least should have noticed. No, he couldn't risk headlights being seen from the road.

So, what did that leave for transporting the body to his vehicle? Saylor took off his glasses and pinched the bridge of his nose. *What would I use?* he asked himself.

A wheelbarrow. Yes. That made sense. Wheel the body down to Mission Road. Near where he would have parked the car. His own wheelbarrow? Or borrow one from the cemetery?

Mrs Stack-Duran might have weighed only one hundred pounds, but, as unpleasant a thought it was, Saylor had to imagine that the corpse was decomposing. He'd wrap her in something. What? A blanket would do the trick. Hell, you could buy genuine United States Army body-bags at surplus stores.

Saylor rooted around in his pants pocket for the rosary beads. They were not worth anything as evidence now. Should he have impounded the Jaguar right when he found them? Gotten a warrant and checked out the car, then Duran's house? Duran could say that the rosary beads had been in their luggage, fallen out in the trunk months ago. Maybe he had his own matching set of beads.

If it was Duran who took his wife's body, then he sure was a cocky bastard – opening the trunk like that. If he killed his wife, then an autopsy could show traces of poison, or a drug overdose. That was certainly a motive for stealing her body.

Duran looked strong enough to handle the break-in at the mausoleum and the removal of the corpse. He said that his wife was certain to die in a very short time. But during that time she could have changed her will. Left Duran out in the cold. How would he react to that? The loss of all that money. Duran. He had a motive. Or, could it have been a mercy killing? Then he panicked when he heard that his wife's son wanted an autopsy and had hired an attorney. Either one of those scenarios fitted. Nothing else did. Unless he had a real crazy on his hands.

'Oh, there was one thing, Chief.'

'What's that?' Saylor asked, zipping up his jacket.

The technician handed him a small plastic bag. Inside was one item. A quarter. A plain American liberty twenty-five cents piece.

Saylor carried the bag outside, examining the coin in the natural light. There was nothing special about it. Minted in 1973. It appeared to have seen its share of pay telephones, parking meters and possibly slot machines.

'Where'd you find this, Tony?'

'Under the coffin. It was lying heads up,' the technician explained. He rolled his shoulders. 'I don't know if it means anything, Chief.'

'Neither do I,' Saylor admitted. The suspect had left nothing behind – no tools, gloves or clothing, and, Saylor was willing to bet, no identifiable prints. 'Why a quarter?'

'Maybe it was for luck,' Tony said jokingly, cutting his laugh short when he saw Saylor's hardening expression.

Saylor hiked over to the maintenance area and peered into the tool shed, an old corrugated iron building that looked as if it belonged on a Second World War military base. He spotted Jarliff Mahoney, the head gardener. 'Just the man I'm looking for. Are you missing any tools, Jarliff?'

'Indeed I am,' Mahoney answered in a brogue thicker than any Irish stew his wife had ever put together. 'A wheelbarrow. You think that bloody ghoul took it?'

Saylor looked back into the shed. Rows of hoes, rakes and shovels hung from the walls. Nine wheelbarrows were parked side by side. Old, battered, chipped and so rusted it was hard to tell their original colors.

Saylor waved an arm out to the hillside. 'Any chance the missing barrow's out there somewhere?'

Mahoney, a small wiry man with thinning hair and a well-trimmed guardsman mustache, was having none of that. 'No way, Chief. My men bring in all their tools every night. Nothing else is missing, not a shovel or a rake.'

Saylor eyed the little Irishman. His khaki shirt and pants were starched and pressed as neatly as a Marine getting ready to go on liberty. A precise man. If he said a wheelbarrow was missing, then it was missing. Saylor fingered the shed door. 'No lock, huh?'

'Never saw the need,' Mahoney grumbled, ''til now.'

'Mind if I borrow one of your wheelbarrows for a bit?'

'As long as you put it back when you're finished, Chief.'

Saylor pushed the wheelbarrow over to the Stack family mausoleum, counting off the yardage as he went. Two hundred and forty-three yards. Not a great distance. But it was now daylight. A sullen gray sky, a cool wind, but daylight. Visibility was not a problem. Saylor knew what it was like out here at one o'clock in the morning. Foggy, cold and dark. No streetlights. Dark as death.

He paused as his eyes swept the terrain again. How had he done it? A flashlight? A single beam of light flashing around a cemetery might draw attention. Infra-red glasses? James Bond stuff? You could buy the damn things at sporting-goods stores.

He had known where to find the wheelbarrow. Knew that the tool shed wasn't locked. He had checked it all out. Then he took the body. Then what? Saylor placed his hands on the wheelbarrow handles again, pulling them up like divining rods. Show me where to go.

I've got a body. I've got to get it out of here as quickly as possible. Saylor pushed off, taking the path of least resistance, hugging the sides of a narrow, winding road.

A black limousine slid by, the capped chauffeur giving him an eyebrow-raised questioning look.

Saylor kept going, counting off the yardage again. Three hundred and seventy-six yards to the chained gate. He must have picked up the chain to slide the wheelbarrow under it. Would Duran have become sloppy? Made a mistake? Saylor took a miniature tape recorder from his shirt pocket and dictated a note to himself. 'Have lab check gate chains for prints.'

He pocketed the recorder and continued his journey, past the dusky-watered pond and the fat-bellied ducks that waddled alongside waiting for someone to throw them bread.

Down to Mission Road. Busy now. Lots of traffic. An assortment of small businesses across the street: an auto repair shop, a roofer, a sheet-metal shop. A quarter mile down the road was a bar that closed at ten o'clock at night.

Saylor closed his eyes, picturing the scene. It was dark, Anona Stack's body lumped in the wheelbarrow. What else? He needed tools to break through the crypt's concrete. A pick, a shovel, drills, something. He'd throw the tools in the wheelbarrow with the body.

Then what? Pushing a loaded wheelbarrow down Mission Road? No. Too risky. Saylor turned around and went back to the pond, turning down a narrow opening bordered on both sides by head-high shrubs and rambling clumps of pyracantha. He bumped the wheelbarrow over a patch of railroad tracks, thick with rust, the line abandoned years ago.

Still, it was a road, which led to a dead end. A good place to hide a car.

Saylor marched off the road's width. At its narrowest, it was barely eight feet. He reached out and touched the branch of a pyracantha plant, pulling back his finger when it made contact. He sucked at the tiny cut on his finger. Sharp. Sharp enough to scratch a car.

Robert Duran's Jaguar was in perfect condition. Not a

mark on it. But someone as savvy as Duran wouldn't be foolish enough to use his own car. But then why were the rosary beads in the trunk of the Jag?

Saylor squeezed his finger, watching the blood bubble up. The cuts and scratches on Duran's hands. Maybe he'd worn gloves at the mausoleum, then took them off once he had the body in the wheelbarrow. That story about being knocked off a cliff in the Presidio and seeing his wife's tattered dress was pretty farfetched.

He crouched down, his hand skimming along the gravel for traces of oil or blood, finding none.

He swiveled on his heels and eyed the wheelbarrow. What if there wasn't a car? What if Duran left his car a half mile or so away? He's got her body, the wheelbarrow and the tools. Saylor scanned the area again. Where's the best place to dispose of a body? In a cemetery. Right here. Just dig a hole, and bury the body in it.

Saylor was pleased with himself as he started maneuvering the wheelbarrow back to Mahoney's shed. He parked it in its proper spot and dry-washed his hands. Then it dawned on him.

What had Duran done with the wheelbarrow? Bury it with the body? That would take a lot of extra digging. Why not just roll it back to the shed? Or just abandon the damn thing behind a tree?

Mahoney's brogue cut into his thoughts. 'Did you find what ya were looking for, Chief?'

Saylor pressed his lips into a kiss of worried disapproval. 'No. I'm afraid I'm right back where I started.'

129

Chapter 14

The dining room table was capable of seating up to twenty-eight people. Jason Lark remembered occasions when the table was filled – mostly with stuffy guests of Conrad Stack. Now he sat by himself. John was at his houseboat in Sausalito, Lisa was avoiding him, Duran was off to work.

He cut into his eggs with surgical care, watching the yolk yellow the plate, thinking about his lunch with Duran's secretary. She hadn't mentioned the Fritzheim case, though Lark had given her enough hints. He'd have to get into the office, have to—

'A call for you, sir.'

George handed Lark a cordless phone.

Lark waited until the butler had left the room before picking the instrument up.

'Yes, what now?' he asked, assuming the caller was his shop assistant, Adam Sheehan. He was wrong.

'Well?'

Mario Drago. He had managed to insert a tone of impatience, arrogance and menace in that single word.

'Nothing positive yet,' Lark said. 'But I'm making progress.'

'How so?' Mario pressed.

'Ah . . . it's difficult to say from this location.'

'Call me within twenty-four hours, Jason. If I don't hear from you in that time, I'll assume you've failed and

131

I'll have to make other plans.'

There was a click and the dial tone began droning.

Lark looked up to see George poised over him with a silver coffee-pot in his hand.

'Bad news, sir?' the butler asked stiffly.

Lark held up his half-filled coffee cup. 'There hasn't been much good news around here for some time, has there, George? Johnny asked me to do an inventory of the house, see if there are any hidden gems that might be worth something. You wouldn't know of any items – old paintings, sketches, that kind of thing, would you, George?'

'No, sir,' the butler replied stiffly.

Lark studied George over the rim of his coffee cup a moment, then said, 'Just before Anona and I split up, we went to France. We stayed at Claude Bresson's château. I vaguely remember Anona having some sketches of the work she did over there, but I haven't come across them.'

The butler's only reply was, 'Will you be needing anything else from the kitchen, sir?'

The sky was pale blue, with just a few scratches of cloud. The bay waters gleamed like dark ice. He sat on his campstool and sketched a dusty-brown pelican who sat hunched on a rotting piling. A pelican. In all his years at Pelican Bay Prison he hadn't seen even one of the species. His eyes drifted over to the Jaguar, then to the pier leading to Duran's office.

Duran had left the house a little after seven, maneuvering the Jaguar through a small throng of media people, and had driven directly to his office.

The pelican arched its neck and stretched out its wings toward the morning sun, rolling them slowly, like a matador taunting a bull. He flipped the tablet and started a fresh sketch.

The radio, TV and newspapers were all trumpeting the

removal of Anona Stack from her mausoleum, but there was no mention of the rosary beads found in Duran's trunk.

The pelican had had enough of the sun and dropped his wings. He flipped back to the original drawing, all the while wondering what Duran would do. Would he make the connection? After all these years? The odds seemed slim. So much had happened since that day in Beverly Hills.

He and Arlene were in the back of the shop, working on a Piet Mondrian geometric oil, *Composition in Red and Blue*. It was one of the easiest works they had ever forged, simple squares of color bounded by black outlines. They were thinking of where to go for lunch when the commotion started. The banging of doors, shouts, then Royce Breamer screaming in that high-pitched squeal of his. Then the policeman stormed into the room, grabbed him, then Arlene, handcuffing them like common criminals. Duran had stood by the door, taking it all in, a satisfied look on his face.

He rubbed his painting hand under his armpit. It was itching. There were pin-points of a rash stretching across his knuckles.

'How much?' a voice asked from behind him.

He jumped to his feet and turned to confront a beer-bellied man in dark glasses, a flower-print shirt and plaid Bermuda shorts.

A heavyset woman who resembled the man was standing alongside him. A sweatshirt with a stencil of Alcatraz Island barely covered her stomach.

The man pointed a pudgy finger at the sketch-pad. 'How much for the picture of the bird?'

'How much would you spend?'

'Put me and the little lady in with the bird and I'll give you ten bucks.'

He laughed. Prison prices – except the guards always

paid him in cigarettes rather than cash. 'All right. Stand over there, by the piling.'

'Come on Margaret, and don't scare the bird.'

Peggy Jacquard swooped by without paying any particular notice to the artist or his subject. Street artists were a common sight around Fisherman's Wharf. She hurried down the pier, as always careful not to catch her heels in the cracks between the boards.

She had spotted Duran's Jag in the parking lot, so she didn't bother using her key when entering the office.

'You're up bright and early today,' she said, trying to put some cheer in her voice. Duran was perched behind his desk, the computer on, a stack of folders at his side. His sleeves were rolled up, his tie undone. His forehead was a washboard of wrinkles. He looked as if he'd already put in a hard day's work. She walked over, gave him a peck on the cheek, then squeezed behind the chair and used her hands to massage his shoulders.

'You're tight, Bob. Real tight.'

Duran rolled his head and her hands dug into his neck muscles. 'Thanks, Peg. I've been going through some old files, trying to find someone mad enough at me to pull a stunt like this.'

'Any luck?' she queried, digging her thumbs into his spinal cord.

'Ouch,' Duran called out. 'Did your halfback teach you that?'

'You don't want to know what he taught me.' She pulled her hands back and went into the alcove to make some coffee. 'Did you come up with any suspects?'

'A few possibilities. I know there are some people who dislike me out there, but not for someone to do this. It just doesn't make any sense.'

'What about the police? Have they got any leads?'

'No, nothing. At least they haven't told me anything. I

played the phone tape we received for Chief Saylor. He didn't seem impressed. The reporters were already out at Stack House this morning. The phones here have been ringing like mad. I took all three lines off the hook. We'll have to put them back in service, just in case the police, or that lunatic who left that song message on the answering machine, call again. But if it's a reporter, just hang up on them. And if any work comes in, politely turn it down, Peg. We're going to concentrate on finding Anona, and who the hell is behind all of this.'

'What about the Fritzheim case?'

Duran massaged his chin. 'I guess we're committed there, but nothing else.'

'Okay,' Peggy called over her shoulder. 'I didn't get to tell you. I had lunch with Jason Lark yesterday.'

Duran leaned back in his chair, locking his fingers behind his head. 'Is that right? Tell me about it.'

'He's a smooth-talking devil. That man can really roll out the patter. He was telling me about what a rat he was most of his life, how he's changed his ways, got it all together now, but all the time he's talking, he's asking questions.'

'What kind of questions?'

'A lot of them were about you.'

Duran leaned forward and settled his elbows on the desk. 'What did Lark want to know about me?'

'Everything. What kind of work you're handling. How the business is doing. I did a lot of talking, but didn't tell him anything.'

'Did he ask about any specific cases?'

'No. He just kind of moved the conversation all around.'

Duran thought back to the meeting with Lark in the Stack House game room. Lark had started to question him about the business then, too. But they were interrupted when Johnny arrived. What is his interest in me,

Duran wondered? Something to do with the will? Was he trying to see just how much money I was making? Or is it something else?

'Peg, was it while you were out to lunch with Lark that the telephone call came in?'

'Right. He took me down the street to Scoma's. When we got back, the message was there.'

'Lark came back to the office with you?'

'Sure did.' Peggy strode over to the window overlooking the line-up of colorful old wooden fishing boats. 'The perfect gentleman, he was.'

'Did Lark hear the message on the tape?'

She turned to face him. 'Yes. I hope that doesn't cause a problem.'

'During lunch, did Lark leave you alone long enough to have made the call and leave the message?'

Peggy pursed her lips. 'Well, he did go to the little boy's room for a few minutes, so I guess it's possible.' She strolled behind the desk and began massaging Duran's neck again. 'What makes you think Jason Lark made the call?'

'No specific reason,' Duran admitted.

Peggy dug her fingertips into Duran's shoulder muscles. 'Tell me about what you've been up to.'

Duran did just that, leaving out nothing, including the fact that he had spent hours digging through his car looking for Anona's wedding band.

Peggy said, 'Whoever the guy is who stole Anona's body, he must be a real creep. I don't remember us ever dealing with anyone that creepy.'

'What time did you meet with Lark?'

'A little after noon. Why?'

'Just wondering.' Duran was thinking of the faxes. Lark certainly had time to send off the faxes to Abbott and Stringer.

'Do you actually think Lark has something to do with it?' Peggy asked skeptically.

'I think he's a no good bastard, who is capable of just about anything if the stakes are high enough. The incident at the trail. That's not Lark's style. He wouldn't risk a physical confrontation with me. I might hit him in that pretty face of his. But let's take a close look at Lark. Run a credit check on him personally and on his business. It's down in Santa Monica.'

'If we eliminate Lark, who does that leave?'

'A psycho. Chief Saylor thought that there was a possibility whoever took Anona's body would call and demand a ransom, but since we haven't had any calls, I think we can discount that. So maybe it's someone who feels they have a score to settle with me.' He patted the folders on the desk. 'These are the possibilities I've come up with so far. You take a look and see what you think.'

'What about the Fritzheim theft? Could that have something to do with all of this?'

Duran's brow knitted. 'I don't see how. We've barely gotten started on that.'

Peggy picked up the stack of folders, carried them to her desk and came back with a thick manila envelope. 'This came in yesterday, from Fritzheim. It's a photograph and the appraisal of the stolen Van Gogh.'

Duran nodded his thanks. Fritzheim had kept the documents in his safety deposit box. The appraisal was a duplicate of the one the insurance carrier had provided Duran.

Peggy leaned over his shoulder and examined the photograph. 'I can see that going for, oh, fifty bucks at a garage sale.'

Duran grinned. 'I keep telling you, you have no eye for art, Peg.'

'If that's art, I should have saved the stuff I drew in kindergarten. It'd be worth millions now.'

Duran studied the photograph, a pale image of the

explosive power of the artist's well-documented imagination, his distorted images and 'devil's furnace' coloring: blood reds, mustard and lemon yellows applied with a strong, varied brush stroke.

Duran shuffled the photograph and documents together and dropped them in his 'in' file, then returned to the computer, accessing old cases, sifting through the reports on the blue-background computer screen. No doubt there were many people who had reasons to dislike him and there had been threats made against his life. There were the heated 'I'll get you for this' cries of frustrated white-collar thieves, often a 'first timer' who didn't really consider ripping off an insurance company a crime. He concentrated on the more exotic cases, where a lot of money was involved and where he had worked with the police, had testified in court and where the suspect had gone to jail. A Monet recovered in Venice. The thief, a mild-mannered security guard at a private museum. He'd been sent to an Italian prison according to the file. That was over five years ago. He was probably out on probation after a year or two. If so, with all the corruption going on it Italy, he might even have his old job back.

There were more museum thefts, in New York, New Orleans, Santa Fe, New Mexico, Dallas and Houston. The Houston case involved a Robert Motherwell abstract that had been insured for over two million dollars.

Duran had eventually found it hanging over the bar of a restaurant in New York's Little Italy. 'Funny thing, just black circles and stripes on white, but I kinda like it,' the thick-necked bartender had told Duran. The owner of the restaurant wasn't all that happy about having to give up the painting. Threats were made, with obvious references to the Mafia.

Duran had had another run-in with the New York Mafia, over Peruvian artifacts smuggled in via a ship that docked in New Jersey. The Mafia was not averse to killing two birds with one stone – the ancient statues were hollowed out and filled with cocaine. Duran figured that if the Mafia had wanted him killed, they would have done it right then and there, but he decided to print out the names and ID of the two mafioso that had been arrested, then found not guilty by a nervous, intimidated jury.

He painstakingly worked his way through a myriad of fraud cases, then into the investigations where he dealt directly with the thieves – buying back the art work at a tenth of its insured value – the thieves often actually working for the owner of the stolen property.

'Ham and Swiss on rye okay?' Peggy asked, drawing Duran's attention from the computer screen.

He stretched his hands over his head and yawned. 'Lunchtime already?'

Peggy set the sandwich and a can of Coke on the desk. 'Did you find anything in the files,' Duran remarked snapping the soft drink open.

Peggy rolled her ergonomic adjustable chair over to the desk and sat down with a sigh. Her nylons rustled when she crossed her legs. Her blouse was cherry-blossom pink and looked wonderful against her dark complexion. Duran told her so.

'Thanks, but you'll have to do better than that to keep up with Jason Lark. I was thinking. Maybe we're looking at this from the wrong angle.'

'What other angle is there?'

'We're looking for someone who has it in for you. What if it's someone who hated Anona?'

'I thought of that possibility, but I couldn't come up with anyone,' Duran concluded.

'No rational person. But remember what happened to her painting the day of the wake at the museum. Somebody tried to ruin *Rondeau #8*. What if it was someone she had wronged. Maybe a long time ago.'

Duran took a sip of the soft drink. 'Yes, the museum

and the cemetery. It has to be the same person. Has to be. But who? You knew Anona. No one hated her.'

'When we were working at the Centennial Insurance Agency, there was a forgery case involving Anona. Didn't Anona go down to Los Angeles and testify against that old Swiss character?'

'Yes, but . . .'

'He went to jail,' Peggy reminded.

'If I remember right he was extradited to a prison in Switzerland.'

'Well, it's a thought,' Peggy said, getting to her feet and smoothing her skirt. 'It might be worth checking out.'

Chapter 15

Carmel is some one hundred and twenty miles south of San Francisco, and, like much of the Bay Area, owes a great deal for its existence to the City of St Francis. Many of the artists and writers who were left homeless by the 1906 earthquake migrated south, finding a home in the small seaside community.

It had become a tourist Mecca, the narrow sidewalks bordering its quaint shops and galleries jammed elbow to elbow with upscale visitors trying to appear casual while they cruise the area hoping to get a glimpse of Clint Eastwood, Carmel's most famous resident and former mayor.

Anona Stack's cottage was on Carmelo Street, just a short block from the beach, near the Carmel entrance to the famed Seventeen Mile Drive.

Jason Lark's first impression of the place had been that Snow White would open the door and the Seven Dwarfs would troop out, Hi Ho-ing their way to work. 'English Cotswold cottage' was the correct description, Anona had informed him. Two stories, cream and chocolate colored, with a steep, wave-laid, shingled gable roof, eyebrowed on each side of the chimney with small dormer windows.

The front garden was a mélange of free-growing fuchsia, yellow flowering marguerite and jasmine. The heavy scent of the Pacific Ocean hung in the air.

The carport was filigreed by an overreaching weeping

willow at the side of the house.

Jason Lark hadn't been to the cottage in years. It hadn't changed at all. Johnny told him that a front door key was kept under the doormat. Lark lifted up the dusty coco mat. It was there, all right. How trusting of Anona.

He took his time, searching through each room, then the small garage. There were some old clothes, garden tools, and golf clubs, but no sketches of any kind, let alone Picassos. Where the hell were they? They must still be somewhere in Stack House. There were so damn many sealed boxes in the basement, and additional boxes in the attic. The problem was the omnipresent butler.

He'd checked the game room, Conrad Stack's library, his old office and most of the bedrooms, including Lisa's.

He'd tried questioning Lisa, but it was obvious she wanted nothing to do with her father. Their conversations were brief, her responses to his attempts at starting a dialogue futile. She still hated him, he realized.

Johnny seemed almost indifferent. He knew nothing of the Bresson sketches. All he was concerned about now was his nightclub, the inheritance – and the chance to remove Duran as executor and eventually out of the will. Lark had encouraged him, suggesting himself as Duran's replacement. More importantly, he'd been able to pry the security code to Anona's studio from Johnny. He'd try the studio later tonight.

The telephone calls and the fax messages accusing Duran of murder had been a stroke of genius. His assistant Adam had balked at making the phone calls at first, but Lark had swiftly won him over with the promise of some high-grade cocaine. The faxes he had sent himself, sure that there was no way to trace the transmissions back to him. The small amount of cocaine base that he'd mixed with Anona's marijuana couldn't have been responsible for her death. Couldn't be, he assured himself. It was only when she was dozing off that he decided to give her a little booster with the coke. But an autopsy would show the traces – cocaine and marijuana. Duran had been supplying her with the grass – Anona had admitted that to him. Duran might never be arrested, but he'd be under suspicion and harassed by the police, which would interfere with his investigation of the Fritzheim heist and give Lark more time to find the Picassos.

Lunch with Duran's sexy black secretary had been well worth the tab. She hadn't been very bright, letting him into the office like that. The Picassos certainly weren't hanging on Duran's walls, but they could be there. In a drawer. A desk. He'd have to get in there tonight, and see what Duran was doing about the Fritzheim robbery. Mario Drago was pressuring him for information. Duran's office, then Anona's studio, though why would she take Bresson's pack of sketches to the studio?

His greatest fear was that the sketches were secreted in a safe deposit box, where he might never get to them.

Lark found a dusty bottle of Chivas Regal in a kitchen cabinet. He poured himself a stiff drink, then leaned against the sink.

The telephone message on Duran's office answering machine that he heard when taking Peggy back from lunch intrigued him. The music: '*I ain't got no body . . .*'. The caller had to be the weirdo who damaged Anona's painting at the wake, the one who took Anona's body. Whoever it is, he's making it easier for me, Lark mused. If Duran happened to turn up dead, the weirdo would be blamed.

The police have to suspect Duran of taking Anona's body. He's under pressure. Enormous pressure. A suicide? Kill Duran, make it look like a suicide? That would satisfy everyone. He swirled the whisky around, watching the amber liquid coat the glass. Except Duran of course.

He raised his glass in a silent toast to whoever it was that had made the phone call and stolen Anona's body.

'Poison oak, sir. That's what it is. You can get dressed now.'

He eased his arms into his shirt. 'Thanks doctor. It itches like hell.'

The physician handed him a small yellow piece of paper. 'This should take care of it. You can get the prescription filled at the pharmacy on the second floor. Where did you pick it up? Doing a little gardening?'

'Yes,' he confessed. 'I guess you could say that.'

Hugh Stringer bulled his way through the knot of television and newspaper reporters in front of Stack House, growling a nasty 'No comment' to their shouted questions.

'Mr Duran has already left, sir,' George informed him when he opened the front door.

'Did he go to his office?' Stringer asked, brushing past the butler as he entered the house.

'He did not tell me where he was going, or when he would return, sir.'

Stringer swiveled to face George, trying to read something in his stoical face. 'What about Miss Lisa? Is she in?'

'I believe she is.'

'Tell her I'd like to see her. And bring me some coffee, please.'

The butler went to a telephone sitting on a low table of hammered brass and buzzed Lisa's room.

'Mr Stringer is waiting to see you downstairs, Miss Lisa.'

He frowned, moved the phone away from his ear and held it out to Stringer.

'Lisa. I must talk to you.'

'But Uncle Hugh,' she yawned. 'I just woke up. Can't it wait until later. I—'

'It's very important, Lisa. I suggest you come down here right now.'

Lisa yawned again. 'No. You come up, Uncle Hugh. You know the way.'

She hung up before Stringer could reply. He settled the phone on the cradle and looked up at the butler. 'Better bring that coffee up to her room.' He started to stride to the hallway, coming to a stop with a hand on the bannister. 'By the way George, a letter has been prepared informing you of the contents of the will.'

'Yes, sir. Mr Duran has been good enough to acquaint me with the details.'

'And I suppose you are satisfied.'

'Quite, sir. It was more than I expected.'

Stringer looked at him sternly. 'Yes. The painting, *Evening Field*. It is worth a great deal of money, George. You're a wealthy man, now.'

'I know, sir. I'll get you your coffee.'

Stringer slowly started up the stairs, grinding his teeth. The painting was sure to fetch over a million dollars, perhaps quite a bit over a million, and Anona leaves it to the goddamn butler, along with the contents of the wine cellar. The cellar was stocked with cases and cases of the best French and American wines, and she leaves it to George. And nothing to me, nothing! Not even the executor's position.

He tapped loudly on the door to Lisa's room.

'Come on in, Uncle Hugh.'

Stringer remembered visiting Lisa in this very room when she was a child. It had been all pink and white, with Alice in Wonderland prints on the wall and animal mobiles hanging from the ceiling, the windows curtained with Disney character drapes.

The change was dramatic. The walls were now covered with life-sized posters of near-naked young men and women holding on to guitars or saxophones or each other.

The carpet was barely visible, hidden by piles of jumbled clothing, books, magazines, and CD albums.

The once pink and white canopied twin bed had been replaced by an Art Deco brass monster set on a pedestal a foot above the floor.

The bedspread was an ivory-colored fur. Lisa was sitting up, a jumble of pillows at her back. Her shoulders were exposed, the sheets barely covering her breasts. She drew deeply on a cigarette and blew the smoke in Stringer's direction. 'Have a seat, Uncle Hugh.'

Stringer looked around for a chair. Lisa patted the mattress. 'Don't worry. It's fake fur. It won't shed on that beautiful suit of yours.'

Stringer perched carefully on the edge of the bed. 'Lisa, perhaps you should get dressed. This is really very important.'

'Did they find Mommy?'

'No. Not yet.'

'Shit,' she said, then leaned over and ground her cigarette out in a crystal ashtray shaped like a reclining nude. The action caused the bed covers to slip to her waist and Stringer jerked his head away and stared at the posters.

There was a light knock on the door and George came in carrying a tray with a silver coffee-pot, two cups and the newspaper.

He set the tray on the bed, then asked, 'Will there be anything else, Miss Lisa?'

'Not for me. Uncle Hugh?'

'No,' Stringer said in a gravelly voice. 'No thank you.'

After George left and had closed the door behind him, Stringer said, 'Lisa! For God's sake. Put some clothing on.'

She cupped her breasts in her hands. 'God, you've seen me with less than this on. And so has old George. And besides, he's like the furniture. He never notices anything.'

Her dark eyes filled with mischief. 'At least he pretends he doesn't.'

Stringer rose stiffly to his feet. 'Put some clothes on, young woman.'

'I don't have to take orders anymore, Uncle Hugh.' She lay back in the bed, stretching her hands over her head. 'From you, or anyone else.' She smiled widely, grabbed the bed sheet and brought it up to her neck. 'Satisfied?'

'Yes. Thank you.'

Stringer poured himself a cup of coffee and carried it over to the window, parting the sheer, flesh-colored curtains, looking out to the street at the bevy of milling reporters.

'Lisa, you're quite well off, thanks to the trust fund your grandfather set up for you, but soon you will be a very rich young woman. I know that your brother has hired Victor Abbott. That's certainly his right to do so, although I thought it was unnecessary. I've always looked out for you, for him, and your mother. I'd like to continue that relationship with you, Lisa. You know how I feel about you. You've always been very special to me. Have you . . . signed anything with Mr Abbott?'

'No. Johnny asked me to, but I'm not sure just what I should do.'

Stringer saw his opening and turned to face her. 'I don't want to come between you and Johnny, Lisa, but you have to look out for yourself. You're an adult. As you said, you don't have to take orders from anyone now. You can make your own decisions. But the estate is quite complex. You'll need legal advice. Good solid advice from someone who has your interest in mind.'

'Like you, Uncle Hugh?'

'Yes, Lisa. Like me.'

'But you're Bobby's attorney.'

'Yes. Because he was your mother's husband.' He put the coffee cup back on the tray and looked into her cat-like eyes. 'Your mother always came first with me, you know that. Your mother, then you, Lisa. Not your brother, and not Robert Duran. You. You're more important to me than anyone else now.'

Lisa slid down into the sheets, so that she was lying almost flat, staring up at the ceiling. 'What about Jason?'

Jason Lark. Her father. Both of the children called him by his given name, not dad, or father. Lark was a stumbling block. 'I'm sorry it didn't work out between Jason and your mother. But you have to look out for yourself.'

Lisa rolled on to her side, grabbing a pillow, pulling it to her, hugging it as if it were a teddy bear. 'You think Johnny and Jason would try and fuck me out of my money?'

Stringer was stung by the wordage. 'Lisa, I'm not saying that, but when there are legal matters involving a great deal of money, millions of dollars, it behooves you to have someone to champion your cause, to take your side, and protect your interests.'

'Is that what you want to do? Champion my cause,' she asked, her voice muffled by the pillow.

'Yes. That's exactly what I'd like to do. I think it would be wise to make it a secure, legal agreement. I have the documents with me today. That way I can make sure that Victor Abbott doesn't try any funny business,' Stringer said, his voice soft and eminently reasonable.

'Did you and Mommy ever . . . you know, do it?'

'Lisa, I—'

'Johnny and I used to joke about you two.' She stretched and raised her hands over her head, causing the sheet to slide down. 'We used to say we'd have to call you Daddy Hugh instead of Uncle Hugh. Did you ever ask Mommy to marry you?'

Stringer fought to keep his eyes from straying to her breasts. 'No. No I did not, Lisa. I did love your mother very much. I have strong feelings for you, too. I want to protect you. To look out for you.'

Lisa threw her head back and yawned. 'Johnny should have talked to me before he hired that attorney.'

'Yes, he certainly should have.' He extracted three neatly folded papers from his suit coat. 'Take a look at these, Lisa,' Stringer proposed. 'I promise you, I'll do my absolute best on your behalf.'

Lisa scrambled up into a sitting position, the bed sheets dropping to her waist. She read each page slowly, then looked up at Stringer.

'What if Bob is . . . involved in what happened to Mommy?'

'If I found out that he had anything at all to do with that, I would stop representing him immediately, and press the police to arrest him, Lisa. Believe me, it's you that I'm most concerned with.'

Lisa held out her hand. 'Pen?'

Stringer quickly handed her his gold Cross ballpoint and smiled inwardly as she scrawled her signature across the bottom of the document.

'You'll never regret this, my dear,' he declared, retrieving the papers and pen. 'Never.'

'Just don't let Johnny fuck me out of anything, Uncle Hugh.'

'You can be sure of that, Lisa.'

He watched her nod, then bury her head in the pillow.

Chapter 16

Jerry Fehring knew that the open field was forty-seven acres in total. Enough room for forty-seven football fields, minus the end zones, or a small tract of homes, or a nine-hole golf course. Room for all of those, but what was going in was another shopping center. Some people called it progress, but he could remember when there were fields like this all over the county. Fields filled with the garden snakes, rabbits, frog ponds, all the wonders of nature that grubby-fingered kids loved to explore.

The land was reasonably flat and covered with a myriad of weeds: quackgrass, soap plant, knotweed, coriander, bull mallow and poison oak.

He bent over his engineer's transit, adjusted the leveling head and began sighting the cross-hairs on the telescope. Freddy, his young assistant, was some seventy-five yards away, holding an eight-foot wooden pole topped by a red flag.

'Back a little,' Fehring yelled, waving his hand forward.

Freddy dutifully followed orders then suddenly disappeared from view.

Fehring pulled his eye from the telescope. 'What happened?'

The boy gradually got up to his knees, brushing off his Levis, inspecting the ground. 'You better come over here, Jerry. This looks weird.'

Fehring cursed softly. The kid was young, eager, but clumsy as a puppy.

'What the hell is it?' he called out, as he carefully threaded his way through the weeds, avoiding the poison oak.

Freddy was still on his knees, rubbing at something with a red rag.

He grinned up at Fehring, showing a row of jagged yellow teeth. 'A piece of cement, with some numbers on it.'

Fehring craned his neck and examined the flat, rectangular-shaped slab of concrete. It was the size of one of those fancy cook books his wife liked to show off on the coffee-table.

Freddy continued to rub the stone with his rag. 'See the numbers? They're real faded.'

'Yeah.' Fehring traced his fingers across the stone, like a blind person reading braille. The indentations were worn down to almost nothing but he could make out one letter and a row of numbers: A26790. He got to his feet and wiped his arm across his forehead.

'What's it for?' Freddy asked.

'I'm not sure. Some kind of a marker. Let's see if there are any more.'

He sent Freddy back to the truck for shovels and the two of them worked for the next twenty-five minutes, clearing brush and weeds and finding two rows of the stones, a total of fourteen – eight in one line, six in another, all laid out neatly – each exactly eight feet from the others. All with a series of one letter – always A – followed by five numbers.

Fehring scanned the field. To the north was a shopping mall. To the south, another mall. West was the highway. To the south, the beginning of the Olivet Cemetery. His stomach gurgled, like bath water going down the drain.

'Freddy. Look around. See if you can find any more of these markers. I better call Mr Sconio.'

★ ★ ★

Robert Duran had been surprised to find out just what having money could do. Especially a great deal of money. Not just the obvious: better clothes, cars, homes, the best doctors, the best lawyers, the best of whatever vice was the one of your choosing. It was the little things. For some reason people wanted to do favors for you. Walk into a bar and some chap who was struggling to put his kids through school and to pay off his mortgage would buy you a drink and bat your hand away when you reached for the lunch check.

Being rich, really rich, somehow put you on a par with being a movie star, rock singer or TV anchor person.

The Centennial Insurance Agency's receptionist, an attractive brunette who looked like a cheerleader fifteen years after leaving college, gave Duran a quick look at first – liking what she saw, she took her time, her shopper's eyes raking him professionally. Rugged-looking, beautifully tailored suit, immaculate shirt, power-tie, and the watch. The watch was what put him over the final hurdle. Thick. Gold. Twenty thousand plus. She flashed her best smile. 'May I help you, sir?'

'I'd like to speak to Peter Fowler.'

The receptionist didn't hesitate a second, even though Fowler was a notorious grouch who had a standing order that he did not want to be bothered with any unscheduled appointments. She fastened her eyes on Duran's watch as she punched in Fowler's extension. 'Your name, sir?'

'Bob Duran.'

'A Mr Bob Duran would like to see you, Mr Fowler.' She tilted her head and cradled the receiver between her shoulder and neck. 'That's right. Bob Duran.'

After a moment she lowered a finger, breaking the connection. 'He'll be right out. Would you care for a cup of coffee?'

The coffee and Peter Fowler arrived at the same time.

'Bob Duran. It's been a long, long time,' Peter Fowler said in a raspy, smoker's voice. 'I never thought I'd see you back here.'

They shook hands in that uncomfortable way old acquaintances, or at least co-workers, do. People who worked together on a daily basis, got to know each other's habits, good and bad, and then drifted apart and became strangers again.

Fowler was a tall, gangling man, his body curved in an academic stoop. Bald, but for some gray strands combed sideways across his scalp. He wore a floppy polka-dot bow tie and baggy pants held up by bright red suspenders.

'Good to see you, Peter. Can we talk in your office?'

'Sure. You must remember the way.'

Duran followed Fowler down a familiar narrow hallway, the filled-to-the-brim coffee cup in one hand. Nothing seemed to have changed. The same honeycomb of offices, all with six-foot partitions – the top half of frosted glass. The hollow doors had slide-in signs with people's names on them. Names Duran did not recognize.

Fowler's office was different than its clones only because of the view. If you leaned just the right way, you could see the Ferry Building clock tower, sandwiched between the city's ever changing skyway.

'Sit down, Bob,' Fowler suggested, whisking out a vinyl-contoured chair. 'Awfully sorry to hear about your wife. That was really tragic. It makes you wonder what kind of a world we are living in.' He collapsed into the chair behind his desk, the chair sighing luxuriously as he did so.

'The episode at the museum,' Fowler said. 'I read about it in the papers. Did they ever find out who was responsible?'

'No, not yet. Whoever did it used one of those paint guns. The kind frustrated soldiers of fortune use when they play those adult hide-and-seek games.'

Fowler's face darkened. 'Have the authorities been able to locate your wife's body?'

'No,' Duran replied coldly. 'I think there's a possibility that someone who I came across in my investigations here at CIA could be responsible. I'd like to run through the old files.'

Fowler pulled a bent-stemmed briar pipe from his jacket pocket and tapped the stem against his freckled teeth. He grimaced slightly. There had been hard feelings when Duran left to start his own firm. He hadn't taken any of CIA's clients with him at the time, but eventually many of them had matriculated his way. 'Can't smoke in here anymore,' imparted Fowler. 'Damned environmentalists.' He gnawed briefly on the pipe stem. 'I don't know, Bob. After all, you're no longer with the company and those old files are in storage.'

'You must keep all the reports on the computer. Even way back then we were using computers.'

'Yes, but—'

'Hell, Pete. If you don't cooperate, I'll just have to buy the company and replace you,' Duran said in a light, joking tone.

Fowler sucked on his pipe for a moment. 'I guess it wouldn't hurt,' he conceded.

Fowler led Duran to one of the cubicles and showed him how to access the computer. Duran explored the index until he found the correct name: Breamer, Royce.

Royce Breamer. A small foppish man in his sixties, barely five feet tall, with an upscale art gallery in Beverly Hills. On Rodeo Drive. He had been doing quite well, selling well-done forgeries to the rich and famous: Stallone, Nicholson, Michael Douglas. He was part of the 'in crowd.' Cashmere and cocaine. Power seats at the Laker's game. All was going well until he was tripped up by a forgery of one of Anona Stack's abstracts, *Blue Leaves*.

The Centennial Insurance Agency had been asked by one of Breamer's Los Angeles buyers to insure *Blue Leaves* for eight hundred thousand dollars. CIA was delighted to sell the policy, except that they had already insured that very same painting for a woman in Tampa, Florida.

Duran had been sent to Los Angeles, where he picked up *Blue Leaves*, then flew it to Tampa. He found the two paintings to be near identical twins. It was only when they were placed side by side that the subtle differences could be detected.

Anona Stack had agreed to fly to Tampa to personally check them out. That was the first time Duran met her. The attraction was immediate. And mutual. She was a lovely woman in her mid-thirties, tall, willowy, her hair a spun-gold color. He still remembered what she was wearing that day: a cool-looking white dress, crocodile-skin shoes and, dangling from her arm, a Hermés canvas and red-calf leather purse that retailed for almost four thousand dollars.

Duran had no clue as to the price of a Hermés back then. Nor did he know that the wafer-thin watch on her wrist was a Patek-Phillipe and cost more than his yearly salary. He was strictly a Timex man in those days.

The owner of the original Anona Stack painting in Tampa was a handsome gray-haired woman who was obviously delighted to have the famous artist as a guest.

The paintings were displayed in her private gallery, a large airy room with a barrel-vaulted ceiling studded with recessed lighting that pinpointed her collection.

Anona Stack's original hung on the wall, between a David Stuart Cubist piece and a John Singer Sergeant watercolour landscape.

The painting that Duran had picked up in Los Angeles was propped up against the wall, directly under the original.

Anona Stack had stood transfixed, hands on hips for a good five minutes, studying both works before she spoke. 'The miserable son of a bitch,' she finally said. 'I'd like to kill him.'

She ran the tips of her fingers slowly across both canvases, moving to her signature, which, in defiance to tradition, was on the top right-hand corner of her paintings.

'He's even got my signature down pat.' She swiveled to face Duran. 'Find out who did this. I hate the thought of someone doing this to me.'

Duran had been booked on a flight back to Los Angeles early the following morning. The Centennial Insurance Agency required all of their employees to fly coach, and the red-eye whenever possible.

Anona Stack insisted that Duran travel with her, first class to San Francisco, where he could catch a commuter flight to Los Angeles.

They spent the flight sipping champagne, talking art and getting to know each other. Although the financial gap between them was of Grand Canyon size, they found that they had a lot in common: they liked the same artists, the same food, and their politics clashed just enough to make it interesting. She was a wonderful raconteur, and had Duran in stitches with stories about the rich and famous. She in turn seemed fascinated when he told her of his background, and his first wife's untimely death.

After they landed at the San Francisco Airport, Duran accompanied Anona to her waiting limousine.

'Go down to Lotus Land and bury this creature, Bob,' Anona Stack said, her voice slightly slurred from the on-board champagne. 'Do that for me, please.' She dug a card out of her expensive little purse. 'Call me when you get back. I want to see you again. No matter what happens.'

What happened was that Duran, cooperating with the

Los Angeles Police Department's Fraud Squad, found that Royce Breamer's real name was Joseph Phelps, that he was a con man wanted in Switzerland and Italy for similar ventures.

Breamer had a long record, all the charges relating to forged art: paintings, ancient manuscripts and rare coins. But there was never any violence involved. He was sentenced to prison, then shipped off to Switzerland, where the charges were more extensive than those in Los Angeles.

Duran remembered Breamer's gallery. A beautiful layout. There had been some really fine paintings on display. He no doubt could have made a good living operating it on a legitimate basis. But once a con man, always a con man.

Duran's work on the Stack case was finished, and he was chasing down a Paul Cézanne painting which had been lifted in broad daylight from the walls of a Boston gallery at the time of the Breamer trial. Anona went down to Los Angeles to testify.

Breamer's employees, the ones who had done the actual forgeries, a husband and wife team, Otto and Arlene Kline, were also arrested.

He closed his eyes, conjuring up a fuzzy image of the Klines – she was short, very attractive, with long dark hair. The husband was tall – his hair almost as long as his wife's. Neither had any type of prior criminal record and when convicted were given minimal sentences.

Duran couldn't imagine Breamer being involved in his current problems, but he printed the entire file anyway.

He followed Duran up in the elevator, standing no more than a few feet away. If he reached out he could touch him. Duran seemed preoccupied, his head dropping toward his chest, eyes cast downward, as if in mourning. Of course, he reminded himself, Duran *was* in mourning.

He watched as Duran walked stiff-legged into the offices of the Centennial Insurance Agency, wondering what he was up to. Picking up a new case? The man was greedy. He was about to inherit a fortune, yet he was out scrounging for work. And all for naught, since he'd never get a chance to spend it.

He waited in the lobby for almost two hours. Then he spotted Duran exiting the elevator. There seemed to be a change in his step as he made his way out to Montgomery Street.

Why the change? The Centennial Insurance Agency. The name was somehow familiar. He hurried out to the street, keeping Duran in sight as he maneuvered through the pedestrian clogged sidewalk. Centennial Insurance. It came to him suddenly. Duran was working for Centennial at the time of the trial.

Joe Sconio eyed the row of concrete tablets with disgust. He was sixty-three years of age, a tall heavy-shouldered man, his stomach bay-windowed from a lifetime of abundant food and wine. He gazed around the open field. His father-in-law had purchased the land from the state in 1938, and had used it to farm lettuce, chard, and sprouts. The old man had been injured in a truck accident over forty years ago. The farm had gone to pot, but the old man wouldn't sell. He had dreams of one day rising from his wheelchair and going back to work on the land.

For years Sconio had tried talking him into selling the property, but with no luck. When the old man died, ownership transferred to his daughter, Sconio's wife. Maria had wanted to sell the land immediately, but Joe Sconio had other ideas now. He had worked as a small contractor for most of his life, now this was his chance at the big time. These forty-seven acres were the last stretch of undeveloped commercially zoned land for miles in any direction.

He scraped his heel across one of the stones. He remembered the old man telling him that the field had once been a potter's graveyard. That prisoners from Alcatraz were buried there. He never paid much attention to the stories. He thought that the old man was making them up. He grimaced and rubbed the palms of his hands across his aching back. If he reported the damn things his project might be held up indefinitely. The state, the coroner, then some do-gooders would probably want to turn the place into a fucking shrine. He couldn't let that happen.

He looked up at Jerry Fehring. Had Fehring guessed? Was he smart enough to keep his mouth shut? Fehring had four kids and needed this job. 'How many stones?'

'Fourteen, Boss. That's all we found.'

Joe Sconio folded his arms across his chest and stared at Fehring. 'Pick 'em up and take 'em to the dump. I don't want anyone else seeing them, Jer. You know what I mean?'

'Yeah, Boss, sure.' He half-turned toward the road. 'What about Freddy?'

Freddy. The young kid. He could be a problem. 'Go over and tell him I want to see him.'

'Yes, sir, Mr Sconio,' Freddy said, out of breath after his run from the company truck to where Joe Sconio was standing.

Sconio pointed a finger at the ground. 'These are old gas line markers. I want them out of here. Taken to the dump. Give Jerry a hand, okay?'

'Yes, sir,' the boy said eagerly.

Sconio put his arm around Freddy's shoulders and shepherded him back toward the company truck. 'I'm going to want this land cleared quickly, son. Starting next week we scrape and level, working day and night. You ever drive a tractor? Cause there's going to be some big overtime and—' He stopped abruptly and pointed toward a thatch of dry waist-high weeds. 'What's that? Is that one of ours?'

Freddy kicked his way into the weeds, dragging out a battered wheelbarrow. 'It's not ours, Boss. Somebody must have thrown it away.' He picked the wheelbarrow up by the handles and bounced the wheel on the ground.

'Well, it's ours now,' Sconio claimed. 'You can use it to load those markers.'

Chapter 17

The printer began sputtering. Chief Saylor waited until it came to a stop then tore off a page along the perforated line.

He carried the single page back to his desk. The rap sheet showed just two entries for Robert J. Duran.

The two arrests carried an 'M' number, the M standing for manual – the offenses having taken place long before the criminal justice system had gone to computers – thus the records had to be searched by hand.

Duran had been twenty years of age at the time of the arrests, which had taken place during a six month period of time. Both were misdemeanours – in San Diego County – for the same charge: battery. Duran had pulled a two month sentence on the second arrest.

The last line of the printout stated: 'Subject has JV record.'

Juvenile charges. Saylor would have to secure a court order to find out what those were.

He leaned back and pulled at a finger joint until it popped. Two battery charges. Jail time. Nothing too serious, but they were crimes of violence.

He dug out the notes from his interrogation of Duran, thumbing through them until he found the notation regarding his first wife's death in New York: 'My first wife, Teresa, died years ago in New York City. An aneurism.'

He picked up the phone and dialed 0 for operator, then asked, 'What's the area code for New York City?'

Peggy Jacquard pulled a pencil from her hair and waved her hand in front of her eyes in exasperation when Duran walked into the office.

'You're lucky you went out. The press got tired of me hanging up on them, so they came over here.'

'And?'

Peggy described the language she used in advising the ladies and gentleman of the press that they were unwelcome.

'Did you find out anything at good old CIA?' she asked.

'Peter Fowler's still in charge. I was able to get a hard copy of the Los Angeles case.' He handed her the file. 'Run a criminal history on Breamer and his two employees. I've highlighted their names.'

'I gave Rachel the information on those people you wanted checked out, those old guys in New York and the ones from Houston, Santa Fe and New Orleans. I'll add these to the list.'

Rachel was a tough-as-nails bail bonds woman in Oakland who was Duran's source for confidential criminal records. A statuesque brunette with a tattoo of a snake coiled around her wrist, Rachel got the rap sheets from her boyfriend, an Oakland Homicide detective. Peggy and Rachel sometimes went out on double-dates. They made an intimidating duo.

'Yes, tell Rachel it's a rush. I'd like the information back as soon as possible. Like today.'

He held up a hand when he saw Peggy was about to protest. 'Tell her we'll pay double the normal rate.'

'You had a couple of other calls.' Peggy scanned her notepad. 'Laura Ralston called twice, and Harry Lawson. He sounds like he's ready to do some dealing.'

Duran called Ralston first. He reflected back on Anona's

wake, Lisa asking him if he was 'fucking' Laura. Lisa's personality had changed since Anona became ill. She had always been a little wild, but once she realized just how sick her mother was, she slipped into a rougher, almost raunchy persona. He often wondered if it was because Anona was certain to die, and Lisa was getting her first real look at death – the death of a loved one. Lisa's grandfather had died years ago, but Lisa was a kid then. She was an adult now. He hoped she'd start acting more like one.

He caught Laura Ralston at her real estate office.

'Bob, thanks for calling. How are things?'

'The police suspect me of stealing Anona's body, Johnny thinks I killed his mother, someone's sending faxes stating that I killed Anona, some bastard pushed me over a cliff yesterday and the TV and newspaper people are trying to corner me. Outside of that, everything is dandy.'

'You sound like a man who could use a drink.'

'You're psychic.'

'How about dinner? I want to talk to you about listing Stack House, the Carmel cottage and your plans for Anona's studio.'

Duran pinched his lower lip between his thumb and forefinger. Dinner. He certainly didn't feel like driving back to Stack House and facing the reporters that were bound to be there. 'All right. I'll pick you up at your office around six.'

'It's a date,' Ralston agreed readily.

Harry Lawson's voice was court-room somber. He spoke for almost five minutes about how sorry he was about Anona. 'But life must go on,' Lawson revealed, as if it was an unknown secret.

'Yes. It certainly does, Harry. You've heard from your potential clients?'

'Yes. They have the merchandise we spoke of. They are willing to return it to the proper owners – after you've had it examined, of course.'

'How much are they asking for, Harry?'

'The usual. Ten per cent of the insured value.'

Duran sighed. The usual. Two point eight million. He didn't want to take the time away from hunting for Anona. 'What time frame do they have in mind?'

'Tomorrow. If not by then, the offer is rescinded and they will find another way to dispose of the merchandise.'

'Where?'

'Here. In Los Angeles somewhere. I'll leave the location up to you, Robert. I would suggest the late afternoon. Four o'clock.'

Duran glanced at his watch. It was almost four o'clock now. That only gave him twenty-four hours. 'I'll have to call the insurance carrier, Harry. I could use a little more time.'

'It's not my decision.'

'I'll have to make arrangements for the money transfer.'

'Do that, Robert. I have advised my clients that you are an honorable man. The usual stipulations?'

Stipulations. A guarantee that once Duran knew where the painting was, he wouldn't call in the cops.

'The usual,' Duran conceded. He had little choice. If he ever did call the police, there'd never be another transaction. Thieves who stole major works of art knew exactly who they were dealing with. Duran's reputation was his credentials. If he slipped up once, word would get around and he'd never be trusted again.

They made their goodbyes and Duran reached for the envelope holding the photograph and appraisal of the painting stolen from Alan Fritzheim's house. Los Angeles. He didn't want to go to Los Angeles. He wanted to stay in San Francisco to find Anona.

But he couldn't think of anyone he could send in his place.

'When did Rachel say she'd have those criminal histories?' he called out to Peggy.

Peggy leaned against the doorframe with her ankles crossed. 'I told her we were in a hurry. She said she'd do her best, but it wouldn't be before midnight.' She gave Duran a wink. 'Her boyfriend doesn't get off until eleven-thirty.'

'Okay. It looks like I'm going to have to fly to LA on the Fritzheim heist. If there is anything interesting on Breamer, I can check it out while I'm down there.'

Duran spent thirty-five minutes on the phone with Dean Talbot, the Chief Executive Officer of Pacific Indemnity.

Talbot wasn't happy about the deal, but he was a smart, realistic individual, and after a solid two minutes of cursing Harry Lawson and his parentage, agreed that there was nothing they could do but accept the terms of the deal.

Duran next called Wendy Lange, an art examiner in Los Angeles. The Van Gogh would have to be authenticated before reaching any kind of agreement with Lawson's clients. There were at least a dozen experts in the Los Angeles area that he had used in the past, but he didn't like using the same expert too often, in fear that the thieves would get to know his selection pattern. Lange's reputation was as good as anyone's in the field. It had been at least two years since he'd done business with her.

'Wendy, it's Bob Duran. I've got an item I'd like you to look at tomorrow. Are you available?'

'Hang on while I check my appointments. What's the item?'

'*Sun and Sky*. The Fritzheim Van Gogh.'

Wendy Lange's voice rose appreciably. 'I'm definitely available for that, Bob. When and where?'

'Tomorrow afternoon, around four. Harry Lawson is handling the action for the bad guys. I'd like to have the painting taken to your studio. Is that all right with you?'

Lange chuckled lightly. 'Dear old Harry. The "Holy Redeemer" strikes again. Okay, my place at four.'

Duran was faxing the appraisal to Wendy Lange when Peggy came into the office, her purse slung over her shoulder. 'I'm taking off.' She laid a thin sheaf of papers on his desk. 'These are the Nexis database checks on Fritzheim's Van Gogh and the credit checks on Jason Lark.'

Duran nodded his thanks. 'Peggy, there's something I meant to tell you. Lisa asked me if you and I were having an affair.'

Peggy's nostrils flared. 'Are you kidding me?'

'No. Her question was a little more blunt than that. She asked about you, and Laura Ralston. Johnny's attorney, Victor Abbott, made the charge that I had committed adultery. Lisa might be Abbott's source, so don't be surprised if he contacts you and asks some questions.'

'Well I hope he comes around. I'll let him know the real score. That girl needs a good talking to.' She crossed over to Duran and gave him a peck on the cheek. 'Maybe Lisa saw me doing that once, or hugging you at the wake.'

'Maybe,' Duran confirmed.

Peggy's smooth forehead knitted in concern. She was worried about Duran. He had gone through so much. It sickened her to think that anyone, especially Anona's children, would doubt his love for his wife, much less think that he had murdered her. 'Are you going to be all right, Bob?'

'Sure. Come on, I'll walk you to your car.'

He scooped the last piece of shrimp from the cup of a hollowed-out French roll. Shrimp, crab, fresh fish, all sold from huge outdoor cooking pots that lined the street. They were all a treat. Nothing like that had ever been on the menu at Pelican Bay. It was when he crumpled the remains of the roll and dropped it into an overflowing garbage can that he spotted Jason Lark.

Lark was standing on the sidewalk across the street between a string of street merchants selling jewlery and T-shirts.

It appeared that Lark and he were monitoring the same location. The pier leading to Duran's office. Who was Lark waiting for? Duran's pretty black secretary? He had seen them together just yesterday.

He crossed the street and melted into a knot of tourists, edging into the entrance of a coffee shop.

Lark looked impatient, bouncing from one foot to the other as if he had to go to the bathroom. Suddenly he froze.

Duran and the black woman were on the street, heading for the parking lot.

Both he and Lark watched as the woman hugged Duran then got into her car and drove away. Duran had a brief discussion with the parking attendant before climbing into his Jaguar.

What to do? Follow Duran? Or stick with Lark? What was Lark waiting for? Was the woman coming back? Maybe she didn't want Duran to know about her and Lark.

Lark suddenly darted across the street, moving swiftly through the crowd, almost vaulting on to the pier leading to Duran's office.

He was curious, but Lark was not his concern. Duran was.

Chapter 18

Duran wanted to go somewhere where he was unlikely to run into anyone he knew or might recognize him and pass the location on to a reporter.

Laura's suggestion turned out to be a good one, a restaurant he'd never even heard of, Ristorante Bacco on Diamond Street in the inner-city of Noe Valley District.

They both tried to keep the conversation as light and casual as possible during dinner but, with all that was going on, it just wasn't possible.

She was wearing a navy and white double-breasted pindot coat-dress. Her hair done up in a French twist. She looked very professional and businesslike, Duran thought. And beautiful.

They slowly worked their way through garlicky versions of marinated calamari, polenta and grilled veal.

As good as everything was, Duran couldn't relax. After the waiter had opened the second bottle of chianti, Laura leaned across the table and said, 'You must be going through hell.'

'It hasn't been easy, Laura. I'm still spinning from the meeting in Hugh Stringer's office. I could tell from the look on Johnny's face that he believes I killed Anona.'

'He's upset, Bob. Everything happening like this. I'm sure he doesn't really think you . . . killed Anona.'

'He does,' Duran contradicted. 'And Lisa, she certainly didn't jump to my defense. She just sat there taking it all in.'

'I can talk to her, if you'd like,' Laura volunteered.

'Thanks, but I don't think it would do much good. The accusations that Johnny's attorneys made – the adultery claim. At the wake, Lisa came up to me and asked me if you and I were having an affair.'

Laura held up her wine glass, her eyes drifting to the persimmon colored walls. 'What ever gave her that idea?'

'I don't know. It certainly didn't come from me.'

'Or from me,' Laura insisted.

'She asked if I was . . . having an affair with Peggy, too.'

'I am going to have to talk to Lisa,' Ralston promised. She sipped some wine, then said, 'Hugh Stringer has asked me to get some appraisals on Stack House.'

Duran was grateful for the change of subject. 'Good news?'

'Not as good as I had hoped,' Laura said, bending over and picking up a slim leather briefcase. 'There are some problems which will affect the sale price. The foundation has some structural damage that will need repairing, and there are potential problems due to the age of the plumbing and electrical systems.'

Duran's mind drifted while Laura described what needed to be done to bring Stack House up to code for a new buyer. What would George do now? He realized he needn't worry about the butler, not with the substantial inheritance Anona had provided for him – but the cook, the gardener, the stream of temporary help . . .

'The bottom line is that our best bet is if we can get a zoning clearance and sell the house to a school or a foreign consulate. There isn't much of a market for houses of this size anymore, Bob. On the other hand,' she continued, 'the cottage in Carmel should sell quickly,' she assured him. 'Then there's Anona's studio – I know it seems silly to bring up such small details at a time like this, but you are the executor. The yearly lease is up next month, and I don't think you'll want to renew it. Hugh mentioned that Anona had some things at the studio. An unfinished painting and some sketches. They could be quite valuable.'

'You're right. I'll stop by and pick them up soon. They're safe at the studio for now.'

Laura paused while the waiter topped off their wine glasses, then said, 'Did you know Johnny considered using the studio for his nightclub?'

'That's news to me.'

'Johnny called me several months ago, and wanted the particulars. Apparently, after looking it over, he decided it was too small for what he had in mind.'

'Did you go with Johnny to the studio?'

'No. I haven't been there in years. And I don't have the key or the security combination. I assume John got them from Anona.'

Duran dipped back into the wine. Laura had made her point. As executor he was supposed to protect the estate assets. Johnny seemed obsessed about money at the reading of the will, Anona's unfinished painting and sketches should be moved out of the studio right away.

'Laura, do you remember Anona going to Los Angeles several years ago to testify at a criminal trial?'

'Do I remember? I was with her, Bob. That was just after she met you, wasn't it? I remember her talking about a handsome investigator who had caught the forgers. She definitely had already made up her mind about you.'

'How did you happen to go to Los Angeles with her?'

'Oh, you know how Anona was. She liked to have friends around her all the time. She kept talking about you, but you were back east somewhere, so I was chosen. We stayed at the Beverly Hills Hotel.'

'What do you remember about the trial?'

'Nothing. I stayed around the hotel and the pool. Jason drove Anona to the court house every day.'

'Lark?'

'Oh, yes,' she confirmed. 'He couldn't do enough for Anona. It was obvious for some months that Jason was trying to get back in with her, but he didn't have a chance.' She smiled at him. 'Anona had fallen for you. Do you think that the trial could have anything to do with what happened to Anona?'

'I don't know,' Duran conceded. 'I'm not ruling anything out. Someone's trying to frame me for taking Anona's body. Whoever he is, he's doing a damn good job. I keep worrying, worrying about what he'll do next.'

The restaurant had no bar and claimed they had no table available for a single diner, so he watched Duran and the woman from the street. An overhanging cottonwood tree obscured most of the window, but what he could see of them was interesting. The woman had been at the wake; he remembered she'd been wearing a tight gray dress. She was attractive: high forehead, straight nose, wide lips, honey-colored hair. Duran had picked her up at a real estate office on Chestnut Street. Ralston Realty. The front window displayed a flattering picture of Laura Ralston mixed in amongst the photographs of available houses and apartment buildings.

He noticed that her eyes almost never left Duran, and she was always touching him. Her hands brushing his side, holding his hand when he had opened the car door. She looked like she wanted to throw him to the ground and mount him at any moment.

It was October eleventh. Just three more days until the anniversary of Arlene's death. Could he use Ralston to lure Duran into the SHU? It was worth thinking about.

Jason Lark fiddled with the key-ring. He'd had duplicates made of all the keys that he'd found in Duran's bedroom. The fourth key turned the lock on the door of Lost Art, Inc.

Lark had noticed when he'd been to Duran's office with Peggy Jacquard that there was no burglar alarm. She had simply opened the door and waltzed in. But Lark wanted to be sure, so he opened the door a crack, then backed off, walking briskly back to Taylor Street, checking his watch every few minutes, waiting for the police or an alarm company to respond.

None did. He made his way back to the office, and once the door clicked shut behind him donned a pair of white cotton gloves. Gloves he'd saved from Anona's funeral. Three rooms, one crammed with file cabinets and shelves bowed under the weight of books and document-sized boxes.

He approached Duran's desk cautiously, walking on the balls of his feet. The Fritzheim file was right there, sitting squarely on the green felt blotter. He eased himself into Duran's chair and paged through the papers and photograph, cursing when he saw that the thieves had made contact. A notation – Harry Lawson will bring *Sun and Sky* to meeting tomorrow. Tomorrow! Jesus Christ. Who the hell was Harry Lawson? Duran planned to go to Los Angeles tomorrow and examine the Van Gogh.

He next read the copy of the fax message to an appraiser named Wendy Lange. He'd never heard of her, but she no doubt was an expert. Tomorrow! He'd have to alert Mario Drago right away.

A small stack of papers sat alongside the Fritzheim folder. A scrawled note lay on top: *Bob – Nexis search on Fritzheim's house and the credit reports on Jason Lark. Peg.*

Lark mumbled a series of curses as he skimmed through the papers – computer printouts of stories from newspapers and magazines. Shit! He knew it would be there. And it was. The article from the spring issue of *Architectural Review*. The architect, Richard Weufer, a puffed-up, egotistical, New York prima donna got most of the ink, but his name was there: 'Weufer used the talents of local interior designer Jason Lark to assist in completing the project.'

Duran would jump on that. He slipped the page out, rolled it into a ball and jammed it in his pocket.

The second document consisted of six pages stapled together at the corner, his name highlighted in yellow – credit reports. His eyes glided across the distressing array of figures – his bankruptcy. The state and federal liens. The collection accounts. There were detailed listings of his company loans, the balances outstanding. He slammed his fist against the desk, causing the papers to flutter to the carpet. Duran knew everything but the amount of cash in his wallet.

He went through Duran's office with a vengeance, but the Picasso sketches weren't there.

Which left Anona's studio, or those boxes in the basement of Stack House.

Laura Ralston had tried coaxing Duran into her condo for a nightcap, but he begged off.

'Next time, Laura. I'm just too tired tonight.'

She leaned across the seat and gave him a kiss full on the lips. 'Let's not wait too long for next time,' she urged, then slipped out of the car.

Duran put the Jag in gear, not sure of just where he was going. Laura was intelligent, beautiful and had been a lifelong friend of Anona's. He admired her, but the last thing he needed now was a romantic attachment. What he wanted was to find his wife's body. And the man who had taken it.

He found himself back at Stack House, grateful that there was no sign of the TV or newspaper people.

He nestled the Jaguar in its stall and entered the house through the kitchen. He checked his watch. A little after nine. The criminal histories Rachel had promised wouldn't be in until after midnight. He decided to shower and change clothes before going back to his office.

The butler called out to him as he was starting up the stairs.

'Ah, Mr Robert, I didn't know you'd arrived.' His eyes regarded Duran gravely. 'The press representatives have been outrageous. I've called the police to complain. They continue telephoning, ringing the bell. It's really appalling.'

'Are either Lisa or Johnny home?'

'I believe Miss Lisa is in the pool, with a friend. Master John is not here.'

'How about Jason Lark?'

'I've not seen him all day.'

Duran took the steps rather than the elevator to the indoor pool, which was situated in the lower level of the house. The smell of chlorine intensifying as he descended.

Someone yelled an undistinguishable chant, followed by giggling, then a splashing sound.

Duran had been consumed by Anona's illness, trying to make her last months as normal and happy as possible. He hadn't paid much attention to the house. Now he noticed the tell-tale signs. Spider-web cracks in the ceilings. The brightly polished hardwood floors were showing their age. A musty, decaying smell permeated the walls. It was as if the building knew it was dying, and wasn't strong enough to put up a fight. Much like Anona had been at the end.

The pool area had been fashioned after the famous Randolph Hearst's indoor swimming pool at San Simeon, with azure and gold mosaic tiles arranged in a variety of intricate patterns on the walls and ceiling. Old man Stack had been wealthy, but he was not in Hearst's league, so the pool was much smaller than the massive eighty by forty foot pool in Hearst's Castle. Duran remembered reading somewhere that Hearst had used tiles faced with real gold. Stack had settled for gold-colored tiles. Anona's acerbic wit had chronicled the room as 'Faux Turkish whorehouse.'

Lisa Stack stood, beautifully posed, balancing herself on the end of the diving board. She was wearing a bikini that was nothing more than a trio of dayglo orange triangles tied at the neck, back and hips. She curled her toes over the edge of the board, stretched her arms above her head and jack-knifed into the pool.

She broke the water with hardly a ripple, surfacing with a shake of her head, spraying water in all directions.

'Hi, Bob,' she called out when she spotted Duran. 'You remember Eric Marvin. He was at Mommy's wake. He works for Johnny at the club.'

Duran hadn't noticed the man at first. He looked to be older than Lisa – late-twenties, cadaver thin, his long, stringy hair plastered to his scalp.

Eric waded out of the shallow end of the pool, picked up a towel and buried his face in it.

Duran shouted a hello, and his face appeared briefly.

Eric nodded, looped the towel around his shoulders, said, 'Hi,' then turned his attention to Lisa. 'I'm going up to change.' He gave Duran a squinting look, then disappeared up the stairs.

'Any news on Mommy?' Lisa asked, pushing her wet hair away from her face.

'No. Nothing yet.' Duran bent down, his knees making popping sounds. 'Lisa. We have to talk. You must know there's no truth to any of the allegations Johnny's been making.'

'Isn't there?' She swung around and effortlessly glided through the water to the shallow end of the pool. She climbed out slowly, turning to face Duran, shifting her weight from one hip to the other.

'Can you get me my towel?'

Duran scooped up a thick white beach towel and tossed it to her, instantly aware of her body, the bikini top seemingly glued on to her skin, the bottom back-string buried in her buttocks.

He tilted his head toward the ceiling, seeing raw plaster patches where tiles had fallen away. 'Lisa, I never gave cocaine to your mother. How did Victor Abbott come up with a crazy idea like that?'

'I don't know. I didn't tell him. About the cocaine, anyway.'

'The adultery charges are false, too. What gave you the idea that I could be seeing Laura or Peggy? Or anyone else, for that matter?'

Lisa's voice was soft, mocking. 'I didn't say you were seeing them. You can look now, Bob.'

She had tied the towel sarong style around her hips.

Duran said: 'Nothing has ever happened between Laura or Peggy and me. You know that.'

'Do I?' Lisa reached her foot out to the pool and wiggled her toes in the water. 'The way they look at you, Bob. The way they—'

A harsh voice interrupted. 'Lisa, are you coming, or what?'

They both turned to see Eric, now dressed in slacks and a white dress-shirt, his hair wet-combed back from his forehead.

'In a minute,' Lisa said angrily. 'I've got to be going, Bob. Uncle Hugh was by this morning. He's going to represent me. He says he can work for both of us, you and me. He thinks that Jason and Johnny are—'

'Lisa!'

Eric Marvin again. This time the look he gave Duran was one of pure hatred.

'What's your boyfriend's problem?' Duran asked, glaring back at Eric Marvin.

'He works for Johnny. Maybe Johnny's been telling him about you.'

'Telling him what?'

'Things. I've got to go.' Lisa strode off, then turned on her heels, her shoulders shrugging, almost pulling her breasts free from the bikini. 'I want Mommy found, Bob. I want her back.'

'So do I,' Duran said solemnly. 'Listen, I'm worried about you. I promised Anona I'd protect you. There's a mad man out there somewhere and there's no telling what he's going to do next. Be careful. Please. Don't leave the house alone. Don't drive by yourself.' He reached out for her hand. 'We can hire a guard, someone to stay with you until this man is caught.'

Lisa jerked her hand free. 'I can take care of myself, Bob. And I have to do what I think is right no matter who it hurts.'

Duran settled his haunches down on the edge of the diving board. 'What I think is right.' What was going on in that beautiful spoiled little head of hers?

Chapter 19

The sky was velvety black, the moon a mellow pumpkin color. October. Anona had often said October was the best of all the months in San Francisco. Late Indian summer. The best month of the year – not the one to die in. Or be murdered. Could someone have poisoned Anona? Why? It always came back to that singular word. Why?

He thought about what Laura Ralston had said at dinner. Anona's studio. Her unfinished painting and sketches. Johnny had a key and the security code. Which suggested that Jason Lark could have them too. Judging from Lark's credit reports, the man was in a deep financial crisis. He looked at the Jag's dashboard clock. The criminal histories wouldn't be in before midnight. He might as well stop at the studio now.

Anona's studio was located on the Embarcadero, a stretch of road bordering the bay waters. The building wasn't very impressive. Three stories of gray concrete streaked with brownish rivulets where the rust from window frames had rain-washed down the walls. The windows were painted black and barred on the outside, giving it the look of a prison.

He found a parking slot a few feet from the studio. The night air was still. He could hear music. Badly played blues, coming from somewhere nearby. It had to be live, Duran concluded. No one would bother recording those sounds.

He inserted the key and opened the door, concerned at first to find that the lights were on, but he theorized that they'd probably been on since Johnny had last visited the studio. John never much worried about things like light bills. Or any other bills, until he opened his club.

Duran deactivated the alarm and hurried up the steps.

The building had originally been three floors – the third floor had been removed, and the studio walls now rose twenty feet straight up to the roof. The first floor was a storage depot for paints, thinners and various supplies.

He rapped his knuckles on the walls as he walked up the stairs. Anona had roamed the woods and hills of nearby Marin and Sonoma Counties for inspiration.

She'd come across a dilapidated, once-red dairy barn and used it as background material in one of her most famous paintings.

When she learned that the farmer was planning to tear the building down, she purchased it and used the rough, pink-gray, sun-sucked boards to panel the studio.

A massive black metal-bearing beam spanned the walls some three feet below roof-level. The major portion of the roof was of slanted glass, spaced between black aluminium girders. Retractable shades of ribbed iron completely covered the glass.

Out of habit, he pushed the control switch and the heavy metal roof shades began screeching as they retracted, revealing the dark night sky.

Duran approached the easel, picking up Anona's canvas, running his hand lightly across the painting – blues and greens against a white background. He estimated it to be three-fifths finished. He took a look around the room, quite possibly his last look, he realized. A narrow pine table littered with cans and tubes of paint, brushes left standing in empty soup and coffee cans, crusted putty knives and palettes, sat alongside the unfinished painting.

One wall was taken up entirely by a closet of sliding doors some ten feet in height.

He slid a panel door open. There were racks of blank canvases, more paint and packing materials.

He rummaged around until he found wrapping paper and string.

When he'd finished bundling up the painting, he dug a large paper bag from the closet and headed for the small room at the rear of the studio, where Anona kept her sketches and research materials. He was thinking that he might need another bag as he approached the room – Anona had so many sketches. They'd no doubt be worth much more money than the unfinished canvas.

He was reaching for the light switch when suddenly his head exploded in pain.

The building was new to him. It appeared to be a small warehouse. Why was Duran coming here at this time of the night? Was there more to the building than there appeared to be? Was it a private club? Or perhaps a whorehouse? A *pied-à-terre* where he met a woman? His black secretary? Or perhaps a man? Or drugs. Was he buying drugs? Maybe that was Duran's secret. He'd learned in prison that all men have secrets.

He leaned back in the van's seat and reached for the sketch-pad.

He had finished his second version of the building when he saw the man burst out of the front door. He was carrying something. A large can, carrying it over to Duran's Jaguar. His body flinched at the sound of the explosion and the flash of light as the fire belched out on to the street.

Duran struggled to his feet, his arm out, groping in the darkness. He felt that he was choking to death. He couldn't breathe. His fingers clawed at his face, feeling paper. He ripped the bag away and stooped over at the waist, sucking in deep drafts of air, then he heard a crashing sound. He saw a yellow-white flash come from the direction of the staircase. There was an explosion, blinding light, then a rush of heat.

Duran ran toward the staircase, finding it engulfed in flames. Dark, oily smoke veiled the doorway.

He backed away. He couldn't make it down those stairs. And there was no rear exit, nowhere to run. Anona had often joked that she preferred the studio that way. 'Just like the Texans at the Alamo. There's no way to back out.'

The suffocating smoke was spilling into the studio. He dug his handkerchief from his pants pocket and jammed it over his mouth and nose.

The fire was all the way up the stairs, working its way into the dry, barn-paneled studio walls. Once it reached the paint and the thinner, the whole room could explode. Duran looked around hopelessly. The glass roof. The roof was the only way out.

He dragged a table over toward the storage locker and used his arms to pull himself up, his fingers clawing at the slick, dusty locker top. He hoisted himself up, rolling on one shoulder, then got to his knees, feeling dizzy, tottering, almost falling back to the floor. He was gasping and coughing, his eyes running. He jumped, reaching up to the bearing beam, his fingers curling around the metal. The edges dug into his hands. He took a deep breath, then, wrapping his hands around the beam, pulled himself up until his head was above the beam, only a couple of feet from the windowed roof.

He heard a roar, then a series of explosions. He glanced down, seeing balls of orange flame bursting through the smoke almost directly below him. He draped an arm around the girder, dangling free for a second. The windows. He had to get out through the windows. The smoke was all over him, in his eyes, his lungs. The beam, no more than six inches in width, had begun to absorb the heat. He swung precariously for a moment, gathering his strength, pulling his legs up, wrapping them tightly around the steel beam. He raised up an arm. His hand touched the glass. He pounded on it with his fist. It wouldn't budge. He pounded harder.

There was another roaring explosion from below. The panic motivated him. Urged him on. His fingers were clenched in a death grip around the warming angle iron. He swung his leg – toes pointed outward. One kick. Sweat blurred his vision and poured from his face, hands and neck, like small rivers. The smoke was deep in his lungs now. He kicked again, and this time was rewarded with a cracking sound. Another kick and glass cascaded down on him, along with the sweet, cool rush of fresh air.

The oxygen-starved fire leapt upwards. He reached out blindly, his fingers finding the edge of the window-frame. Jagged shards of glass ripped into his flesh.

He heard another series of explosions. He could feel the fire itself, hot, burning. He braced his foot on the angle iron and launched himself upwards.

A sudden burst of energy swept through him as the fresh air surged into his lungs. His hands were slick with blood, his grip loosening.

He pushed his right hand out, the fingers grabbing, wrapping around something round. Solid. He pulled himself up, letting go of the window-frame with his left hand, praying as it joined his right hand. Don't slip, don't slip, now. Do it! Do it!

His arms and back ached from the effort, but gradually he moved upwards, his head and shoulders were above the roof, then his chest. Without warning his blood-drenched left hand slid free for a moment. He dug his elbows into the window-frame, using every bit of strength he had left to hang on, to lever himself forward.

He wasn't sure if it was imagination or not, but his feet were getting warm, as though the fire was burning the soles of his shoes. He shook away the images of the fire, of his falling, and being swallowed by the smoke, the smoke that was billowing out through the broken glass all around him. He focused his watery eyes on his hands, which were gripping a short pipe. Some type of an air vent. He dug his fingers into the metal, willing his fingertips to impale the pipe, then gave a final pull, inching forward until his hips were through the opening, then his legs. He rolled free on to the gravel edge of the roof, landing on his back, his mouth open, gasping, staring at the black sky.

He lay there, sucking air into his lungs, trying to get his strength back, while he categorized his wounds. He ached all over – legs, neck, arms, back, but nothing seemed to be broken. He held both hands in front of his face, saw them smeared with blood and wiped them on his pants.

He heard the sirens and struggled to his feet. He skirted around to the edge of the roof, avoiding the window areas. There was no fire escape. He'd have to wait for the firefighters to rescue him. The red lights on their trucks were visible now. His feet were feeling warm again. Would the roof collapse? He saw a battery of firemen position a ladder alongside the building.

What little energy he had left drained from his body as he staggered to his knees, watching the frenzied activities of the firefighters.

He noticed one lone figure across the street. A tall man in a basketball hat. He was looking up toward Duran and clapping his hands together, like a spectator at a basketball game.

Johnny Stack downshifted the Porsche and tapped his foot on the brakes. He was just a few feet behind the boxy station-wagon that had been hogging the road.

He blinked his highbeams on and hit the horn, but the

driver of the station-wagon held to a steady forty miles an hour.

Johnny saw his chance to pass, gave the horn another blast then glided into the oncoming traffic lane and accelerated, feeling the wind in his hair and his spine being pressed into the back of the bucket seat. He caught a quick glimpse of the white-faced station-wagon driver, then saw the headlights of an oncoming car. He swerved to the right, almost clipping the station-wagon's front bumper.

He stuck his right arm up in the air and extended his middle finger in response to the blaring horn. The speedometer wavered between fifty-five and sixty as he negotiated the next turn.

The road flattened out, taking him on to Bridgeway and through the downtown area of Sausalito. At this time in the morning it was deserted – the busloads of tourists, exhausted from a day of shopping and souvenir hunting were all safely tucked away in their dingy motel rooms.

He loved Sausalito. It had a certain old-world charm. He liked leaving his club late at night, driving across the Golden Gate Bridge with the convertible top down, regardless of the weather, challenging the road, the curves. Unlike the old fool in the station-wagon, driving a cautious few miles under the speed limit, a death grip on the steering wheel.

He liked having the bridge between him and San Francisco. Between him and Stack House. He throttled down as he moved through town, past the Sausalito Inn, toward the bobbing masts of the Yacht Harbor, then home, just beyond the Second World War site of the Kaiser Shipyards. The electric mix of upscale houseboats and old, abandoned derelicts suited him just fine. The fact that only a handful of people knew his address was a plus. He needed time to himself, to think, to create.

You don't have to paint to be an artist, his mother had often told him.

Johnny had tried painting, sculpting, and writing, but found he had no talent for any of them. Then he tried music, but the tedious piano and guitar lessons quickly bored him. Promoting, that was his forte, finding talent, refining it, showcasing it.

The Bay Area was ripe for a new Bill Graham, and he saw no reason why he couldn't be the one to fill those shoes.

His club, Stack's, was just a start. Just the beginning, he assured himself. Once he received his share of the estate, he could expand. Start bringing in some top-name acts to bolster the yet unknowns, his 'discoveries.'

He notched the Porsche into the carport, turning the collar of his leather jacket up as he walked over the wobbly planking leading to the pier.

The drawback to living in a houseboat came at low tide. The smell of raw sewage wafted over the oily bay waters as he carefully dodged rotting planks and dog droppings.

His houseboat was just that, a small house that had been fitted on to a barge and floated to its berth.

He was whistling softly, looking forward to a beer and a smoke. He had scored some high-grade grass at the club from Eric Marvin. Marvin was becoming a problem. He knew the business and could deal with the food and laundry suppliers, the unions, the kitchen staff, but he was beginning to act as if he was a partner, rather than an employee. And now he was making it with Lisa. His sister was becoming a pest, hanging around all night, sticking her pert little nose into everything, especially the band, the . . .

Suddenly he saw movement out of the corner of his eye. 'Hey, what—'

The first blow caught him squarely between the eyes. He grunted a protest, then there was a second blow to the top of his head. He fell, his arms dangling uselessly at his sides, his face hitting the decking at full force with a loud, squashy sound.

He felt himself being dragged, the rough wood tearing at his skin. He managed to get a glimpse of his assailant before he hit the water, the shock causing his mouth to drop open. He tried to shout, then the darkness closed over him, the water running into his nose, finally covering his fear-glazed eyes.

Chapter 20

The paramedic was a serious-faced young man of twenty-five. He used a pair of tweezers to pull a sliver of glass from Robert Duran's palm. 'I'd suggest that you see your own doctor, sir, though I don't think any of these cuts need stitches.'

'Thanks. I'll do just that,' Duran assured him. He was feeling light-headed, perhaps because of the elation of surviving the fire trap, perhaps due to the pure oxygen that the medic had given him.

Duran was sitting on the rear bumper of an ambulance. He watched with interest as the firemen went about their duties. There were no signs of flames now, just smoke rolling out of the roof – charcoaling the sky, before sinking down to ground level.

Three brightly-polished red fire-trucks surrounded the building, their silver-colored metal ladders extended into the air, a fireman clinging to the tip, directing a powerful stream of water on to the skeletal shell of the studio.

Fire hose was strewn like spaghetti all over the street, which was Vaseline–shiny from the water.

Duran winced as the paramedic sprayed a disinfectant across his palm, then began wrapping it with gauze.

A man in knee-high fireboots, a black canvas turnout jacket and a battered leather helmet that had ARSON SQUAD stenciled across the crown, sank down next to Duran. He lifted the helmet from his head and tossed it casually toward his feet. He was a solid, weatherworn man in his forties with thick sandy-colored hair, his face darkened by soot except for the areas around his eyes, nose and mouth which had been protected by an air mask. 'We've got the fire licked. Are you the man who was on the roof?'

'Yes. That's right. Bob Duran.'

'Lieutenant Jack Powers.' He craned his neck to watch the paramedic go about his work. 'Looks like you ruined a nice suit.'

'Yes. I'm lucky that's all I ruined.'

'I guess you are. Do you want to tell me about it?'

Duran pointed his unbandaged hand toward the building.

'My wife's studio was in there. She's an artist.'

Powers's voice tightened. 'Was she with you tonight?'

'No. She died a few days ago.'

'Wife's name?'

'Anona Stack.'

Powers pulled his right foot from its boot and began massaging his arch. 'Anona Stack. Yes, sir. She was indeed an artist. So why did you come down here tonight?'

'There were some sketches and an unfinished canvas in the studio. I was going to bring them back to the house.'

'Shit,' Powers barked. 'There's no way anything could have survived the fire.' He wiggled his foot back into the boot. 'So you went inside about what time?'

'I guess it was a little after eleven.'

The paramedic climbed out of the back of the ambulance and both Duran and Powers stood up to give him room to close the doors.

Powers stooped down and picked up his helmet. 'Mr Duran, I looked at the building entrance. There's some type of alarm system, isn't there?'

'That's right. A standard touch pad. The code must be

192

entered within thirty seconds of opening the door or the alarm will go off.'

'And you used your key?'

'Right.'

'And who else has a key?'

'Well, I've just learned that Anona's son, John Stack, looked at the studio a while back. He was thinking of taking over the property.'

'So he had a key and knew the alarm code. Anyone else?' Powers asked courteously.

'I'm not sure,' Duran responded guardedly, not liking the way the questions were going.

'When you entered the building, did you close the door after you?'

'Yes. It locks automatically when you do that.'

The ambulance driver tapped Powers on the shoulder. 'We've got another call. There's been a shooting over in the Bayview District. We're taking off.'

'Yeah, okay. Send me a copy of your report.' He turned his attention back to Duran. 'So, Mr Duran. You're inside the building, then what happened?'

'I was in there a few minutes. I wrapped my wife's painting, the unfinished canvas in paper, then headed back to a room where she kept her sketches.' His hand went to the back of his skull. 'Then I got busted on the head. I don't know how long I was unconscious, but when I came to, I couldn't see. Someone had slipped a paper bag over my head.'

'Paper bag?' Powers asked skeptically.

'I was carrying the bag to gather up the sketches. I tore the bag off, heard a crashing sound, then I saw the fire in the stairway.'

'A crashing sound? Like what? The door being kicked open? Something falling?'

'I'm not sure.'

'And you saw the fire right after that?'

'Yes. Immediately. I still can't believe how fast it moved.'

They had to detour around a hose connection that was leaking, spurting a mini-geyser of water in a ten foot circle.

Duran was impressed at the amount of activity. There were over a dozen fire-rigs spread out on the street now, some with hoses connected to each other. The smell of their diesel engines merged with the soot and ashes from the fire.

'Then what happened?' Powers prodded.

'There was no other way out. I couldn't get down the stairs. I climbed up on top of a cabinet, broke through the glass ceiling, and managed to get out through the roof.'

Powers jammed his helmet on. 'The roof. You were lucky, Mr Duran. Real lucky. Did you see anybody in the street prior to the fire?'

'No. Not a soul. What kind of accelerant was used?'

Powers's eyes hardened. He was surprised at Duran's terminology. *Accelerant*. A technical term. Most people would ask if it was gasoline, or paint thinner.

'We're not sure yet, but my guess is that it was paint thinner.'

'There was thinner in the studio,' Duran said. 'Some of it was upstairs, and there were cans of it stored down on the ground level.' Suddenly his legs felt wobbly. He wanted to sit down. Or lie down. Paint thinner. Someone tried to kill him this time. It wasn't a prank telephone call or a push off a trail. It was a calculated attempt at murder.

'I want to thank you and your men for getting to the fire so quickly, Lieutenant.'

Powers pointed down the street. 'Someone pulled a street alarm box or we wouldn't have made it in time. In time to get you off the roof, anyway. What are your plans now, Mr Duran?'

'I'm going to go home and slop into bed, Lieutenant. I'm exhausted.'

'Yeah. I'll bet you are. How are you figuring on getting home?'

'Oh, I'm all right. I can drive.'

Powers waved his helmet at the Jaguar. 'Is that your vehicle over there?'

The car was parked where Duran had left it. A fire engine had jumped the curb in front of the Jaguar, its hose bed now empty, the fire hose now coupled to the side of the rig, weaving a path like a child's scribble toward the studio.

'Yes, that's my car.' He shoved a hand into his pants pocket, grateful to feel the car keys.

'We found a trail of accelerant, Mr Duran. It ran from the front of the building, along the sidewalk, to the rear end of your car.'

'Lieutenant, whoever set that fire was inside when I entered the building. And no one knew I was coming to the studio. No one. I just decided to stop by a few minutes before I got here.'

'So what do you think this "someone" was doing in there?' Powers asked.

'I don't know. Maybe he was after my wife's sketches.'

'The lights were on, but you didn't think that someone might be inside?'

Duran shrugged. 'I knew Johnny had been there checking the studio out. I just assumed he'd left the lights on.'

'That's possible,' Powers contended. 'The trail of paint thinner, it stops, or possibly started, by the Jaguar. Maybe he was thinking of torching your car too, is that your guess?'

Duran didn't have to guess. He cursed himself. After finding the rosary beads in the trunk of his car, he should have had the locks changed. Damn. The bastard wanted to make it look like I started the fire and accidentally got burned to death.

Duran unlocked the car door. 'I have no idea, Lieutenant. You must have read the papers, about my wife's body being stolen from the cemetery. Perhaps it's the same man. I just don't know. I really don't.'

'Would you mind if I took a close look at your car, sir? Maybe whoever did this spilled some paint thinner on the tires or under the hood. You never know.'

'Not tonight,' Duran said with an edge to his voice. 'Call me tomorrow. I'm not feeling well. I've got to get out of here.'

'I can call an ambulance or have one of my men take you home, sir.'

Yes. And go through my car, and maybe find a can of thinner in the trunk. 'No, thanks, Lieutenant.' Duran hit the ignition and the engine growled. 'I'll talk to you tomorrow.'

Powers stood back and watched Duran maneuver the Jag from the curb and around the fire-engine. He was tempted to impound the car, right then and there, but he just didn't have enough to justify it. Maybe there was something inside the building. Maybe a body. Duran's wife's body. Was that his reason for torching the place?

It had all the earmarks of a botched job. An amateur pouring paint thinner all over the place, then getting caught in his own trap. But not many amateurs were as lucky as Duran.

Chapter 21

Jason Lark's fingers moved slowly, methodically over the yellowing ivory keyboard. He was playing Gershwin, but in a manner he was sure Mr Gershwin would not have approved of.

He had raided Anona's wine cellar, dear old George's now, he corrected himself, for a vintage bottle of Burgundy. He was reaching for the wine when he heard a door slam.

'Is that you, Johnny? Lisa?' he called out.

Lark narrowed his eyes, making crows feet, when the tarnished image of Robert Duran entered the room. 'Jesus Christ! What the hell happened to you?'

Duran's clothes were blackened and torn. His face was smoke stained.

'There was a fire. At Anona's studio,' Duran informed him. 'I almost got killed.'

Lark swiveled on the piano seat. 'Let me get you a drink, man. You look like you could use one.'

'How long have you been here, Jason?'

'Oh, an hour or so.' Lark went to the drink cart and poured a stiff slug of cognac into a balloon snifter. 'Here. I know you don't like drinking with me, but under the circumstances, you can make an exception.'

'Where were you? Before you came back to Stack House?'

Lark ran a finger across his ear, pushing away an errant

lock of hair. 'Out seeing the town. Having a few drinks. One or two too many, perhaps.' He straddled the piano bench. 'You look like hell. What happened?'

Duran studied Lark's features. He looked shocked. Shocked at how I look, or that I had survived? He wondered. 'I told you. There was a fire at Anona's studio. When were you last there?'

'Me? Oh, maybe ten years ago. Is it still on the Embarcadero?'

'Yes. What about Johnny? Were you with him tonight?'

'Johnny? No. He's too busy with his club to spend the night with his poor old father.' Lark settled his fingers back on the piano keys. 'Why all the questions, Bob? Are you suggesting I had something to do with the fire?'

'Did you?' Duran drained the cognac and settled the glass on the grand piano. 'Whoever set fire to the studio tonight had to have a key to get into the building. And the code for the alarm system. I know Johnny was looking at the studio a while ago.'

Lark kept his eyes on Duran as he reached slowly for his wine glass. 'Johnny? You think Johnny is going to burn down the studio? What the hell for? You're losing it Bob. You're getting paranoid. Who do the cops think started the fire?'

'When you were with John, did he ever give you the key and security code for the studio?'

Lark's face blanched. 'Why would I want them?'

Duran ignored the question. 'Anona went to a trial in Los Angeles several years ago. She stayed at the Beverly Hills Hotel. I'm told you went to the court house with her.'

'Who told you that?' Lark asked, tinkling out the first few notes of *A Foggy Day*.

'Did you or didn't you?'

'Sure,' Lark confirmed. 'Anona was on a crusade against the people who forged her painting.' He smiled up at Duran. 'You're the one who found it, weren't you? The forged painting, I mean.'

'What happened at the trial, Jason?'

'What happened? Law and order prevailed. The bad guys went to prison.'

'I know that, but what about Anona? She testified. Were there any threats made, or any other problems?'

Lark shrugged his shoulders and reached for his wine glass.

Duran batted his hand away. 'I asked you if there were any problems.'

Lark started to get to his feet, then sank back down on his haunches. 'Temper, temper, Bob. There were no problems. The guy, not the old geezer who owned the gallery, but the guy who actually forged the painting, he was all pissed off at Anona, I remember that.'

'Why was he mad?' Duran pressed.

'I think it was because he tried to play Prince Valiant, and it didn't work. He asked the judge to let him serve his wife's time, too, but the judge wouldn't go for it. Anona had made some cry-baby plea to the judge about how terrible it was to see your art copied like that. She said it was like being raped. Apparently the woman had done some of the work on Anona's forgery, too. Anona wanted her punished.' He laughed lightly. 'That old Catholic upbringing, I guess.'

'I think it's time you moved out of Stack House.'

'Not now,' Lark said heatedly. 'Not until Anona's found. The kids, Johnny and Lisa, they need me now.'

'You were never around when you were needed,' Duran said coldly.

'A few days, I'll just stay a few more days. Is that too much to ask?'

The two men stared at each other in a stiff, formal silence, then Duran turned his back and left the room without answering.

★ ★ ★

Duran had found it almost impossible to get to sleep. He arrived at the office a little before five in the morning. The criminal histories were waiting in the fax machine.

The first two were of the 'longer than my arm' type, and Rachel had scribbled a series of question marks and a short note across the page: 'What the hell are you into, Peg?'

Angelo Belardi and Anthony 'Tony Dope' Viscoti. New York mafioso, both in their seventies now. All of the arrests were in New York – the charges ranging from strongarm, to attempted murder to bookmaking. Neither man had an entry in the last three years. Had they retired? Gone straight? Hired better lawyers? Died?

The checks relating to the museum thefts in Houston, Santa Fe and New Orleans had proved inconclusive – the thieves, all first timers, had served their sentences and hadn't been heard from since, as far as the criminal justice system was concerned.

The owner of the Beverly Hills gallery, Joseph Phelps, aka Royce Breamer, Ron Breamer, Joseph Lally, Sidney Harris, William Morries, William Breener, had arrests dating back to 1958. Breamer-Phelps moved around the map, Delaware, Washington, DC, Philadelphia. The same sad story followed him around – arrests – but no convictions. There was a gap of some ten years between the arrest in Philadelphia and the art fraud charges in Beverly Hills. Duran surmised that the lapse between charges had to be during the time period that Breamer had operated in Europe.

The notation following the Los Angeles County arrest showed he was convicted, given a six year sentence, then, seven months later, extradited to Switzerland.

The next two histories were for Otto and Arlene Kline, the two artists who actually forged the paintings for Phelps.

Arlene Kline was twenty-nine at the time of her conviction. Her husband thirty-three. Both had received identical sentences – two years, which normally would mean they'd be out in a year.

The second arrest on Otto Kline's record caught Duran's eye: 4501 Penal Code – Assault with deadly weapon by prisoner. Kline had been given a ten year sentence for this offense.

There was no mention on the sheet as to whether or not he was still in prison.

Duran massaged his chin. Ten years. Pretty stiff. Was he still in custody? Could the additional charge have anything to do with Anona? With him? How? The wife would have been released years ago. Where was she now?

The computer gave him some of the answers. He modemed into a database and entered the California driver's license ID numbers listed on the rap sheets for both Otto and Arlene Kline.

Arlene Kline's license had expired and showed a nine-year-old address in Burbank. It also showed her as deceased.

Otto Kline's license had expired six years ago and showed the same Burbank address.

He moved to another database, checked the state death register and found that Arlene Kline had died in Los Angeles County just eight months after she'd been sentenced to prison. She died in prison! On October fourteenth. Almost seven years ago to the day.

Duran rechecked the rap sheets. Otto Kline's assault charge was listed as taking place one day after his wife's death.

He was mulling over the possibilities when the phone rang. He picked it up cautiously.

'Mr Duran?'

'Yes.'

'This is Jack Healy at the *Chronicle*, I'm calling about—'

Duran slammed down the receiver and made up his mind quickly. Los Angeles.

'Nice flight, Mr Duran?' asked the shaggy-haired limousine driver.

'Not bad. First stop is the Los Angeles Police Department headquarters on West Sunset Boulevard.'

'Yes, sir. My name's Lenny. No luggage?'

Duran patted his briefcase. 'Just this.' He settled into the Lincoln's back seat, opened the briefcase and fingered the contents.

Paul Haber, the Los Angeles police sergeant who'd been involved in the Breamer-Kline arrests had been upgraded to captain and now worked out of Homicide. Firstly, Duran congratulated him on his promotion.

'Thanks, Bob. It's been a long time. I read about your wife. My condolences. What have the San Francisco investigators come up with?'

'Not much. That's why I'm here.'

Haber had put on some weight and lost some hair since Duran had last seen him. He gestured Duran into his office, pointed to a chair, then said, 'What can I do for you?'

Duran told him everything he knew about the Klines.

'And you think this has something to do with your wife?'

'I'm checking out every possibility, Captain.'

Haber picked up a pencil and ran it through his fingers. 'I haven't thought of that case in years. You're sure this Otto Kline got into trouble while he was in prison?'

'Positive,' Duran confirmed.

Haber pursed his lips, then got to his feet. 'Let me go see what we've got.'

He returned fifteen minutes later carrying a small batch of computer printouts.

'You weren't kidding about Kline getting in trouble. He

damn near killed a guard while he was at the state prison in Chino. He got a stiff sentence and was shipped up to Pelican Bay.'

Duran's eyes narrowed. 'Pelican Bay. It sounds familiar.'

'It's been in the news a lot. Toughest prison in the state. Maybe in the whole country. It's up north, just a few miles from the Oregon border.' Haber glanced down at the printouts. 'He was released last month.'

Duran's back stiffened. 'Last month?'

'Right. The scoop on his wife is that she committed suicide. Right here in the county jail. She hung herself in her cell.'

Duran leaned back in his chair, trying to digest the information. 'Does it show where Arlene Kline is buried?'

Haber shuffled through the papers. 'No. You'd have to check with the county on that.'

'How about a current address on Otto Kline?'

Again Haber went back through the printouts. 'No. Nothing. Just the prison.'

'Do you know anyone at Pelican Bay?'

'Not personally.' Haber chuckled. 'I've sent them a few customers since I've been here at Homicide. Do you want to talk to someone up there?'

'Very much so,' Duran confided.

Chapter 22

Jason Lark drove until he spotted a pay telephone in a gas station parking lot. He used his credit card for the Las Vegas call.

'Yes?'

'It's me, Jason.'

'Everything is being taken care of,' Mario Drago assured him. 'We're pleased with the information you provided.'

'Is there a possibility that Duran could . . . meet with an accident at the meeting this afternoon.'

'Do you think that's necessary?'

Lark studied his reflection in the smudged phone booth window. 'I thought I had . . . taken care of Duran last night, but it didn't work out.'

'Yes. I know about the fire, Jason. The story was on television here.'

'Duran was asking me a lot of questions last night. After he got home from the fire. I think that he—'

'He's connected you to the Fritzheim robbery,' Drago said flatly.

'I'm not sure,' Lark qualified. 'I just didn't like the way the conversation was going.'

'And you want us to handle him.'

Lark pressed his point. 'If Duran is eliminated, I can go ahead with the job I was telling you about, the woman with the—'

'Very well,' Drago cut in. 'I'll let them know.'

Lark hung up and rubbed his hands together like a man anticipating a gourmet meal. He still hadn't found the Picassos, but at least Duran would be out of the picture. He was whistling as he walked back to his car and didn't notice the man in the white van with the sketch-pad.

Duran used the limousine's phone to call Peggy.

'I got your message, Bob. You got out of town just before the posse. The press, some guy from the fire department and that Colma cop have been calling. You're a popular man. Your picture is on the front page of the *Chronicle*. A fireman helping you down a ladder. Are you all right?'

'Yes.'

'Really?'

'Really,' he assured her. 'I think your hunch on that old CIA case turned up positive.' He told her about Kline's prison experience and his wife's suicide. 'I just went through the Medical Examiner's file. Arlene Kline hung herself in her cell at the county clink. Run a driver's license check on Barbara Linker. Forty-two years of age, born on August eleventh. She was in the cell with Mrs Kline the night of her death.'

'Where are you now?'

'I'm on my way to the cemetery where Arlene Kline's buried.'

Peggy moaned softly. 'You're not thinking that—'

'I'm thinking it's worth looking at, Peg. I've got a Los Angeles police captain trying to get me in touch with someone at the Pelican Bay State Prison. Call your buddy Rachel. See who she knows in the prison system. Call everyone you can think of. I want to talk to someone up there at the prison, anyone who can give me some information on Otto Kline. Spend whatever's necessary.'

'All right. What about the Fritzheim case? You've got a

four o'clock appointment with Harry Lawson and Wendy Lange. Do you still want me to call Lawson with Wendy's address?'

'Yes.' Lawson wasn't going to learn about where the painting was to be examined until just before the meeting. Duran glanced at his watch. 'Call Harry at three-thirty. He'll be sitting on the phone, with the Van Gogh cradled in his lap. I should still be able to get to Lange's place on time.' He read off the number labeled on the phone. 'Call me as soon as you have anything on Barbara Linker.'

Duran stretched out his legs and gazed out of the limo's window, not noticing the passing scenery, thinking of Arlene Kline's death. 'Incomplete suspension' was the way the attending coroner had described it. She had cinched her bra around her neck and fastened it to the upper berth in the two bed cell, then while lying down, had leaned out and over the bed far enough to compress the blood vessels of her neck and shut off the supply of oxygen from reaching her brain. She'd stuffed a piece of her shirt in her mouth, apparently to keep from awakening her cellmate or drawing the attention of the guards.

It was an incredibly difficult way to die. No quick fracture of the neck – a long, slow, painful, self-induced strangulation. What had driven her to it?

According to the ME's report, Barbara Linker, her cellmate, claimed she heard nothing and knew of no reason for Arlene Kline to kill herself.

'We're here at the cemetery, Mr Duran,' the driver announced on the speaker.

'Let's find someone who knows where the bodies are buried.'

It wasn't much of a cemetery, Duran noticed, once he was out of the Lincoln. The lawn looked in need of a trimming. The grave markers were small, some just knee-high crosses.

'I'm looking for a grave,' Duran told a man bent over the engine of an industrial-sized lawn mower.

The man straightened up. He was tall and gaunt. Dark sweat marks showed at the armpits of his hickory shirt. 'You came to the right place, mister. Any particular grave?'

Duran smiled lightly. 'The woman's name is Arlene Kline. She died in—'

'I know the grave. Over that hill.' He pointed to the west. 'There's a pond, then a small meadow. It's the one with the big new headstone.'

Duran was impressed. He put his hands on his hips and surveyed the area. The sky was cloudless, that peculiar yellowish smog almost blotting out the brassy sun. The distant hills looked as if they were shielded behind saffron curtains. 'There must be thousands of people buried here. Have you got them all memorized?'

'Nope. I just laid in the new headstone for Mrs Kline a few weeks ago.'

Duran dug out his money clip and pushed out a twenty-dollar bill. 'Would you mind showing me just where her grave is, Mr . . .?'

'Linszky.' He waved the money away and hopped on to the seat of the lawn mower. 'Follow me.'

Duran climbed back into the limousine. 'Follow that lawn mower,' he said with a grin.

Linszky was right. There was just one new headstone. The others were nothing more than upright slabs.

Duran scanned the stones. Except for Arlene Kline's the burial dates were twenty and thirty years old.

'This here is a potter's graveyard,' Linszky informed him. 'Jailbirds. The old timer's called it God's back yard. The county don't bury them anymore. They cremate 'em, it's a lot cheaper.' He reached out and fingered the polished gray marble slab standing guard over Arlene

Kline's remains. 'This is the first new one I can remember. Her husband paid for the burial. Wanted her in the ground, not up in smoke, I guess.'

Duran fixed his eye on the tombstone. Arlene Kline's name in chiseled cursive script, the words: At First Thought Sweet.

'At first thought sweet,' he said aloud. 'It sounds familiar.'

Linszky shrugged his shoulders. 'You got me. That what was ordered, that's what I put on it.'

Lenny, the limo driver solved the puzzle for Duran.

'It's poetry. John Milton. "Revenge at first thought sweet, bitter ere long back on itself." It's from *Paradise lost*.'

Duran arched his eyebrows in a questioning gesture.

'One thing about my job, I get a lot of time to read,' Lenny revealed.

Duran turned to Linszky. 'Did you ever meet Mr Kline?'

'Nope. I saw him just once. A few days or so ago. He spent about six hours at the grave. Brought his lunch and everything.'

'What does he look like?'

'What's your interest?' Linszky countered.

'I think he may be trying to kill me.'

The gardener's eyes widened sharply. 'God's truth?'

'God's truth,' Duran pledged.

'He's a big, gangly guy. Hair cut real close to his scalp. He didn't look friendly, and I didn't get very close.'

'The tombstone. How did he pay for it?'

'He called on the phone, told me what he wanted. I gave him a price and he sent a United States Post Office money order.' Linszky put his hands over his eyes to screen the sun as he peered at Duran. 'Why do you think he's trying to kill you, mister?'

★ ★ ★

The girl who came to the door had long carrot-red hair that streamed below her shoulder blades. Her eyes were topaz colored and doe-shaped. She was taller than Duran, thanks to her spiked heels. Her macro-mini beige crocheted dress hung from two narrow straps looped around her neck.

Duran figured if he had a dollar for every year she was over sixteen he wouldn't be able to buy a Big Mac.

'I'm looking for Barbara Linker. Is she home?'

A scratchy voice called out from inside the apartment. 'Who the hell is it, Paula?'

'I don't know,' the girl answered softly.

The door was yanked open wider and a woman appeared, pushing Paula out of the way. Paula's companion was short, her gray-brown hair scaled down into a crew cut. Her skin was leathery. She wore jeans and a red and black flannel shirt, the sleeves rolled up to show a series of tattoos on each of her thick forearms. 'What'd you want?'

'I'm looking for Barbara Linker.'

'What for?'

'I just want to talk to her.'

The woman leaned her shoulders against the door jamb and frisked Duran with her eyes. 'You're too fucking good-looking to be a vice cop.'

'I'm not a cop,' Duran acknowledged. 'I'd like to talk to Barbara Linker, and I'll pay her for her time.'

'Just to talk? You can get that from one of those phone-sex operations.' She stuck her head out the door and looked down the hallway. 'Maybe you want to talk to Paula, huh?'

'No. It's you I want, Barbara. It's about Arlene Kline.'

Linker's mouth started to move, then stopped. 'Kline? The push that hung herself in jail?'

'Yes. That's the one.'

Linker held up a finger. 'Wait a sec.' The door closed.

Duran could hear her ordering the girl to go to her room. The door reopened and Barbara Linker waved him inside.

'You said you'd pay, didn't you?'

'Indeed I did.'

The walls were covered in black leather, the ceiling mirrored. There were two zebra-striped couches against one wall. A wooden cross with handcuffs dangling from the edges sat in the middle of the room. A cobra-like leather bullwhip was coiled neatly alongside the cross.

Duran massaged a fifty-dollar bill between his fingers and held it out to Linker.

'Talk's not cheap, honey. Two hundred dollars.' She pushed her hand out and wiggled her fingers for the money. 'Three hundred, if you want Paula to join in.'

Duran dug out his wallet. 'Just tell me why Arlene Kline killed herself.'

Barbara Linker leaned back against the wooden cross, sliding her fingers in and out to the cuffs. 'That happened a long time ago.'

'Yes. And there is no way you could be held responsible. I just want to know why she did what she did.'

Linker pursed her mouth in a gesture of contempt. 'Are you one of those kinky bastards that digs snuff films and all that shit? Is this the way you get your kicks?'

'It's a kinky world, Barbara. You know that. Tell me about Arlene Kline.'

Chapter 23

'Sorry it took so long to get back to you, Chief, but this stuff was really buried, you know what I mean?'

Although the New York police detective he was talking to on the phone couldn't see it, Saylor nodded his head vigorously in agreement.

Saylor had ended up speaking to nine different divisions of the NYPD before he got Detective Regelio to help him.

Being the chief of a small town in California had pulled no weight with his first eight contacts, but Regelio was planning a vacation to San Francisco around Christmas time. Saylor's offer of showing him the town had sparked Regelio's interest.

'It's like dis,' Regelio informed him in a thick New York accent. 'The woman croaks right in the hospital. We don't even get a call on it. They prep her right then and there. The autopsy confirms an aneurism. Case closed.'

'Nothing at all suspicious?' Saylor asked.

'Nothin'. Except . . . let's see. The doc lists contusions on her elbow, knees and shoulder. The husband claimed she fell while jogging around Central Park a couple of days before she assumes room temperature. Case closed. We didn't even give it a sniff.'

'Okay, Detective. Do you think you could fax that out to me?'

'Fax? Shit, we're lucky we got phones. I'll drop it in the

mail to you. And Gina likes Chinese.'

Saylor grunted in confusion.

'My wife. Chinese restaurants. I hear you got some good ones out there. See you in December.'

Wendy Lange decided a cup of tea was just what she needed to calm her nerves down. She had celebrated her thirty-eighth birthday the night before. Perhaps overly celebrated. Long-legged, with a shapely figure and eyebrow-length bangs, she always projected an abundance of energy. Today, more so. She was excited about examining the Van Gogh. Just holding the painting, if it was authentic, would be the best birthday present she could have possibly given herself.

Her combination office-residence was a neat white-brick Regency home on a quiet tree-lined street in Los Angeles. She entered the kitchen and turned on the tap. No water. She fiddled with the faucet handles, then cursed and checked the bathroom sink. Still no water.

She was marching toward the telephone when the front door-bell rang. She peered through the peekhole. A stocky man with a drooping mustache dressed in a tan shirt and hat was on her porch.

'Yes? What is it?'

'Water Department, ma'am. We've had a rupture up the street. Are your pipes working?'

'No.' Wendy slipped the lock. The man was short, stocky, and had a tool belt sagging at his waist and a City of Los Angeles Water Department logo stitched on his shirt.

'I just tried the faucets. Can you tell me how long this is going to take? I'm expecting—'

'It all depends, ma'am. I looked at your meter connection. You're lucky you haven't had problems before. Come on, I'll show you.'

Wendy hesitated. 'I've never had any trouble with—'

The man pulled something from his tool belt. It took Wendy a moment to realize it was a gun. She opened her mouth to scream.

'Don't do it,' he warned. 'I really don't want to kill you.'

Lange backpedalled slowly into the house. The man waved the gun at her. 'Turn around and get down on your knees.'

She felt helpless. 'Listen, I—'

'Just do what you're told, Wendy. I just want the Van Gogh. You won't be hurt.'

'But, I—'

'Down,' he shouted, as if commanding a dog to obey.

She sank to her knees, biting on her lip to try to curtail her shaking. She heard the door open again, footsteps. Something wet, cold, bitter-smelling was forced against her face.

The man in the tan shirt turned to his companion. 'Grab her arms. She's fighting it.'

Wendy Lange felt a wet cloth being ground into her nose, her mouth. Her skin was burning, her eyes were hot and watering. She made a final effort to free herself, then suddenly went limp.

The man kept the towel in place for several seconds, then said, 'She's out. Let's drag her into a back room.'

'How long have we got to wait?'

'Duran and Lawson are supposed to be here at four. Grab her feet.'

He rolled his palm across her breast. 'She's kind of pretty. Too bad you put her out. We gonna do her?'

'No. Lawson and Duran are due at four o'clock. We just do Duran.'

'Good. I hate doin' women.'

'Sorry about the traffic, Mr Duran. I can get off the freeway in about a mile and take an indirect route.'

'Do what you think best,' Duran suggested. He checked

his watch. Four-forty. It would take Wendy Lange an hour or two to authenticate the Van Gogh, so there was no reason to worry.

Harry Lawson knew he could not contract a deal without Duran's approval. He reached for the mobile phone and called his office.

'Nice timing,' Peggy advised. 'I think I've got you a connection with a guard at Pelican Bay.'

'Who through? Captain Haber?'

'No. I haven't heard a word from Haber. Rachel's boyfriend has a friend, who has a friend, you know how it goes.'

'I know. Time and place?'

'That's the hard part, Bob. The only time this guard can meet you is before he goes to work in the morning. That means you'll have to be up there before seven.'

'No problem. Book me a flight directly from Los Angeles.'

'That is a problem. You have to fly into Crescent City, a few miles from the prison. United's got the only direct flight, and the first one doesn't get there until ten after eight.'

'Hold on.' Duran tapped the headrest behind the driver's seat. 'I need a charter plane. A jet to get me up to Crescent City early in the morning. Know anyone that can handle it?'

Lenny caught Duran's eyes in the rearview mirror. 'Sure, but it will be expensive.'

'The flight's taken care of,' Duran informed his secretary. 'Fax me down the information on the prison guard I'm meeting with.'

'Will do, Bob. How are you fixed for cash? The guy you're meeting with will expect a donation.'

'How much?'

'Rachel suggests three hundred dollars.'

'All right. Any other calls?'

'The fire investigator, Lieutenant Powers, he was by in person an hour ago. He's not a happy camper.'

'What's his problem?'

'Not being able to talk to you. He was threatening to go to the District Attorney if you don't cooperate.'

'Who else?'

'Laura Ralston called twice and your attorney Hugh Stringer. He says it's important that he talk to you right away.'

'Okay. Barring any complications with the Van Gogh, I'll fly into San Francisco tonight and talk to Stringer and the fireman, then go on up to Crescent City in the morning.'

Duran recognized Harry Lawson's pearl gray Cadillac sedan parked in front of Wendy Lange's house. Every time Duran had dealt with Lawson the attorney had been accompanied by his driver-bodyguard, a huge, former professional wrestler with a beach-ball face.

Duran rang the doorbell and waited. He rang again, then knocked on the door and shouted out Lange's name. Still nothing.

Duran tried the handle. The door was unlocked. He pushed. Something was blocking the door. He pushed harder, grunting at the effort, calling out first Lange's name, then Lawson's.

The door finally budged enough for him to squeeze his head in. Harry Lawson's bodyguard was sprawled on the floor. A thin line of blood spiraled down from under his cap, puddling in the crease of his neck and shirt collar.

'Is there a problem?'

Duran's head jerked around. It was Lenny, the limo driver.

'Call 911.'

It was nine-thirty that night when Robert Duran watched Captain Paul Haber and the uniformed policeman who had been guarding the door to Wendy Lange's room walk out of the lobby of the hospital.

He rode the elevator up to the seventh floor.

A nurse, gritty-eyed with tiredness, called to him from her work station. 'You can't go in there. Ms Lange is not receiving visitors.'

'I'll just be a minute,' Duran promised. 'Captain Haber forgot a couple of questions.'

Wendy Lange was propped up in bed. Her eyes were puffy and there was a raw red circle around her nose and lips.

'I'm sorry about this, Wendy.'

'Me too. I saw my face. I look like the flag of Japan. Any word on the Van Gogh?'

'No. Not yet.'

Duran snapped open a folding chair and set it alongside the bed. 'How did it go with the police?'

'I told them everything I know, which wasn't much. I just saw the one man, but there were two of them.' She told Duran just what she had told Lieutenant Haber, including the description of the stocky man with the tool belt. 'They were planning on killing you. Just you, Bob.'

'You're sure about that?'

'Positive. I heard them. Whatever it was that they used on me, the police think it was some kind of ether. It didn't put me out right away. I heard them. They were discussing whether they were going to "do me." One of them was a real charmer. He said he didn't like "doing women." "We just do Duran." That's what they said.'

'What else did they say?'

'The one who came in first, he said he didn't want to hurt me. He just wanted the Van Gogh. They knew everything about the meeting, you, Harry Lawson, and the time. Someone had to tell them,' Lange prompted.

Duran shook his head slowly from side to side. 'I told the insurance carrier that I had a meeting set up with

Harry Lawson. I didn't give them your name or the time.'

'Then it had to come from Harry's end. He dealt with a lot of crooks.'

'Yes. But he was valuable to them. Why would they kill Harry?'

'Maybe they thought Harry was pulling a double cross?' Lange suggested.

'Maybe,' Duran conceded. He got to his feet. 'Is there anything I can do for you?'

'Find the Van Gogh, Bob. I'd really like to look at it.'

The wary nurse gave Duran a withering look as he headed to the elevators. He pushed the down button and stared at his image in the smudged brass elevator doors.

They wanted to kill me. Why? 'Just do Duran.' Then why kill Lawson? They could have just as easily put him out with ether like they did Lange. Why kill anyone?

During his session with the police, Captain Haber had informed him that the killings were done by a professional hit man. 'A .22, probably a semi-automatic with a silencer. One shot behind the left ear of both Lawson and his bodyguard. There was no exit wound. A .22 isn't powerful enough to exit the skull, but it ricochets around like a pinball.'

Haber had offered a theory that Lawson may have been killed because of the bodyguard being parked out front of the house. Wendy Lange's backyard abutted a neighbor – there was no way to get out of the house except through the front. The bodyguard would have spotted them. So he had to be drawn into the house. And killed. 'They must have gotten nervous waiting for you, and decided to split.'

Wendy said that the killer mentioned Lawson and Duran by name. But not the bodyguard. Lawson always had his guard with him. Which meant that the killers knew nothing of the attorney. Except his name and the time of the meeting.

The hospital was cool, almost cold, but Duran felt a

trickle of perspiration roll down his spine. The notorious Los Angeles freeways had been responsible for an untold number of deaths. But today, the traffic jam had saved his life. If he had gotten to the meeting on time, he would have been killed.

'We just do Duran.'

Why? And how was it connected to Anona? Or to the fire last night?

The elevator pinged open. Two tall men dressed in business suits looked out dispassionately at Duran. He took one step toward the elevator, then stopped, wheeled suddenly and headed for the stairs, his heartbeat pounding in his ears.

The men in the elevator – probably doctors going off shift, or friends coming from a visit with loved ones. His feet made sharp cracking sounds on the steps, the words 'We just do Duran' echoing in his brain.

Chapter 24

The chartered jet touched down in Crescent City a little before six in the morning, giving Robert Duran time to rent a car and drive out to view Pelican Bay Prison. The morning was dark and damp. From the road, the flood-lit prison resembled something out of a science-fiction movie – gray concrete walls and dark blue gun towers, razor-tipped wire fences encircling the entire complex. Just looking at it gave him a cold, eerie feeling.

He drove back to town, to the agreed-on meeting place, Yvonne's, a glorified coffee shop adjacent to a Spanish mission-style motel with a sagging red-tiled roof that catered to truckers by the look of the parking lot.

Duran picked out his guest as soon as he entered the restaurant. Junior Erwin looked typecast for what he was – a prison guard. In his forties, short, heavy-set, with ruddy, porcine features, his head topped by a high-walled crew cut, no doubt scissored by a trustee at the prison.

The nature of Duran's job put him in constant touch with law enforcement personnel of every stripe: local, sheriff, FBI, customs, raw recruits, veteran sergeants, battle-scarred detectives, lieutenants, captains and chiefs. And he got along well with most of them.

But not prison guards. He had a hard time understanding why a man would voluntarily take a job that placed him behind bars for forty hours a week.

Erwin was dressed in spotless gray slacks and shirt.

Duran stood up and signalled to him. The guard gave him a wide grin and shambled toward the booth, a cigarette dangling from the corner of his mouth.

'Nice of you to take the time to meet with me,' Duran said, gesturing for Erwin to sit down.

Erwin flopped into the duct-tape-patched booth with a thick-bodied slump. 'They said you was real anxious to see me.'

Erwin ground out his cigarette in a coffee-cup saucer then immediately lit another.

The waitress, a lush-bodied young woman in a snug brown and white uniform came by, to clear the table.

'You want the usual, Junior?' she asked, bending over to pour coffee, giving Erwin a catbird's view of her cleavage.

'Nah. Just a piece of pie, honey.'

The waitress questioned Duran with her eyes.

'Just coffee, thanks.'

Duran reached into his coat pocket, pulled out a business-size envelope stuffed with fifteen twenty-dollar bills and slid it across the table. It was not the first time he'd offered a civil servant an envelope. A 'green subpoena' was the description his first boss at the Centennial Insurance Agency used to describe the package. 'A little something for your time.'

Junior Erwin's ample stomach caused his uniform shirt to stretch open at his navel. He burped lightly, then said, 'I appreciate that, Mr Duran. What's your interest in Otto Kline?'

'I think he may be involved in a case I'm working on.'

The waitress arrived with Erwin's pie which was covered with a melting ball of vanilla ice cream.

Erwin swooped the envelope into his lap before sampling the ice cream. 'Otto Kline. He was a spooky bastard. Hell of a talented painter, though. He did a mural in the guard's mess room.' Erwin raised an arm above his head.

'Floor to ceiling, all blue sky, sunsets and trees. It's really something.'

'Did Kline ever do any other painting? Canvasses?'

'Sure. He kissed ass pretty good. He did a few things for the warden. Paintings of the beach, waves rolling on to the shore, crap like that.'

Erwin took a final drag on his cigarette, snubbed it out and dug a fresh one from his shirt pocket. The cigarettes were like a sixth finger, almost never leaving his hand. As soon as one burned down, he'd grind it out and light another one with a red plastic disposable lighter. 'I do a little moonlighting, repairing boat engines. I gave Kline a picture from *Field and Stream Magazine*. It showed a boat at a dock. I wanted Kline to paint my name and something like the picture on my beat-up camper shell. Kline taped the picture to the side of the shell and damned if he didn't copy the thing, just about perfect.'

'What kind of a man is Otto Kline? Tell me what brought him here to Pelican Bay.'

Erwin leaned across the table and winked. 'He fucked with a guard. Down in some fruitcake lockup in LaLa land. He choked the guard, kicked him around some. You fuck with a guard in this state, you come to us. You're a member of the Aryan Brotherhood, or some Mex or Black jive ass prison gang, you come to us. We ain't here to rehabilitate these sleezeballs, we punish them, Mr Duran, that's what we do. We gave Kline some SHU time. A year-and-a-half of it. That always takes all the juice right out of their balls.'

'Shoe time?'

Erwin slid the ice cream off the tip of the pile with his fork. 'S-H-U. Solitary Housing Unit. The boys call it "the hole," things like that.' Erwin used his fork to saw off a third of the pie, then shoved it in his mouth. 'Some guys spend two or three years in the SHU. By the time they get out, they're cream of wheat, tapioca. No visitors, no books, no TV. Nothing.' Erwin belched, then gouged out another hunk of the pie. 'Kline, he was scared shitless.' Erwin smiled, showing a ragged set of blueberry-stained teeth. 'Hell, they're all scared, but Kline, all a guard had to do was shake a club at his hands and he'd jump out of his skin.' Erwin slid his right hand, fork and all, under his left arm. 'Every time you got near Kline, he'd hide his hand like this. I guess it was 'cause he's a painter and that was his paintin' hand. Kline wasn't used to doing time, especially hard time. He'd cry like a baby when you brought him his food. Beg for you to talk to him, that kind of shit. He was always whining about his wife. She hung herself, you know, in some pussy-palace dyke cooler down in Southern California.'

Duran took a sip of the over-strained coffee while Erwin demolished the last of the pie. 'What did Kline say about his wife? Did he blame himself for her death? Or did he blame someone else?'

'Hell, I don't know. I don't pay any attention to their bitching, Mr Duran. They're all scum. No matter who they are, the SHU changes them, I can guarantee you that. They become zombies. Kline was an exercise nut. Running back and forth in his cell all the time. It was kinda funny to watch. He could only take about three steps one way, three the other, then he was lying on the floor, doing all those exercises. We gotta give the sleeze-balls an hour a day in the yard. They're by themselves, of course, and we strip search them before they leave the SHU and when they return. Otto Kline, he spent the whole time out there running around in circles. Except when he was playing at being sick. He was always bitching about headaches.'

'So Kline did his time in the SHU, then what?'

'Then he went into the mix with the rest of the prisoners. If you've got some skills, you can get into Level One, meaning you can work. For each day you work, you get a day off of your sentence. If you're a real good boy, we might let you have a radio. But, you've got to have earphones.' Erwin smacked his lips. 'That way we don't have to hear whatever these pukes are listening to. So Kline, when we found out he was good with a brush, we put him to work.'

'Was Kline able to sell any of his paintings? To someone on the outside?'

'No, I don't think so, but I'll check, if you want me to.'

'Yes, I do,' Duran answered as Erwin took a drag on the cigarette then almost immediately shoveled a spoonful of ice cream into his mouth. 'What about friends? Did Kline have anybody special?'

Erwin wiped his sweating face with the restaurant napkin. 'You mean a hump? Hell, everyone in there has someone to love. Even if it's only their own hand.' He held up his palm, closed it into a circle and made an obscene pumping motion. 'You know what they say. "Close your eyes and this is the girl of your dreams." But we don't allow no Vogues inside.'

'Vogues?' Duran queried.

'Yeah. Like the magazine, you know. Models. They make hot pants out of their dungarees, paint their faces, lipstick, make-up, the whole routine.' His face wrinkled in disgust. 'We don't allow none of that stuff up here. When I was down in Soledad, it was different. You should have seen some of those perverts. You'd have to be pretty horny to get the old cobra up to strike at those babies.' He flicked the cigarette in his hand. 'These are still as good as money inside. By the time Otto went home, he had a couple of cases of smokes in plus.'

'Plus?' Duran asked, tiring of Erwin and his prison jargon.

'Yeah, plus. Coming to him. The warden, us guards, we didn't want to give him no money for the stuff he painted, so we gave him smokes.'

'So Kline had nobody special.'

'Oh, he had someone special all right,' Erwin conceded. 'Old "Ramblin' Nose" Firpo.'

'Tell me about Firpo.'

'Ken Firpo. A tough old bastard. He's spent more of his life inside than outside. He comes from a family of scumbags. His old man died in prison, they say. He's got a big nose, a real honker, broken more than a couple of times. That's how he got the nickname, like the song, you know, *Ramblin' Rose*. So Firpo's Ramblin' Nose. Though, nobody calls him that to his face. At least none of the prisoners.'

'What was their relationship?'

'They may have been fuckin' each other. I don't know for sure. They were cellmates for most of the time Kline was here, that is after he got out of the SHU. Firpo kind of took Kline under his wing.'

'What kind of man is this Firpo?'

'DFW as far as the cons go. Don't fuck with. Big bastard. Strongarm man, burglar. He did SHU time. Handled it pretty well. He and Kline used to spend their lunch hour in the sandpit. That's where the exercise equipment is, barbells, that kind of crap.'

'Is Firpo still in prison?'

'Yeah, he's got more time to do.'

'Does he keep in contact with Kline? Would he know where Kline is now?'

'I don't know. They're all scum. We treat 'em all like ducks, if you know what I mean.'

Duran wasn't at all sure what Erwin meant and he didn't want to find out. 'What does Firpo do in prison? I mean, does he have a job?'

'Oh, sure. They'll do anything to get a job, 'cause like I said, it can cut down their time. Firpo works in the library. Funny spot for a guy like that, but that's what he wanted. Always reading. Even uses the computer,' Erwin offered, as if there was something wrong with people who did such things.

'I'd like you to question Firpo. See if he's heard from Kline.'

Erwin's features creased in apparent pain. 'Well—'

'Naturally I'll reimburse you for your time. I'm interested in anything else you can find out about Kline. Especially an address. His DMV still shows the prison address.'

Erwin bowed his head down, his voice dropping to a confidential whisper. 'That's kind of confidential stuff, You got to realize—'

'I've got another envelope in my pocket. I need that address.'

'I kind of figured you might.' Erwin pulled a crumpled piece of paper from his shirt pocket, unfolded it and spread it on the table as if it were a treasure map. 'I don't know how good it is, these pukes move around like gypsies, but this is where he's at according to our records and his probation officer. Some half-assed, half-way house. 276 Turk Street, San Francisco.'

Duran grabbed the paper, San Francisco! Kline was in San Francisco.

'Who determines where a prisoner goes? Does his probation officer pick a place, or is it up to the released prisoner?'

'It's up to the puke. Usually they go where they got family or a job possibility.'

Duran tossed the second envelope on to the table. 'I'd like any information you can dig up about Kline. Why he picked San Francisco, who he knows there, any living relatives he may have. If he sold any of his work to someone outside the prison. The names of any visitors he may have seen. And some background on his cellmate, Firpo.'

Erwin stubbed out his cigarette in the puddled remains

of the ice cream, and hefted the envelope in the palm of his hand. 'I'll see what I can do.'

'How old is your camper shell, Mr Erwin?'

'My camper shell? Why? I don't—'

'You get me this information in a hurry, and I'll buy you a new one.'

'You shittin' me?'

'No.'

Erwin shook a cigarette from its pack, scorching it half-way down its length in lighting it. 'I think that Firpo was from Frisco, or some place down that way.'

Chapter 25

'You're an iron man, George,' Jason Lark praised. 'Don't you ever take a day off?'

The butler placed a plate of sausage and scrambled eggs in front of Lark.

'Will you be with us much longer, sir?'

Lark ignored the impertinent question and reached for the pepper shaker. 'Did you see the morning paper? Our hero narrowly missed being killed. What do you think is going on with Duran?'

'I'm sure I wouldn't know, sir.'

'Hold on a minute, George, don't leave. Johnny told me about the will. You're getting *Evening Field*. Perhaps I can help you there. Have you thought about how much you'd want for it?'

'I've no plans to sell.'

'You should think about it, George. I know some people who would be interested. Very interested. I'm sure I could get you top dollar.'

The butler's only response was, 'More coffee?'

Lark grunted a negative reply and watched George's stiff-back departure. He turned his attention to the newspaper article – DOUBLE KILLING IN LOS ANGELES

Well-known attorney Harry Lawson and his personal assistant, Gregory Alante, were assassinated late yester-day afternoon at the home of art appraiser Wendy Lange.

Lange was rendered unconscious prior to the shootings and is recovering at Los Angeles General Hospital.

A police source said that the killings were 'gangland style' – bullets to the back of the head.

The bodies were discovered by insurance investigator Robert Duran. Duran is the husband of the renowned artist, Anona Stack, whose body was stolen from the family crypt in Northern California, and is still missing.

Duran had been scheduled to meet with Harry Lawson and Wendy Lange to discuss the theft of a Vincent Van Gogh painting, Sun and Sky, *taken from the home of movie producer Alan Fritzheim.*

Harry Lawson had a reputation for negotiating deals involving art thefts.

Neither the police, Lange nor Duran would comment as to the possibility that the painting had been in Mr Lawson's possession prior to the shootings. The whereabouts of the Fritzheim Van Gogh is still unknown.

Jason Lark had a good idea as to what happened to the phony Van Gogh. It went up in smoke. Destroyed. He wondered how the thieves who boosted the painting from Fritzheim's house were feeling now. Their stolen painting stolen.

He pushed the sausage on his plate around with a fork. Duran. What did it take to kill the bastard? He survived the fire, and now this. How hard would Duran dig into the Fritzheim theft now? He just wouldn't give up. It wasn't the bastard's nature to give up. Even jiggle-head Danielle Fritzheim recognized that. So he'd continue his investigation, and discover that Lark had been the Fritzheim's decorator.

Duran still had to be dealt with. He sampled the sausage and sighed. He'd been in a near panic over his inability to find the Picasso sketches, but the fact that no one else seemed to be aware of their existence was encouraging. If he could find them, he could just pack the sketches up and run off. The hell with Mario and Duran.

George was the problem. The old fart seemed to be everywhere. He'd caught Lark looking through drawers and closets several times, but Jason had been quick to make up a line about looking for old snap shots of the children. And now the jibe: 'Will you be with us much longer, sir?'

Duran was pushing him to leave. Lisa didn't seem to care if he lived or died. And Johnny. Where the hell was Johnny? He had to get to John before Duran did, to make sure Johnny didn't tell Duran that he'd given his father the alarm code for the studio.

Johnny wasn't at his club last night. Lark had called the Sausalito houseboat, but all he got was Johnny's answering machine.

Where were the fucking Picassos? He had managed to search Lisa's room. No Picassos. Just rock posters and closets bulging with clothes. And they weren't at Anona's studio, either. He had managed to pilfer a dozen of her sketches from the studio. But selling them would be difficult, at least right away. He'd have to wait a while, maybe years to put them on the market at a decent price.

Lark hurriedly finished his meal then moved swiftly toward the stairs leading to the basement. Those boxes stacked near the luggage. He had to check the boxes.

The butler's voice boomed out as Lark was within a foot of the steps.

'May I be of some assistance, sir?'

Lark felt the back of his neck redden. 'I'm going for a swim, George. I think I can manage that myself.'

He decided to wait for Duran at his office on Fisherman's Wharf. He liked the cover of the crowds. The streets were filled with tourists of all sizes and ages – and languages – he recognized the French and Spanish, the guttural

German, but there were others that he'd never heard before. He was even beginning to attract a following of customers. Yesterday he'd made over a hundred and seventy dollars doing caricatures of children for their parents – some of whom communicated with him by pantomiming their requests and holding out handfuls of coins and dollar bills.

He hadn't read the morning paper or watched television, so was unaware of the killings in Los Angeles. All he knew was that he hadn't seen Robert Duran for two mornings in a row. Where was he? It was October twelfth. Two more days. Not much time left. No more time, really. He had to take Duran now. Before the Lark got to him.

He slipped his hand under his armpit, the fingers digging into his flesh. Lark's fire had failed and there was no way he was going to let Lark rob him of Duran. No one was going to take Duran from him.

He'd seen Duran's black secretary show up for work at nine o'clock. Less than half an hour later the policeman from Colma had arrived, the one who had found the rosary beads. He'd gone into Duran's office, only to come out a few minutes later, and walk a half block away, where he was now, leaning against the fender of his car.

Waiting. Waiting like I am, like Lark is, he thought. For Duran. He'd have to move soon. He lost Anona. He wasn't going to lose Duran.

The address Junior Erwin had given Robert Duran for Otto Kline was located in the Tenderloin, one of the raunchiest districts in San Francisco, dominated by adult movie houses and book stores, rough and tumble bars, prostitutes and drug dealers.

Duran slipped his watch from his wrist and jammed it in his pants pocket. The watch would be a magnet with the bizarre street parade: trolling, sallow-faced hookers of both sexes, hunched-over old-timers walking off the effects of a night spent sleeping in a doorway and mean-eyed street dealers who took one look at Duran and made him as a policeman. Which didn't bother Duran at all.

He kept his eyes straight ahead, weaving between the hostile stares, his shoes making light kissing sounds on the sticky, refuse-strewn sidewalks.

Groups of bright, happy-faced Vietnamese youngsters ran and roller-skated through the raunchy crowd as though they didn't have a care in the world.

Number 276 Turk Street was an old hotel, the Excelsior, which some fifty years ago may have worn a coat of respectability. Now the glass windows were grime-coated. In the lobby elderly men and women, bundled up to their chins, sat in fissured sofas, staring blankly at the outside world. An accordion-wire gate secured the front entrance. A stout-bodied black man was leaning against the gate. He wore an Australian-style outback coat that stretched to the tips of his shoes and was swinging an aluminum baseball bat back and forth in a slow rhythm.

'Morning officer,' he said with a wide smile. 'What can I do for you today?'

'Open up,' Duran commanded.

'Who you looking for? Maybe I can help you.'

'Otto Kline.'

The man's forehead knitted. 'Kline? I don't know that name.'

'Are you telling me his parole officer lied to me?'

'I ain't telling you that. Just the name don't mean nothing to me.' He rested the bat against the wall. The metal screeched as he opened the gate. A redhead in a bare-shouldered green dress elbowed past Duran, who noticed the long, curvy legs under black fish-net stockings. The red wig was tilted at an angle and a beard was beginning to show through the rouge.

'Morning Justice,' the redhead said in a high falsetto to the man.

'Mornin' darlin''. Come on officer, I'll see what the book says about your Mr Kline.'

Duran followed the black man over to a check-in counter. The top half was wire mesh and extended to the ceiling. There was a horseshoe-shaped cut-out arch for the passing of keys and money.

Odors of sour food, spilt beer and urine hung in the air. Duran watched as the black man poked a long arm through the cut-out and grabbed a journal.

'Justice. With a name like that you should have joined the force.'

Justice gave a tambourine laugh. 'Yeah. Saved me a whole lot of trouble if I did. Who you with? I ain't seen you before.'

'Homicide,' Duran supplied. 'Which room is Kline's?'

Justice pulled a pair of glasses from his coat pocket. One bow was missing and he had to hold the ramshackle glasses to his eyes to read. 'You know the smoke here, huh?'

Duran had no idea what Justice was talking about. 'Remind me.'

'The first five floors is for the old folks there. The next two are the half-way house. The rest is for guests.' He moistened a finger with his tongue and turned a journal page. 'Oh, yeah. Here's the dude. Otto Kline. He ain't been here but a couple of weeks. Room 704. Now I know the guy. Always drawing people. He's good, too. He did one of me. Made me even better-looking than I really am,' he said with a loud chuckle. 'What's your interest in Kline? He can't be too bad, otherwise you'd have your partner with you.'

'Routine questions,' Duran said, realizing he sounded like a TV policeman.

'I can't give you the key, man,' Justice disclosed. 'You want me to see if he's in?'

Duran nodded his head and Justice picked up the

house phone. He shook his head negatively after a minute. 'He must have gone out early. I was at the door at nine.'

'Is someone on the door around the clock?'

'Nah.' Justice craned his neck and peered through the mesh. 'The manager's supposed to have somebody there, but he don't. I get off at five, then Sheo, the manager's brother, hangs the door 'til he gets tired of it.'

'I thought there were bed checks for the people in the half-way house project.'

Justice laughed and slapped his hand on the check-in counter, leaving a moist imprint. 'Oh, there is. Once a week they change the sheets and make sure the bed's there.'

'I don't want Kline to know I'm interested in him, until I see him myself. You understand?'

'Yes, sir. Officer. I understand perfectly.'

Peggy Jacquard heaved a massive sigh of relief when she saw Duran coming through the office door. She jumped to her feet, ran over and gave him a big toothpasty kiss full on the lips.

'You're going to be the death of me,' she said when she pulled back. 'The fire. Then those murders in Los Angeles. That poor old scoundrel Harry Lawson.' She blotted her eyes with the back of her hand. 'What's going on, Bob?'

'I wish I knew,' Duran admitted. 'I'll tell you what I learned in Pelican Bay as soon as I get a cup of coffee.'

Peggy ran her hand over his chin. 'You could use a shave too. The phone's been going crazy and that policeman from Colma was by a while ago. He said he'd be back.'

'And here I am,' Chief Bill Saylor announced from the door.

Duran said, 'Any news of my wife, Chief?'

'Anona Stack? No. Nothing yet. I read about what happened in Los Angeles. Trouble seems to have a way of following you around. I had a long visit with a San Francisco Fire Department arson investigator, Jack Powers. He's a little upset that you've been avoiding him.'

'I'm not,' Duran said. 'I had to go out of town. What did Powers tell you about the fire?'

'That someone started it deliberately.'

Peggy handed Duran a steaming cup of coffee then offered Saylor a cup.

'No thanks. Do you want to talk here, or down at my office, Mr Duran?'

'That sounds like a threat, Chief.'

'It does,' Saylor granted. 'I want to talk to you. Uninterrupted.'

Duran nodded his head toward his office, then said, 'No calls, Peggy.'

'Why don't we take a walk?' Saylor suggested. 'It's a beautiful day.'

Chapter 26

'Come in, come in, Lisa,' Hugh Stringer said, cupping her elbow and ushering her over to the high-back leather chair directly in front of his desk. She was wearing skin-tight jeans and a masculine charcoal pinstripe suit-jacket – no shirt or blouse – Stringer could just make out the white V of her bra.

'Your secretary said you were busy, Uncle Hugh.'

'Never too busy for you, dear,' Stringer said with a professional smile.

'I'm worried about Johnny. He's disappeared.'

'Disappeared? Surely you mean he's just not been around to the house, Lisa.'

'No. He hasn't been at his club, either. Eric has been trying to get him too, but—'

'Eric?' Stringer broke in.

'Eric Marvin. He's Johnny's manager at the club, and a friend of mine.'

'I'm sure John's just visiting someone, or—'

'No,' Lisa said adamantly. 'He wouldn't stay away from the club.'

Stringer flipped a palm back and forth. 'Johnny isn't involved with drugs again, is he? I thought that the rehabilitation program I arranged for him had straightened him out, Lisa. If John gets caught using drugs again, I'm afraid he'll end up going to jail.'

'I'm really worried, Uncle Hugh.'

'I don't think that—'

'First Mommy died, now Johnny's disappeared. What if something really bad's happened to him? And someone's trying to kill Bob. If something happens to them, then I'd be the only one left. Just me. Maybe I'll be next.'

'I'll check on John if you wish, but I think you're jumping to conclusions, dear. He's probably staying with someone from—'

'No,' she insisted. 'I know Johnny's friends. I've checked with them. He was supposed to meet with Eric two days ago to talk about plans for the club.'

'Do you really think John might be in some danger?'

Lisa closed her eyes for a moment and brushed her finger across her lips. 'I'm frightened. For Johnny. For me. Whoever is out to get Bob, may be after us too!'

Lisa got to her feet and put her purse under her arm. 'The fire. Bob was almost killed in the studio and he just missed being murdered in Los Angeles. You said you'd protect me, Uncle Hugh.'

'And I will,' Stringer assured her. 'Is Jason still at the house?'

'Yes.'

'Maybe he knows John's whereabouts,' Stringer said.

Lisa dug her nails into the back of the leather chair. 'Jason. Everything's gone to shit since he got here.'

'Lisa, surely you don't think your father would—'

'I want him out of the house,' Lisa said adamantly. 'Get him out of Stack House, Uncle Hugh. Now!'

A strong wind was blowing in off the bay, whipping up whitecaps and fluttering the dresses of the tourists waiting to board the ferry for Alcatraz Island.

'Why were you so anxious to get me out of my office?' Duran asked Saylor, feeling he already knew the answer. Saylor would be afraid there was a tape-recorder somewhere in the room.

Saylor ignored the question. 'I've been doing some digging, Mr Duran.'

'I hope you came up with something.'

'Do you? I started digging in New York City.'

Duran pulled to an abrupt stop and stared at the policeman, whose eyes were shielded by his tinted glasses.

'What about New York?'

'Your first wife. She died of an aneurism, like you said, but the coroner's report showed that she had some bruises and scrapes.'

Duran took a breath and counted to ten before responding. 'Teresa took a spill in Central Park while she was jogging.'

'Is that right?'

'That's exactly right,' Duran said angrily.

'I never asked. Were there any other marriages? Between New York and with Anona Stack?'

'No. Are you trying to paint me as some kind of a Blackbeard that goes around killing his wives?'

'I'm not a painter, Mr Duran. I'm a cop.' Saylor brushed off a spot on a pier railing before settling his elbows on it. 'Lieutenant Powers says that the fire at your wife's studio was definitely arson.'

'That's not exactly news. Somebody knocked me out and set the place on fire.'

'Yes, they used an accelerant,' Saylor said, stressing the last word in the sentence.

Duran tried looking beyond the policeman's tinted lenses. 'Is that what's bugging Powers? The terminology I used? Accelerant? I handled a lot of arson investigations when I first got into the insurance racket, Chief. I know the jargon, it's as simple as that.'

The ferry horn tooted four times, then the boat started edging away from the dock. A group of youngsters began waving at Saylor.

He waved back. 'Everyone loves a uniform,' he

observed. 'Almost everyone. What was in the studio worth destroying?'

'Me,' Duran said pointedly.

'Someone knocked you out, you say. If they wanted to kill you, they could have done it right then and there.'

'They wanted to make it look like I set the fire and then got trapped inside the building.'

'*They*? The they that put the beads in your trunk? That pushed you over that cliff? Are they the same ones who killed those people down in Los Angeles? I'm trying to splice the arson in with the disappearance of your wife's body. But I just can't seem to do it.'

'You won't find any answers in New York.'

'Lieutenant Powers has been trying to get in touch with your stepson, John Stack. You told Powers that the boy had a key and the combination to the studio.'

'John's living on a houseboat in Sausalito.'

'Yeah, Powers knows that. And about his nightclub, too. You think the boy would have done this? Knocked you out and set the place on fire?'

'No. Not a chance, Chief.'

'So who else? Was there something besides you in the studio worth destroying?'

Duran closed his eyes and tilted his face to the sun. 'No. And if you're thinking that my wife's body was there, you're wrong. If it was, there would have been trace evidence left, you should know that, Chief.'

'Oh, I do know that. Maybe there had been something in the studio. And it was moved. And whoever put it there wanted to destroy any evidence of its having been there.'

Duran blinked his eyes open. Saylor's head was centered between the massive fog-capped terracotta-red towers of the Golden Gate Bridge. He thought of bringing up Otto Kline's name now, but held back. He wanted to be sure of Kline before he talked to the police.

Saylor straightened up, whisking the sleeves of his

uniform jacket. 'I told Powers I'd talk to you, see if you knew where he could find your stepson.'

'I'll ask his sister,' Duran responded. 'Any other questions, Chief?'

'Yes. Why were your prints all over your wife's coffin?'

'I closed the coffin lid,' Duran said in a measured tone. 'At the funeral parlor. For the last time. Or what should have been the last time. You can check with the funeral director on that.'

'Let's talk about motives. You're an investigator. You know the drill. Jealousy, revenge, profit. You say your wife didn't have any real enemies – so we cross off jealousy. Revenge. For what? So we eliminate revenge. Now we're at profit. There's been no ransom demand, so we scratch a loony-tune being responsible. I talked to your stepson's attorney, Victor Abbott. He showed me the fax – the one claiming you murdered your wife.'

'My attorney received one, too. It was sent from a pay fax-machine in the Hyatt Regency Hotel.'

'So who's the person sending the faxes and making the calls?'

Duran turned toward Jefferson Street. A stream of bicycle-driven rickshaws were showing off the wharf to sore-footed tourists. A man was sketching a youngster in the backseat of one of the rickshaws.

'I don't know, Chief. I don't see anyone profiting from the damn things.'

'Unless someone thinks he or she can prove that you did what the faxes claim. That would knock you out of the will. That would narrow the benefactors down to two.'

'I don't believe either Johnny or Lisa would do that.'

'No? Maybe a friend of theirs?'

'Friend?' Duran scoffed.

'A relative,' Saylor hinted.

'Jason Lark? I've run this around and around for days, Chief. It doesn't stick.'

241

'Then that leads us back to the profit motive. If your wife was killed, and an autopsy would prove it, then that's a damn good motive for someone taking the body.'

Duran reacted testily at Saylor's emphasis on 'someone'. 'Damn it, I'm tired of your accusations. If it'll get you off my back, I'll take a lie detector test. I'll take as many of the damn things as you want, but stop wasting your time on me and find my wife!'

Saylor kicked the remains of a hot dog over the pier and into the oily green water. He wasn't impressed at Duran's offer. The lie detectors were useless, especially to anyone who knew their function – knew how to beat them. 'I'll be in touch, Mr Duran.'

Duran started to walk away, then skidded to an abrupt halt. 'What if I posted a reward? A hundred, two hundred thousand dollars for finding Anona.'

'You'd send a hillside full of nut cases digging up my cemeteries. I wouldn't like that.'

'Then find my wife, Chief,' Duran said firmly.

'I'm trying,' Saylor replied sharply.

'Try harder,' Duran pressed.

There was a hazy, floating circle of light around the boy's head. 'I'm sorry,' he said. 'I can't finish this.' He ripped the sheet from the sketch-pad and handed it to the ten-year-old in the back of the rickshaw.

'Hey,' his father protested. 'I'm not—'

'No charge,' he muttered with annoyance, widening his stride to catch up with Duran. Duran and the cop had been arguing. For a moment he thought that the policeman was going to bring out his handcuffs and arrest Duran.

The pain had been building ever since he'd first seen the cop. Building slowly, the way it always did before a massive attack. Throbbing, pulsating, as if his brain were being squeezed by an unseen hand. He had to lie down. Somewhere dark and quiet.

★   ★   ★

There was a look of relief on Peggy's face when Duran returned to the office.

'I thought I was going to have to call Rachel and get her to bail you out.'

'It may come to that,' Duran admitted. 'Peg, the murders at Wendy Lange's house, Harry Lawson and his bodyguard, and the theft of the Van Gogh. I want to be certain that the leak didn't come out of this office.'

'How could it?'

'The day you had lunch with Jason Lark. He walked you back here. Did he have time to look at anything? Files? Reports on your desk?'

Peggy shook her head vehemently and a strand of hair fell a twist of wire across her cheek. 'Lark was here for just a minute. He didn't get a look at anything,' she said indignantly. 'He was on his way out the door when I played the answering machine tape of that crazy phone call. He heard the call, but he didn't see anything.'

'Easy, Peg. I had to ask. They were waiting for me at Wendy Lange's house.' He gave her a brief synopsis of his conversation with Lange and the Los Angeles policemen. 'They were going to "do" me. No one else. Take the Van Gogh and kill me.'

'It must have been someone in Lawson's circle,' Peggy insisted.

'Then why kill Lawson? Harry was too sharp to let something like that slip out. He went to Wendy's with the painting. He was living up to his end of the bargain. The bodyguard may be the thing that threw the killers into a panic. Maybe he tried to be a hero, I don't know, but they knew about the meeting, Peg. Wendy heard them. They were coming for *me*.'

'They must have been afraid you'd recognize them, Bob. Maybe it was someone we've dealt with in the past.'

'No. We've never dealt with professional hit men, and

that's what this crew were. Pros. Someone hired them to get the Van Gogh and kill me. Why? They had the Van Gogh. It's something that I know, or that I'm likely to find out. The fire here in San Francisco. That was a totally different thing. I surprised someone in the studio. No one knew I was going to the studio that night, I . . .'

Peggy leaned over to catch Duran's eye. 'What is it?'

'Laura Ralston. When I had dinner with her, she mentioned the studio and suggested that I pick up Anona's paintings and sketches.'

'Did she know just when you were going?'

'No. I dropped her off at her place, then went home before driving to the studio. She couldn't have known when I'd go there. But the fire. That was a spur of the moment thing, someone acting on an unexpected opportunity. The shooting in Los Angeles was planned. Entirely different.' He rubbed a hand through his hair, then his face. 'An entirely different MO. Different people. Why? What the hell could the Los Angeles attack have to do with Anona?'

Peggy raised her arms to the ceiling in frustration. 'I don't understand what's happening!'

'Join the club. Saylor is confused, too. Except he still thinks I took Anona's body. We've got a lot of work to do. I'm waiting for some information to come from a guy in Pelican Bay, and—'

'You mean the guard, Junior Erwin?'

'Right. He's called already?'

Peggy grinned and tapped the top of her desk. 'He faxed these a few minutes ago.'

Duran picked up the papers which, except for one, bore the letterhead for Pelican Bay State Prison. The complete dossiers on both Otto Kline and Kenneth J. Firpo. The other document was a copy of a magazine ad for a pickup truck camper shell.

Chapter 27

The prison files were fascinating to Duran. Otto Kline's life history had been condensed into three pages. Born in Iowa, then schooling in New Mexico, Oregon and Southern California. A short stint in the army followed by marriage. No children. Work as a painter – a house painter for a short time – then a range of jobs from hamburger flipper to bicycle messenger to waiter.

Duran had found that many artists struggled much the way actors do – taking part-time jobs, making just enough money to keep going, waiting for a break. And, like actors, there was just too deep a well of artistic talent out there for most of them to scratch out a living.

There was a reference by the prison psychiatrist about Kline's wife's background: Arlene Dore – born in Paris, France. Another artist.

Duran tried to picture the two of them in his mind. Not old, but no longer young – the sparks, the passions diminished – the realization that they'd probably never really make it big – all those plans, those hopes, taken away day by day until they were reduced to forging paintings for a Swiss con man.

Royce Breamer was probably paying them peanuts, while he himself lived a jet-setter's life.

There was nothing in the report about Arlene Kline's suicide, but Barbara Linker, her cellmate, had described Arlene as a 'push' – frightened to death most of the time, an easy mark for the hardcases. Duran remembered his few months in jail. If you let them push you around, you soon found yourself on your knees. Literally. Barbara Linker had made it clear that's exactly what she and her friends had done to Arlene Kline.

The medical profile on Otto Kline showed that right after his wife's suicide, he'd spent four weeks in the Southern California prison hospital for his assault on the guard. Duran had no doubt that Kline had been severely punished after the assault. Following his transfer to Pelican Bay, there were thirty-six scribbled entries, all listing the same complaint – migraine headaches.

There was nothing in Otto Kline's past history to link him to San Francisco. No relatives or past employment.

Kenneth Firpo was another story. He was born in Montara, a sparse coast-side community some twenty miles south of San Francisco.

Firpo's criminal history was a steady input of felonies: burglary, robbery, kidnap, rape. As the prison guard Junior Erwin had told him, Firpo was following in a family tradition. The report indicated that Firpo's father had died in prison. Alcatraz. And that his grandfather had been killed while running away from the police.

Alcatraz. Duran swiveled his office chair around and looked directly at the former prison. Once known as the toughest prison in the world. Now that honor belonged to Pelican Bay.

Otto Kline, whose wife killed herself in her cell, ended up with a lifer whose father died in prison. They must have had some bizarre discussions in their cell. What did Kline learn from Firpo?

The prison file cleared up another thing that had been bothering Duran – Arlene Kline's tombstone. Otto Kline had paid for it with a money order. Where had the money come from? A one-sheet 'personal assets form' for Kline listed a Seiko watch, leather wallet, dark blue suit, white shirt and tie, and passbook savings with a Los Angeles branch of the Bank of America. Kline had eleven thousand four hundred and forty-two cents in the account when he was released from prison.

It explained the tombstone. What else would Kline do with the money? Transportation. Duran kicked himself for not thinking of it earlier. A car. He'd rent or buy a car.

He put the computer to work, getting into the proper database. The DMV files were updated weekly. He clicked in his account number, his password, Kline's name and x'd the square alongside – Vehicle Registration.

Within seconds the information flicked across the screen. Kline had purchased a 1976 International Truck from Honest Ed's Used Vehicles on South Van Ness two weeks ago. Kline's address was listed as a postal box in Crescent City.

The phone rang and Peggy called out from her desk: 'It's Hugh Stringer.' Duran picked up the receiver and said hello.

'Robert, remember me?' Stringer chided. 'I'm your attorney. At least I was, the last time we spoke.'

'I apologize for not contacting you sooner, Hugh. But things have been pretty hectic.'

'Yes. I read the papers and watch TV, however, it would be nice to get the story from my client.'

'You've made your point,' Duran conceded. 'This is what happened.'

Stringer listened patiently, interrupting occasionally with a technical question.

'Why didn't you tell Chief Saylor about this Otto Kline creature?' Stringer asked when Duran had finished his narration.

'I want to be sure about him, Hugh. I'm going to his place on Turk Street tonight.'

'I hardly think that's wise. If he's as dangerous as you say, then the police should be involved.'

'They will be. When I'm sure about Kline. One thing that Chief Saylor and I agree on – the theft of Anona's body can't have anything to do with that trap that was set for me in Los Angeles, where Harry Lawson and his bodyguard were killed.'

'Lawson. I hate to speak ill of a fellow barrister, but Harry Lawson had a dubious reputation. A well-earned dubious reputation.'

'But the plan was to kill me, not him,' Duran reminded.

Stringer made a coughing noise, then said, 'Some good news, Robert. Lisa has agreed to my representing her in the estate dispute. That certainly gives us some leverage against John's attorney. Lisa is quite worried about John. She hasn't seen him in a couple of days and says that his friends haven't either.'

Duran leaned forward, his chair creaking in protest. 'I told Lisa it would be a good idea for her to have a bodyguard. I was never able to get in touch with John. I'm worried that whoever it is who's trying to kill me, may go after the kids.'

'More reason than ever to turn this over to the police,' Stringer insisted. 'Lisa was also quite concerned about her father. She wants Jason out of Stack House.'

'She's not the only one. I've done some checking on Lark. He's in heavy financial trouble. Has Lark been pestering Lisa for money?'

'She didn't say. Her comment was that, "things have turned to shit since he arrived." '

Duran took a few seconds to respond. 'That's hard to argue with. I'm going home in a bit. If Lark's there, I'll talk to him.'

'Yes. Do that, Robert. And for God's sake, take care. And tell the police about Kline. You can't survive many more of these attacks.'

He clamped his eyes shut and rolled into a fetal position.

After fifteen minutes he knew it wasn't going to work. The noise – constant voices from the hallways, shouts, a radio booming out rap music angered and enraged him.

At least his cell had been quiet. Even the SHU was dark and quiet when the attacks came.

Someone began pounding on his door. He shouted out an obscenity, but the pounding continued.

'Hey, Otto man. It's me. Justice. Open the fuck up.'

'Go away,' he groaned.

'It's important, man. Some cop was here looking for you.'

He dragged his legs across the mattress, struggled to his feet and shuffled over to the door.

'Man, you look like shit,' Justice said when the door was opened. 'You been doin' some bad acid or something?'

'Headaches. What's this about a cop?'

Justice slipped into the room, grinning like a cat. 'The dude said he was a cop, but he didn't act like one. The more I talked to him, the less I think he is a cop, you know? I tell him you're not in your room and he believes me. Doesn't shove my ass in the elevator and make me prove it. And he's all alone. Cops don't come in here alone unless they're looking to steal a piece from one of the whores. He wanted you, Otto. Said it was "routine".'

'What was his name?'

'What you been up to, Otto?' He picked up the sketch-pad. 'Drawin' dirty pictures or something?'

'What was his name?' Kline repeated.

Justice tilted the pad to the light coming from the street. 'I like this one. Cute little kid.'

He jammed his hand in his pocket and pulled out a roll of cash – his take from the day's sketching.

Justice plucked at the money with two fork-like fingers.

'He didn't give me a name. Dark hair, tan, blue eyes. Big scar over one of those eyes, like maybe he got hit with somethin'.' Justice waggled the aluminum baseball bat. 'Somethin' like this, maybe.'

Otto Kline felt his throat constrict. 'What time was this?'

Justice carried the roll of bills to the window and began uncurling them. 'Oh, 'bout ten this morning.'

'I need some help, Justice.'

'Yeah, I bet you do, Otto. I bet you sure as shit do.'

The chili-pepper-red sign spelled out *Stack's* in a lazy script over the burnished copper doors.

Jason Lark trudged down the steps. He was worried about John. He'd been to his houseboat in Sausalito. It was locked. John's neighbor, a middle-aged sunburned drunk, said he hadn't seen Johnny in a couple of days, yet John's Porsche was parked in its stall.

He flinched at the volume of the music once he was inside the club. Three men, all in their early twenties, each wearing ragged jeans and murky gray T-shirts, were grouped on a tiny, elevated stage. Their hairstyles were identical; long-curled Kenny G lookalikes.

Two of them raked at electric guitars, their jolting body movements indicating to Lark that there had to be a short in the wiring leading to the huge amplifiers bracketing the stage.

The third man held a cordless microphone to the tip of his chin. He stood mannequin still, eyes closed, head tilted back shouting something Lark couldn't decipher.

The cavernous room had a rough-surfaced ceiling showing the marks left by the wooden framework. The walls were all brick, with concrete oozing out between the bricks. Black plastic tables and chairs were stockpiled along the walls. Lark had tried keeping an anguished look from his face when his son told him how much he had paid a decorator to design the club.

Eric Marvin sat astride one of the chairs at the back of

the room, his face wreathed in cigarette smoke.

'Have you heard from John?' Lark called out over the music.

Marvin slid his eyes over Lark, then back to the stage. 'Who let you in?'

'I asked if you heard from John?'

Marvin shook his head slowly from side to side. 'His sister's worried about him.'

'So am I.'

'Johnny's probably holed up somewhere with some nectarines.'

Lark hated to appear unknowledgable, but he had no idea what Marvin was talking about.

'Nectarines?'

Marvin's head was jerking back and forth with the music. 'Yeah, half a peach, half a plum.' He leered into Lark's confused eyes. 'Half a boy, half a girl. Maybe a couple of each.' He pointed his cigarette at the stage. 'What do you think of them? They want a thousand a gig.'

'I think they should be eliminated as soon as possible, so they don't start breeding. Is Lisa around?'

'No. She'll be in later.' Marvin stood and waved his arms like an umpire calling a base runner safe. The screeching music veered to a halt.

'Okay guys, you're in,' Marvin advised them. 'Be ready to kick on at ten o'clock.' He turned his attention back to Jason Lark. 'Lisa doesn't want you around. She told me that, so you better be gone before she gets back.' He sauntered toward the stage, then stopped, as if he'd forgotten something. 'You don't have much luck with your kids, do you Jason?'

Chapter 28

The Excelsior Hotel's sign of faded vertical orange lettering had several blank spots so that it flashed X ELS R
off-and-on every few seconds. The darkness muted the
graffiti and the neighboring storefronts wore a coat of
neon make-up.

The chill wind hadn't influenced the dress code: the
hookers still wore thigh-high mini-skirts, hotpants and
thin, tight blouses and tank-tops.

Robert Duran had dressed down for this visit. Cords,
turtleneck and a suede casual jacket – his gold watch
again safely tucked away in his pants pocket.

A smell of danger wafted through the exhaust-tinged
air. A rubied string of tail-lights cruised the street at
loitering speed, the drivers pulling over to the curb,
rolling down their windows to conduct their transactions.

Young men with soft smiles and hard eyes were positioned at every other doorway, cliques of two or three of
them monitored each corner. Many of them, like Justice,
had aluminum baseball bats dangling from their hands.
There was a feeling that at any moment someone would
say the wrong thing to the wrong person, or a shoulder
would come into innocent contact with the wrong shoulder, and violence would erupt.

Justice wasn't working the door to the Excelsior Hotel.
A dark-skinned man in baggy pants and a blue hooded
sweatshirt was holding the fort.

Duran ignored a half-dozen or more 'Hi, how about a date?' queries from the collection of prostitutes on patrol, deciding to turn the corner before picking out a prospect.

He found a girl slouched against a parking meter on Jones Street. She had tightly spiraled hay-colored hair. Her skin was white and putty-soft. Her black leather pants had silver dollar-sized peephole grommets running up the outside of both legs. Her nipples looked ready to drill free from the glittery midriff-bearing blouse. She was tottering on her platform shoes, shoulders hunched up, hands clasped at each elbow.

Her spiel was the familiar, 'Hi, want a date?'

'Maybe. Do you know the place around the corner? The Excelsior Hotel?'

'Are you a cop?'

'No.'

'My name's Candy. Sure, I know it, honey. But I got a better place.'

'I want to go there.'

She shrugged her thin shoulders. 'You'll have to pay extra for the room.'

'That's not a problem.'

She tilted her head to one side and surveyed Duran. 'Okay, I'll have to ask Tyrone.'

'Ask him.'

'It's a hundred dollars. Twenty-five for the room. Up front.'

'I'll pay you when we're in the elevator,' Duran said firmly.

She hugged her arms to her chest and shivered. 'Okay. Let me check.'

Duran watched her skip across the street. The window of a bright red Corvette hissed down an inch or two. Candy leaned on the car's roof for a moment, then came running back to Duran.

'The party's on,' she announced.

Candy kept up a nervous line of patter as they walked together back to Turk Street: What's your name? Where you from? What do you like? Do you want me to bring a friend?

Duran saw her flash a signal to the man in the hooded sweatshirt and baggy pants – first two fingers, then five.

He nodded his head and smiled lazily at Duran. 'Have fun children,' he advised, then pulled the metal gate open.

Candy hurried to the check-in counter and quickly passed a bill to a man who looked as if he could be the brother of the night-time doorman.

He slid a key through the cut-out, not bothering to look at Duran.

As soon as the elevator doors clanged shut, Candy held her hand out. 'You said you'd pay when we were inside.'

'Indeed I did. What's the room number?'

She turned the key over and rubbed a bony finger over the engraved numbers: '816.'

Duran peeled seven twenty-dollar bills from his money clip, then pushed the buttons for floors seven and eight. 'Give me the key. You go on up and wait for me, I'll be right up.'

Candy started to protest until she counted the money. 'Sure, honey, sure,' she said eagerly.

The elevator walls were battle-scarred with initials and obscenities. Even Candy's overpowering dosage of perfume couldn't disguise the stench coming from the soggy carpet underfoot. It came to a jarring halt at the seventh floor. 'See you in a few minutes,' Duran said exiting the elevator.

Candy smiled and waved at him. A goodbye wave. She couldn't believe her luck. Or how stupid the guy was.

Duran heard the elevator grind up a floor, stop, then begin its descent immediately. Candy hurrying back to Tyrone.

He made his way to room 704. The door was warped.

The numbers stenciled in wavy, fading black ink. He leaned his ear against the door for a moment, then rapped it lightly with his knuckles.

'Otto,' he said in a husky whisper. 'Otto.'

Duran had thought of bringing a gun. There were still several of Conrad Stack's hunting rifles and shotguns in Stack House. He hadn't fired a weapon since leaving the army. He selected an elegantly hand-engraved Bertuzzi double-barrelled shotgun with exposed hammers. There was something about the exposed hammers that seemed intimidating. The shotgun was now tucked away under a blanket alongside the passenger seat in the Jaguar. He couldn't think of a way to conceal the weapon for his visit to the hotel, so he'd settled for a foot long pry bar he had found in the garage. He slid the bar from his belt and knocked louder. 'Otto.'

He tried the door handle, his mind flashing back to Wendy Lange's house. It was locked. He tried the key Candy had picked up in the lobby. It slid easily into the lock, but wouldn't turn the cylinders.

Over the years, Duran had investigated so many burglaries and museum thefts that he'd become adept as most burglars at forced entries. Slipping locks with credit cards had become popular in movies and TV, but seldom worked in actual situations, so Duran went about his task using the same techniques professionals did – breaking the connection between the door and the frame. He edged the end of the pry bar into the slim opening alongside the lock then gave a quick tug. The door resisted momentarily, then opened with a slap.

He charged into the room, the pry bar cocked at shoulder height. Light imprinted the floor with a shadowy X from the hotel sign. There was a single bed, the blankets tangled and cascading over the floor. A lone pine dresser, on top of which sat an electrical stove burner.

Duran closed the door behind him and leaned against

it, watching the neon X flicker through tattered window curtains. He fingered the wall for the light switch. A pair of naked electric bulbs spotted with fly droppings threw an ugly glare from the ceiling fixture.

The closet door was ajar, showing nothing but empty wire hangers and dustballs. Duran searched the bureau, reverting to a burglar's technique of starting at the bottom and working towards the top, thus saving the time of closing one drawer before starting on the next. All empty. Either Kline had skipped, or Justice had given him the wrong information.

He tore the blankets from the bed, then raised the mattress from its spring. A piece of paper had fallen between the mattress and the wall. Duran picked it up eagerly. A caricature of a young boy's innocently smiling face. In the background was a watchtower that Duran recognized immediately. The Ghiradelli tower at the Cannery on Fisherman's Wharf. Less than a block from his office.

Duran rolled the paper in a slim cylinder and slipped it into his pocket while glancing around the room. Something was missing. A telephone. Justice had told him he'd called Kline's room from the hotel lobby.

The hotel manager's basset-eyes looked at Duran with indifference when he slid the room key through the check-in cut-out.

'Have you seen Justice?' Duran asked.

'Who?'

'Your daytime doorman.'

'You have a problem with Justice?'

Duran crinkled a pair of twenty-dollar bills between his fingers. 'I owe him some money.'

'Ah, I see. I would be happy to deliver it to him on your behalf.'

Duran pushed his hand into the cut-out. He tugged

back when the manager's hand clamped on the bills.
'How do I know you'll pass this along to Justice?'

'I am an honest man, sir.'

'Then maybe you can clear something up for me. Otto
Kline, in room 704. He's not in. The door was unlocked.
It looks like Kline moved out.'

'I have no record of that, sir.'

'Why don't you check your log just to make sure.'

He was shaking his head negatively when Duran
opened his fingers and the money fluttered to the counter.
The manager swiftly pocketed the two bills then reached
for a hotel journal. He licked his fingers as he turned the
pages. 'No. I have no record of that.'

Duran snatched the journal out of his hand and looked
at the entry. Room 704. Otto Kline. Checked in three
weeks ago. He began flipping through the pages. 'What's
Justice's room number?'

'Oh, he does not reside here, sir.'

'Where can I find him?'

'On duty tomorrow morning, God willing.'

Duran's shoulders slumped in defeat. He couldn'
envision many instances where God exerted much influ
ence in the Excelsior Hotel. Justice must have tipped of
Kline. Where would Kline go now? What would he do?

From the sketch in Kline's room, Duran knew Klin
had been down by the office. Duran remembered hi
conversation with Chief Saylor yesterday. A man wa
sketching a youngster in a rickshaw. Could it have bee
Kline? Kline was watching him – stalking him.

Justice clicked the highbeams on and shifted the va
down to first gear. 'Shit, Otto, how'd you ever find thi
place? This is the fuckin' boondocks.'

'Keep going,' Kline moaned from the passenger sea
peering at the road from the barest of slits in his eyelid
The pain was intense and the nausea rolled through hi

stomach every time the van went over a bump. 'Up the hill, then left when you reach an opening.'

'We'll be lucky if we make it up this hill,' Justice predicted. The road was narrow, bordered by expanses of towering trees. It was like driving through a tunnel. He mentally kicked himself for agreeing to drive the goofy bastard. Drive him down to this hell-hole, then he'd have to drive himself back to the city.

The plan was for him to come back in the morning. Kline had agreed to pay him a hundred and fifty dollars cash for each trip. Which meant he had at least that much money in his pants or his one crumby suitcase.

The van bellied into a ditch, the undercarriage making a loud, scraping sound.

'Man, we better get to your spot soon. I'm gettin' tired of this shit.'

'Just a little further,' Kline promised, his voice a painful croak.

'What you got? Some kind of withdrawals? Maybe I can fix you up with something.'

'No. It's a migraine. I just need someplace dark and quiet.'

The ground leveled out and Justice pulled to a stop. Low-flying clouds towed their shadows over a bare stretch of weeds and dirt.

'Where's the house, man? I don't see a house.'

'Over there. To the left.'

Justice shoved the gear shift into park. The dashboard lights barely showed the flash of steel from the knife that magically appeared in his hand. 'Otto. I got to tell you, you need some help man. Let me help you.'

He was leaning toward Kline's cowering figure when he heard the unmistakable double click of a gun hammer being cocked.

'You must think I'm awfully stupid,' Kline whispered, narrowing his eyes, trying to keep the fun-house mirror image of Justice from moving too fast, too far.

'What's you talking about, man, I—'

Justice made a quick, powerful move with the knife, the blade slashing toward Kline's left arm.

Kline pulled both triggers of the Derringer. The bullets entered Justice's throat inches from each other.

Justice's head jerked back, then the knife slipped from his hand and fell harmlessly to the floorboard.

Kline reached over, turned off the van's lights and the ignition, then rolled out the door, landing in a heap on the soft weather-slicked weeds. He crawled slowly on his hands and knees towards his destination. The van and Justice's body could wait for the morning. When he reached the truck he used the back bumper for leverage, climbed to his feet, and lurched inside, his knees coming into contact with the iron-bunk ribbing. He collapsed on to the bare mattress and hugged his knees to his chest. The SHU. He never thought he'd ever be happy to see the SHU again.

Chapter 29

The crowd was three- and four-abreast and curved from the stairway out to the parking lot. The mix was almost fifty:fifty male to female, the age group from late teens to mid-twenties.

Robert Duran felt out of place as he skirted the line. A broad-bodied Samoan dressed in a lavender up-collared polo shirt and black tuxedo jacket was working the door.

He eyed Duran's progress and stuck his chin out as Duran approached him. 'You got business, brother?'

'I'm Johnny Stack's stepfather. Is he in?'

'I ain't seen him,' the bouncer said. 'You say you're the stepfather?'

'Right. Bob Duran.'

'Well, he better show up soon. He owes me a week's pay.'

'Is Lisa here?'

'The sister? Yeah. She's here.'

Duran started down the stairs. There was a chorus of boos and catcalls from the crowd. The bouncer raised his arms like a priest granting benediction. 'Peace, brothers and sisters. Keep the peace. Your time will come.'

The noise hit Duran first – a combination of decibel screaming music and the plangent babble of the crowd. He could understand the line outside now. There hardly seemed space for one more body. He elbowed his way

261

through a sea of denim, leather and flesh, swiveling his head, hoping to spot Lisa.

The elevated bar took up an entire side of one wall. He'd stepped on several sets of toes, some in shoes, some bare, by the time he reached the bar.

The musty scent of marijuana mingled with the odors of beer and alcohol. He waved a ten-dollar bill at a sullen-faced bartender and ordered a Scotch on the rocks. His drink arrived five minutes later and the bartender collected the money, not bothering to return with his change.

A young woman with spiked tomato-red hair and dark stains under her eyes nudged Duran with her elbow. Duran could see her lips moving, but couldn't hear what she was saying. He leaned down and soon found her teeth fastened on his ear lobe. 'Want some blow?' she asked, when she opened her mouth again.

'No, thanks,' Duran said, thinking that if Johnny didn't hire better security people, the cops would be closing him down. He pushed his way to the end of the bar and stood on the tips of his toes scanning the dance floor. The music seemed to get louder with every tick of the clock. Strobe lights flashed in random sequences, bathing the dancers in red and blue puddles of color.

He finally spotted Lisa, her head rocking back and forth, her knees bent slightly forward, her hips gyrating in an attempt to keep up with the staccato bursts of the music. She was wearing a black spider-web-knit dress. Thick silver bracelets encircled her wrists. Her dancing partner was at her back, pelvis thrust against Lisa's buttocks, hands holding on to her bare shoulders.

Lisa twisted her head, her hair swishing in front of her face, then swishing back, as she licked at one of her partner's hands.

They moved in a slow half-circle and Duran was able to catch a look at her partner. Eric Marvin, his narrow face sweat-sheened, his hair lacquered into place.

The music ended in a discordant, measureless frenzy of high-amp clamor. There was a brief moment of silence, then the crowd erupted in foot-stomping applause and shouting.

Duran held his space against the tide surging toward the bar. Lisa and Marvin melted into the throng. He moved in the general direction of where he'd last seen them, finally spotting the pair in a brass-buttoned red leather booth near the bandstand.

Their heads were close together, Marvin's mouth on Lisa's neck.

Duran rapped his knuckles on the formica-topped table. 'Lisa, I need to talk to John.'

Lisa pulled her head away and looked up, her eyes glassy. 'Hey, Bob. What are you doing? Slumming?'

Eric Marvin's eyes weren't glassy. They stared daggers at Duran. 'We're busy,' he snarled. 'Go away.'

Duran ignored him. 'I'm worried about John, Lisa. And you, too.'

Marvin got to his feet and stood with his hands on his hips. He was wearing designer jeans and a black and red plaid lumberjack-style shirt. 'Why don't you get the fuck out of here. You're not wanted.'

'I've got something to say to Lisa. And to you, too, Eric. Sit down.'

Marvin opened his mouth to say something, then pushed Duran out of the way and swaggered off toward the bar.

'Somehow I get the feeling he doesn't like me,' Duran said, sliding next to Lisa.

She rested her elbow on the table and propped her chin in the palm of her hand. Duran could see she was as high as a kite. 'He thinks you stole Mommy's body, Bob. You didn't do that, did you?'

'Of course not.' Duran extracted the sketch he'd found

in the Excelsior Hotel room. 'Have you seen anyone around doing sketches, like this one?'

Lisa tilted her head as she examined the drawing. 'Who's this? Is this one of the sketches Jason is talking about?'

'Jason? He was asking you about sketches? Is he here?'

'Everybody's been here. Everyone but Johnny.' Lisa's flushed cheeks dimpled. 'His attorney was here a few minutes ago. Did you talk to him?'

'You mean Victor Abbott?'

A tress of hair dropped down in front of Lisa's face and she blew it away. 'He sure looked funny. Wearing a suit in here.' Her bracelets chimed together as she covered her mouth and gave a soft burp. 'No one wears a suit in here. You look nice, Bob. I like that suede jacket. You always look nice.'

'Lisa. The drawing. I think the man who drew it may be the man who took your mother's body from the cemetery. Does the name Otto Kline mean anything to you?'

'No. Why would he take Mommy?'

'I'm not sure yet. What did Victor Abbott want?'

Lisa reached out and touched Duran's glass. 'May I, stepdaddy dearest?'

Duran opened his hand in approval and Lisa grabbed the glass, draining it until the ice clicked against her teeth.

'What did Abbott want?' Duran repeated.

'He wants Johnny. Just like all of us.' Lisa put the glass down and buried her hands in her hair. 'I don't know where he is. I don't know where Mommy is.' She parted her hair and peered at Duran through her fingers. 'Where is she, Bob? Where's Mommy?'

'Look at the drawing again, Lisa. Think. Did you ever see anyone around you or Eric sketching? Where have you—'

Duran felt someone grab his shoulder. He looked up and saw the face of the bouncer from the street.

'Hey, brotha. Eric says you're leaving.'

Marvin was standing alongside the bouncer, a triumphant look on his face.

'In a few minutes. After I've talked to Lisa.' Duran turned back to Lisa who was having trouble keeping her eyes open.

The bouncer's hand increased its pressure, causing Duran to wince. 'Now, brotha.'

'All right, all right,' Duran said between clenched teeth, climbing slowly to his feet.

Maybe it was the way Eric Marvin was glaring at him, his lips spread apart as if he was ready to spit, or maybe it was the over-confident look on the bouncer's face, who was twenty years younger, and had him out-weighted by over a hundred pounds, but when Duran tried pushing the Samoan's arm away, only to find the huge fingers digging deeper into his flesh, he couldn't help himself. He raked his heel down the man's shin, and when his shoulder freed from the vice-like grip, brought his knee up to the bouncer's groin, and followed it with a quick-left hook to the head. Pain shot through Duran's bandaged hand.

The Samoan bent over at the waist and groaned in agony and astonishment. He straightened up and snarled, coming at Duran with both hands open, going for his head, planning to squash it like a coconut.

Duran ducked inside and threw two quick left-right combinations to the man's well padded belly, feeling his hands sink in to the wrist, and followed it with an uppercut to the man's massive neck.

He stepped back ready to fire again, but the Samoan's mottled face told him the fight was over. He sank slowly to his knees, gasping as he tried to catch his breath.

A group of customers had circled the table. A tall man in a business suit bumped into Duran.

He pointed a finger at the man on the ground. 'I think

I'll give him my card,' Victor Abbott announced in a formal voice. 'He may want to consult with an attorney.'

The Bentley was missing from its parking spot. Jason Lark slipped the rental car in an open slot and hurried into the house. He cruised through the vacant kitchen and the front room. There was no sign of George. Finally, the old bastard had left the house.

Lark returned to the kitchen and selected an eight-inch carving knife then made his way to the basement. He began going through the unmarked boxes, slitting the neatly taped creases, finding mostly household items such as cookware and linens until he cut open the last box. It was crammed with papers: scribbled papers. He recognized the stick figures and smiling-faced suns, childish distorted versions of cartoon characters, authored by John and Lisa, remembering how Anona had encouraged their interest in art.

He sank back on his haunches and scraped the tip of the knife along the cement. The Picassos. He had a sudden vision of Lisa and Johnny filling in the master's work with crayons.

Lark climbed quickly to his feet. He'd searched through most of the house. What was left? The west wing – the staff's residences. At one time there had been a full-time cook and several young maids and butling apprentices working under George. Now there were only temporaries. Except for dear old George.

He silently cursed, fearing that some goddamn Mexican maid or swishy housekeeper had somehow made off with the Picassos.

Lark made his way up the stairs. George. George had always supervised the packing of suitcases in the old days. He also took care of the returning luggage, sending the soiled clothing to the cleaners or the laundry.

He dropped the knife in the kitchen sink and peered

out the window overlooking the garage area. The Bentley hadn't returned. He took the steps two at a time to the third floor, past his 'guest' room and into the west wing.

George occupied the corner suite. Lark knocked on the door and called out George's name. He tried the knob. Locked.

He moved down the hallway to the adjoining room. It was vacant, stripped bare of rugs, not a stick of furniture. He went to the window, opened it and leaned out, looking down to the shadowy dark green mass of the garden. A narrow stone ledge skirted the house's beaded-brick exterior wall.

Lark took a deep breath, then carefully climbed on to the ledge, his mind picturing himself as a suave jewel thief about to steal the crown jewels. Once he was on the ledge and inching his way forward, that image vanished, replaced by one of him falling to the tangled hedges some thirty feet below. He kept his eyes tracked on the slowly approaching window to George's room, his head to the wall, the bricks rubbing at his ear, his fingers moving jerkily for a grasp on the next brick lining.

The journey took no more than two minutes, but to Lark it felt like an hour. Finally he was there. The heavy brocade drapes were tied back. He pushed the sash up far enough to allow him entry and slipped through, falling to the carpet with a grateful thump.

The suite's decor resembled an English gentleman's club, burgundy leather chairs, burgundy carpeting and a paisley couch in front of a limestone fireplace.

Lark's eyes quickly inventoried the walls – prints, inferior copies of Toulouse Lautrec's music-halls and streets of Paris.

Lark moved swiftly into the bedroom – briefly noticing the four-poster canopied bed, his eyes drawn as if by a magnet to the framed drawing hanging over the nightstand, the paper now saffron-colored from age – a small residential building on a cobblestone street. Lark gazed lovingly at the address printed along the bottom of the work – 11 boulevard de Liche. An address known by anyone who'd studied modern art. Picasso's studio in Paris!

Lark's hands were trembling when he carefully slipped the frame from the wall. George. Stuffy, stodgy, pompous, boring old George. He had the Picassos!

Chapter 30

Junior Erwin ran the tip of his baton across the cell bars. 'Hey, Firpo. Are you missing your old buddy, Otto Kline?'

The prisoner was stretched out in his bunk, hands behind his head, a passive expression plastered on his face as he responded to the big-bellied guard. 'Not much.'

'I got a paintin' job for him. Know how I can reach him?'

Firpo swung his legs on to the floor and stood up. What was Erwin fishing around after Otto for? 'He didn't tell me what his plans were.'

Erwin's baton thunked out a ribbon of notes against the bars. 'That's too bad. How you like bein' alone? We was talking about you. We think it's about time to get you another roomie. Some of the guards was sayin' they'd like to see Jumbo move in with you. What do you think of that?'

Firpo shrugged his heavily muscled shoulders. Jumbo Garcia was the leader of the prison Latino community, a scar-faced killer who hated white men. 'It might be a tight fit.'

'More ways than one, huh?' Erwin winked. 'You two old bulls would probably kill each other. Then again, I hear there's a pancake getting out of the SHU next week. Cute little feller, just twenty-four. The kind you like to take under your wing.'

Firpo gauged the threat. 'What kind of job have you got lined up for Otto?'

'Oh, it's a good one. He'd make some big money, and be doin' me a favor.' Erwin slipped his baton into its belt holder. 'And maybe you too, Kenny. I hear this pancake is going to need a lot of nursing.'

Firpo laced his fingers through the bars. 'Kline told me something about going down to San Francisco.'

'I know about the half-way house. I just thought you might have some other ideas – like where he was goin' to look for a job, or some friends of his he might visit.'

Firpo squeezed his fingers around the bars and stared into Erwin's pig-like eyes, then relaxed his grip. Otto was gone. And he had four more years to serve. He'd never make it if they shoved Garcia in his cell. They'd end up at each other – and it didn't matter who'd win. That was the beauty of the system as far as the guards were concerned. They had everyone by the balls. A fight would automatically extend your sentence and both the winner and the loser would do SHU time.

'What's the pancake's name?'

Honest Ed nodded toward a truck at the end of the lot. 'Yeah, I remember. He bought a bread truck. Like that one down there. Only that one's in tip-top shape. Damn nice vehicle. He bought this old beat-to-shit thing ready for the bone yard. Kline thought he was screwing me on the deal, but I was ready to ship it out to the junkers.'

'Did he say why he wanted the truck?' Duran asked.

'Nah. And I didn't ask. He paid cash.' Honest Ed grinned wickedly. 'He could have got it five hundred bucks cheaper if he knew how to bargain.'

'Was he alone?'

'Far as I could see. Skinny guy. Looked kind of like Ichobod Crane, long neck, big Adam's apple.'

'What color was the truck?'

'Once it was blue and white. With a checkerboard running around the top. Kilpatrick's Bread. It's all nicked up and rusty now.' Honest Ed narrowed his eyes and lowered his voice. 'I really dumped that thing on him good. Real good.'

Duran thanked him for the information, then walked directly to the truck the salesman had pointed to.

So far the day had been a disappointment. Justice wasn't at the door of the Excelsior Hotel. Everyone he questioned said they had no idea of where he could be found.

The door to room 702 hadn't been repaired. There was no sign of Kline. Both of them had disappeared. Hugh Stringer still hadn't heard from Johnny. Nor had Victor Abbott, according to Stringer, when Duran called him at his office.

'Abbott told me about the incident at Johnny's club,' Stringer had chided. 'Not very bright under the circumstances, Robert. You're just giving Abbott more ammunition. He's threatening to call the police.'

The bread company's name had been wire-brushed off the sides of the truck, leaving swirling waves of bright steel. Duran walked around the vehicle. Why a bread truck? It was big and bulky. And a bread truck parked in one spot for a long time was going to draw attention.

He opened the back door and climbed inside. The racks had been removed – Duran's head almost touched the ceiling. A portable studio? Someplace he could store his sketching and painting materials.

A sudden gust of wind slammed the truck doors closed behind him. Duran swiveled around, hands up in a defensive position. It was pitch black, confining. Like a cell. He hastily pulled at the door handle, jumping out on to the pavement.

He wiped his sweaty hands on his pants legs as he stared into the back of the truck. Like a cell. Kline. The son-of-a-bitch bought himself a prison cell.

* ★ *

The voice on the other end of the phone had a strange, garbled, high-pitched tone.

'Mr Duran isn't in at the moment,' Peggy Jacquard said cautiously. 'Whose calling?'

'No name. I'll call back. Tell him we want the painting back.'

'And which painting are you talking about?'

'Our Van Gogh, lady, *Sun and Sky*. You tell Duran we want it back.'

'Would you like to leave a number where he can reach you?'

'Very funny, lady. You just tell Duran I'll be calling in an hour.'

There was a buzz, and the connection was severed.

Peggy tapped the linebar with her fingernail, then dialed Duran's carphone number.

'You just got a doozy of a call, Bob. I think it's the guy who stole the Van Gogh from Fritzheim.'

'What did he say?'

'He wants the Van Gogh back. He says he'll be calling back in an hour.'

Duran looked at the Jaguar's clock. 'Well, he'll be disappointed. I'm headed for Colma to talk to Chief Saylor.'

'Okay. What do I tell him when he calls again?'

'I'll leave that up to your imagination, Peg. But keep the door locked. I'll be back as soon as I can.'

Peggy took Duran's advice and double-locked the office door. Back at her desk, she began flipping through the Fritzheim file. It was obvious the caller thought that Duran had the painting. She could almost understand their convoluted thought process: Wendy Lange drugged and tied. Their contact, Harry Lawson, and his bodyguard killed. Bob untouched, arriving on the scene after all the damage was done. He must have the painting.

All that plotting, planning, scheming. They committed the perfect crime, then the Van Gogh was snatched back.

Pacific Indemnity had been less than pleased with the results of Duran's investigation. The claims manager was threatening to withdraw any future assignments until the Van Gogh was recovered.

Peggy read through Duran's notes, his fax to Wendy Lange, the appraisal figures, the logged times of the calls with Harry Lawson. It wasn't much of a file. She had never examined the Nexis check on Fritzheim's property, and wondered if Duran had had time to look it over.

Simply by entering Fritzheim's name, and then coupling with Van Gogh, the computer database had pulled up seven pages of stories starting from when Fritzheim had purchased the painting three years ago from a Christie's auction, to numerous articles trumpeting the movie producer's lifestyle and new home.

Peggy skimmed through the computerized clippings with little enthusiasm until she came to the bottom of page four. The storyline jumped from an interview with Danielle Fritzheim to a feature on the construction of the house. It took her several seconds to realize that there was a page missing. Page five. She shuffled the papers again, but it wasn't there. Had Duran found something of interest on page five? Removed it from the file?

She put the computer to work, re-entered the Nexis request and in a matter of seconds the computer began coughing up documents. Again, seven pages, the first four identical to the ones in the file.

She studiously reviewed page five. It didn't take her long to spot the paragraph mentioning that the architect employed by Fritzheim had 'used the talents of local interior designer Jason Lark to assist in completing the project.'

'Holy shit,' Peggy said, loud enough to startle herself as she reached for the phone.

* * *

The cameo-faced woman behind the thick bullet-proof glass window gave Duran a patronizing smile. 'Chief Saylor is out.'

'Can you get in touch with him? It's important,' Duran assured her.

'He's up in Sacramento and won't be back until this afternoon.'

'It's related to the disappearance of my wife, Anona Stack. It's very important. Can't you page him?'

'I can try, Mr Duran. He's attending a statewide chiefs' convention.'

'Try. Please. Have him call me.' Duran took out a business card and scribbled his carphone number and the Stack House number on the back. 'Tell him I have a lead on the man who took my wife's body from the cemetery.'

Chapter 31

He thrust the shovel downward into the soft ground. Justice's knife had made a gash, but the bleeding from the cut on his arm had been minimal. More importantly, the migraine was now gone and his head felt clearer than it had in weeks.

He had a purpose now. A single purpose. Robert Duran. Somehow Duran had figured it out, had identified him.

He hadn't expected that. He'd underestimated Duran.

Otto Kline tossed the shovel aside and climbed out of the hip-high hole, crossed over to the van and grabbed one of Justice's ankles, pulling him from the vehicle and dragging him over to the makeshift grave.

Justice's gray, marble-like eyes stared vacantly up at Kline.

He bent down and searched through the dead man's pockets, retrieving the roll of cash he'd given him last night, a collection of keys and his wallet. The wallet held almost six hundred dollars in cash, several credit cards and a driver's license in the name of J. Allen Wells. He nudged Justice's body into the hole with his foot, then picked up the shovel, scooped up some loose dirt and sprinkled it over Justice's face.

When he finished with the burial he jammed the shovel into the ground, and thought about saying a prayer. When a prisoner died in Pelican Bay, the warden made an announcement over the speaker system, ending with a short non-denominational prayer.

Kline remembered his church years as a child. The word 'amen' concluded each prayer. Ken Firpo had a better ending. 'Goodbye asshole.' He missed Firpo.

Peggy Jacquard jumped when she heard the clicking of a key in the office-door lock. She quickly got to her feet, only to sink back down into her chair when she saw the familiar profile of Robert Duran through the slanted window shades.

'Did he call back?' Duran asked once he was inside.

'No, not yet.' Peggy had contacted Duran on his car phone and told him of the missing Nexis page.

She handed him the documents. Duran saw Jason Lark's name and thumped his forehead with his fist. '*Menso*,' he said, the gutter Spanish word for idiot somehow popping into his mind. 'Lark has had the run of the house. He must have gone through my room, found a set of spare keys. He'd have keys to the office and the Jaguar. Why the hell didn't I think of that earlier?'

'After reading that article, I thought of it too, Bob. I called a locksmith. He's coming over to change the locks.'

'Great,' Duran grunted, remembering how he had criticized Alan Fritzheim for 'locking the barn after the horse was stolen.' 'And get a security guard posted at the door – and I want him to go with you to and from your car and follow you in from your house in the morning.'

'That's going a little too far, Bob,' she protested.

'I don't think so, Peg. I found this in Otto Kline's room.' He showed her the sketch, with the nearby Ghiaradelli Tower in the background. 'Kline could be out there right now. Watching, waiting.'

'Is there a connection between Kline and Jason Lark?'

'I don't know. Lisa had a point when she told Hugh

Stringer that everything has gone to shit since Jason arrived.'

'Jason must have been involved in the Fritzheim theft,' Peggy asserted.

Duran snapped his fingers nervously. 'Yes. He was involved all right. Somehow he got into this office. Saw that file, saw his name in the Nexis search. And he saw everything else, including my fax to Wendy Lange indicating the time and place of our meeting, and that Harry Lawson would be there.'

Duran headed for his office, stopping at the doorway, his shoulders suddenly slumping in dejection. 'Let's back up, Peg, we're missing something here. Lark is working at the Fritzheim house. He sees the Van Gogh. Tells his accomplices about it. Tells them the Fritzheims' schedule: the husband is always away at the studio, Danielle is out denting the cash registers in Beverly Hills most afternoons. He tells them that the maid is usually alone in the house. Lark's buddies pull off the heist. They have the painting. They want to sell it to Pacific Indemnity. They contact Lawson. Everything is working out perfectly. What would make them steal it back?'

'Maybe Lark's partners double-crossed him,' Peggy suggested.

Duran pinched his lower lip between thumb and forefinger. 'The maid, Eleana, said the two men who came to Fritzheim's door were both tall, young, and looked enough alike to be brothers. Wendy Lange heard two men talking, but she saw just one of them. She described him as short, heavy-set.

'Both jobs were done by two men. But with completely different MOs. Eleana said they treated her softly, told her not to cry, made sure that the ropes weren't too tight, apologized for having to gag her, promised her that they wouldn't harm her in any way. They brought the ropes to tie her with.

'Wendy got a face-full of ether, then was trussed up like a steer with strips of sheets from her bed. One of the men made a comment about her being pretty, and it being too bad they had to put her to sleep, as if he wanted to rape her.'

'A gun was used in both instances,' Peggy reminded.

'Yes, a "*grande pistola*" according to Eleana. Like a cowboy's gun. The LAPD says that a .22 was used to kill Lawson and his driver. A professional killer's gun. Probably with a silencer attached. They were two different teams on those jobs, Peg. I was the target in LA. They wanted to kill me. Now this clown who took *Sun and Sky* from Fritzheim's bedroom wall thinks I've got the Van Gogh.'

Peggy's eyebrows cocked in a questioning arc. 'You think that Lark told them—'

The chirping of the phone cut her off. She picked it up, then cupped her hand over the receiver. 'It's him,' she told Duran, 'the man with the strange voice.'

He nodded, reached over and pushed the phone's speaker button. 'This is Bob Duran. What can I do for you?'

'Give us back our painting,' was the off-pitch reply.

Duran gave an exasperated sigh. 'I don't have the Van Gogh, and it isn't yours in the first place. It's Alan Fritzheim's.'

'We want—'

'I don't have what you want. Why don't you ask Jason Lark?'

There was a long pause. 'Who?'

'Your partner. Or ex-partner.'

'The only partner I have is standing three feet from me, mister. Cut the shit. You set up Harry Lawson. Harry had a lot of friends. Friends who aren't happy about what happened.'

'Harry was a friend of mine, too,' Duran exaggerated.

278

'And I couldn't do business without him.'

Another long pause, then: 'We've done business together before. Through Harry.'

Duran wasn't surprised at the admission. 'And I've always played straight. I don't have the Van Gogh and I had nothing to do with Harry's murder. You can believe that or not, I really don't give a damn.'

His finger stabbed at the phone, breaking the connection.

'That voice. It was one of those electronic gadgets, wasn't it?' said Peggy.

Duran nodded in agreement. A voice changer, originally developed by law enforcement to protect witness identification. As usual, the crooks found it suited their purposes just as well.

'Call our source at the phone company. Get a record of Lark's phone calls. Both at his office and home. The addresses are on those credit reports.' He paused for a moment, marshalling his thoughts.

'Get the Stack House toll calls too, for the past few days, since Lark has been here.'

Peggy nodded, reaching for the phone.

'And check our office numbers, too,' he added. 'The bastard had the gall to break in here, maybe he used the phones.'

The store's name intrigued him: Big & Tall. The sales clerk fitted both descriptions – perhaps a former football player gone to pot, he theorized. He let the clerk select slacks, a sports coat, tie, and shoes for him, hardly glancing at the prices. He'd already verified that Justice Wells's Visa card had a credit line of fifteen hundred dollars. He chose one item himself, a modified western hat, the type he remembered seeing President Johnson wear.

His next stop was the barbershop located in the street-level floor of a towering financial building on Montgomery Street.

The frustrated barber protested that there wasn't much that he could do, other than contour what was there.

'It will take three or four appointments for me to get your hair to where it should be.' He fluttered his hands over Kline's scalp. 'Who did this? You must have been in a jungle somewhere,' the barber said jokingly.

'Some place worse,' he assured him.

A young manicurist worked on his fingers while a tired-eye Latin buffed his new shoes. The barber evened out his hair, trimmed his eyebrows, gave him a shave and applied a soothing 'unisex' cologne.

Kline examined himself in the mirror while the barber fussed over brushing his immaculate blue blazer.

The changes were subtle, yet rewarding. His hair had a razor-straight part and was close to what the barber described as his 'executive cut.' Rather than resembling a country bumpkin or a middle-aged boot camp sergeant, he looked like a businessman – a rather prosperous businessman. The type that Laura Ralston would welcome as a customer.

To add to the illusion, he stopped at a print shop and had business cards made up in the name of J. Alan Wells. President of Wells, Inc. He made up a Dallas, Texas address. Dallas – oil – Wells. If he'd had a sense of humour, he would have grinned over the combination.

A tapping sound caught Laura Ralston's attention. She looked up to see a tall, neat-looking man standing at the door holding a hat in his hand.

'Are you Laura Ralston?'

'Yes. Can I help you?'

'I hope so. I'm looking for a house for me and the wife. Something nice. And vacant. We need it in a hurry.' He walked toward Laura with long loping slides, and handed her a card. 'J. Allen Wells, ma'am. Pleased to meet you.'

Chapter 32

The security guard had shown up at Lost Art, Inc., and had been advised of his duties. Duran was preparing to leave when Peggy announced Hugh Stringer's arrival.

Duran was surprised to see Stringer standing shoulder-to-shoulder with Victor Abbott. He motioned both men into his office.

'Victor and I are on our way to John's houseboat,' Stringer explained. 'No one has been able to make contact with him. We thought you might have a key.'

'No, I've never had a key to John's place.'

Victor Abbott trailed his hand across the arm of a high-backed cane chair. 'When was the last time you saw my client?'

'At Hugh's office. The day of the reading of the will.'

'The day your wife's body was taken,' Abbot confirmed.

'That's right. What about Lisa? Has she seen John?'

Hugh Stringer cleared his throat, then said, 'I've spoken to Lisa. She hasn't seen John in days. She's quite concerned. She's been to the houseboat. It's locked and John's car is in the carport.'

'I'm going to bring the police into it,' Abbott said sternly.

'Good idea,' Duran responded quickly. 'What about his father? Have you spoken to Lark?'

Abbott gave a quick nod. 'He's worried about his son, too. If something has happened to my client, something

serious, I intend to pursue the civil and criminal conse-
quences to the end, Mr Duran. To the very end.'

'Good for you, counselor. My suggestion is that we all
go to the houseboat and kick in the door. John may be
sick.' His eyes caught Stringer's again. 'Does Abbott know
about John's drug problem.'

'There was no problem,' Stringer objected. 'It was a
one time thing. I think that all—'

'I think we're wasting time,' Duran cut in. 'Let's go over
to the houseboat. If we don't get a response, we can just
break in.'

Abbott seemed surprised by Duran's directness.

Stringer hunched his shoulders. 'I'd feel much more
comfortable if we had a key.'

'Call the fire department,' Duran advised. 'They'll
break in the door.'

'Yes. You've had some experiences with fire departments,
haven't you,' Victor Abbott said with heavy irony.

Duran ignored the sarcasm. 'We're wasting time, gentlemen. Let's go.'

Abbott held up his hand like a cop stopping traffic. 'I
think it would be advisable if just Mr Stringer and I
handled this.'

'Have it your way,' Duran conceded. 'But do it.'

Abbott turned to Stringer. 'I'll see you in the car.'

Stringer waited until Abbott was out of the building
before speaking. 'What's with the security guard, Robert?'

'I'm worried about Peggy being alone in here.'

'Have you had any more information on this . . . criminal you were telling me about?'

'I'm getting closer to him. I'm waiting for a call from
Chief Saylor.'

'John's disappearance. Could this creature be involved
somehow?'

'It's possible, Hugh. Let me know what you find out in
Sausalito.'

★ ★ ★

'Do you want to follow me in your car?' Laura Ralston asked the tall Texan.

'No. I'd just get lost, ma'am.'

They took Laura's white BMW. Laura had spent thirty minutes in her office with J. Allen Wells. His business card showed him as president of his own company. Money did not seem to be a problem. He was looking for a large house. Wells was in a hurry. He wanted something right now.

They had gone through the multiple listings forms, and Laura pointed out properties in the Marina, Sea Cliff and Pacific Heights area.

Wells had shown interest in three of the houses, the lowest asking price of which was one and a half million dollars.

'How did you happen to choose my office?' Laura asked, once they were in her car and driving to the first property on Casa Way.

'Your last name. Ralston. It's my wife's maiden name.'

Laura glanced at Wells out of the corner of her eye. He had one hand tucked under his armpit and a pained look on his face.

'Are you feeling all right, Mr Wells?'

Otto Kline took off his hat and began massaging the area above his right ear. 'Just a headache, ma'am. I'll be okay.'

Duran circulated through the Tenderloin area again, dispensing ten-dollar bills to various grifters in and around the Excelsior Hotel. No one had seen Justice, or Otto Kline. Kline's room was still vacant.

He used the carphone to check in with Peggy. There were no calls from Chief Saylor. Hugh Stringer had phoned in a message. Johnny wasn't in his houseboat and Victor Abbott had officially notified the police of his absence.

Duran returned to Stack House, hoping to find Jason Lark.

'He left early this morning,' George informed him.

'Did he say where he was going?'

'No, sir. His clothes are still in the guest room, so I assume he will be back.'

'What about Lisa?'

'She drove off with a gentleman friend less than an hour ago.'

'The gentleman. Do you know him?'

'I believe she called him Eric, sir. He's been around quite a bit lately.'

Duran nodded his thanks and hurried upstairs to his bedroom. He checked through the armoire drawer. The plastic, see-through bag of spare keys were still there, in with the jewelry. He emptied the keys on to the bed and stirred them with his finger. The Stack House front door, car keys for the Jag and the Jeep 4x4. And the key to the office door.

All present and accounted for. Which meant nothing. Lark could have easily had duplicates made.

There was a light tapping on the bedroom door. George's head appeared. 'A policeman to see you, sir. I put him in the living room.'

Duran found Chief Saylor standing with his hands clasped behind his back, head tilted to one side, examining Anona's painting, *Leaf in Transit*.

'What do you think?' Duran asked.

Saylor turned his head slowly in Duran's direction. 'Your wife did this?'

'Yes. Like it?'

'I'm not sure,' Saylor reflected.

'It's part of the estate, Chief. It will probably go up for auction.'

Saylor looked back at the painting. 'How much you figure?'

'A million dollars. In that ballpark.'

'That's not my ballpark,' Saylor said with a lopsided grin. 'My office says you've been trying to get ahold of me.'

'Yes. I've got some information in my car, I'll be right back.'

When Duran returned with the prison records of Otto Kline and Kenneth Firpo, Saylor was again staring at *Leaf in Transit.*

'I've decided. I do like it.' He extended a hand. 'What have you got?'

Duran hesitated. 'These are from a confidential source, Chief.'

Saylor gestured with his fingers. 'Let's see what you got.'

Saylor settled into a chair, tilted his hat to the back of his head and began reading. He went through each page thoroughly, some more than once, before looking over at Duran.

'So. According to these documents, this Firpo character is still in prison. The other guy, Kline, just got out. What ties either one of them to your wife?'

Duran filled Saylor in on everything, including Anona's testimony at the trial and Arlene Kline's subsequent suicide. 'Kline suffered a head injury after he jumped on that prison guard in Los Angeles. He was then transferred up to Pelican Bay. It gave him time, lots of time, to plan his revenge.

'I saw Arlene Kline's grave in Los Angeles, Chief. It's in an old potter's field. The cemetery caretaker called it God's backyard. Kline just put up a tombstone. The inscription reads: "At first thought sweet." It's from a poem: "Revenge at first thought sweet, bitter ere long back on itself".'

'And that makes you think Kline stole your wife's body and is trying to kill you?'

'Yes, I do.'

'It still doesn't add up in my book.' Saylor folded the documents neatly and fanned them under his chin. 'Your confidential source is either a prison official or a probation officer who could be in a lot of trouble for giving you these.'

'Kline came to San Francisco when he got out of prison. A half-way house on Turk Street. He's moved. His room was empty.'

'Who spooked him?'

'Me,' Duran admitted. 'I've been there. He was out. The doorman, a guy named Justice, gave me his room number. He called Kline's room from the lobby, said there was no answer. When I checked the room later that night, I found there was no phone.'

'Have you talked to this Justice again?'

'I've been back twice. He's gone, too.'

Saylor drew a patient breath, then said, 'You've been busy, Mr Duran, I'll give you that. But it all doesn't add up to a hell of a lot. What'd you say the cemetery guy called the spot where Kline's wife was buried?'

'God's backyard.'

Saylor bulged his lower lip with his tongue. 'Where the hell have I heard that before?'

Chapter 33

Remove George. That seemed to be the only reasonable solution, Jason Lark decided. But what if George had stashed the rest of the Picassos in his safety deposit box? Or given them to a friend? Did George have a friend? Lark could never remember seeing him talk to anyone but the Stack family and the household staff.

Lark had started to search George's suite, stopping when he'd heard the sound of the front door slamming. It had been George returning home, all right. And as far as he knew, the bastard hadn't left the house since.

He stirred the olive slowly through the Martini. Dispose of George. He was an old man. It shouldn't be too difficult. Of course he wouldn't do it himself. Perhaps Mario Drago could recommend someone to him. Mario had expected Lark to kill Duran. Now that they'd gotten the Fritzheim Van Gogh back, was it still necessary to kill him? Would Duran continue to poke his nose into his affairs once Anona's body was found?

Lark knew the answer only too well. If Duran got even a sniff that he was somehow involved in the Fritzheim theft, he'd be after him with a vengeance.

He popped the olive into his mouth and circled his finger around the glass to signal the bartender he was ready for a refill.

He was drinking too much. He knew it. The cocaine he'd brought with him from Santa Monica was gone. He knew no one in San Francisco he could trust. And someone had removed Anona's stash of marijuana right after her death.

Surely John would know someone who sold reliable drugs. All those young barbarians that frequented his club looked like they were stoned. Where the hell was John, anyway?

He'd made a hint to Eric, Lisa's friend, about scoring some coke, but Eric had laughed at him. 'Get your own shit, old man.'

Old man. Lark studied his reflection in the barroom mirror, liking what he saw, subconsciously protruding his chin so that his neck remained taut. He gave himself a knowing smile. In a few years perhaps he'd go in for a nip or tuck, but certainly not now. It wasn't necessary.

There was a young brunette who had been sending him signals for the last twenty minutes, sandwiched in between two swarthy, husky, sweater-clad bores at the opposite end of the bar.

He sampled the fresh drink. Forgeries. It wouldn't be hard for a professional to forge the Picasso hanging in George's bedroom. Mario had always supplied the forger for the jobs in Los Angeles, a quiet, bald, weak-chinned man with liver spots on his skin. Lark would let him in the house, then he'd spend a half hour or so photographing and scanning the painting. In a week he'd return with the replacement.

Lark didn't even know the forger's name. Or how to get in touch with him. Except through Mario. And he didn't want Mario, or anyone else, to know about the Picassos.

So it was back to finding the rest of the Picassos. The *Cinq Putains*.

He noticed the sweater-boys had left the brunette all by herself. She gave him a rueful smile. She really was beautiful. Early twenties, he estimated, wearing a black dress with a brassy over-sized zipper that stretched from cleavage to knees. She was tempting. But he had more important things to do.

Ken Firpo had told him to use a gun on a man, but a knife on a woman. The sharp blade intimidated women much more than the barrel of a gun.

Laura Ralston showed him through the spacious tiled kitchen, the living room, then the dining room.

'Is this anything like what you had in mind, Mr Wells?'

'It's nice. Very nice. Where are the owners?'

'In Arizona. A job transfer. They hated giving up the house.' She pointed to the staircase. 'The bedrooms are upstairs.'

'I don't have to see them, Laura.'

'Then you don't really—' She went rubber-legged at the sight of the knife that had suddenly appeared in his hand without warning.

'Please, Mr Wells, my office knows where I am, they can—'

'They don't know shit,' he said, tossing his cowboy hat to the rug. 'Drop your purse, Laura.'

'Please, I—'

He moved in, waving the blade rhythmically back and forth in front of her face. He could see the sweat start to form on her upper lip. Her eyes were riveted on the movement of the knife.

'Drop your purse like a good girl. I'm not going to hurt you. It's your boyfriend I want.'

Laura clutched her purse to her chest. It was the closest thing to a weapon she had. Her cellular phone was inside, her beeper. She could—

The knife-blade flashed toward her, the tip settling on her nose. 'Don't be stupid. You're a pretty woman. You want to stay that way, don't you? Drop the purse.'

Laura released her fingers. The purse barely made a

sound on the thick carpeting. She expelled her breath slowly when the knife was withdrawn a few inches.

'Why are you doing this to me? Why—'

'Why me?' Kline chuckled. 'Everyone says that, Laura. Everyone. It's not you, it's Duran. Sit down. Make yourself comfortable.'

'Sporting World.'

'I'm calling for Junior Erwin,' Duran said.

'Hang on, buddy.'

Duran did just that, for about two minutes. The prison guard had called the office and Peggy had relayed the message. ' "Junior's got something hot," is what he said, Bob. He's calling from a sporting goods-store in Crescent City.'

So Duran waited. The meeting with Chief Saylor had gone well. Saylor was interested in the information on Otto Kline. Not fascinated, but interested.

Like Duran, Saylor could not figure out a connection between Otto Kline and the Los Angeles killings.

Kline. His just getting out of jail, his cellmate Firpo having been born and raised in San Mateo County, Firpo's father dying in prison. That's too much coincidence, Duran had contended.

Erwin came on the line. 'Hi there, Mr Duran. How you doin'?'

'Just fine, Junior.'

'I did what you asked. Talked to old "Ramblin' Nose" Firpo.'

The line was silent for several moments. 'And?' Duran prompted.

'I was just looking at this electronic fish-finder. Damndest thing. It's like sonar on a submarine. You trail it in the water and the fish show up on a screen. Can't miss with these suckers.'

'If what Firpo told you is of any help to me, you can

put the salesman on the phone and I'll pay for it right now on my credit card.'

'I think it'll help,' Erwin said, trying to sound casual. 'Firpo says he and Kline used to talk a lot about his grandfather, and his father, the one who died in Alcatraz. Grandpa was a moonshiner down there. Some place called Montara.'

'Moonshiner? That had to be in the twenties.'

'Right,' Erwin agreed. 'Grandpa had a hell of a business goin', according to Ramblin' Nose. He got caught in a chase one night and got himself killed.'

'What does all this ancient history have to do with Otto Kline?'

'Well, Firpo says his father kind of kept the family business going for a while. Switched from moonshine to smuggling drugs, even some Chinamen once in a while. Firpo's father made a mistake of getting in a shoot-out with the cops. Wounded one of them. That's what landed him in Alcatraz. The thing is, Grandpa Firpo kept his stills spread out all over the place in these caves up in the mountains down there. Hold on a minute.'

Duran could hear the rustling of paper. 'San Vincente Creek Road. Firpo's family owned the property. It went for taxes years back, the state sold it to some lumber company. Only thing is, there's a moratorium or some damn thing. They can't cut down the trees. Firpo says the land is vacant. Not much good for anything. 'Cept hiding still, I guess.'

'This doesn't sound very promising, Junior,' Duran objected.

'Well, there was one particular spot that Firpo says he told Kline about. Got a pencil?'

Duran reached for a pen. 'Go ahead.'

'You drive south on the Cabrillo Highway. Turn on 16th Street in Montara, just when you get to the lighthouse. Then turn right on San Vincente Road. You go for two to two and a half miles. You go over a couple of rickety bridges on the way. There's a bunch of small dirt roads off to your right, and they branch out into a bunch of other roads. Firpo says that's where the caves are. Dozens and dozens of 'em, honeycombed all over the place.'

Duran dropped his pen in disgust. 'Junior, no disrespect intended, but Firpo was pulling your leg.'

'No, sir,' Erwin blurted belligerently. 'He wasn't. Firpo was lying low there 'fore his last arrest, that was a few years ago. He says he knows they're still there.'

'And why would he give this information to you?'

Junior responded with a coarse laugh. ''Cause I gave him two choices for his next cellmate. A young baby, a pancake just out of the SHU, or the toughest, ugliest Mexican in Pelican Bay.'

Duran leaned back and pondered the information. 'Okay,' he finally said. 'Put the salesman on.'

Chapter 34

Laura Ralston stared up at the man's beady eyes. He'd used thick, silver-colored tape to secure her ankles and wrists.

'I'm just going to say this once, Laura. I'll dial Bob Duran's number. You tell him that you have to see him right away. It's very important. Something about Anona. Something that someone told you, that you don't feel comfortable talking about on the phone. You'll give him this address. If he's not there, leave a message. Make it brief. But get him over here.'

He trailed the dull edge of the blade down her forehead and across her nose, scraping her skin.

'If I don't like the way you talk to Duran, if I think you're trying to warn him, I'm going to cut your nose off. Do you understand?'

'Yes,' Laura said, her voice parched and hoarse.

'Good.' He took Laura's cellular phone from her purse and touch-toned Duran's home number. When the butler answered, he put the phone to Laura's face, edging his own next to hers so he could listen in.

'George, this is Laura Ralston. Is Bob home?'

'Yes. He's on the other line, however. Can I have him call you?'

Laura questioned Kline with her eyes.

He gave a curt nod.

'No. Just tell Bob I have to see him right away. I've got

some information about Anona. I'm at 132 Casa Way, in the Marina. Tell him it's important, and that I'll wait for him here.'

Robert Duran furnished the sporting goods salesman with the information from his credit card, and was informed that he'd just spent six hundred, eleven dollars and forty-three cents for a fish-finder.

'Anything else I can do, just let me know,' Junior Erwin volunteered when he came back on the line.

'Keep after Firpo. Let me know if he receives any mail from Kline.'

They said their goodbyes and Duran had an image of the prison guard combing the sporting-goods store for his next reward.

There was a knock on the door and the butler entered the room.

'You had a call. Laura Ralston. She said it was quite important. Some good news on Mrs Anona.'

Duran reached for the phone.

'Miss Ralston said she was at an address.' He glanced at the notepad in his hand. 'Number 132 Casa Way. In the Marina, and that she'd wait for you there.'

'She didn't leave a phone number?'

'No, sir.'

Duran got to his feet. 'Has Jason Lark returned?'

'No, sir,' George replied with a hint of relief in his voice.

Duran began rummaging through the desk for a map book, wondering why Laura hadn't left a phone number.

Chapter 35

Duran recognized Laura Ralston's white BMW parked in the driveway of the three story, stucco fronted, Art-Deco style home.

The tunnel-like entrance lead to a tilted stairway. The heavily varnished front door was ajar.

'Hello. Laura,' he called, leaning his head into the threshold.

The living room was void of furniture – faded areas on the pale-white walls showed where paintings or mirrors had once hung.

'Laura? It's me, Bob. Where are you?'

He made his way into the kitchen, then heard a thumping noise from above.

A narrow wrought-iron circular stairway led to the upper floor. Duran skimmed his hand along the banister as he trekked up the stairs. 'Laura? Are you up there?'

The thumping noise again. Duran momentarily thought of retreating, going back to the Jaguar for the shotgun – then there was a crash followed by a muffled wail.

Duran ran up the steps. Stumbling in his haste, he careened off the hallway wall. He was trying to regain his balance when he spotted Laura Ralston, pinned and dangling from a door, half naked, her breasts exposed, her head up toward the ceiling, her feet inches above the floor, kicking out in desperation.

Duran wrapped his arms around Laura's waist, seeing the brassière knotted around her neck. Her face was crimson, contorted in pain, her eyes rolled up in their sockets. A swatch of silver-colored tape covered her mouth.

Suddenly she fell loose, into his arms, the weight of her body pulling him down, her legs entangled with his as they tumbled to the floor.

Otto Kline slipped from behind the door, seeing the woman in Duran's arms, Duran's hands and legs fighting to become free. Kline hit him once across the forehead with a taped piece of pipe, snapping Duran's head back, then took his time, circling Duran as he tried to get to his feet. He brought the pipe down on Duran's left shoulder joint, feeling the metal penetrate the cartilage and tendons and make solid contact with the ball and socket bones.

Duran cried out in agony, bending over at the waist as Kline casually selected his next target – the down tip of the temporal bone behind Duran's ear.

Duran's body jerked upwards for a second, then he collapsed, his head making a cracked-iced sound when it contacted the floor.

Once Kline was off the freeway and through the small community of Montara, he stabbed the accelerator. He enjoyed punishing the car, grinding through the gears. He'd done it! Anona had cheated him, but he had Duran! Had them both now. When he reached the turnoff, he jammed the transmission into low, his foot only grazing the brake when necessary. The Jaguar's sleek hood-ornament jounced up and down, like a ship's bowsprit in heavy seas as he steered between the silent rows of redwoods and pine trees.

He hit a deep pot-hole and the car bucked under him, his head bouncing up against the roof.

He pulled off his hat and slapped it against his thigh and yelled a croak-voiced 'Yahoooo.'

The pain jarred Duran awake. He opened his eyes. It was pitch black. He raised his head a few inches and it bumped into something hard.

He tried opening his mouth, but it was impossible. The scene at the house came back to him. Laura, hanging from the door. Laura. What happened to Laura? She was alive when he held her in his arms, her bra tightly knotted around her neck. He'd gotten just a brief glimpse of the man who hit him. Tall, long-faced, dark hair. Otto Kline. In the flesh. The all-too-solid flesh.

Duran moaned as he tried moving his arms. His shoulder was on fire. The slightest movement brought more pain.

He lay still, fighting to breathe slowly, normally. The air felt thick, confined. For a moment he imagined he might be in a coffin, but there was a sensation of movement. He tried moving his feet. They were bound and his hands were fastened behind his back.

There was a strong smell directly in front of his face. He inhaled sharply – holding the air in his lungs as if to analyze it. Rubber. It smelled like rubber. He ground his nose into the smell, feeling the rough surface – corrugations. A rubber mat. A car mat. He was in a trunk. The Jaguar's trunk? With Kline driving? Driving where?

Duran drew his knees up and tried moving, stopping almost immediately when his head hit something soft. He probed at the softness. Someone moaned. He wasn't alone! Laura? It had to be Laura. She was alive!

He could feel the car slowing down, then tilting as if they were going up a grade, his body sliding backward, the pain in his shoulder throbbing relentlessly. The car bucked and weaved, the chassis scraping the ground.

Duran imagined the setting – a rough unpaved road, in

a desolate wooded area. Kline was taking him to the mountain, Firpo's old mountain. Taking him to his bread truck prison cell. To his SHU.

The trunk lid popped open. 'Enjoy the trip?' Otto Kline asked innocently. 'A little crowded in there?' He reached down and ripped the tape from Duran's mouth.

'You can shout and scream all you want. It won't do you any good.'

Duran felt Kline's fingers gouge into his legs and drag him from the car trunk.

He fought a losing fight to keep his balance and flopped back against the Jaguar's fender.

The sun had set, but Duran could see the outline of trees in the background.

Kline grabbed Duran by the belt-buckle, then pushed him to the ground. He used the knife to cut through the tape on Duran's hands and feet, then backed away, sliding the knife back into its sheath, picking up the shotgun, Conrad Stack's shotgun that Duran had left in the Jaguar. He waved the weapon at Duran. 'Nice of you to leave this in the car for me. Now get up and start moving. That way.'

Duran struggled to his knees, then pushed himself upright with his right arm. His left arm was numb, useless. He stumbled forward. The ground was flat, covered by scrub weeds. Then he noticed the fresh mound of dirt.

'Anona. You bastard.' He dropped back to the ground, his right hand clawing at the dirt.

Otto Kline chuckled, then the chuckle grew to a hearty laugh. 'No, that's not your wife's grave, Duran. Your wife is someplace special, and you'll be joining her soon.'

Duran dragged his hand through the dirt, palming a marble-sized rock before getting back to his feet.

'What are you going to do to Laura?'

'She's served her purpose. Get moving!'

Duran lurched forward, dragging his feet. He had to take a chance soon. Once Kline got him into his bread truck prison cell, he was as good as dead. 'What about Johnny. What did you do to Johnny?'

'Johnny? Her son? Nothing. Or the daughter. Just Anona. And now you.'

'Is this Firpo's place, Otto?' he asked in a controlled voice. 'Where his grandfather hid his stills?'

Kline cocked both hammers on the shotgun and drilled the barrels into Duran's back. 'How do you know about that?'

'Ken Firpo told me. Told me all about it. I met with him up at Pelican Bay.'

'Ken would never talk to you,' Kline shouted. 'Keep moving!'

They were coming to a stand of trees. Duran could see ruts in the dirt, then a flash of bright metal. Kline's SHU!

'You've been making too many mistakes, Otto. That fire at Anona's studio. You left your prints on the paint thinner cans.'

'Nice try,' Kline scoffed. 'That wasn't me. I wasn't ready to kill you yet. Tomorrow's the day, Duran. Tomorrow. October Fourteenth.'

'Firpo got a new cellmate. Someone like you were. Just out of the SHU.'

'You're lying! You never talked to Ken!'

They were into the trees now. The shiny metal doors on the back of the bread truck were spread open. Duran could see a brassière dangling from the interior ceiling. He fought back a shudder and turned to face Kline.

'I saw him, Otto. He's an ugly bastard with a big, rambling nose. He told me everything.'

Kline brought the shotgun to his shoulder and stared at Duran over the barrels. 'You're a liar.'

'How do you think I got your name? Junior Erwin, the prison guard got me to Firpo. He also told me about your time in the SHU, Otto. And Ken told me about Arlene. How she died. I visited her grave. I saw the inscription on the tombstone. I saw it all. And I told the police everything, Otto. They know about this place, too.'

The shotgun sank slowly until the barrels were pointed at the ground.

'Firpo's new cellmate. A "pancake" is what Erwin called him. Just out of the SHU, like you were, Otto.'

Kline shook his head slowly. 'Ken would never talk about me, he would never—'

Duran hurled the rock at Kline then dived at his legs.

Kline flinched when the rock struck his cheekbone. Both barrels of the shotgun went off simultaneously, a portion of the buckshot spraying the truck's steel doors in a deadly pattern.

Duran felt his knee being ripped apart. He crashed into the dirt, grasping at his leg, spinning around in pain, his eyes searching for Kline.

A cluster of the shotgun pellets slashed across Kline's abdomen, knocking him backwards, his head smacking against the tangled trunk vines of a redwood tree.

Duran tried to get to his feet, but his legs wouldn't hold him. He started to crawl, jamming his elbows into the turf, using them like ski poles to propel himself toward Kline. He reached out, grasped Kline's foot and twisted it savagely.

Kline clasped the shotgun in both hands and swung at Duran's arms. 'Let go,' he screamed. His left hand groped at his stomach, feeling the sticky ooze of his own blood.

Duran joined his fists together and brought them down as hard as he could into the bloody mass at Kline's belt line.

Kline howled in anguish, swung the shotgun around and pounded the barrel against Duran's skull.

Duran grabbed for the gun, twisting the barrel

viciously, hearing a cracking sound as Kline's fingers snapped.

The intense pain acted like a surge of adrenalin to Kline. He kicked himself free of Duran's grasp, pulled his battered and broken fingers from the shotgun's trigger guard, the weapon falling to the ground. He rolled on to his back and aimed his heel at Duran's head, feeling it make solid contact, he kicked out again, then again, stopping only when he saw Duran quiver and go limp.

Kline lay still for a moment, staring up at the interlaced tree branches. He held his hand in front of his eyes. His right hand. His painting hand. The index and middle fingers were broken, the bones slanted in unshapely angles, the flesh torn, bleeding, the knuckles turning a deep, purple-blue. His painting hand!

He inched over to Duran. The vein on Duran's neck was beating out a slow, steady pulse. He wrapped his left hand around Duran's windpipe and began to squeeze, feeling his nails burrow into the soft flesh. He slowly released his grip. It was better if Duran was alive. He wanted Duran to see Anona. See his wife, before he killed him and put him in the ground with her.

Kline flopped back on his side. The pain in his head was intensifying with each second and he could feel the blood draining from his stomach. He looked at his mangled fingers again and began sobbing.

The building dated back to the late nineteenth century. 'Historic' Old Molloy's. The history included several bare-knuckled prizefights involving the likes of the great heavyweight champions Jack Johnson, Battling Nelson and Jack Dempsey.

The strains of a Dixieland band greeted Chief Saylor as he pushed his way into the bar. Six intense senior citizens, decked out in red candy-striped shirts and straw hats were finishing up an upbeat version of *Sweet Georgia Brown*.

The crowd gave them a rousing cheer then turned their attention back to the bar.

Saylor spotted his target, Dave Cassel, at his customary table, shuffling a deck of cards. Cassel had been the chief of the Colma Police Department when Saylor joined the force as a rookie almost twenty-five years ago.

Cassel was in his early eighties, a lean string bean of a man with parchment-colored skin stretched over his hawk-like features.

'Hi, Chief,' Saylor said genially, sliding into the hard-back chair next to Cassel. 'How's it going?'

'As long as it's going, it's good, Bill. How's you? Find that missing body yet?

'No, not yet,' Saylor admitted. 'I thought I might pick your brain if you've got the time.'

Cassel grunted. 'Man my age has nothing but time in some ways, Bill, and no time in others. Whatcha need?'

'Ever hear of a family of crooks that worked on the coast – out by Montara, last name of Firpo? The father supposedly died in Alcatraz, the son, Ken, he's in his mid-fifties now, is doing time in Pelican Bay.'

'Firpo,' the old man snorted. 'Miserable bunch of cusses, and it goes all the way back to the grandfather. He was big in the moonshine business.'

'Moonshine? I thought that was something they did in Oklahoma.'

Cassel riffled the edge of the deck of cards. 'They did it here, too, son. Big time. Dan Firpo had stills hidden all over the coast. They caught him one time in a barn in El Granada. One of his stills blew up. They found twelve thousand gallons of mash whisky in a nearby cave. Firpo got away that time, but they caught him with a truckload of bourbon, chased him to San Bruno, the truck went off the road and blew up, killing the bastard.'

'We're talking ancient history,' Saylor said.

Cassel began shuffling the cards slowly. 'Nineteen

twenty-eight. Then the kid, Dan's son, can't think of his name, he was another rotten apple off the same tree. He was into drugs. The boats would bring the stuff up from Mexico, and this Firpo would go out and meet them, bring it ashore. He smuggled more than dope, too. People. Mex's and Chinamen. Sold 'em like cattle. He shot a Fed. Customs man. That's what sent him to Alcatraz.'

'There was one more rotten apple on the tree,' Saylor reminded. 'Ken, the one now in Pelican Bay.'

Cassel shuffled the deck of cards, then said, 'What's all your interest in this?'

'It might have something to do with the missing body thing, Chief. Ken Firpo had a cellmate, man named Otto Kline. His wife and he were convicted on a forgery charge, the wife killed herself while in prison. She was buried in a potter's grave in Los Angeles. The caretaker called it God's backyard.'

Cassel ran a playing card across his stubbled chin as if it was a razor. 'God's backyard. Yeah, that's what they used to call 'em. We had an old potter's graveyard for the men that died in Alcatraz. This Firpo bastard was probably buried there.'

Saylor leaned forward, the chairlegs scraping the weathered wooden floor. 'Where, Chief? Where was this place?'

The old man cut the deck of cards and began dealing himself a solitaire hand. 'Somewhere up by Junipero Serra. I can't rightly remember, but it's around where they're putting in another one of those damn shopping centers.'

Chapter 36

Bright diesel-powered field lights illuminated the cool night air. Half of the field had been skimmed smooth, the other half was still a knee-high jungle of weeds. Chief Saylor signaled the bulldozer to a stop.

'Where's the boss?' Saylor asked.

The young man in the 'dozer's cracked and sun-faded vinyl seat looked nervous. 'Why? We ain't done nothing wrong.'

Saylor cocked an eyebrow. When a man opened a conversation with a denial of wrongdoing, it usually meant he'd done something wrong. 'What's your name, son?'

'Freddy.'

'Mind turning that thing off?'

The motor died with a jerk and noisy sigh. Freddy untied the bandanna from his neck and used it to mop his forehead.

'I'm looking for a body, son. Have you come across anything that looked like a grave?'

'Grave?'

Saylor could see the sweat popping out on the young man's forehead. He was frightened.

'If you know something, now's the time to tell me.'

'Well, I didn't see a body, but I saw the marker stones. I tripped over one when we were plotting the land. I figured out what they were. Mr Sconio doesn't think I know what they were, the markers, I mean.' He held his hands out to shoulder length. 'Flat kinda tombstones, that's what they looked like to me.'

Saylor lowered his eyes and stared at the weeds surrounding his shoes. 'I'm not interested in old graves. Just a new one.'

Freddy started to climb back up on his rig. 'I ain't seen nothing like that.'

Saylor put a hand on his shoulder. 'Have you run across anything unusual? Like some fresh diggings? Or an old wheelbarrow?'

'Yeah, a beat-up old wheelbarrow. How'd you know about that?'

'Exactly where did you find it?' Saylor asked, keeping his tone low and casual.

Freddy jutted his jaw to a part of the field still blanketed with weeds. 'Over there somewhere. I didn't steal it. Mr Sconio had me put the wheelbarrow in his truck. Mister, it was old. Somebody just dumped the damn thing.'

Saylor hitched up his gun belt. 'I'm going to talk to your boss. You do your best to remember just where you found that wheelbarrow, son.'

Otto Kline dropped his head on to the Jaguar's steering wheel for a moment. It seemed to take all his strength just to raise it back up. He looked out the windshield, wondering what had happened. The field was different now. So different. The lights. He focused on the bulldozer, his eyes tearing. Most of the ground had been plowed and was just flat dirt.

Kline's blood-smeared left hand slipped off the door handle twice before he was able to lever it open. He literally slid out of the blood-slick driver's seat, tilting forward a few scant inches, then falling back against the car fender.

The fingers on his right hand were throbbing, and he gently slipped them under his armpit. The shotgun. Where was the shotgun? Somewhere in the car? Had he left it in the trunk with Duran and the woman?

He tilted his head back and looked up at the gray-black sky. It was like a prison. Another prison. The whole world was a prison.

He drew in a rasping breath, then pushed himself off the car and lumbered forward.

Chief Saylor had been documenting the crime lab crew's activities as they went about their work. They were wearing long smocks, head-caps and face masks as they prodded at the dirt with round-nosed shovels.

'I think I've got something,' one of the crew called out. Two other lab workers joined him, dropping to their knees and hand-scooping dirt from around what appeared first through the crusty brown soil: a finger, a hand, then an arm.

Saylor kneeled down, a queasy feeling rolling through his stomach. A woman's arm. There was a gold band on one finger.

'Let's get some pictures before we go any further,' one of the lab men suggested.

Saylor barked out his agreement, then got to his feet. 'What the hell—' Saylor broke off his sentence when he saw the man, one hand clamped under his arm, the other clutching his belly, blood streaming through the fingers. He was rocking from side to side in a stiff-legged manner that reminded Saylor of a Frankenstein's monster caricature. Droplets of blood marked his weaving trail.

Saylor drew his gun and moved toward the man. 'Stay right there, mister. Right there.'

Kline hesitated, wobbling on his feet like a tree ready to topple. 'You found her,' he said between clenched teeth, abruptly bending over at the waist, coughing up blood.

'Someone call an ambulance,' Saylor ordered. He approached Kline cautiously, worried that there was a gun in the hand cupped under his arm. He placed the tip of his revolver against Kline's shoulder. 'Easy, sir. An ambulance is on the way. Just let your right hand drop free. Let me see that right hand.'

Kline straightened up. He smiled, his teeth foam-laced with blood. He slowly pulled his hand free and held it up to Saylor. 'My painting hand,' he said, then crumpled to the ground.

'For someone who's supposed to be so tough, you sure get beat up a lot, Bob,' Peggy Jacquard pointed out.

Duran's left eyebrow lifted slightly. It was about the only part of his body he could move without feeling pain.

'Your bedside humor needs work.'

Duran grimaced and the eyebrow slipped back into place.

His head was bandaged and his left leg was in a cast. The double vision had subsided, but doctors were still concerned about the concussion. Another sharp blow to the head might cause permanent damage.

The surgery on his knee had been deemed a success by Dr VonRogov.

'There's not much cartilage left. We may have to go in there again in a year or so, but outside of having a slight limp for a few months, you should be all right.'

Duran was willing to settle for a slight limp. He considered himself fortunate to be alive. In addition to the shotgun pellets in his leg and the contusions and cuts on his head, the results of Otto Kline having kicked him repeatedly, the doctors found five deep bruises on his neck, bruises matching up to Kline's fingers.

Chief Saylor had found Duran unconscious in the trunk of the Jaguar, heaped on top of Laura Ralston.

Laura was alive – tied, gagged, dehydrated, her neck

and throat muscles badly damaged from Kline's attempt at hanging her.

During Duran's stay in the hospital, he'd been kept busy: appearances by doctors, nurses, police and district attorney officials, as well as visits from Peggy, Lisa, Hugh Stringer, and George the butler.

Stringer had seemed ill at ease, his main concern the re-burial of Anona in the family crypt, and the psychological effect that all this, including the fact that John Stack was still missing, was having on Lisa.

Stringer claimed he had tried to keep the police from performing an autopsy on Anona, but the District Attorney had insisted and Stringer's legal challenges were quickly overruled by a judge. The autopsy showed that Anona did indeed have traces of alcohol, marijuana, cocaine and a lethal dose of a tricyclic antidepressant.

Dr Feldman had prescribed an anti-depressant, Improvane, for Anona months ago.

The police and District Attorney had decided not to open an investigation into Anona's death, the implication being that she had committed suicide.

There were veiled threats about the police looking into how she had acquired the illegal drugs, but Stringer had assured Duran that nothing was going to come of it.

John Stack's disappearance was still a mystery, though the police had found traces of his blood and hair on the dock near his houseboat. DNA tests of the hair, taken from samples from John's hairbrush had been positive. The predominant theory was that Otto Kline had killed John, disposing of his body in the bay. The police didn't seem to be interested in putting much effort into the investigation until John's body was found. The Coast Guard had searched the area around Sausalito for days, with nothing to show for it.

Duran didn't buy into the Kline killed John theory, though he feared that John had been murdered.

Kline had told him he hadn't harmed John. If he had done so, he would have bragged about it. Duran informed the police of Kline's statement, but they seemed to disregard it. 'He was probably playing mind games with you,' one detective offered. 'He was a nutcase. He may have killed the kid and not even remembered doing it.'

Kline had denied setting fire to Anona's studio. There was no reason for him to lie about that. He was preparing to kill Duran. At a certain time and certain date. It wasn't until after his knee surgery that it dawned on Duran that the day Kline intended to kill him was the October fourteenth. Kline had mentioned the date. It was the anniversary of Arlene Kline's suicide. So he had definitely planned on the exact day to murder him and bury him with Anona. So who set the fire?

Duran strongly suspected Jason Lark was responsible for the fire. The missing Nexis page in his office – that had to be Lark. And Lark had alerted his accomplices about the meeting in Los Angeles. But John Stack? Lark kill his own son? No. Lark was closer to Johnny than he was to Lisa. He had a better chance of worming his way into his son's wallet than his daughter's.

Would Lark have given Anona the cocaine? The wine? She rarely got more than a few sips of wine down every night. The autopsy results showed more than that.

'You look tired, Bob. Maybe I should get going,' Peggy said.

'No. I was just thinking. Have you seen Laura?'

'Yes. She's home. She still looks pretty shaky.' Peggy reached over and gently touched Duran's hand. 'I'm glad it's over, Bob. I'm glad that bastard is dead.'

'Kline's dead, Peg. But it's not over. I want you to do some things for me.'

Peggy took a pen and pad from her purse and began writing down Duran's requests. When he was finished she rose reluctantly from her chair. 'When are they going to release you?'

'The doc says two more days. Is the security guard still stationed at the office?'

'No. I didn't think he was needed anymore.'

'He is. Get him back, Peg. And have them send a man over to Stack House.'

She bent over and brushed her lips across his. When she leaned back there were tears in her eyes.

'You're sure all this is necessary?' she asked softly.

'Positive,' he confirmed.

George Montroy appeared to be his usual implacable self, dressed in an immaculately pressed charcoal-colored suit, standing stiff-backed alongside the Bentley, which was parked in the passenger loading zone at St Francis Hospital.

The nurse pushed the wheelchair to the curb and assisted Duran to his feet.

'Good to see you, sir,' George said, opening the Bentley's back door.

Duran hobbled over to the car with the help of a cane and climbed awkwardly into the back seat.

'Home, sir?' George inquired.

'No. The cemetery.'

The Bentley purred to a stop near the mausoleum and George assisted Duran out of the car. The smell of drying concrete hung in the air inside the mausoleum. Duran made his way to Anona's crypt, running his hand across the rough surface.

He bowed his head and said a prayer, the words to the Hail Mary escaping him, so he improvised, talking directly to Anona, his failed Catholic beliefs suspended. He truly hoped that there was a heaven for his wife and that there was a hell – a fire and brimstone hell – for Otto Kline.

A coughing sound brought Duran out of his reverie. He shifted his cane and turned to see Chief Saylor.

'How are you feeling?' Saylor asked.

'Lousy.'

Saylor's eyes swept the mausoleum. 'It looks a lot nicer than when I last saw it.'

Duran nodded his agreement.

'Do you still think it was me, Chief?'

'You mean do I think you poisoned your wife? It doesn't much matter what I think, Mr Duran.'

'It matters to me.'

Saylor removed his sunglasses, then looked over his shoulder to see if anyone was within hearing distance. 'Do I think you did it? Yes. I know your wife was sick, and in pain, and was going to die. Still, in my book that doesn't give you, or anyone else, the right to kill her. I know Otto Kline was a raving lunatic, and the world is a much better place with him gone, and there's no doubt he took your wife's body; but I have trouble swallowing him as being the whole package: the arson fire, your missing stepson, the murders in Los Angeles. It just doesn't fit.'

Even though Duran agreed with Saylor, he played devil's advocate. 'He hated my wife, Chief. Maybe he thought he was getting back at her that way. Maybe he planned to kill the whole family. Kline was, as you say, a "raving lunatic". Who knows what was going through his mind.'

Saylor swung his sunglasses by one bow. 'But he was a smart raving lunatic, with a definite mission.'

'What happened to Kline? His remains, I mean.'

'Cremated. No God's backyard for Otto Kline. So long, Mr Duran. I don't think we'll be seeing each other again.'

Duran leaned on his cane. 'You never know, Chief. You just never know in this life.'

Chapter 37

'Will you be staying with us again, sir?' George asked as
Jason Lark slipped past him into Stack House.

Lark had returned to Santa Monica for a day-and-a-
half to take care of business.

'I believe so, George. My clothes are still in the guest
room, I hope.'

'I took the liberty of packing your belongings, sir. Just
in case.'

Lark jammed his hands in his pants pockets, telling
himself now was not the time to knock the silly old fart on
his ass. Not while he had the Picassos.

'Why is there a security guard in front of the house?'

'Mr Duran's orders, sir.'

'Has there been news on Johnny?'

George shook his head as if it weighed a ton. 'No.'

'Is my daughter in her room?'

'She is,' George acknowledged. 'Her young man is with
her.'

Lark started toward the stairs, pulling up when he
noticed the blank space on the living-room wall.

'Where's Anona's painting?' he demanded. 'What happened to it?'

'Mr Duran had it removed and put in storage at the
bank, sir.'

Lark wheeled to face the butler. 'What about your
painting, George? The one from Anona's bedroom.'

'Also at the bank. Temporarily,' he added with heavy irony.

Lark's fingers were moving in his pockets as if counting change. 'Have you made a decision about selling the painting? When I was at my office I mentioned it to a client. He was very interested. In fact, my client might be interested in any other . . . mementoes you might have stored away somewhere. Old drawings, sketches, that kind of thing.'

'I will keep your offer in mind,' the butler said stiffly. 'Mr Duran is in the library. I believe he wants to talk to you, sir.'

'After I see Lisa.'

Lark found the door to Lisa's room opened. The change was dramatic. The carpeting was clean, the posters on the walls had been removed. She was lying on her bedspread, dressed in jade-colored satin lounging pajamas.

Eric Marvin lay beside her, one arm laced around her shoulders.

'Lisa, how are you feeling today?' Lark asked.

'Oh, hi, Jason. I'm fine, just a little tired.'

Jason. 'Daddy' hadn't lasted long. Before he left for Santa Monica, Lisa had been coming around; all during the ceremony for Anona at the cemetery, she hung on to his arm, literally used his shoulder to cry on, even called him 'Daddy' once. Now it was back to 'Jason'.

Lark sank down on the foot of the bed, his hand going to Lisa's naked foot.

'I'm sorry I had to leave town. I was down at my office. I'm closing it up, moving here.'

'That's nice,' she said with little enthusiasm.

'I'd like to be alone with my daughter for a few minutes,' Lark told Eric Marvin.

Marvin started to protest, but Lisa sat up, swung her feet to the floor and said, 'Eric, why don't you take a swim? I'll be down in a little while.'

Marvin opened his mouth, thought better about what he was about to say, and exited the room.

'Are you and Eric . . . serious?' Lark asked.

'No. Not really.' She got to her feet and began pacing back and forth. 'He's keeping Johnny's club open. Running it. With my help.' She paused at the windows, parting the curtains with her hand. 'The police think Johnny's dead. Uncle Hugh does, too.'

'I'm afraid it's a strong possibility, but we have to keep hoping.' He tried to catch Lisa's eyes. 'If . . . if something did happen to John, then it's just the two of us now, Lisa. You and me. We're all that's left of the family.'

'Family? You weren't much of a father, Jason.'

'I made mistakes. Stupid mistakes. I'd like to make up for them. That's why I sold my business. I want to be here. With you. Help you.'

'Help me? How? You weren't here when I needed you. I don't think I need you now.'

'Lisa,' Lark pleaded. 'I'm your father. I'm not perfect, but I'm your father.'

'Do you think that man killed Johnny? The crazy man?'

'Otto Kline? That's what the police are saying.' He reached out his arms toward her, but Lisa pushed past him and flopped back on to the bed.

'What about Mommy? Who killed Mommy?'

Lark clasped her hand and began kneading it in his. 'Lisa, I think we have to face it. Anona committed suicide. She wasn't herself at the end. You could see that.'

Lisa wrenched her hand free and looked at Lark accusingly. 'I don't think Mommy would do that.'

Lark reluctantly got to his feet. 'Lisa, I want to help you. Very much. In any way I can.'

Lisa rolled over on her stomach and burrowed her head into the bedspread. 'I'm tired now, Jason. Maybe we'll talk later.'

Lark clenched his teeth, then tip-toed out of the room. Duran must have gotten to her. Or that little prick Eric.

Or it could have been her sessions with the psychiatrist? Hugh Stringer had insisted she see a doctor. He could imagine his daughter's sessions with a quack – all those father-daughter conflict theories – repressed memories: 'Did your father ever touch you here? Or there? Did he beat your mother?'

Shit. He never should have gone to Santa Monica. But he had to – had to put out the brushfires, especially with Mario Drago. Drago wasn't satisfied. He was still worried about Duran. But it was Drago's people who screwed up by not waiting for Duran and killing him along with the attorney and his bodyguard.

Drago wanted Lark to come to Vegas. It was a trip that Lark knew could end up as a oneway journey. He had to accept the fact that his connection with Drago was finished. He owed more money on the inventory in the shop than it was worth. His bank accounts were down to nothing. He had placed the sketches he took from Anona's studio with a dealer in Los Angeles, but at a rock-bottom price – forty-thousand dollars. Enough to keep him going until he unloaded the Picassos.

He had managed to stall Drago, stop him from sending someone to escort him to Vegas, with the promise of a new job. The old woman in Beverly Hills. 'I talked to her this morning,' Lark had assured the Vegas gangster. 'She's expecting me there in the next couple of days to finalize the contract for the redecorating job. There's a Renoir, a Rembrandt, and a fantastic Caravaggio, Mario. They're all magnificent.' Actually, the old bitch had decided to put off the redecorating until next year.

'Call me in a week,' Drago ordered. 'I won't wait any longer than that.'

A week. Five days now. Lark had spent almost a full day making inquiries on the Picasso sketches. The response was overwhelming. One New Orleans dealer he spoke to made an offer of six million dollars, much less than what the Swiss dealer Gerhow had projected – but in cash. Six million in cash!

Lark saw the back of George's head disappear toward the kitchen. They were in George's room. Somewhere in there. They had to be.

'Lark!'

Jason's head hooked around. Duran was standing in the hallway, leaning on a cane.

'Come in, Lark. We have to talk.'

Duran was perched on the edge of old man Stack's desk when Jason entered the library. It was, he had to admit, a beautifully appointed room – three of the walls were lined from floor-to-ceiling with shelves filled with gold-tooled, leather-bound books. Lark had wasted the better part of a day going through each and every one of those books looking for the Picassos. The fourth wall was taken up by a gun case of varnish cherrywood with polished brass inlays, holding Conrad Stack's collection of shotguns and hunting rifles. The couch and chair were of saddle-brown leather. Lark knew he could peddle the rare Swedish Empire desk with gilded winged sphinxes for sixty thousand dollars.

'You look like you're feeling better,' Lark offered.

'How were things in Santa Monica, Jason?'

'I sold my business.'

'Come into some money, have you? Or are you expecting to?'

'It's time for a change, that's all.' Lark looked over at the gun cabinet, noticing the open slot – the slot where the shotgun that had almost killed Duran once rested.

'I was in Santa Barbara yesterday, Jason. I spoke to the Fritzheims. Mrs Fritzheim said to say hello to you.'

Lark swiveled around slowly and stared at Duran. The physical contrasts between the two were strikingly pronounced: Lark, immaculately attired in a tailored camel-haired sports coat, black cashmere turtleneck and matching slacks – his hair sprayed helmet-hard in calculated disarray, a slight sweat sheen appearing on his finely-drawn features – Duran, his nose and forehead showing bruises and scrape marks, the back of his head bandaged, shirt-sleeves rolled up past his elbows, one leg of his pants cut away to make room for the cast.

Lark broke the standoff. 'How is Fritzheim dealing with the loss of the Van Gogh?'

'I was stupid,' Duran admitted. 'I should have gotten a list of people who'd worked in the house from Fritzheim. Should have dug a little deeper. If I had seen your name right away, I would have pieced it all together a lot quicker. How much money did you make off the deal, Jason? And how many other paintings have you stolen?'

Lark shrugged his shoulders and wandered over to the gun case, watching Duran's reflection in the glass. 'I'm afraid you took one too many blows to the head, Robert. I'm told one more hit might just do you in.'

'Yes. Either that, or if I'm caught in another burning building. That was you, wasn't it?'

Lark held his hands out, like a priest granting benediction. 'Me? You're not going to get anyone to believe that I had anything to do with the fire. That was your playmate, Otto Kline.'

'No. It wasn't Kline. It was you. You sent those faxes and had someone make the phone calls to Johnny saying that I killed Anona. You gave Anona the cocaine, and the overdose of the medicine.'

'That's preposterous! I didn't kill Anona! I didn't kill anyone! I had no reason to harm Anona. But you did, Robert. You certainly did. And now Johnny's missing. That doesn't hurt you at all, does it? Just Lisa's left and, believe me, I'm not leaving until the will is finalized, and there's no longer a motive for you to harm her.'

Duran rested his cane on the desk top and brought his hands together in a series of claps. 'Danielle Fritzheim told me she thought you should have been an actor. And you are, in your own way, aren't you?'

'I'm not going to—'

'Shut up!' Duran commanded. 'It took me a while to figure it out. The Van Gogh stolen from Fritzheim's house was a forgery. The original was already stolen. You switched it, then when the forgery was stolen, you panicked. The new thieves were going to try and sell a forgery back to the insurance company. You found out I was hired to get it back. Danielle Fritzheim told you I was working for the insurance company. Once I knew it wasn't authentic, I'd start checking. And find you, Jason Lark. So I had to be stopped. Or the phony Van Gogh destroyed. Or both. That was the setup in Los Angeles, wasn't it? Kill me and snatch the forged painting. You made copies of keys from the spares in my room, got into my office, saw the Fritzheim file and set up a killing ground in Los Angeles. You made a dumb mistake, Jason. Taking the one page from the Nexis search with your name on it.'

Lark started toward the door. 'Now I know you took too many hits to the head.'

'You go out that door and you're finished,' Duran promised. 'I'll run you down. I'll check every job you've worked on for the past five years, Jason. You know what I'll find.'

Lark stopped short, looking at Duran over his shoulder. 'You're bluffing.'

'I'm not. Just how far I go into the investigation depends on you. Who are you working with? You haven't got the spine to actually handle the killings in Los Angeles. Who are your partners?'

'I'm telling you, you're crazy.'

Duran limped around behind the desk and slipped carefully into the padded leather desk chair. 'I've got your phone records, Jason. I'm going to run the numbers you've been calling, see who they're listed to. Then I'll go through your bank accounts – not just the credit reports that you saw in my office – but your bank accounts. Then I'll talk to Adam, your assistant. Knowing you, you're probably paying him next to nothing. A little pressure and he'll open up, then I'll—'

Lark held his hands up in mock surrender. 'There's nothing there. You'd just be wasting your time.'

'It's a good thing you didn't decide to become an actor after all, Jason. You're no good at it. I haven't gone to the police . . . yet.'

'Why? Because of our family ties?' Lark mocked.

'Because I want to know if you gave Anona that overdose.'

Lark leaned across the desk until his face was less than a foot from Duran's. 'No. I didn't kill Anona.'

Duran held his eyes for a long moment, then said, 'What do you think happened to John?'

Lark's head jerked back. 'I'm afraid that Kline killed him.'

Duran reached for his cane and used it to thrust himself to his feet. 'I'll give you a day, Jason. Twenty-four hours. Because of Lisa. I'd just as soon you aren't here when you're arrested. Then I go to the police. One of the men who swiped the painting from Fritzheim's house called me after Harry Lawson was killed. He thought I was involved, that I had the Van Gogh. I told them to talk to their partner. To you, Jason. I spoke to Alan Fritzheim about my theory on his Van Gogh having been being switched earlier, by you, before the robbery, and the insurance company, too. The genie's out of the bottle. Your partners, whoever they are, aren't going to be very happy with you, Jason.'

'You don't give a man much wiggle room, do you?' Lark said.

'You're not much of a man. Have you enough money to find a deep hole to hide in?'

Lark nibbled at one of his carefully-manicured nails. 'Does that mean you're going to give me a head start? Get out of town by sundown? Something like that?'

'Because of Lisa, and only because of Lisa, I'll get you some money. Enough to travel a long way from here.'

'You're starting to sound like old Conrad Stack, Robert.'

Duran paused at the door. 'I'm going out for a couple of hours. I'll have your money for you by morning. Then I want you out of here. For good.'

Chapter 38

Lark flopped down into the chair Duran had just vacated. He wasn't sure how long he sat there, his mind traveling back to the first years of his marriage with Anona. The early years had been wonderful. Exciting. Travel. All the money in the world. Then the children came along and Anona changed. Much more than he thought she would.

He swept his arm carelessly across the desk, sending the phone crashing to the carpet. He picked the phone up gingerly, as if it were a bomb. It was a bomb, Lark realized. A live, ticking bomb. Duran wasn't bluffing about getting his phone records. He'd zero in on the calls to Las Vegas. He had called Drago's number from his office dozens of times. Duran, or the police, would make the connection. Then it would be a race to see who got to him first – Drago or the cops.

Lark rose unsteadily to his feet. He had to get away. Far away. And for that, he needed money. Real money. Not whatever piddling amount Duran had in mind.

The Picassos. They were his only chance now.

He hurried out to the kitchen and looked into the garage area. The Bentley was gone. Duran said he'd be out for a couple of hours. He couldn't drive himself with his bad leg, so George was undoubtedly chauffeuring him.

He hurried up the inside stairway, racing to George's room. The door was locked again. He moved swiftly to the adjoining room and retraced his earlier route, out of the window, along the ledge and into George's suite.

He entered the bedroom, taking Picasso's drawing of his flat in Paris from the wall, then began combing through the places he'd missed on his first visit, his fingers clawing at shirts, sox, underwear. Then the closet, fingering suits, jackets, dozens of shoe boxes.

He was panting like an animal after a race. There was a chest of dark wood, banded by iron at the far end of the closet. He pushed the hanging garments out of his way and dragged the chest forward. He unlocked the clasp and raised the lid. It was jammed with multi-colored papers. There were more of Johnny and Lisa's crayoned drawings, old photographs, stacks of letters rubber-banded together.

Lark burrowed through the maze, then he spotted the brick-colored packet. Claude Bresson's packet! It had to be!

He yanked the packet free, his trembling fingers undoing the ribbon, folding back the lid, carrying the contents over to George's bed.

He spread the sketches across the bedcover. The first was a one-dimensional rendition of Bresson's château. The next an equally bad Paris street scene. Then the women. He arranged the five sketches in a neat line. Five young women. Three showed only their faces, the other two were full-figured nudes. *Cinq putains*. He'd found them!

Lark turned the five sketches over, his eyes narrowing as he tried to decipher the French inscriptions. Then the initials. PRP. Why hadn't Picasso signed his name? Was it because the models were whores? Had he intended to give them to the women? Perhaps as payment for their services?

He slipped the sketches back into the packet, then tidied up the chest, slid it back into the closet, and gave the room a quick once-over. He debated with himself briefly, then rehung Picasso's drawing of the Paris flat. George could keep that one, he decided.

He silently thanked George when he saw his suitcases neatly stacked at the foot his bed. He slipped the packet with the Picassos into the smaller of the two bags then used the phone, dialing information first, getting the number for United Airlines.

'I want to get to New Orleans in a hurry.'

'There's a flight leaving at six fifty-five,' he was informed.

Lark glanced at his watch. More than enough time.

'Is there anything available in first class?'

Chapter 39

The airline clerk, a slim elfin-faced woman in her twenties, said: 'I'm afraid that there's a problem with your VISA card, sir.'

Jason Lark managed to look offended. 'You must be mistaken.'

She gave him a tired smile. 'They won't accept the charge on the flight to New Orleans.'

Lark smiled ruefully and pulled out his wallet. 'I've been out of the country so much lately, I guess my accountant has screwed up. Here. Try American Express.'

Lark kept a confident look on his face, while he fumed inwardly. His feet were bracketing his carry-on case with six million dollars' worth of Picassos in it, and the lousy credit card couldn't handle a nine hundred and ninety-seven dollar one way first class ticket to New Orleans.

'That did it, sir,' the clerk said with a professional smile, handing Lark back his American Express card.

She hummed softly to herself while she wrote up the ticket.

'Have a nice trip, sir. Your flight number is 372, leaving from gate 86 in an hour and ten minutes.'

'Where's your VIP lounge?' Lark queried.

He could feel a surge of adrenalin and beads of sweat break out on his forehead when the carry-on was placed on the conveyor belt and scuttled through the X-ray machine.

He didn't feel comfortable until the bag was safely back in his hands. As soon as he picked it up, someone bumped into him and he clutched it to his chest like a fullback recovering a fumbled football. He needed a drink. His first-class ticket awarded him entry to the airline's VIP lounge, a large, narrow room with smoked glass windows and polished chrome and leather furniture.

A ping pong-sized table groaned under the weight of dozens of bottles of liquor, wine and platters of unappetizing looking *hors d'oeuvres*.

Lark helped himself to a generous measure of Johnny Walker Black Label and collapsed into a chair near the windows.

He wedged the bag between his shoes, took a large sip of the whisky and relaxed. He had made it. Another hour and he'd be in the air. Then New Orleans.

It had been years since he'd been there. He tried to recall the name of the top hotel. Senestra? Something like that, right on Bourbon Street. Brennan's was the restaurant to go to back then. He wondered if it still was.

'Do you mind if I sit here?' a voice asked.

Lark's eyes twitched open. The woman was tall. Her long sable-colored hair framed a perfectly-formed face. She wore a smartly-tailored green dress with a velvet collar.

'That man across the room, the fat one, thinks he's Romeo and I'm Juliet.'

'Be my guest,' Lark offered. He looked over to the bar and saw a heavy-set man in an ill-fitting dark blue suit. The man gave him a strained look, then did an about face and marched out of the room.

'It looks like you scared him away,' the woman beamed. She offered her hand. 'Jessica Savage.'

'Jason Lark.' Her hand was satiny feeling. The diamond ring on her finger looked to be at least two carats.

'He was behind me when I checked in,' she explained.

'Unfortunately I think he's going to New Orleans, too. If his seat assignment is next to mine, I may ask for a parachute.'

'I'm going to New Orleans. Maybe we can arrange to sit together,' Lark suggested.

'That would be wonderful.' She looked at the glass in his hand. 'The least I can do is get you a drink. What's your poison?'

'Scotch. Black Label.'

Lark watched her saunter to the bar. Firm body. Nicely dressed – not flashy, but there was no doubt that there were a hundred and ten pounds of goodies under that expensively-wrapped package. Jessica Savage. It had a theatrical sound. Movies. TV. Commercials. He could bring in Alan Fritzheim's name to give her a charge.

'Here you are, kind sir,' she said when she was back with his drink, a glass of white wine clutched in her other hand.

'Cheers.' Lark sampled the Scotch. 'You're so beautiful, you must be in the movies.'

'I was about to say the same about you, Jason,' she said playfully. 'What is your game?'

'I'm an art dealer.'

'How fascinating.'

Lark told her just how fascinating it was for a few minutes, then he noticed her features start to blur. His lips were feeling numb.

It appeared that she was moving in slow motion when she reached out and took his glass.

'I . . . I'm not feeling . . .'

She pushed her lips together and made soft kissing sounds. 'Not feeling well? Poor baby.' She leaned closer, her voice barely a whisper. 'I wasn't kidding when I asked you what your poison was, Jason. To tell you the truth, I can't remember the name – some new designer drug, but they say if you have to go, this is the way to do it.'

Lark fought to keep his eyes open as the girl got to her feet, leaned down and kissed him lightly on the head, then, as an afterthought, slid the bag from between his legs.

'Mario said to say goodbye. So goodbye, darling.'

Chapter 40

'Robert, I wasn't expecting you, come in, come in,' Hugh Stringer invited.

He stood back to allow Duran room to maneuver into the apartment. 'I wish you'd called, I was getting ready to go out.'

'I won't be long, Hugh,' Duran promised, pausing to take a look at Stringer's digs. A curving, cantilevered staircase was silhouetted against a background of shuttered windows. The walls were a soft beige, with white trim scalloped moldings around the ceiling. The carpeting was of yellow and red fleurs-de-lis. Two embroidered chairs sat alongside a white-tiled fireplace.

Dark, brooding, baroque-style portraits of bearded men in ruffled collars dotted the walls.

'Very nice, very nice indeed,' Duran said, turning to face Stringer.

The attorney was wearing a dark cardigan sweater over a white shirt. A scarf at his neck clashed with his dour image. It was the first time that Duran had seen him dressed in anything but a business suit. He looked somehow larger, and Duran now remembered that Anona had told him that Stringer had been an All American football player in college. He had a half-filled wine glass in one hand and a thick Madura wrapped cigar in the other.

Duran noticed a similar glass resting on the glass-topped coffee table near the fireplace.

'Am I interrupting anything?'

'No, no,' Stringer assured him. 'A friend just left. Can I fix you something?'

'Sure, Hugh. Whatever you're having.'

Duran caned himself over to the windows, pulled the shutters back and walked out on to a balcony with a spectacular view of San Francisco Bay.

'Here you are,' Stringer said, handing him a glass. 'Fonesca Port.'

'You must like heights, Hugh,' Duran observed. 'Your office, now this. Forty floors.' He leaned over the railing. 'I bet on a clear day you can see my office from here.'

Stringer puffed on his cigar. 'I must admit that I've never had the urge, Robert. What can I do for you?'

'I have some questions about the estate,' Duran said.

'The estate? It's hardly the time to—'

'I think it is,' Duran countered. 'How much cash is available now?'

'Cash? What do you need cash for?'

'I want to give Jason Lark fifty thousand dollars.'

Stringer's face registered confusion. 'Whatever for?'

'Travel money. I want him out of here. Away from Lisa.'

'Well, it's your money, Robert. I don't know what Lisa would think.'

'I wouldn't want her to know,' Duran explained. 'The money would come out of my share of the estate. Can you arrange it? Right away?'

'Where's Jason now?' Stringer queried.

'Stack House. The sooner he's out of here the better, Hugh.'

'Why this sudden concern for Lark? Why the urgency to give him money?'

'Because I think someone will try to kill him very soon. And I don't want his blood on my doorstep.'

'Why on earth would anyone want to kill Jason?'

'He's been involved in some shady art deals.'

'If you supply him with money, you could be considered to be an accessory,' Stringer said in a professional tone.

'I'll take that risk. How long will it take to get the money?'

'I can move some things around, some of the bonds, and have it for you tomorrow, if you insist.'

'I do. First thing in the morning. Have you heard anything about John?'

'I spoke to the police. They've nothing new. They think that he's dead and that Otto Kline killed him.'

'Is that your assumption, Hugh?'

'I'm afraid we have to consider the worst. And until we know for sure just what happened to John, the estate is going to be in suspension.'

'What about Victor Abbott?'

Stringer compressed his lips. 'Right now, he doesn't have a client. I don't know how he could pursue litigation.'

'Kline didn't kill John,' Duran said bluntly.

The attorney waved a hand vaguely. 'It makes the most sense, Robert. Who else would have a motive?'

'What do you know about Eric Marvin?'

'Eric? Lisa's friend? Nothing. Surely you don't think he had anything to do with John's death.'

'He's been cozying up to Lisa and he's running John's night club.'

'Well, it's a possibility, I guess.'

'There's another possibility. Lisa.'

Stringer's mouth dropped open. 'Lisa? That's ridiculous.'

'Is it? She and Johnny haven't gotten along for some time. Maybe it was an accident, or maybe she said something to Eric about John, something that Eric took as an invitation to do something on his own.'

'Lisa loves John. I know she does.'

'But Eric didn't. I heard that they had some pretty

heated arguments about how the nightclub should be run.'

Stringer's heavy jowls shook as he moved his head from side to side. 'We're not even certain that John is . . . dead. But, if you're so sure that this Kline creature wasn't responsible for whatever happened to John, then I suppose that Eric Marvin could be a suspect. I refuse to believe that Lisa is involved. But this Marvin fellow. You could be right. Have you mentioned any of this to the police?'

'Not yet.' Duran leaned against the balcony railing. 'I'll bet you can see all the way over to Sausalito. With the right telescope you might even be able to zero in on John's houseboat. I've hired an investigator. Did I tell you that? A former Coast Guard Commander. He said that John's body could still be out there somewhere in the water, maybe lodged in the mud and sludge at the bottom of the bay, or caught under some debris: an old ship, a tree trunk, or, it could have drifted out from the pier, gotten caught up in the rip tides of Raccoon Straights' – he used his cane as a pointer – 'right there by Angel Island, and was swept out to sea. Never to be seen again.'

'I'm very much afraid that may be just what happened, Robert. Since John hasn't surfaced by now, I just don't think there's much hope.'

Duran picked up his glass and took a sip of the port. 'Umm. Good. As good as anything in the Stack House cellar, I'd bet. And those paintings. Very nice, Hugh. Originals? One of them looked like a real Van Eyck.'

'No, no. Just copies, Robert. I can't afford an original.'

'Really? You always have done pretty well. This place must rent for what? Four or five thousand a month?'

'I make a decent living. And being a bachelor, I can indulge myself. But you're not here to talk about me, I'm sure.'

'Are you?' Duran countered. He put his drink down on

an ornate iron table, then hooked his cane around the balcony railing. 'A bachelor. You never married. At your age, and especially in this town, you know what that makes people think, Hugh.'

'I don't pay attention to what people may or may not think, Robert,' he replied huffily.

'Well, personally, I never gave it any thought. Anona told me that you proposed to her. That was just before I met her, wasn't it?'

One of Stringer's thick eyebrows shot up. 'I was very fond of Anona. I made no secret about it.'

'What about John's houseboat?' Duran asked, in a quick change of subject.

'What about it?' Stringer responded sharply, the annoyance in his tone obvious.

'If John is dead, it will become part of the estate: George drove me over there this morning.' He patted his leg cast. 'It was the first time I'd been there since Johnny's open house. Remember that party at the houseboat? Anona tried to christen it with a bottle of champagne, but she was so weak that John had to take the bottle from her and smash it against the houseboat wall himself.'

'Yes, I remember, Robert, but I really don't see why we're even discussing this now, and I—'

'That was the only time that I visited the houseboat. Until this morning. You must have been there to see Johnny a couple of times.'

'No,' Stringer said, impatiently. 'Just that once, that is until the day I went with Victor Abbott.'

Duran's face tensed. 'That's interesting, because when I got there today, I couldn't find John's place at first. Neither could George. He'd been at the party, too. We checked with the harbor master. He told us that John had his houseboat moved over two piers a month ago. It seems his neighbors didn't care for the parties and loud music he was playing. So he moved two piers over, Hugh. Yet

Victor Abbott contends that you took him directly to John's houseboat that day. That you knew exactly where it was.'

Stringer flicked the remains of his cigar over the balcony, watching until it disappeared from sight. 'You spoke to Victor Abbott?' he replied bitterly.

'Oh, yes. Several times. Abbott's investigator is in Sausalito now, knocking on houseboat doors, with a picture of you. Just in case you were there before, asking questions about the location of John's houseboat. Did you do that, Hugh? Or did you follow him there that night? Shoot him, knife him, or just beat him to death before you pushed him into the bay?'

'You're mad,' Stringer shot back in an angry voice. 'Your doctors are concerned about your head injuries. Obviously they have reason to be. You're hallucinating.'

'No,' Duran replied calmly. 'You did it. Hugh Stringer. Dear old "Uncle Hugh." The trusted family attorney. John crossed you up hiring another attorney. Victor Abbott, the kind of attorney who'd look after the interests of his client, who would check into the estate assets and would wonder why it wasn't as large as it should be. My hunch is that you've been misappropriating funds since Conrad Stack died. Maybe even before that, but we won't know for sure until Abbott's investigation is complete. With Conrad gone and Anona sick, you had full control. I didn't involve myself in Anona's business affairs. And she trusted you, Hugh. Really trusted you. Did you slip Anona the overdose? Who was next? Me? Lisa? Or was it just John?'

Stringer dropped his glass to the cement floor and slammed one large hand into an open palm. 'I think it's time for you to leave, Robert. I'm going to forget this. For now. But if you ever bring up these ridiculous charges again, I'm going to make life very unpleasant for you.'

'It's unpleasant now, Hugh. I've lost my wife, and—'

'I never touched Anona! I loved that woman. More than you or that ridiculous peacock Lark ever did!'

'Then why did you steal from her all those years? Why did you kill her son? Why did—'

Duran was caught off guard by the speed of Stringer's lunge. The attorney's heavy hands grabbed him by the neck and lifted him from the ground.

Duran lashed out with his good leg, making contact with Stringer's knees, but missing his target, the groin.

Stringer bulled Duran into the balcony railing, using his strength to lift Duran higher, edging him backwards.

Duran clawed at Stringer's face, his thumbs searching for his eye sockets.

Stringer screamed out in pain, his grip loosening.

Duran dropped to the floor, gasping for breath, his throat on fire, watching as Stringer shook his head violently from side to side, like a bull preparing to make a final charge.

He pushed himself to one knee, his left hand reaching out to the dew-slick railing, coming in contact with his cane. He wrested it free as Stringer came at him, arms outspread, his lips peeled back from his teeth, shouting an unintelligible curse, slamming into Duran with his knees.

Duran fell on his back, swinging out wildly with the cane, the hooked end catching Stringer's ankle, causing the attorney to stumble forward. Duran yanked hard on the cane and Stringer lost his momentum, his arms flailing, fighting for balance, then he stumbled backwards, hitting the balcony, his weight carrying him over the edge. He hung there for a moment, then teetered over the side, his hands making a desperate grasp at the narrow vertical metal balcony posts.

Duran turned on his side, still lying on the floor, his head now level with Stringer's, on the opposite side of the balcony.

'Help me,' the attorney croaked. 'Help me.'

Duran shuffled over and extended his hands through the balcony railings, out to Stringer, clasping him by the forearms. 'Hang on!' He dug his fingers into Stringer's meaty flesh as he struggled to his knees, leaning backwards for leverage.

Their eyes locked together. Stringer was slipping, pulling Duran to him, until his face was pressed against the posts.

Duran's arms felt as if they were about to pop out of their shoulder sockets. 'I can't hold on much longer,' he said, his face now grinding so hard into the railing the flesh was bleeding. 'Try and drop to the balcony below. It's the only—'

Stringer's left hand slipped free. He was dangling by one arm, his free hand scratching at the concrete siding of the building.

Duran joined both of his hands around Stringer's forearm, feeling it slowly slither through his fingers until he was holding Stringer's wrist, then his hand, finally his fingers.

Their eyes met again. The attorney opened his mouth to say something, then he was gone, cartwheeling down into the blackness.

Chapter 41

'So, Stringer actually admitted to killing John,' Victor Abbott stated.

Duran's reply was slow in coming. They were seated in Conrad Stack's library, Duran behind the desk, the attorney across from him.

Duran had spent most of last night and a good portion of the following morning in sometimes heated discussions with the two Homicide inspectors from the San Francisco Department.

Jason Lark being found dead at the airport had surprised Duran. Why hadn't Lark waited at Stack House at least until Duran gave him the promised money? What had spooked Lark? Who got to him? Who were his mysterious partners?

Questions, questions – some of which he was sure he'd never get the answer to.

He took a deep breath before responding to Abbott. 'Yes, Stringer admitted it.'

Abbott sliced the air with his hands. 'But the police have only your word as to what really happened.'

'Then I guess they'll have to settle for that. Have you found any evidence that Stringer was embezzling funds?'

'Stringer was playing games with your wife's fortune, all right, but I don't know if I'll ever be able to prove it. Money churned through the stock and bond brokerage accounts. And the real estate deals. They were something

339

else. Stringer was working with Laura Ralston. He'd buy a piece of property for your wife, under her name, hold it for a year or so, and during that time he skimmed the hell off the rent, then sell it at a loss to one of a series of dummy corporations he and Ralston set up. Then their dummy corporation would resell it at a neat profit.'

'What does Laura say to all this?'

Abbott gave a grudging nod. 'Just what she should say. Talk to my attorney. And she's got herself a damn good one: Carol Ventura, so it's going to take some time to get any of this to stick to Stringer and Ralston.'

'It doesn't really matter much now,' Duran said with resignation.

'It'll matter like hell if the cops decide to go after you for Stringer's death.'

Duran's hand went to his bandaged head. 'I'm counting on you to persuade them not to.'

Abbott got to his feet. 'I'm working on it. And we're still digging into Stringer's records. I think we can recover some of the money. He has no heirs, so we'll be fighting with the good old United States Government and the State of California. This is going to complicate the hell out of your wife's estate – the Feds are already insisting on a full scale accounting.'

'Do whatever you think best,' Duran instructed, suddenly feeling exhausted.

'I'll do just that,' Abbott advised, assembling the financial documents he'd taken from Conrad Stack's desk and file cabinets and slipping them into his briefcase.

'My investigator didn't turn up anyone who saw Hugh Stringer around the houseboat. You know, Duran, I had you figured for John's death. I really did.'

'I'm a popular target, counselor. Tell me something, now that you're in my employ. Those accusations you made at the reading of the will – the overdose of drugs and the adultery. Where did they come from?'

340

Abbott's mouth approximated a smile. 'The fax messages were all we had on the drug charges. The adultery idea came from John. He was just guessing, but it seemed reasonable under the circumstances, so I thought I'd run a bluff on you.'

'It didn't work.'

Abbott shrugged his shoulders in mock defeat. 'Hey, that's the law. Sometimes you win, sometimes you lose. I'll be in touch.'

Duran nodded, watching the attorney exit the room, then he slumped into a comfortable position and closed his eyes. Moments later he heard footsteps and saw a shadow over his shoulder.

He put his hands up in a defensive gesture, lowering them when he recognized George Montroy, the butler.

'I thought we might have a drink together, sir. I'll be leaving in the morning.'

'For good?' Duran queried.

'Yes, sir. I'm moving back to Boston. My sister's home.' He placed a silver tray on the desk and whisked a snowy-white cloth from a bottle of wine.

It was the dustiest bottle Duran could ever remember seeing.

'A 1948 Mouton-Rothschild,' George said almost reverently as he wiped the bottle clean with the cloth. 'It's the last one in the cellar.' He used a waiter's corkscrew to carefully peel back the wrapper and work the cork free. 'It should really be decanted and breathe for an hour or two.'

'Pour away, Mr Montroy. It's waited long enough.'

George carefully spilled the wine into two glasses, like a scientist working with hazardous materials. He took a cautionary sip, then handed Duran his glass.

'I really feel rather badly about the size of my inheritance, sir.'

Duran sniffed the wine. 'You mean because you killed Anona, George?'

The butler's long gray face blanched. 'I want you to know that if you, or anyone, was ever charged with Miss Anona's death, I would have come forward.'

'I don't doubt that, George. I don't doubt it at all.'

'When . . . how long have you known?'

Duran swilled the wine around in its glass, watching it cling to the side. 'You were always a possibility, George. It became a case of elimination. At first I thought Jason Lark might have done it, but no, he wouldn't be up to something like that. The kids? No. No way. Then there was Hugh Stringer. Once I crossed him off the list there wasn't anyone else left. Anona asked you to do it, didn't she?'

'Yes. It was during one afternoon. On the patio. You know how she liked to sit out there in the sun, admiring the roses. She . . . she was in such pain. Such terrible pain.'

'So she asked you to do it.'

The butler took a long sip of wine before replying. 'She asked me if I knew anything about poisons, about overdoses of particular drugs. How much would be needed, which worked quickly, and, more importantly, that would not raise anyone's suspicions. She presented it this way: "George, I want to die. As soon as possible, but I don't want to make a fuss, or get anyone in trouble." ' His hand started to tremble and he slowly put the wine glass back on the tray.

'So you decided to kill her.'

'It wasn't an easy decision. Believe me, it was not. Miss Anona was . . . very special. Always. Even as a small child, she had the gift, not just for painting, but for life.

'Mr Stack was rather a bore. He spent most of his time away on business, and poor Mrs Stack, I had hardly got to know her before she passed on. But Miss Anona treated me as one of the family from the beginning. When she was a young girl I accompanied her to the zoo, the park, concerts. She was just . . . very special,' he finished lamely.

'You won't get any argument on that from me,' Duran confessed.

'I do feel awkward. The will, I mean. Her magnificent painting, the Bentley, the contents of the wine cellar. I don't deserve any of it.'

Duran raised his glass in a toasting gesture. 'I'm sure Anona didn't feel that way,' he ended softly.

Raising Cain

Gallatin Warfield

There is trouble in the mountain valley in Maryland where attorney Gardner Lawson practises. A mysterious religious cult has arrived, settling in an abandoned granite quarry deep in the hills.

Known as CAIN (for Church of the Ark, Incorporated), this fanatical group attracts media attention after an elderly black man dies in unusual circumstances.

The dead man's son is police detective Joseph Brown, who's convinced that CAIN was responsible and begins secret investigations. When the CAIN leader is also found dead, 'Brownie' becomes the prime suspect for murder. Gardner Lawson now decides to resign as State's Attorney in order to conduct his close friend's defence.

Lawson's subsequent inquiries and a high-tension trial compel many to confront their innate prejudices – and force hidden secrets out of the shadows.

0 7472 4507 X

The Weatherman

Steve Thayer

A major serial killer thriller . . . a tour de force

Chief among all the complex and original characters in this astonishing novel is the shifting weather and landscape of Minnesota – demonic, majestic, bizarre, magical. And on Minneapolis-St Paul's 'Sky High News' it is TV weatherman Dixon Bell, a hulking eccentric uncannily precognitive of the elements, who pulls the highest ratings. His alter ego, busy breaking the story of a killer who snaps the necks of local young women, is hard news producer Rick Beanblossom, a Vietnam veteran like Dixon, a Pulitzer Prize winner who hides his napalmed face with a mask. Rivals for beautiful, ambitious anchor queen Andrea Labore, they develop an ambivalent friendship when Dixon becomes a suspect in the killings and Rick sets out to prove him innocent.

Electrifying, from the opening rollercoaster of a flash tornado to a cataclysmic and controversial death chair scene, *The Weatherman* grips like a vice and has more twists and turns than the Corniche.

'I read *The Weatherman* with mounting excitement and a sense of involvement which few novels can elicit in me these days . . . This is a wonderful story, one that will stay in my memory for a long time' Stephen King

0 7472 5083 9

HEADLINE
FEATURE

A selection of bestsellers from Headline

BODY OF A CRIME	Michael C. Eberhardt	£5.99	☐
TESTIMONY	Craig A. Lewis	£5.99	☐
LIFE PENALTY	Joy Fielding	£5.99	☐
SLAYGROUND	Philip Caveney	£5.99	☐
BURN OUT	Alan Scholefield	£5.99	☐
SPECIAL VICTIMS	Nick Gaitano	£5.99	☐
DESPERATE MEASURES	David Morrell	£5.99	☐
A CERTAIN JUSTICE	John Lescroart	£5.99	☐
GRIEVOUS SIN	Faye Kellerman	£5.99	☐
THE CHIMNEY SWEEPER	John Peyton Cooke	£5.99	☐
TRAP DOOR	Deanie Francis Mills	£5.99	☐
VANISHING ACT	Thomas Perry	£5.99	☐

All Headline books are available at your local bookshop or newsagent, or can be ordered direct from the publisher. Just tick the titles you want and fill in the form below. Prices and availability subject to change without notice.

Headline Book Publishing, Cash Sales Department, Bookpoint, 39 Milton Park, Abingdon, OXON, OX14 4TD, UK. If you have a credit card you may order by telephone – 01235 400400.

Please enclose a cheque or postal order made payable to Bookpoint Ltd to the value of the cover price and allow the following for postage and packing:

UK & BFPO: £1.00 for the first book, 50p for the second book and 30p for each additional book ordered up to a maximum charge of £3.00.

OVERSEAS & EIRE: £2.00 for the first book, £1.00 for the second book and 50p for each additional book.

Name ....

Address ....

....

....

If you would prefer to pay by credit card, please complete:
Please debit my Visa/Access/Diner's Card/American Express (delete as applicable) card no:

Signature .... Expiry Date..............